Pride Publishing books by AE Lister

Persuasions
Various Persuasions
Various Distractions

Northern Horizons
760 Miles

Collections
Dark and Deadly: Skeletal Equation
We Three Kings: A Spoonful of Sugar

I0691652

760 Miles
ISBN # 978-1-83943-779-3
©Copyright AE Lister 2022
Cover Art by Erin Dameron-Hill ©Copyright March 2022
Interior text design by Claire Siemaszkiewicz
Pride Publishing

Published in 2022 by Pride Publishing, United Kingdom.

Pride Publishing is an imprint of Totally Entwined Group Limited.

Northern Horizons

760 MILES

AE LISTER

760 MILES

Dedication

To those who understand that gold isn't solely
dug from the ground.

Preface

A word about historical accuracy.

Although I researched the area and time period to the best of my ability and have included what I feel are accurate details of the landscape and setting, this story remains a fictional account that takes liberties with the realities that would have been encountered in the Yukon, in Canada, in the year of 1906.

Chapter One

Dawson City, 1906
"A good heart is worth gold." ~ *William Shakespeare*

Meetings come in many forms. Some are expected and looked forward to. Others are dreaded. Many of them leave you mostly inconvenienced. Once in a while, an unforeseen encounter will change your life.

Jimmy

The stench of Dawson City hit me before anything else. My wagon full of supplies for Mr. Henley had merged with more traffic several miles before, so I must have been getting close to civilization—or what passed for civilization in these here parts.

And by more traffic, I only meant there was one other wagon and a couple of horses with riders on the road ahead of me. Most who traveled this country in the summer months used the river systems instead of picking their way through the tricky overland passes and uneven ground.

I liked the risk of it, seeing as how this was a safer way of living than anything I'd done o'er the past twenty years. I was traveling the straight and narrow now, trying to be an honest, hardworking man. I'd wasted the glory of my youth with a band of no-good thieves and murderers, doing their dirty work for nothing but a smile and a kick to the trousers. Yeah, I'd had a place in the world, but it hadn't taken long to realize t'wasn't a good one. Problem was, it had taken more time to figure out how to leave that life behind than it had to realize that I wanted to.

But I had found a way out, and my theories on how much I was worth to them had been correct. Nobody had lifted a finger to find me. I was nothing to them and always had been. Spook, Whitlaw and the gang were rotten, immoral men who used folks then tossed them aside when they weren't of use no more — or simply didn't care if those people decided to quit them.

Even though it stung, since there'd been a time that I'd imagined they'd liked me and maybe thought of me as a valuable addition to their circle, t'was a blessing. Because if either of them had decided t'was in their best interests to get me back into the gang or to make sure I didn't go joining any other gangs, I would have been disposed of a long time ago. But I figured they didn't care one way or another what I was doing now, and they'd probably rounded up a couple of greenhorns to train into the life the way they wanted, doing their dirty work and being witness to more cruelty than they could ever imagine.

Now I was hauling supplies on the regular by way of the Overland Trail and doing it for less money than Mr. Henley would pay a riverboat captain. It didn't leave much extra for me, but it paid for keeping up the horses and the wagon, gave me something to do that I enjoyed and a way to be my own boss. My life was my own, small as t'was, and I was eternally grateful for that.

T'was rough terrain I traveled, and there were wild animals that would kill me if I wasn't on the lookout. But I loved this country, and I knew it from twenty years of roaming and outlawing with the gang before I'd left that life in the Yukon dust.

The gold rush that had mobilized half the continent was long o'er, and most of the folks left were simply hanging on. To what, I wasn't rightly sure. I'd been delivering supplies to Mr. Henley for a couple of years, since 1904, and 'The Paris of the North' had long since failed to live up to its name. The city just kept getting dirtier and the people more desperate. What little economy was left centered around small shops and mining operations that remained, trying to make sense of a world where towns were built up then abandoned in the blink of an eye, when better offerings were found elsewhere.

The city was on the decline and full of desperate people.

There were one or two decent hotels left, so after I'd unloaded the wagon at Mr. Henley's store with the help of his son, I made my way to the Miner's Rest Hotel on Front Street in the middle of all the action. By 'action', I meant the dubious operation of a number of saloons and cathouses that were left o'er from the gold rush days. But, where they might have enjoyed a brief time of luxury and the illusion of respectability, now they languished in a sorry state of lefto'er offerings and a dank sense of necessity.

There were still miners in and around Dawson City with gold to spend, but they were few and far between, and a far cry from the gold dust that had flowed for a few years at the end of the century. That gold had made this city, and now t'was dying without it. T'was a shadow of its former self, and I knew that because I'd seen it at its height, back when I'd been with the gang. We'd make the occasional trip into town after a good job and spend our money on whores and liquor.

The whores in those days had been personable, intelligent and outspoken women—lots of them pretty, many of whom were in Dawson to mine the gold out of the miner's themselves, make their fortune on their backs and head back to the places they'd come from, to lead respectable lives with no word as to how they'd gotten their money. They were a special breed, these young women, hardy and enterprising. But they'd left to follow the gold and the miners to Alaska when the pickings got slim in Dawson, and now the only ones left were the ones who had no other choice but to do the work they did. I'm not saying a man couldn't find a good one, and some of the cathouses had higher standards than others in terms of cleanliness and the way they did business.

But things were different now, and the town was dying of neglect.

Even as I stabled the horses and left the wagon in the care of a stableman at the hotel, I saw a young fella in grimy clothes and worn shoes swipe an apple from where it sat on the wagon bed, where it must have tumbled out of one of the boxes I'd delivered to Mr. Henley. T'was hard to guess his age under all the filth—probably an adult, although barely. He looked awful young to me...and scraggly.

I met his gaze, and he froze like he thought I'd go after him or mention him to the stable hand. But I wasn't gonna do that. I held his wary gaze for a whole second, trying to let him know I didn't have anything against him, and I wasn't gonna tell anyone about the apple. He narrowed his eyes at me as his grimy hand tightened around the bruised fruit, and he took it and turned tail, moving fast into the street so he wouldn't get caught if I changed my mind.

A shiver snaked down my spine because I'd seen a desperate look like that before. Those eyes knew pain and abuse, hunger and hopelessness. I hated everything about those eyes and what they meant— that this youngster was reduced to the most basic of human needs and even those weren't being met. But I shook it off, because there was more than one desperate, starving fella in this town, and I couldn't do anything about it. And there wasn't no use worrying about any of them.

In the hotel I paid for a large room with a double bed because I had the money and I was sick of camping on the ground. Mr. Henley had paid me and given me a bonus because he was pleased with my punctuality and the quality of the goods I'd delivered. So, goddammit, I was gonna spend a few days living in style.

First off, I needed a bath then a meal. Then I was gonna get myself a whore and fuck all the hardships of the past few weeks of rough travel out of my system.

* * * *

The hotel maid had two young men bring up a tub and three buckets of hot water, which they poured into the tub before leaving. The maid herself brought a bucket of cooler water for rinsing and left it on the floor beside the tub, giving me a towel and a bar of rough soap.

"Anythin' else you need, mister? And don't say a woman, 'cause you can get one o' them down the street and I ain't got nothin' to do with that."

"No, ma'am. I only need what you brought me — and thank you for that."

She huffed, as if she didn't believe me, then left me to myself.

It felt good to take off my dirty clothes and leave them outside the door for the maid to wash. I had some clean ones in my pack that I got out and set on the chair for after my soak. I stretched to one side, then the other, making my old bones creak in the process. I was thirty-six and had wasted most of my life doing things I wasn't proud of. How I'd got myself involved with the likes of Spook and Whitlaw was an old story of misguided loyalty and misplaced trust. They'd impressed me with their skills at shooting and robbing before I'd been introduced to the coldness with which they dispatched their victims in the name of completing a job. Spook especially had a tendency toward torture that I'd found extremely off-putting. But by the time I'd realized the depths of their depravity, t'was too late. I was a fixture in the gang, and I didn't know how to escape it.

I was valued for my strength and my willingness to do whatever they asked of me, no matter how humble. For the longest time I'd thought they'd hunt me down if I left and either kill me or drag me back, until I realized that they didn't even care enough to do that. T'was a cruel joke to me when I'd finally gotten the balls to take off and leave them, that I could have done it ages before without a problem.

They'd ruined my life and for what? For nothing. My presence in their gang had meant nothing, only that

I bore witness to the cruelty and carelessness of evil men with no solid plan for the future. They were aimless, simply living for the next job and the next — killing, raping and torturing for the privilege of scrounging a few dollars that they soon spent on drink and women.

T'was a rude awakening for me that life was only what you made of it.

And I was determined to make something of mine now.

* * * *

I slept the sleep of the dead that night and woke up late the next morning. All that travel had worn me out. I hoped the horses were recovering with good feed and attention in the hotel stables. They'd need a few days' rest — and so would I.

I popped in after breakfast to check on them.

"Hey, there. My horses doin' okay?" I asked the lad in charge of the stables.

"Yes, sir. They've enjoyed their time to rest, and I reckon they'll be ready to go by tomorrow or the next day, sure enough."

"Good. I know you take good care of 'em."

Dixie, the brown mare with the stripe down her face, was the only thing I'd got worth any value from my time with the gang. I'd worried they'd come after me to get her back because she was a damn good horse, strong and young enough to have a lot of good years left in her. But the gang had enough horses, and they could always get more since they had no problem stealing anything they took a shine to. They probably figured t'was more bother to chase me down than to find a random horse if they needed one.

As part of our contract, Mr. Henley paid for their stabling and me a salary to bring goods from the depot in Whitehorse to Dawson. It saved him a couple of hundred to bring them supplies overland rather than pay the high prices of river transport. He owned a sleigh that I used in the winter months, and t'was a cold and harsh journey, except for the roadhouses that were scattered along the trail where I could get a warm bed, a couple of hot meals to shore me up and shelter when the weather was bad. I was getting used to it, but I still didn't look forward to the cold and dark of a Yukon winter. Still, t'was good, honest work and I was living a respectful life.

That in itself was worth its weight in gold.

I reckoned I had one more trip with the wagon left before I'd have to switch to the sleigh. Winter came early up north, and t'was late August now. By mid-September to early October, temperatures would plummet, and the snow would come, coating everything in a frigid white blanket and bringing the threat of frostbite and hypothermia with it. Still, I was happier with the weather trying to kill me than I ever was treading lightly around Spook and Whitlaw, who could've murdered me for the heck of it at a moment's notice. The weather seemed more honest and predictable than them two.

While I leaned against the stable door, I saw that young man again—the skinny one covered in dirt and grime with the tragic eyes and likely more tragic backstory. This time he slunk along the side of the mercantile across the street, eyeing a pretty girl in a coat and bonnet whose purse dangled by strings from her dainty wrist. There weren't a lot of respectable women in Dawson, but she was one of them, and it looked like she had the wealth to keep her place in society.

I stood up straighter, narrowing my eyes at the wraith, trying to tell him with a look that he was getting in o'er his head with her. She wasn't gonna let a dirty street rat steal her money, and if she caught him red-handed, she'd have the law on him in a heartbeat.

I caught his eye and shook my head once back and forth, like I was his daddy telling him to behave himself, but he didn't pay any attention—only licked his lips and focused in on that lady's purse, inching toward her as if he'd be able to slip it off her, when t'was tied on fast with a pretty green ribbon.

I rolled my eyes and stepped forward, crossing the street quickly and doffing my hat. "Ma'am," I said, attracting her attention as the street rat's eyes widened and he shrank back. "Sorry to bother you but watch your step. There's a nasty puddle here in your way. Allow me to help you," I said, putting on my most gentlemanly manners to assist her when she was perfectly capable of making her way along the street without my assistance.

"Well, aren't you kind? Thank you so much, Mister...?" Her brown eyes flashed up at me with a query.

"Downing. Jimmy Downing," I said, glancing at the skinny fella who'd melted into the shadows with an angry frown.

I let the lady take my arm and guided her around the puddle. She let go and flashed me a smile. "Thank you. Good day," she said, releasing my arm and walking off as I moved back along the street to the last place I'd seen the young man.

I found him huddled in a doorway, regarding me warily with blatant hostility.

"Why'd you do that? That was my mark, and you knew it."

"What's your name, boy?"

"I ain't a boy. And I ain't gonna tell you my name."

I took a breath. "Why don't you come with me, and I'll get you somethin' to eat. You look hungry."

"Yeah? Well, you look like you enjoy gettin' in the way of other people who's just tryin' to get by."

I narrowed my eyes. "If you'd gone after that lady's purse, she'd have called the law on you. That what you want?"

He sighed, and it looked like a shudder went through his wiry frame. "Don't matter. Why don't you leave me be?" He sounded so tired and about done with everything, so it seemed futile to continue.

"Fine. Suit yourself." I moved off and went about my business, done caring about what happened to the dirty little bastard. He'd said he wasn't a boy, and I'd figured that, but he didn't look much older than eighteen or nineteen, in my opinion, and what was the point of arguing, anyway? I'd offered to get him some food and he'd declined, so that was that.

I had some small errands to do, and t'was mid-afternoon by the time I made my way along Front Street to the old Monte Carlo theater, which, in its heyday, had been the star attraction in Dawson City, where many a lucky miner had squandered his gold on entertainment and loose women. Now t'was a run-down, dirty establishment that housed a slew of working women who, while not the cream of the crop of young dance-hall girls that had plumbed the pockets of the miners, but who were a step above what I'd find a street or two o'er in Paradise Alley and Hell's Half Acre.

The front room was a saloon where a man could grab a cheap drink before heading to the back and availing himself of meatier offerings, and t'was where I planned to spend a relaxing minute or two before satisfying the hunger that had built inside me for weeks. There were brothels in Whitehorse, sure enough, but they weren't as plentiful as here, and t'was harder for respectable men—or men who were trying to become respectable—to avail themselves without drawing the attention of a disapproving public.

Here in Dawson City in 1906 nobody cared how men spent their time, because things had been so wild and unhindered in them gold rush days. This was a sorry and desperate town now, and the people who lived here had lower standards than most—or could turn a blind eye easier. So I saved my whoring for Dawson City, even though I could have used a more regular relief than waiting for two or three weeks to pass between a brush of the intimate kind.

As I trod the wooden sidewalk in the fading afternoon light of a late August afternoon, my head was filled with the delights soon to be available to me, and I wasn't prepared for the sight of the disheveled street rat lurking in the shadows of the doorway as if he were about to go in himself.

Chapter Two

Lost Boy

"Jesus, not you again. What's your angle? You goin' in?" I said, remembering my first visit to one of these places and how scared I'd been. Maybe I could grease the wheels for him, make it easier. I could do that much, since he'd refused my help earlier. I didn't begrudge him his attitude. If I were starving in the streets of Dawson City like an abandoned dog, I'd be surly too.

I could see him better in this light, and the way he looked at me with eyes wide and cheeks hollow like he hadn't had a square meal in days made me uncomfortable all of a sudden.

"What's it to you?" he said, his voice soft and sallow, like he could barely rustle the energy.

"Ain't nothin' to me, son. Suit yourself," I said, shrugging and grabbing the door handle.

"Wait. You sure you want to go in there?" he said, making me pause, even though I was pretty damn sure I did.

"What?"

The fierce-eyed youth scrubbed at his face like he was trying to scrape some of the dirt off. I could smell him now, and t'wasn't pleasant. It looked like he hadn't had a bath in months.

He threw a gaze at me then, like he held a secret close and he was about to share it. "Maybe *I* can help you."

I stared at him for a long moment, wondering what the hell he was talking about, until his gaze slid down my shirt and locked on my groin. Even as dirty and skinny as he was, the jolt that ran through me was considerable. I must have been plumb horny to swell at that look, that's for sure. Better I got inside and got me a plump girl right fast if I was gonna respond to something this questionable and...well, *wrong*. But it made sense in a way, that he wasn't hanging around out here to spend money but to make some.

"What are you talkin' about?" I said in a whisper, glancing around to see if anyone was near. But t'was only me and the young fella out there, and goddamn it if I didn't suddenly have a curiosity and a need firing up inside me that threatened to burn down the whole town. Because I knew what he meant. Of course I knew. And hell, by now I'd done way worse things than have my cock sucked by a starving street rat.

Except this street rat seemed barely old enough to sit at a bar, and that made me wary.

He licked his filthy lips and tried to smile, though it came off more like a grimace. "I can help you out for a few dollars, mister. Less than you'd pay inside — and quicker, too." He gave me a half-hearted leer that came off more pitiful than anything else. "I know what I'm doin'."

"How old are you?" I asked, squinting into the darkness to get a bead on him.

"How old do you want me to be?" he said, the crack in his voice touching me in places that weren't connected to my dick, finally.

"Look... I ain't... I ain't lookin' for that. You shouldn't be out here offerin' yourself to strangers," I said.

He stared at me for a long time then he said, "Fuck you. And I will if you'll pay me to. You wrecked the mark I had earlier, so you owe me. I ain't got no other choice. I need somethin' to eat, mister, and if I gotta eat your cock before I get a meal, that's just fine."

The way he said it, with resignation, logic and a cold pragmatism that hit me right in the gut made me hesitate. We stared at each other for another long minute. I took my hand off the door handle.

"You don't have to touch me. I'll get you somethin' to eat, son."

"What?"

"I said, I'll get you somethin' to eat. Come with me." I told my dick to settle the fuck down, that it would have to wait a while for any action and I stepped away from the building as another man came up and gave me the stink-eye, grabbing the door handle and yanking it open. The sounds of music and people talking, laughter and singing were out of place with the atmosphere out on the street between me and the starving youngster.

"I ain't coming," he said.

"Why the fuck not? You gonna go inside and offer yourself?" I looked him o'er with deliberate disdain. "They ain't gonna want you, the way you look." I wrinkled my nose. "You smell like a cistern."

His face drooped and his mouth opened like I'd taken away the last of any hope he'd ever had. A full-body shiver took him, even though t'was warm out there in the heat of the August afternoon.

Tugged at my heart strings it did. Guess I wasn't as cynical and hard-hearted as I'd thought.

"Come on. I've got a room at the hotel. You can have a meal and a bath and get cleaned up."

I glanced at the whorehouse, then back at the grimy fella. "If you want to come back here tomorrow, at least you'll have more to bargain with."

Maybe, in the meantime, I'd be able to convince him that t'wasn't the answer he thought t'was. I'd seen enough of the world to know it would be a step on the way to disaster and disease and a miserable fucking life.

I started walking, not even glancing back to see if he'd follow. He was like a skittish horse, and the best way to earn his trust was confidence and care. After a little while, I stopped suddenly and waited. Sure enough, he almost walked into me, and I had to turn quickly as he cursed and recovered.

"Careful there."

"What the fuck are you doing?"

"Making sure you're coming. You might as well. I don't think you'll get a better offer tonight."

He stared at me for a long moment, clutching his arms like he was cold. I wondered when he'd eaten last. His dirty clothes hung on him like he was a scarecrow.

I took pity.

"My name's Jimmy. Jimmy Downing. I haul supplies to a man in town. Just dropped off my load and was aimin' to relax and find a pretty girl that don't cost much. But I figure I can do that tomorrow." I looked him o'er. "What's your name?"

He blinked like he had to think long and hard to remember. "Oscar."

I smiled, trying to show him I could be kind. "That's a good, strong name. Now come on before you fall o'er, Oscar. You need a proper feeding, and I aim to get you one."

Oscar nodded, like he'd given up trying to oppose me. "Fine."

"You can stay with me tonight. I got a room at the hotel," I said. "After that, you're on your own."

He nodded and shivered again. I hoped to God he wasn't sick with anything catching.

As we rounded a corner, a man on a horse came near and Oscar stepped out of the way and almost tipped right o'er. I quick grabbed a fistful of his soiled shirt and held on to him.

"Easy, there."

"Shit."

He side-eyed me like he still didn't trust I wasn't hauling him off somewhere to fuck. But I wouldn't ever do that. Guess he wasn't sure, and I didn't blame him. He was lucky it'd been me who found him.

He was lucky. I wasn't sure about me at this point. He was a surly little animal, but I couldn't really blame him, 'cause it looked like he'd had it rough lately and who knew for how long. There was something about him that made me want to look after him, anyways.

My heart was about breaking at the state of him by now, and I wanted to get him inside and fed, first of all. Then a hot bath and maybe arrange for some decent clothes somehow. If I could do all that and he got a good night's sleep, maybe I could live with myself taking off the next day.

True enough, he wasn't the only starving person in this town. True enough, I couldn't save them all. But maybe I could stop at least one of them from taking desperate measures that would ruin their life forever.

After the gold rush a few years before, this town had taken a nosedive. So many people had lost their livelihoods and savings on a fool's errand, coming all the way out here when all the promising land had been claimed already. Most of them had turned around and gone back home, but some of them stayed and tried to make a living other ways. It didn't always work out. I wondered what Oscar's story was. He seemed too young to have come out on his own

He stared at my hand like he didn't trust what t'was going to do to him, then pulled away roughly, out of my grasp, almost falling, but he recovered himself.

"I ain't no delicate flower," he spat, snarling at me like a rabid cur. I had to stop myself from really laying into him, because he was being so disrespectful. But he was obviously in dire straits and probably not right in the head.

"I know you ain't. But you're so exhausted and weak that I don't believe you're payin' attention to your surroundings much. You'll end up under a horse or in a mud puddle, and you're dirty enough already." I smiled to make it sound kinder.

"I don't need your charity, mister. If you'd let me suck your dick, you could have paid me and it would have been a fair exchange. I don't want to owe you."

Red heat flushed my face as I processed his words and glanced around to see if anyone had heard him, but nobody was paying us any mind, and we were almost at the hotel.

"A fair exchange, huh? How much you think a guy'd pay for that? Enough for a room and a meal and a wash and a new set of clothes, maybe? I doubt it."

"You never know."

I looked him o'er and made a skeptical sound. "Anyway, I don't want that, and neither do you. I'm offerin' you some kindness here, and I suggest you take it." I offered my hand to help him, since he seemed so unsteady.

He rolled his bottom lip between his teeth, looking between my face and my hand until he finally shrank in defeat. "Fine. But I ain't takin' your hand."

"Fine," I said, trying not to laugh.

God, he was a fiery colt. He gave me a look that would have killed a less experienced fella than I was.

"You sure you don't want to suck my dick, mister? You can do it after I get that wash, if you're picky." He wiggled his ass in front of my face and almost fell, grabbing my arm reluctantly. "You pay more, and you can do more. I gotta lot of things I can do for you."

My cheeks flamed, and I couldn't deny I was looking at his ass in those dirty trousers, but not with anything but the urge to tan it ten times to Sunday. This boy could use a good spanking to tame that smart mouth and teach him not to trade himself for money no more.

"Stop tryin' to get me to do that. I don't wanna go near your little dick right now — or any day. I was looking for a woman when you got in my way, not a man. I ain't like that — and maybe neither are you."

I didn't doubt he'd figured out the best way to score some cash, and it didn't say anything about what he actually wanted. Surely, t'wasn't that.

I'd been around enough that I knew some men wanted that, and I had no problem with it at all. Can't say sometimes I didn't think about it, too, with a shiver and a guilty conscience. But I didn't have much time for anything but hauling supplies, let alone chasing other men for comfort. T'was easier to pay a whore and get some level of satisfaction that didn't require too much moral questioning.

Anyway, who was I kidding? When had I ever tried to be a moral man? Except for now. Now I *was* trying. And I'd be damned if this bratty little bastard was gonna ruin that.

I watched his face twist into an expression of real hate and anger now.

"It ain't *little*," he seethed, and I wondered if I'd struck a nerve. "It maybe ain't a horse cock like you prob'ly got, but it's just fine, thanks. And I should go right back to that whorehouse and find me a man who'll pay to get his cock sucked or somethin' else. I aim to earn my keep."

I stared at him with barely concealed contempt that shifted to pity as I watched his lips twitch with the effort to keep from crying. I didn't know how to deal with his attitude, and I was quickly losing patience.

"Fine. You wanna go back there, go on. I'm goin' inside and gettin' a table and orderin' some beef and potatoes, maybe dessert, if they got it. You wanna join me, you're welcome to. I'll leave it up to you."

I turned and headed for the hotel, which was only a few buildings away, hoping he'd follow but giving him the choice. I wasn't gonna force him to do anything. That wasn't my style. If he wanted the dignity of choosing his own path, I'd give it to him. Wasn't no skin off my nose. Would make things a hell of a lot easier for me, actually.

But as I stepped into the darkness of the hotel, I hoped he would let me help him. For some goddamn reason, the state of him out there and the fact he was trying to hustle for a buck made me sad and frustrated with the state of things.

Chapter Three

A Hearty Meal

There were a lot of people in the hotel restaurant, but a woman in a brown skirt, blue blouse printed with white flowers and a gray apron greeted me and directed me to a table in the corner by the fireplace. T'was a small table for two people, which was all I needed. Hell, maybe t'was more than I needed.

I sat in the chair facing the door, hoping Oscar would make the right decision and let me look after him for one night—get him fed and cleaned up and clothed properly—maybe give him tips on jobs he could do that wouldn't involve praying on the baser instincts of strange men.

The lady in the flowered blouse brought me a beer and a plate of bread, and I hoped to hell Oscar wasn't lying out there in the mud or trying to walk back to the cathouse. I'd done what I could, in any case, and if he didn't show at that door soon, I had my answer. I tried to let it go, and I thought I had until the door opened and the filthy fella stepped into the hotel, looking like a lost calf, his eyes all big and his legs barely holding him up. My heart jumped into my throat, and I stood, lifting my hat off the table and waving it so he'd see me.

He caught sight of me and couldn't hide his relief, which made me thrill a bit. He *did* need me, at least for something as basic as a meal and a bed — and that was enough. T'was something I could do for him, and I wanted to do it. I was glad he had the sense to take what was offered him.

He made it to the table, almost crashing into the woman in the flowered blouse, who was carrying plates of food.

"Mind yourself," she scolded as she swerved around him, wrinkling her nose as she caught the stench of him.

He didn't pay no attention but continued to the table and collapsed into the other chair, making a sound of surrender and splaying his filthy hands out in front of him.

"I ain't got no other place to go, mister. So, I guess I'll take your charity."

I nodded. "Good. You don't have to call it that, though. I only wanna help."

He gave me a look. "Why?"

He stank, but our table was a ways from any other, so I buckled down to bear it. I'd smelled worse things in my time.

His blatant inquiry made me smile, because I didn't rightly know. I shrugged and sipped my beer as the server slapped another one on the table in front of Oscar and he looked at it like t'was the holy fucking grail or something.

"I don't rightly know why but I do, and you might as well shut up and take advantage of that fact and stop questioning it," I said, pushing the mug of ale closer to him.

"Fine," he said, his eyes going dreamy as he looked at the amber liquid.

"Fine."

He picked up the mug and brought it to his lips, closing his eyes and gulping the drink down in long, sensuous swallows. The sight of the ball of his throat moving back and forth made me feel funny, and I wasn't used to feeling that way looking at another man. A woman's elegant wrist or a glimpse of her naked ankle, sure—but not a man's goddamn throat.

And this fella was barely a man, which made it a hundred times worse. What two adults wanted to do together was nobody else's business. I put the blame square on him for talking about sucking my dick so much. I didn't want to think about it.

I cleared my throat and focused on enjoying my own beer. The lady in the flowered blouse came by then and plopped two plates of supper down before us.

"You got a room for the night?" she asked me.

"Yep."

"What's the number? I'll put this on your tab."

"Sure. Number two-oh-five. Can I have a tub of hot water brought up in an hour? And is there a way I could get a set of clothes for my" —I cleared my throat, thinking fast. If he were related to me it wouldn't seem so strange bringing him up to my room later—"cousin here? His are"—I glanced at Oscar, who had noticed the food and picked up his fork, ignoring us completely—"beyond repair."

The woman wiped her hands on her apron and covered her nose as she looked Oscar o'er. "I'll see what I can do. Might be able to find him something for a small fee."

I nodded. "I'll leave that in your hands, then. Thank you."

She grabbed Oscar's glass to fill up again. When she'd gone, I watched the poor wretch shovel food into his mouth like he hadn't eaten in a week. For all I knew, it had been longer. His eyes had glassed o'er, and he didn't seem aware of anything but the food going into his mouth. He choked and coughed, but that didn't slow him down none.

I glanced up and noticed people starting to stare. Not that I cared, but I thought he might.

I put a hand on his arm and nodded at his fork. "Hey, slow down. This ain't goin' nowhere. It's yours."

He focused on me, a dribble of gravy snaking down his chin as he tried to slow his actions. I knew I was right, and he'd been starving...actually starving.

"Also, you'll make yourself sick, and it'll all come back up. Not much good if it does that."

He seemed to think about that logic and slowed. But he looked as if he didn't trust that all this food would wait for him to eat it in his own time.

"Now I want you to answer some questions for me. Maybe that will slow you down." I said, chewing on some potato before I spoke. "Since I'm payin' for this here meal, I figure I have the right to a few basic answers."

He swallowed and narrowed his eyes. Then he nodded curtly, resuming his eating. "Fine," he said with his mouth full.

"How old are you?"

Maybe I was worried about the thoughts I was having, and if he was older than eighteen that would help me to feel better. It's not like I was planning to do anything, but even thinking about him that way was beginning to disturb me, since I'd never had sexual thoughts about a particular fella before, only random fantasies involving men instead of women.

He looked me up and down and smirked as he swallowed his potato. "I'm twenty-one."

I gaped at him, and he smiled, the first time I'd seen him do that. It lit up his face like a light had started shining inside him, stoked by the hot food and warmth of the room. Don't know if I was shocked more by his smile or by what he'd said his age was.

"Get out. You're not a day older 'n twenty," I said, because he didn't look it at all. Honest to God, he didn't look even that old.

"I don't got any papers to show you, mister, but I'm twenty-one. I know I don't look it. Most men *like* that."

I focused on my food so I could ignore that comment. "I told you my name. Why are you still callin' me 'mister'?"

He shrugged, looking me o'er as if he'd only now been able to fully see me, now that he had food in his belly and his brain had started working again. "Mister's easier. I already forgot your name."

"It's Jimmy."

"All right. I ain't got any papers to show you, Jimmy."

I nodded. "I believe you're what you say you are. It's simply that you look younger than that."

His smile turned into a grin that made me feel something else again. "Yeah, I know. I'm way too skinny, and these clothes are too big."

I was pleased to see his ability to smile and converse developing. The food and beer were doing him good. If he were truly as old as he'd said, well, that relieved me, although I could hardly believe it. But at least I was having these thoughts about a grown-ass-adult man and not a child—whatever they were—and I didn't want to examine them too closely. I'd gotten him to trust me, finally, at least a bit, and I wasn't going to take

33

advantage of this situation. I wanted to help him out, not add to his problems.

His smile disappeared as quickly as it had come, and a strange expression o'ercame his features. He shifted in his chair and put a hand to his belly.

"You okay, son?" I said, even though he'd told me he was old enough to be married and have a son of his own.

He shook his head. "I don't know," he said, gaze flicking to mine, then darting about the room. "I ain't eaten much for a while. Maybe it's not agreein' with me."

"You gonna hurl?" I asked.

"Maybe. Dunno."

I nodded. "Come with me, then."

"But if we leave, they'll take our food away —" He looked horrified at the thought, even though it had started to make him sick.

"No, they won't. I'll tell the serving girl."

He looked like he was about ready to toss his stomach, so I moved quick and took him by the elbow, leading him through the restaurant. As we passed the lady with the flowered blouse, I told her my cousin wasn't feeling well and I was taking him outside, but we would return to eat the rest of our meal — or at least I would. She gave Oscar a skeptical look but nodded.

I got him outside and steered him to the bushes beside the hotel. He clutched his stomach and bent o'er, and I prepared to watch him vomit up everything he'd eaten, but it didn't happen. We stood there while the sun moved closer to the horizon and the electric streetlamps came on, illuminating the narrow street in the dim evening light. I laid a steadying hand on his back because he was obviously not feeling well, and I felt awful for him, being so damn hungry and not able to eat a lot without upsetting himself.

"You okay? You gonna hurl?" I said.

He breathed deeply and carefully for a bit. "I think I'm okay. Thought I was gonna hurl, but I'm feelin' better." He looked at me with a blatant vulnerability that touched something inside me. "You were prob'ly right about me eatin' too fast."

I nodded. Well, at least he'd admitted it. "You wanna go back in?"

"Yeah. But I'm gonna watch you eat for a bit."

"Sounds like a good idea."

I moved to take his elbow out of concern for his ability to stay upright, but he shook me off.

"I'm all right now."

"Fine."

We sat back down at the table, and I finished my potatoes and beef, then ate the green beans while Oscar watched me closely. I wondered what he was thinking. Probably cursing me for being able to eat when he couldn't.

"Why don't you try eatin' some of your beans now?" I said, urging with my fork. "Maybe t'was the beef on your empty stomach."

He nodded and sighed. "I couldn't help myself. Long time since I had any meat." He forked a bean and put it in his mouth, chewing slowly and carefully before swallowing it and waiting.

"Well?" I asked.

"S'okay. I just have to go slow."

"I reckon you're right."

By the time Oscar had finished his beans, he looked much better. He had color in his face now under all the grime, at least. And that brought me to my next mission.

"Come on. Let's go up."

He regarded me warily but stood and followed me to the wooden stairs by the hotel entrance that led up to the second floor.

I motioned for him to go up first, in case he wobbled and fell. He was obviously weak and pretty damn bone tired, and I wasn't taking any chances.

He moved up the steps, taking his time as if he was sixty-four and not twenty-one. Poor fella was in a sorry state, and I aimed to fix that.

I fit the key the matron had given me into the lock and twisted, pushing the door open. When Oscar followed me in, he stopped and stared.

"What?" I asked.

"It's big."

"I know it. I've stayed here before. You get your money's worth."

I shut the door behind him. There was a sizeable bed in the corner, and a dresser and washstand under a large window that looked out o'er the street. T'was clean, too, and warm. Someone had built a fire in the grate, and it crackled and popped while we looked around. I was pleased to see there was a large tub already placed in front of the fire with steaming water in it.

"There's a bath," he said in a voice filled with wonder.

I nodded. "I asked them to bring it. I've already had one, so that there's for you. I usually ain't quite so clean as I am now."

He looked me o'er from top to tail and took his time about it, making me wonder if he was truly looking for a man to fuck and not doing it because it paid well. His gaze made me feel goose-pimply and shy, and I both liked it and didn't at the same time—probably because of what that said about me and what I might be wanting.

If only I'd run into Oscar after *leaving* the cathouse, I would've been spent and satisfied and not looking for anything alive—barely, in Oscar's case—to warm my sorry dick. Maybe. I shook off that thought and figured I'd have time after he fell asleep to take the edge off, at least, as long as I did it quietly.

He looked o'er at the tub and back at me. "You gonna watch, mister? I mean, Jimmy? I don't care if you do, just be honest about it."

Well, that made me blush and stammer. "I may watch, but it's only to make sure you don't fall full asleep and drown in that thing. You're barely standin' straight. When's the last time you slept?"

He scrunched up his face as he started to unbutton the soiled shirt that hung on his thin frame. "Don't remember. Hard to sleep when your belly's eatin' you from the inside."

I nodded and took off my hat, laying it on the bedside table beside a little bowl holding a handful of peanuts. "I reckon that's true."

He watched me as he finished unbuttoning his shirt and let it fall to the floor. "You ever been that hungry?"

I nodded. "Yeah. Couple of times. It ain't pleasant."

"No, it ain't. So that's why I was lookin' for a dick to suck, by the way. I ain't never done that for money before. Only ever when— Never mind," he said, looking at me kind of shyly now. "Thought you should know that."

"I'm glad to hear it." And I *was* glad. Although the fact he'd sucked dick at all made me wary...and strangely aroused.

God, I'm a goddamn mess.

"You think it's wrong?" he said, eyeing me cautiously.

"Do I think it's wrong to suck a man's dick for money? Yeah, sure do. But I guess starvation can drive a person to extremes."

He shook his head, laughing with a sort of sadness at the same time. "No, I mean for a man to *want* to suck another man's dick.

I realized what he was asking. "Oh," I said, and cleared my throat.

He undid his trousers and let them fall from his thin frame, standing naked in the dim light from the fire and the lamp I'd lit. He was fucking dirty and skinny. There was no denying that. But he stood tall and proud, naked as the day he was born while I looked him o'er, wondering why my cock was getting hard and figuring I'd fuck almost anything right now, barring an animal or a child. But I wasn't gonna fuck him, even though I kind of wanted to see what it'd be like.

I sat down on the bed and swung my feet up, crossing my boots and my arms behind my head. "I've seen enough of this world not to get upset by anythin' like that. What folks do in private ain't none of my business. I'd rather see a fella get his dick sucked by another man than get shot or shoot someone else, if you want an honest answer."

Oscar seemed surprised by the statement, and I couldn't blame him. Lots of folks thought that kind of thing was worse than murder. But not me. Because I'd seen murder up close and personal and didn't never want to see that again. Two fellas being physical together for relief or the goddamn joy of it was nothing I was worried about — except now it seemed I was more curious about that than I'd thought. And I didn't really know how I felt about it if it involved *me*.

Oscar blinked quietly, thinking, then said, "I appreciate you bein' honest."

His dick lay soft and small, nestled in a bed of thick dark curls that matched the black hair on his head. I was glad of that, for some reason I couldn't name and didn't want to. I wondered how much bigger it got when he was horny. And why the hell did I care?

I cleared my throat again. "Best get in there before the water cools down."

"Yes, sir," he said, and that just about made all the blood rush to my face, and I didn't know why. What the hell was wrong with me? "I reckon that's a good idea."

Goddamn it, that was the first reasonable thing he'd said to me, and I felt a relief that I couldn't pinpoint. But I was glad he'd stopped fighting what I was trying to do for him, at least for the moment.

"I'll keep an eye on you. If you start to fall asleep, I'll throw a peanut at you. How about that?"

The corner of Oscar's mouth crooked up, and he sighed a laugh. "Fine. You do that. What-the-fuck-ever."

And the attitude was back, but more playful than before, and I liked it. I liked it a lot. More than I wanted to, in fact.

As Oscar sank into the warm water, he made a noise of pure pleasure that went right to my cock, and I couldn't really deny anymore that whatever this young man was doing to me, I was a willing participant. Figures I'd stumble on a wayward fella with an attitude that pushed all my buttons, right when I was determined to be good and lead an honorable life.

Chapter Four

Temptation

I picked up my hat from the table and put it on, tilting it forward so I could watch Oscar in the tub without him seeing exactly how closely I was paying attention. I figured there wasn't any harm in enjoying watching him get clean. I hoped the interest I felt was simply because I knew he'd look and feel so much better and not related to anything else.

He sank into the water up to his chin and sighed. "Goddammit. You just might kill me with this here bath."

My lips twitched but all I did was grunt.

There was silence for a bit and gentle splashing. I peeked from under the brim of my hat to see him vigorously washing his hair with the soap the maid had left. There was a louder splash when he ducked into the tub and rinsed his hair off, then sputtered up to the surface. Things got quieter, and I thought the water must be cooling by now, but he stayed in there. It took me a while to notice a jerky shaking of his shoulders, and I realized he was crying silently and hanging onto the sides of the metal tub with white knuckles.

Before I knew what I was doing, I'd gotten up and walked o'er there, crouched and put my hands on his wet shoulders, the dripping strands of his dark hair against my cheek as I murmured into his ear. "Hey, hey, s'okay. Oscar, yer okay."

I don't rightly know where it came from, this need to comfort and calm him, but doing it satisfied something inside me deep down. There wasn't anything sexual about it, except something hovering quietly in the background, and I didn't examine that too close. I simply did what I needed to do this second for Oscar and let it soothe something wild in me, too, because...why not? There wasn't enough comfort in this world to go around, if you asked me.

I almost expected him to toss me off, but he didn't. He raised a hand and wrapped it around my forearm, holding on to me like if he let go he'd drown or dissolve or something terrible. I wanted to kiss him like my momma did me when I was upset, but I didn't, because it'd seem strange, and I didn't want him to think I wanted something more.

The water had turned brown with all his dirt, and t'was getting cold, just like I'd thought.

"Hey, we better get you out of this cold water. You don't wanna catch a chill. And we still need to get you rinsed."

He seemed to settle himself after a few more moments and nodded.

"All right. Sure."

He gazed at me with swollen eyes that widened with a lost look. "What do I do? It's so long since I had a proper bath that I don't remember."

And I about melted, but I didn't want him to see that emotion in my eyes, so I pulled back and got up. "You need to stand up, and either you or I gotta pour that lukewarm water onto you," I said, gesturing to the floor where the maid had left a bucket for rinsing.

"Can you help me? I'm still wobbly and weak—and tired. So goddamn tired."

"Of course," I said, glad he was accepting my help and not fighting it anymore. I hoped I'd soothed all the fight out of him with good food and a warm bath. All he needed now was a solid night's sleep and he'd feel so much better. I was sure of it. At least I could give him that before we parted ways. I suppose he was a little like a stray dog I'd found, and that was why I was having these soft feelings. I wanted to help him, but I'd have to let him go.

I kicked his dirty clothes o'er to beside the door and went to get the bucket of clean water. Setting it beside the tub, I took hold of his arm and helped him stand. He felt shaky for sure, so I held on to him with one hand and lifted the small bucket with the other. It had a lip on it so I could hold it with one hand.

"Ready?"

"Sure."

He gasped as I tipped the bucket o'er top of him. The cooler water ran o'er his thin frame, making a louder noise than I'd expected but taking all the remaining dirt and soap suds with it. I kept him steady while I lowered the bucket, then helped him step out onto the wood floor. I should have thought to put a towel down, because water dripped everywhere. At least there was one to dry him off, and before I even thought about it, I was rubbing him briskly with it, o'er his body, everywhere that was wet, as if he were a small child.

"Hell, I prob'ly could have done that myself," he said, and I froze.

I looked up and he was watching me with a curious, half-amused look out of sleep-droopy eyes.

"Sorry," I said, clearing my throat and handing him the towel, trying not to look at his naked body. Now that he was clean, I could see he had some muscle on him, even though he could use a lot more—and some fat besides. This man needed feeding something fierce or he'd fade away to nothing.

"Don't gotta be sorry," he said, the hint of a smile on his face. "T'was nice."

He held my gaze for longer than I was comfortable with, so I looked away and rubbed at my forehead with a finger, puzzling o'er whether he should get into bed naked or if I had something he could wear. The serving girl hadn't come up with any clothes yet, and besides, Oscar needed sleep more than anything else right now.

But I didn't think having him naked beside me in that bed was a good idea, the state I was in. I wasn't gonna do anything, but what if I fell asleep and had one of my horny dreams and cozied up to him, thinking he was a girl and—goddamn it—I'd done worse things in my life. But that wouldn't exactly endear me to him, and for some reason I wanted to be his friend more than anything, even if we did have to part ways soon.

"I should prob'ly thank you for that and everythin' else you done for me." He gazed at me with what might be the beginnings of affection, and I took it and held it close to my cold heart. "Nobody's looked after me like this for a long time. And I'm sure nobody will again for exactly as long. So, thank you kindly."

I nodded, the lump in my throat making me cough and stutter. "You're welcome. I'm surely glad to." He swayed a bit, and I steadied him. "Here... I got a clean shirt in my bag. You can wear that for the night. I asked them to see if they could get some clothes for you, so you don't have to put them dirty ones back on."

"Sure. Thank you."

"Maybe they can find some that fit you better."

"Maybe. I'm kinda small for a grown man, though," he said shyly as I helped him into my cotton shirt.

"You ain't that small. You're almost as tall as I am when you stand up straight. Just skinny. You got some muscles."

He looked down at himself and spread his arms to the sides, the shirt billowing out like a sail. "I do? Where the hell are they at, then, 'cause I sure as hell don't see 'em."

And I laughed suddenly, feeling like he was deliberately jerking my chain.

Sure enough, he looked up with an impish expression on his face, and I noticed the dimple in his cheek, and the tiny mole on the other side and his soft brown eyes that looked clearer, although still a bit glazed with exhaustion.

As if reading my mind, he moved toward the bed and fell onto it, stretching out like a cat and grabbing the pillow. "Jesus, I gotta sleep, Jimmy. Sorry I ain't good company."

He yawned and I swear to God he was asleep before I could take another breath. I stood there watching him, now that I had a chance to really look without worrying he'd notice.

Although skinny and shorter than me by a few inches, Oscar wasn't exactly small. And what I'd seen of him without his clothes told me he was a grown man, sure enough. He had a man's dick, even if it seemed on the smaller side, and a spatter of hair between his thighs, thick as thieves o'er whatever he was hiding underneath—a pair of balls bigger than mine, probably. I would never have the courage to stand outside a whorehouse offering myself up for cash. Never, no-how. To be fair, it had probably been more desperation than anything else. When you were that hungry, nothing else much mattered at all.

I knew a bit about what men did to other men in the dark of hidden alleyways, and it didn't sound pleasant to me, even though it must be, somehow, for them to want it. I couldn't deny the thought of Oscar's sweet lips on my cock was more of a distraction than I wanted it to be. But men were beasts. They'd take anyone's damn lips around their dicks if t'was on offer, because t'was plenty easy to close your eyes and pretend whatever you wanted.

And what did it mean that I thought it beneath him to offer himself for cash, when I was going on in there to hire a whore for the night, so I could take care of myself the way I wanted and not with my own hand in the moonlight like most nights? What about that woman? Was it the life she'd have chosen for herself? *Probably not.* Would I have been taking advantage or helping her not to starve by having her mouth on my cock in exchange for a wad of cash? If I really cared about her, I'd just give her the cash.

So, t'wasn't honorable what I'd been doing, either. I had no right to make any judgments about Oscar when I'd been about to dip my stick in the common ink. Because t'was a woman, did that make it more acceptable somehow?

The way I saw it, normally men had more options than women. T'was hard for women if they'd never married or their husbands died or up and left them. There wasn't a whole lot of honorable things a woman could do to make a living, at least one that kept her out of the poorhouse. I figured cathouses were a necessary evil, and I guess I did think I was helping these women by availing myself of their services.

But seeing Oscar there, all skinny and dirty and starving, looking like a boy more than a grown man, had triggered something in me that didn't want to see him that way, didn't want to think of him trading himself for cash, didn't want to think of him doing things he might not have wanted to do, because he needed the money so desperately. Even if they were things he might want to do with another man he chose, because that man looked nice or spoke well or wanted to dote on him, well, that was another thing entirely. Those two things were not the same and I knew it — and he did, too.

There was a soft knock on the door. I didn't want Oscar to wake up, so I answered it quick and quiet. The serving girl stood there with a pile of things in her arms and a pair of boots dangling from one hand.

"I got some clothes for your cousin, Mr. Downing," she said, giving me a saucy look as she tried to peek around me into the room. "He looked damn wrecked. Hope you'll look after him and treat him right."

She gazed at me with a false smile and a fierce look in her pretty eyes that made me think she had the idea I'd brought Oscar here to get up to nonsense with him, and I wanted to straighten her out right there.

"Thank you. I recently got back from out of town and didn't know things were this bad, so I'm getting him cleaned up and — " I didn't know what to say about that but I pushed on. "Then I'll be taking him with me so's I can keep him safe."

She raised her eyebrows as I took the clean clothes from her.

"Well, that's mighty thoughtful of you, Mr. Downing. Not many men would do that, even for a blood relative."

She still sounded like she didn't believe me, but she was happy to drop it.

"The clothes'll be another two dollars that I'll add to your tab."

"Yes, ma'am. Thank you. Can you take these dirty ones away?" I asked, grabbing the soiled clothes off the floor and holding them out to her. I figured these ragged clothes had a long history and that Oscar would be glad to be rid of them. Wasn't much left to them anyway.

She wrinkled her nose, and I couldn't deny they smelled pretty bad. But she took them. "That'll be another fifty cents, Mr. Downing."

"Fine. I'd like this room for another night and possibly one after that. Not sure when we'll be pushin' off."

"Suit yourself. I'll let the innkeeper know."

"Thank you kindly."

I closed the door softly and placed the clothes on the chair beside the bed. Oscar hadn't moved a muscle.

Before I did anything else, I pulled the blankets up o'er him before he caught a chill. The man needed a good night's sleep, and I was determined he'd get one — maybe two if I decided to offer him my company for another night. We'd have to see about that. He might wake up more ornery than he'd been earlier, and if that were the case, well, he could go back to whatever life he wanted for himself. T'was his damn choice.

I walked o'er to the clothes the serving girl had brought and lifted the top piece to have a look. T'was a decent shirt and looked about right to fit him better than the other one — and better than my spare one did. The trousers were basic brown but made of strong material and without any holes or worn parts to them. Same thing for the undergarments.

I had to hand it to this hotel. They knew how to please their guests. I didn't mind so much being charged two whole dollars for these here clothes. The boots were sturdy and definitely used but looked like they might fit, too.

I was taken suddenly with the urge to see him dressed in them and how he might look. I don't know why the idea made my dick swell. Well, I suppose I did, but I didn't want to think about that right now. I had to take myself in hand before he woke up, so I could stop having these thoughts. Then maybe I could get a bit of sleep myself. I had a brief idea of leaving him there and going back to the cathouse to get some real relief, but somehow that wasn't appealing to me anymore. Whether that was because of what I'd been thinking earlier or because now I'd got other ideas of what would please me, I didn't rightly know. But the truth was I didn't want to leave him there alone, in case he woke up and didn't remember where he was or what had happened.

I walked to where the fire was still burning strong and opened my trousers, just enough to slide my hand in there and grab my cock, making a soft noise as the pleasure took me and it swelled the rest of the way, hard as anything. I leaned my other arm on the wood mantel and peeked o'er my shoulder to make sure Oscar was still sound asleep, which he was. I turned back and focused on a rough knot in the wood while I played with myself and got harder and harder and needier and needier.

Flashes of different things went through my mind, and I didn't focus on them or question them, either. A man's desires were a private thing, and I had every right to them. When I was getting close, I eased things with a bit of spit and tried to be quiet, but t'was hard. It'd been a while since I'd spilled my seed, and that was pretty obvious. Didn't take long at all to get close, and when it took me, I swallowed a gasp and a moan as my body shuddered with it real hard. I tried not to think of things, like what it would have been like to have Oscar suck me and what kind of a man did that make me, and did it really fucking matter at this point? I'd never be able to get into Heaven after all the things I'd already done, so what were a few more sins? If I was going to hell anyway, I might as well get some pleasure out of my life.

T'was a nice thought, but I wasn't kidding myself at all. Truth was, I was determined to be on the straight and narrow now and somehow make up for all the terrible things I'd witnessed.

Maybe that was the reason I wanted to help Oscar out so much. T'was penance — penance for the life I'd lived up to now, and for things that had happened that I'd never meant to have happened and that I couldn't barely think about without sobbing like a child.

But that wouldn't help anybody right now. I couldn't change anything about that and there was no point trying. I could only change what I did from now on, and I was determined to do that. And it would take more than a trash-talking brat without two cents to his name to waylay me.

Chapter Five

Revelation

Turned out I was awful tired, too, so after I'd handled myself and they'd come and taken the tub out of the room, I got into bed. I took off my boots and socks and shirt but kept my trousers on in case I got affectionate in my sleep to save the poor fella from waking up to a big fat cock on his back, which he could thank me for later. I was sure I'd be hard again by morning, but there wasn't much I could do about that, was there?

I woke off and on through the night, simply from being in a strange place, but each time, Oscar was sound asleep in the same position, snoring enough to wake the dead. I'd camped with enough men o'er the years to be able to shut out all the snoring and farting anyone could come up with, so that didn't bother me, and I went back to sleep, no problem. By sun-up, I figured he'd be awake, but he was still dead to the world, and except for the snoring, I might have thought he was actually dead, because he slept so deep and still.

I got up and peeked out of the curtains to the early dawn, shivering in the cold since the fire had died in the night. The town had begun to wake up, and I watched for a bit before deciding I could do with another hour of sleep and getting back under the covers where t'was warm and cozy.

The next time I woke up, I didn't rightly know what was happening, except there was something familiar and not familiar going on. It took me a little while to figure out what. I seemed in a dream state for a long time, feeling pleasure and heat and wetness before I really woke up and tried to take stock of things. I heard my own groan before I realized what t'was, and I blinked at the ceiling as someone swallowed my cock and made me cry out into the dimness.

I didn't dare to look, but I didn't tell Oscar to stop, neither. I was too far gone by then, and I couldn't bear to. What that said about me, I didn't rightly know, but I was too o'ertaken to examine it.

Oscar's mouth on my cock — for that was the only thing it could possibly be — felt too goddamn good, and his tongue did wicked things to me that couldn't possibly be legal and didn't feel much like what a woman usually did down there.

Before I knew it, I'd spilled with another desperate groan. He kept me inside his mouth, of all things, and swallowed what I'd given him. My eyes stayed wide open, staring up at the rough wood beams of the ceiling in shock and bliss and confusion and horror — and every other goddamn emotion I could name.

After soothing me with a gentler touch of his talented tongue as I came down from my pleasure-high, he slid off my sorry cock and smacked his lips like he'd done after last night's meal.

I blinked as my heart raced and my breathing stuttered. I couldn't move and I didn't want to, because then I'd have to face what had happened square on, and I wasn't ready to do that yet.

"Jimmy," Oscar said, sidling up beside me and poking me on the hip, "you okay?"

Am I?

I didn't rightly think I was. Maybe I was still dreaming or having a weirdly pleasurable nightmare. Oscar looked sinful in nothing but my white shirt, his lips swollen from having my cock in his mouth, cheeks flushed in the most bewitching way.

I didn't answer.

Then a hand wrapped around my chin and turned my face, so I shut my eyes tight because I couldn't rightly bear to see him right now, after what had happened.

"Jimmy," he said again. I felt his hot breath on my face before he pressed his lips to mine.

My eyes flew wide, and I shoved him away from me.

"What the holy hell you *doin'*?"

My voice was rough and low and shaky, and Oscar stared at me like a dog that had been kicked in the head.

I watched the different emotions skitter across his face while my focus was drawn to a bit of my semen on the corner of his mouth. I shuddered and ran a hand o'er my face, wondering how to deal with this.

"Goddammit," Oscar said, his voice tight with anger. "I was only tryin' to thank you for what you done for me, that's all. I thought you'd like it, from the way you looked after me n'all. The ways you were lookin' at me last night, I thought— Never mind!"

He sounded so frustrated with himself, beat down and like he wanted to crawl under the blankets and hide. So I met his gaze, wanting him to know I was confused, a little shocked and a lot embarrassed at how much I'd liked it, that I didn't rightly know what to say or do.

I shrugged, as if him sucking me off was nothing. Then I apologized, because it had been real nice and friendly of him in a very strange and not-strange way.

"I'm sorry. I didn't mean to sound ungrateful," I said, then collapsed on my back and laughed because what a fucking thing to say, and who the hell was I, anyway?

He shook his head sharply. "Forget it. I made a mistake. I'll get dressed and leave now."

Before he could slide himself off the bed, I shot out my hand and circled his wrist, holding him firm. The sleeves of the shirt puffed out so much above where they were rolled at his elbow that it made his arms look more delicate than they were. He had a sinewy strength to him.

"Don't you run off now."

He tried to pull away, but I held him.

"Stop your squirmin' and listen to me. I got somethin' to say."

He settled down some and huffed a breath.

"Didn't you wonder why I kept my trousers on?" I asked.

"Figured you did it 'cause you thought you might want to get up to mischief with me if you didn't."

Well, I'll be goddamned. Fella was smarter than he looked.

"Maybe I did it because I wasn't comfortable bein' naked with another man in bed? Did you think of that?"

He laughed short and relaxed onto his side. "Didn't seem to have much problem eyein' me all o'er when I got out of the bath — or towelin' my bits."

Is this my fucking life? What the hell is happening?

"For fuck's sake. I was tryin' to help you, Oscar. I'm *still* tryin'."

I let go of his arm, but he didn't move. I couldn't meet his eyes now.

He snorted this time. "Yeah, right, sure. You finished pretty fuckin' hard just now with your cock in my mouth, Jimmy."

The fire that raced up my body from my dick to my face shocked me with its sudden and vicious heat — shame and embarrassment and a lot of remembering exactly how good it had felt, too.

"Fuck," I said.

"Yeah? You wanna?" He traced the wrinkles in the bedsheets idly with his finger, licking those sinful lips that made me want to kiss him all of a sudden. I didn't know what to do with those feelings. The truth of it was that now he was clean and wide awake, Oscar had a certain appeal. His dark brown hair fell softly against his cheeks and forehead, mussed from being in bed, and his brown eyes sparkled with clarity and intelligence. He had barely any facial hair, and what he did have was soft and sparse, and that made him look younger than his twenty-one years. I doubted he'd ever had a shave, in fact.

He reminded me of a lost foal that had been hidden by its dam for its own safety but got up and wandered away from its hollow, and now had become vulnerable to all sorts of danger.

"Stop it."

"You wanna fuck me, say so. I ain't got no problem with it. Hell, the size of you'd make me — "

"Oscar, stop." I used his name on purpose and swiveled to meet his gaze. His eyes were pools of darkness with depths to them I'd not anticipated from how glazed they'd been in his half-starved face the night before. Seemed I would drown as he looked at me and my dick firmed up again, and what the fuck was happening? I reached down, tucked myself in and zipped up my trousers, not breaking eye contact.

Oscar nodded and licked his lips. "That's what I thought. You want to, but you're stoppin' yourself for some reason."

I gaped at him. "For some — for *some* reason?" I sat up on my elbow and watched his eyes track down my naked chest and lock on the swell of my cock under my trousers.

Jesus fucking Christ.

I forced myself to lower my voice, even though I was mad that he was questioning me, because I didn't want nobody else in this hotel to hear what I was saying.

"Maybe for the fact you were half dead with starvation and exhaustion, and I thought you were" — I cleared my throat — "younger than you are when I first noticed you. And maybe for the fact I never thought in my wildest dreams I'd want to do anythin' like that with another man in my lifetime. And maybe because even though you can't get hanged for it no more, they can still put you in the clink for plowin' another man's ass if they find you doing it. You think those're enough *reasons*?"

He blinked and licked his lips, his cheeks flushing even more in a way I was pleased to see, because it meant his blood was flowing well and he was alive. Hadn't been so sure that'd be the case, yesterday.

"Goddammit, Jimmy. You're somethin' when you get riled up."

My brain went blank. "What does *that* mean?"

My gaze followed his hand as he reached down and slid his shirt—*my* shirt—up past his pale hip until he revealed his cock standing there, arched against his belly, very interested in what was going on right now.

"I guess I like it. Even though you're pissin' me the fuck off right now 'cause you don't accept what you want and go for it. I'm sittin' right here. *Hard*. See?" He wrapped his hand around it and gave it a couple of pulls, his eyelids drooping with the pleasure of it. "I might be a bit small, but I'm thick and I'm eager, an' that can make up for a lot, I reckon."

But my gaze locked onto something else, and I didn't reply.

Oscar's mouth opened in surprise as I leaned forward and pushed his hand away, because I wasn't going for what he thought I wanted. I laid two fingers softly against the massive blue bruise on his hip.

"What's this from?"

I suppose t'was still tender, since he made a little hiss when I touched it. It looked goddamn awful, that was for certain. The light must have been too dim for me to notice it last evening.

"It's nothin' but an old bruise. Never mind it," he said.

My gaze shot up to his, and his eyes widened because maybe he saw the no-nonsense demand in my eyes, all of a sudden. "It ain't nothin'. You been manhandled or somethin'." My voice went quieter. "Did somebody violate you?"

He held my gaze for a long moment then cackled a laugh so loud that I drew my hand back.

"Did somebody *violate* me? Who the fuck are you, my Granny Bea? You mean, did I get raped? Did some fella put his dick in my ass without askin' nice?" He sobered up a bit at that. "Well, no, not actually." He looked down at his poor cock that had begun to deflate. "Almost, maybe. But I got in a good kick, you better believe it." He laughed again, this time quieter. "He's prob'ly still tryin' to find his balls, actually."

I blinked hard and looked at that vicious bruise again. "I ain't gonna touch your dick, so you might as well put it away. And I ain't gonna touch you anywhere else right now, so don't get any other ideas."

He opened his mouth to argue but I held up my finger.

"I'm not sayin' I don't want to, mind, just so you know. You seem to know I do, anyhow, and you were right about earlier. I *did* like that, and I can't say I didn't. But I ain't going further with that right now, and you can stop askin' me to." I figured it was best to be straight with him.

He nodded and moved the shirt to cover himself. "Can I ask you one thing, Jimmy? I think I know what the answer is, but I wanna check. And I want you to be honest."

"I'm always honest." Barring answering detailed questions about my outlaw past, that is. I told the truth when I could, and these days, that was most of the time.

He made a weird noise. "Then you ain't like most of the folks I've knowed up to now."

"No, I prob'ly ain't."

He looked up at me from under his dark eyelashes, and t'was all I could do to keep my hands to myself, knowing he was okay with me touching him but trying to remember I wasn't. "Do you like the look of me?"

"Jesus Christ," I said, rolling my eyes. "What the fuck does *that* matter?"

He seemed offended and frowned. "It matters to me."

And suddenly he was the half-starved, exhausted, lost boy again, and my heart about melted into butter.

"Yeah, I like the look of you—more'n I want to." I scratched at my chin as if it were itchy and not because I needed to do something to take away some of the awkwardness I felt admitting that.

He seemed cautious. "You don't think my cock's too small, do you?"

I laughed, then sobered at the look he gave me—all narrowed eyes and indignation. "Too small for *what*?"

"You know…to have fun with. That kind a thing." He chewed his lip. "Some men tease me 'cause it's small. And I don't know that if the man is nice otherwise and takes care of me good…I don't know that I mind, really." He shook his head. "It's weird. Never mind."

I frowned, having a look at his cock as it stood from the nest of curls. T'wasn't that small, I didn't think.

"Seems okay to me. I've seen a lot of other men in my time, and there's a lot of variety in dicks, not that I looked that close."

Or maybe I did? I was starting to rethink a lot of my past behaviors right now.

Watching the smile come out on his face was like seeing the sun come up on the day you got out of jail. I couldn't help answering it with one of my own. A small one, mind, because there were still a lot of things about this arrangement that made me uncomfortable. Seemed they were starting to matter less and less, though.

"Good. 'Cause I sure like the look of you," Oscar said.

This shocked me, and I must have looked it, too.

He nodded. "Yeah, I do. All strong and gruff and hairy... You gotta nice big cock, too, and your ass? Whoa, that is somethin' all of itself."

My mouth dropped open and I wondered how in tarnation he could talk about stuff like that so easily. The way he casually referenced my ass made me nervous, though. It must have showed on my face.

"Don't worry. I don't mean I want to fuck you or anythin'. I'm more wantin' you to do that to me." He waggled his eyebrows but held up a hand. "No hurry, though, if you ain't comfortable with it yet."

"If you like the look of me so much, how come you were actin' like such a brat last night? You ain't never said one nice thing to me, and you were fightin' me so hard 'till I got you in that tub."

My voice came out soft and hesitant because I couldn't even believe we were talking about this.

He blushed so pretty then that I could have kissed him, and where the hell had that come from? Goddammit, did it only take one pretty man with a cocky attitude to get me o'er to the other side?

Oscar snorted, rolling onto his back and lacing his hands behind his head, which made the shirt ride up and almost expose his dick again.

"I was so hungry and so tired I couldn't even think straight, though I 'spect you knew that or you wouldn't have been so nice to me. And to be honest, I didn't really know what you wanted. Never expected you to be so damn kind. Never expected anybody to be so kind. Not in this goddamn town, anyway, and I don't much know about anyplace else."

I nodded. My gaze teased the hem of that shirt where it lay high on Oscar's pale, lightly haired thighs, and I wanted to move on him and push it out of the way.

Instead, I cleared my throat and said, "You grow up here?"

He grinned, and I swear he knew what I was fighting and that it amused him. "Most of my life, yeah. My folks came lookin' for gold when I was fourteen. They never found it. Spent the rest of their lives tryin' to make do with whatever they could. My pa ran a shop for a while, until some townies burned it down. He was Ukranian, and they didn't like that. Didn't like me neither—or my ma."

"Shit," I said. "I'm sorry."

He shrugged. "Is what it is. Folks are mean and stupid. Learned that pretty quick."

"Well, I ain't," I said, feeling the need to defend myself.

"I know you ain't." He played with the hem of his shirt, drawing my eyes there again. "Never met a man nicer'n you."

"I ain't perfect, though. Nowhere near," I said, my mouth going dry. "I done things…"

He raised an eyebrow. "Worse than spillin' in a man's mouth?" he asked with a quirked lip, making me blush again.

I rolled my eyes. "Stop sayin' stuff like that. Have you no *shame*? *Really*?"

Now he rolled his eyes at me. "I ain't got no use for shame. All shame does is make people feel bad about what they wanna do. If what I wanna do ain't gonna hurt nobody, then what's wrong with it? Tell me *that*." He was fierce now, his eyebrows drawn together and lips tight, so I knew he cared a lot about what he was saying. And I understood that point of view, for sure.

But then maybe I should have been a lot more ashamed of what I was doing with my life when I had been Oscar's age, and I sure hadn't been. And look where it had got me.

"Anyway, ain't nothin' wrong with words like cock and jizz and fuckin'. They all mean things that ain't bad, only private. Only I like to say them 'cause they make me feel saucy and brave and dirty. An' I like that."

Jesus Christ, this young firecracker would be the death of me. My dick felt like iron in my trousers now and he fucking knew it, leering at me like the devil himself come to tempt me.

"Stop it, now, you hear? How come you're such a rude fella, you tell me that, now? How come you're such a brat?" I don't know where this was coming from except as an honest question, but the way he reacted to me saying those words was something to see, honestly, even if I didn't understand it.

His face got all red—I mean, *really* red—and he started squirming like he didn't know what to do with himself, and I could tell his cock was as hard as mine, and what the fuck did that say about us both?

"Fuck it, Jimmy. You almost made me spend just now. How do you know exactly what to say to me?"

I was able to see the humor in a situation, so I kind of huffed a laugh, even though my face was as flushed as his and I was having trouble keeping my hands off him, all of a sudden.

"You like that?" I said, trying to figure him out. "You like it when I call you a brat, Oscar? 'Cause that's surely what you are, and I oughta haul you across my knee and give you a hidin' you won't forget."

My breath came in harsh little pants, and Oscar gaped at me like he'd discovered Shangri-la, and I didn't know what was happening. I couldn't keep up.

But Oscar seemed to, because he grinned and nodded and said, "Yeah, I think that would do me good."

We stared at each other for a few seconds as flames lit inside me. I pushed up into a sitting position and patted my lap, not sure what the hell was wrong with me but glad to be able to spank some sense into this foolhardy young man before he ended up getting himself killed. I ignored my throbbing cock and figured I was only hankering for a bit of justice, and I was still so horny I was almost mad with it, so what-the-fuck-ever.

"Hell, Jimmy. Really?" he said in the smallest whisper that made my blood boil so hard I thought I might die.

"Get o'er my lap. *Now.* You been askin' for this since last night, and I aim to give it to you."

Chapter Six

Wantings

I felt a bit bad for wanting to spank some sense into him when he still had that bruise on his hip, but I'd stay away from it. I also knew he was still tired and probably would be hungry again soon, and I felt bad about that—but not bad enough to stop.

Now it seemed like the spanking was only an excuse to haul him onto my lap, but I didn't want to think about that. I only wanted to put him o'er my knee and honor be damned...at least for this morning.

When Oscar moved toward me, I reached out and wrapped my fingers around his wrist. We froze in that position for several moments, our gazes locked. His eyes held fire in them and a good deal of mischief, too, and I liked it. Can't say I didn't thrill to it more than I ever did to the sight of a naked whore, which confused the fuck out of me. Was this all I'd ever wanted? Seemed to be a strange thing to want so bad, but I thought I might cry if he said no.

But he wasn't saying no. He squinted at my lap, nodded as if to himself, then laid himself out across my knees and nestled his head on his crossed arms and sighed.

"I reckon I deserve a hidin'," he said.

When he glanced back at me with those dark, liquid eyes, I almost came to orgasm right then, and I was sure glad I had my trousers on.

Before I knew what I was doing, I put a trembling hand on the back of his thigh and slid my fingers up, higher and higher, pushing the edge of the shirt — *my shirt* — o'er his bare ass while holding my breath like I wasn't ever gonna take another one — and maybe I wouldn't.

The skin there was as pale as the skin of his face, and there were some small dark moles there as well. He clenched, causing his cock to bump my leg.

"Holy hell," Oscar whispered. "I reckon you been wantin' to do this for a while. Lucky we found each other."

I grunted. "Maybe. Or unlucky? I ain't never thought I'd wanna do anythin' like this," I said, tracing my fingers along his ass, which was about the plumpest thing on him.

He bit his bottom lip and closed his eyes like he was savoring every moment.

I didn't understand any of it, but that didn't mean I wasn't getting off on this, more than I had on anything before in my whole entire goddamn life, except maybe spilling in his mouth that morning.

"I might spill on your leg." Oscar panted. "I'm likin' this so much." He squirmed under my hand, making the most delicious sounds.

I ain't even spanked him yet. I was a bit scared, to be honest — scared of how much he'd *like* it, scared of how much *I'd* like it. But not scared enough to keep from lifting my hand and bringing it down hard on that pale, plump skin.

I did not expect him to groan like he did, and the sound went straight to my trapped dick, making it twitch and throb.

"Oh fuck, that's good. Do it again."

I blinked and gasped, then brought my hand down again. He groaned even longer this time and rocked himself on my lap, rutting against me like a horny dog. The sight of that damn near killed me.

"Jesus, *Jesus*," I swore, about ready to spurt with what I was seeing, what I was doing. "You gonna be a good boy, Oscar? You gonna behave after I tan your hide?"

I didn't know where any of it came from, but it didn't seem to matter.

Oscar made a noise and said, "Yes, I will, Mr. Downing. I'll be a good boy. Don't worry. I'll be such a good boy, Mr. Downing, such a" — he left off with a gasp, rocking against me, fucking my leg and breathing hard, and t'was only a matter of time — "good...good... boy!"

He froze for a long moment as the wetness of his release soaked my trousers, and he gave a choked cry and shuddered against me. My hand that was holding his thigh felt the tremble go through his whole body, and t'was humbling that I'd done that for him. I'd done it in a strange way, but I was glad of it — glad for him to have this little bit of happiness when t'was obvious his life hadn't been so good recently.

My mouth was dry, and I couldn't speak. My cock throbbed like it might spill any second. And when Oscar looked back at me with a sated gaze and squirmed against my crotch, rubbing on me, it *did* spill, right inside my trousers as I opened my mouth and made a sound so helpless and lost that it would echo in my head for days.

We sat there for a bit, trying to calm down and not knowing where to take it now that we'd both spilled and ruined my trousers from two directions. I was trying to parse it, trying to figure out what was so goddamn exciting about spanking this bratty fella, this street-smart young rascal who had come into my life and upended it so spectacularly that it felt like I was the one with my ass in the air, not him.

"I'm sorry," I said, because now that my cock was shrinking and my crazy, ruinous desire had been sated, my trousers felt wet and clammy, and I couldn't help feeling bad about spanking him when he was still, probably, not well.

He quick scrambled up and put his face close to mine, bringing up his hand to cradle my cheek as he regarded me with something more than plain affection — except it couldn't be more than that, since I'd only seen him for the first time a day ago. Maybe t'wasn't even that, and I was hallucinating.

"What're you sorry for?"

"I don't rightly know," I said, shaking my head and experiencing more emotions than I'd had at one time for what seemed like centuries. "I just feel sorry."

He looked sad all of a sudden.

"Are you sorry we did that? 'Cause I ain't!"

He got that fierce look on his face that I'd seen a few times before.

"And I don't want you to be sorry, neither. There ain't nothin' wrong with it, Jimmy, I promise. I done it before with some men I liked, but t'wasn't nothin' like this. T'was somethin' more like playin', when *this* felt *real*. It felt so real, and I liked it so much."

I turned my face away from him, though it hurt me to do it.

"Ain't no point in you likin' it, 'cause it can't happen again. Besides, I got to take the wagon back to Whitehorse and get another load of supplies for Mr. Henson."

He nodded, but he looked so sad that it hurt my heart.

"Is that what you do?" he asked, and for a second I thought he meant the spanking, which I'd never ever done before. But he meant for a living.

"Yeah. That's what I do...now." I cleared my throat like something was stuck in it.

"What did you do before?" he said. He was still on my lap, and it looked like he didn't never want to leave. But now he was sitting up and gazing at me with those wide-open brown eyes.

"You don't wanna know," I said with a sigh.

"Maybe I do."

"You don't." My voice was firm now.

He quirked his lips up in the corner. "Jimmy, I do —"

I slapped him on the ass like t'was my new job and he squeaked. My hand didn't land right because of his changed position, but it had the effect I wanted.

"Do I need to give you another one, or are you gonna stop badgerin' me?"

"Ho-ly shit. You sure know how to treat a boy." His face was flushed with color, and it looked good on him, compared to how pale he'd been yesterday.

I blinked then laughed. He was so funny, and this whole situation was ridiculous.

"This really what you like, Oscar? Bein' o'er my knee and takin' a spankin'? E'en though you say you're twenty-one?"

He blushed again. "Do you even gotta ask? I spilled all o'er your trousers. I *loved* that. And what the hell has my age got to do with it?"

I shook my head, not even able to parse it. "But...*why*?"

He shrugged. "I don't know. 'Cause I really am a naughty brat, and I need someone to mind me? 'Cause it's nice to know someone cares enough to make me behave? 'Cause the feel of your big, strong hand on my ass makes me so fucking hard?"

"Stop it," I grunted, feeling my dick start to take notice again.

He lifted his chin and gave me a sultry stare. "Make me."

"I ain't gonna make you. We need to go down and get some breakfast."

He nodded and frowned, looking down at my trousers. "Shoot, I kind of ruined them."

"Well, I didn't help, did I?" I said, gesturing at my crotch where the spunk had made a dark spot.

"Oh shit, did you spill too?"

I thought he'd known that.

"Yeah. Right after you."

"Holy shit. You liked that as much as I did." His eyes were wide with surprise, and he smiled a slow, long smile that made my heart melt.

I cleared my throat. "I reckon that's true, as much as I don't understand it."

"Maybe you like makin' brats like me be good? Huh? Maybe that's all that is." He looked at me with moony eyes again, trying to get me hard, I knew it. If t'was up to him, we'd stay here all day and he'd get nothing to eat again. I don't know how his priorities were so messed up, but I knew he needed feeding, even if *he* didn't.

"I got another pair of trousers," I said, getting out from under him, so he rolled off me and sat with his legs crossed, watching me move gingerly o'er to the bag to get my other trousers. I cursed and blushed.

"I ain't spilled in my trousers since I was fourteen years old. Don't rightly know what happened just then."

Oscar laughed. "I think you found your wantin'. And it matches pure smooth with mine. You know how rare that is?"

"What's a 'wantin''?" I asked. "And how can I have one for so long without knowin' what it is?"

He winked and put a hand down to touch his spanked ass. "Well now, it's a particular thing you really like to do with someone else that might look strange to anyone seein' it but feels right to you. Lots of people have 'wantin's', only they don't indulge them very often…or not at all. More's the pity."

My gaze was locked on that hand of his, rubbing on his sore bottom. "Hmm. Not sure it seems 'right' to me. Not now, anyway."

"But while we were in the middle of it? And you were spankin' your very naughty boy? Did it seem regular and right to you at the time?"

He knew the answer to that and so did I.

I lifted my hands in a hopeless gesture. "But how could I have gone so long without discoverin' it?"

He laughed and crossed his arms o'er his chest. "You shared beds with a lot of wild fellas like me? Who know what they want and ain't ashamed of it?"

I shook my head. "No, I guess not. Shared a lot of campfires, though. And those men were wild — there ain't no denyin' it — but not in that way."

He nodded slowly, his expression calculating. "Those men you shared campsites with — what'd they do?"

"Nothin' you want to hear about," I said, pulling a clean pair of trousers from my bag.

"They thieves and murderers? That what you been talkin' about by not talkin' about it?"

I hesitated. I didn't really want to tell Oscar about all that. "Maybe."

"You a thief and a murderer, Jimmy?" he asked. I could see he was serious, but he didn't have a lick of fear on him when he asked it.

I ran my hand o'er my face, feeling my pulse quicken as the guilt and shame came o'er me. But I tamped it down and met his gaze.

"Not anymore. I'm tryin' to be an honorable man now."

"You are an honorable man. I know it," Oscar said.

I laughed sharply. "Don't feel so honorable right now with your spunk on my trousers."

Oscar smiled and the sight of that was an absolution. "Ain't nothin' dishonorable about givin' somebody pleasure, no matter how you do it."

He was something, this strange, half-starved creature who seemed to want my essence more than he cared for nourishment. T'was seductive and scandalous, and it grabbed me where I was vulnerable. A shiver went up my spine as I recalled stories I'd heard about succubi and incubi, demons that would fuck you till you couldn't give no more, and they had everything you ever were then left you an empty husk. Maybe he was one of them.

"Not sure most folks would agree with you."

Thing was, if that's truly what he was, I didn't almost even care. I'd sacrifice myself to his hunger if it meant more fun like we'd had. I didn't much care about the consequences at the moment.

"Not sure I give a good goddamn about most folks," he said, crossing his arms and flashing a scowl so severe that I had to laugh.

He didn't seem like an incubus then — simply an angry youngster who was disappointed with the world and what it had promised him. I felt my heart loosen in my chest more than it had in years…maybe in forever.

"You are somethin', y'know that? I ain't sure exactly what, yet, but you make me confused and happy and horny, all at the same time. I don't understand it at all."

"You said 'yet'. That mean you ain't gonna show me the door?"

With so much hope in his voice, I could see he was preparing himself for my answer, whatever t'was.

I wasn't thinking with my head right now. Hadn't been thinking with my head since yesterday, probably. I only ever intended to give him a hot meal, a bed and a bath, then send him on his way the better for it. I ain't never thought any of *this* was gonna happen, or how I'd feel about keeping him with me for a little longer. I'd assumed he was younger than he was, and if that had been so, I wouldn't have let myself get carried away. Because whatever I was, I wasn't the sort of deviant who would look to children for satisfaction.

"I don't know," I said, watching him closely. "Let's get you dressed, and we'll go down, get somethin' t'eat and I'll think on it. Truth is, I got a job to do, and if I bring you with me, it'll be pretty distractin', I figure."

His eyes widened and he couldn't help grinning, the hope laid out there plain to see, and it made my heart ache. But I gave him a firm look.

"Not because of that. That ain't happenin' again anytime soon, so don't think it will. I mean because you're a badly behaved, argumentative, mischievous brat, and I don't know if you'll be more of a hindrance to me than anythin' else."

I thought he'd be upset with me saying those things, but he simply nodded and looked kind of smug. Fella had my fucking number. There was no denying it.

"I sure am, Jimmy." He sighed, getting up off the bed and standing there with his head hanging, like he was actually ashamed and not simply trying to manipulate me, like the little bugger he was. "I'm such a naughty brat, and I know I'm a handful."

He peeked at me from under those thick eyelashes, and my mouth went dry, my cock got hard and my hand itched to pull him o'er my knee again.

Jesus fucking Christ.

"Stop it," I said.

He shrugged, then glanced to the pile of clothes on the dresser. "T'was awfully good of you to get me some decent clothes to wear. I s'pose we should make sure they fit me."

Before I knew it, he had the shirt pulled off and stood there naked in front of me, in the full light from the windows. I clenched my hands into fists but couldn't help my gaze coasting o'er him like he was a whore I'd paid for and had every right to examine like that. I swallowed thickly, remembering how he'd felt on my lap.

He knew I was looking and raised his arms up o'er his head, stretching out to one side, then the other, and yawned.

"Yeah, why don't you do that. Get dressed, Oscar," I said, my voice weak and shaky. *I might have to revisit the incubus theory.*

"Sure will." He sighed as he walked slowly to the pile of clothes, and my gaze tracked him. "Shit, I ain't never felt so clean before, I don't think—not since I was a child."

He picked up the thing on top of the pile, which was an undergarment made of light cotton with a string looped through holes at the top. He stared at it for a long moment. Then he looked up at me with a puzzled expression.

"What the hell is this?"

I couldn't help a laugh escaping me as I fastened my clean trousers and pulled on my shirt from yesterday. "Those're your drawers. You put them on under your trousers."

"*What in tarnation?* Really? Seems like a waste of material."

"You tellin' me you ain't never worn 'em before?"

"Well, not like this. I used to wear long underwear in the winter, but in summer I just put my trousers on o'er my naked ass."

His innocent look belied the knowledge of how those words must affect me.

"Jesus *Christ*, Oscar."

"In fact, I don't rightly know how they go on. Can you help me?"

"No," I said, so quick that t'was pretty funny. "No, I ain't gonna do that. You best use your brains and figure it out. You sure ain't stupid now you got some sleep and a meal."

He laughed and sighed. "Fine. I'll do it myself. You can watch, though."

"I ain't gonna watch," I said, but I didn't look away.

"Ain't you?"

"Jesus, Oscar, you— I can't even keep track of you. You keep pullin' all my strings, like I'm your goddamn puppet or somethin'. I don't know if I'm comin' or goin'."

He smiled at me with that childlike gaze that was so truthful and open that I couldn't hardly take it.

"I wish you were *comin'*." He winked. "But you better not be goin' unless you're takin' me with you."

I hugged out a ragged breath full of disbelief. "We'll see about that. I ain't makin' no promises."

He nodded, figuring out the underthings then pulling on the trousers and doing them up. And for the first time in a long while, I sighed with relief.

"I'm good with horses. I can cook a bit, too. I could be your camp boy, Jimmy. I could do lots of chores to make campin' out easier and more comfortable for you."

I cleared my throat. "I bet you could."

He scoffed, as if my putting a sexual spin on that offer was below contempt.

"I didn't mean that. You sure got a dirty mind, doncha? One soft spankin' and a bit of a lark, and you think you can do all kinda things to me whenever you want."

I felt ashamed and embarrassed as I tried to backpedal. "No, I don't. I'm sorry, Oscar. I didn't mean to take that the wrong—"

But he was grinning at me now and trying not to laugh, and I realized he'd got me.

"You little bastard," I said, feeling taken and a bit peeved and more amused than anything. But I was stopping this nonsense. "Now look here... You get yourself into them clothes, shut your mouth for ten minutes and get your ass down to breakfast with me."

His eyes widened, and his hand went to the front of his trousers as he sighed. "Oh, my. You do know how to talk to a boy."

I sat on the edge of the bed and grabbed my boots, pulling them on and scowling at him. "Quiet now. That's enough."

"Fuck," he said. "Yes, sir. I'll be quiet."

"And besides, you're a man, not a boy. You need to start actin' like one."

"True enough. But I feel like a boy when I'm with you, Jimmy."

At that point, I damn near knew I'd be taking him with me.

Chapter Seven

All the Pretty Little Horses

For now, though, I took him downstairs and got him breakfast, which he gobbled up without any stomach issues this time, I was pleased to see.

"Now, I got to shop for supplies today. You want to come with me, or rest up in the room? I figure you'll be bored outa your skull if you come shopping, and you could prob'ly use some more rest."

He'd yawned several times during the meal.

"You mean, you trust me to stay in that room all by myself? With all your things there? You don't think I might rob you?" He seemed shocked.

I couldn't help the short laugh that escaped me. "What are you gonna get if you do? I got my pouch with me. The only things I've got up in that room are some personal items and a soiled pair of trousers." I lowered my voice. "That *you* soiled, by the way. Take 'em if you want."

Oscar blushed a deep shade of pink but grinned. "I seem to recall we both soiled 'em. Well, fine, I'll stay and mind the place while you're gone. I ain't had this much leisure in ages. I'm usually so busy chasin' down food."

He looked sober all of a sudden. "Thank you...really. For all you done. For this here meal. For supper yesterday. And for the top-shelf hospitality you give me."

Now I was blushing, because I knew exactly what he meant by that.

"You're welcome."

I laid out some coin on the table and followed Oscar to the stairs. "You need me to get anythin' for you while I'm out?"

He froze with one foot on the stair and his hand on the railing. "What?"

I cleared my throat, trying not to look embarrassed. "You want me to get you anythin'? You don't got nothin' to your name right now. Might be nice to have one thing — or two, even."

He stared at me, and something passed between us. "You don't need to buy me nothin'."

"But if I want to?"

I saw him fight the smile that threatened. "Then you get me some sweets. I ain't had sweets for...fuck, Jimmy. For *years*. Figure I could do with some licorice or some of them gumballs they keep in the glass jars, if you'd be so kind."

We were talking low, so's nobody would o'erhear, and I'd leaned in close to pick up what he said. And suddenly, t'was like he was my best friend, and I wanted to please him with something he'd like more than anything in the world.

"Okay. I will."

This time, the smile won out.

"Now, you go on up there, lie down on that bed and try'n sleep. Or rest, at least. The maid should have started the fire, and you'll be cozy and safe and warm."

He nodded. "I will. And thank you."

I shook my head and watched him climb the stairs. At the top he looked back and flashed that smile again before heading down the hall.

And why did that smile light a burning warmth in my chest that made me catch my breath? I turned and headed out of the front door of the hotel, my step light and my heart happy.

* * * *

When I'd finished my shopping and got back to the room, the hotel was quieter than it had been that morning. There wasn't anyone in the dining room since t'was after lunch and only a maid wiping down the stair rail in the entry.

I nodded to her as I passed. "Good day, miss."

"Good day, mister. You got someone in that room of yours upstairs?"

I froze, not knowing what to say. Was it against the rules for a person not paying for the room to be in it alone? That didn't seem to make sense.

I turned and smiled. "Yes, I do. My cousin."

She smiled and gestured up the stairs. "He's been singin' off and on. He can carry a tune pretty well."

As I was trying to process this astonishing piece of information, a mesmerizing tenor voice drifted down the stairs.

"Amazing Grace, how sweet the sound
That saved a wretch like me.
I once was lost but now am found,

Was blind but now I see."

T'was Oscar's voice, but like I'd never heard it before. T'wasn't wisecracking, trying to manipulate me or breathless from excitement. That voice was pure and wholesome and strong.

I tried not to look as surprised as I felt. "Yes, ma'am. He's a good singer. Is he too loud? I'll ask him to be quieter."

"No, I like it. Makes my work go easier," she said. "Does he take requests?"

"I don't rightly know," I said, secretly stunned that the voice coming from upstairs belonged to Oscar. Maybe she was wrong and t'wasn't coming from our room, after all.

"Tell him I really like *Goodbye, Dolly Gray*, if he knows it."

"I surely will, ma'am." I nodded awkwardly and hastened up the stairs.

I wasn't used to talking to women who weren't paid companions, honestly. Even though a hotel maid wasn't much of a step above that, when it got down to it, her attention still made me nervous. Did she suspect Oscar was more to me than a cousin? But why would she?

I pushed them thoughts out of my head and continued to the room. When I knocked on the door, Oscar stopped his singing. In a moment the door flew open, and he stood there in only my shirt again and blushed like a maiden.

"Hi."

He eyed me up and down while I stared at him in that billowy white shirt and remembered everything we'd done that morning. My cock started to plump up as his gaze locked on the small bag in my hand.

"Oh, my goodness. Is that what I think it is?" He licked his lips and reached his hand out.

I swallowed thickly and dragged my mind out of the gutter.

"Yeah."

I passed it to him and closed the door behind me, taking deep steadying breaths and determined not to give in to my desires.

He took the bag and pounced onto the bed, making the wire frame creak in a terrible way. He crossed his legs under him and opened it, staring inside like it held the richest of treasures.

He was a grown man. I knew that. But seeing him there, cross-legged on the bed, staring into that bag of candy like a child on Christmas morning touched something pure and wondrous in me, and t'was easier to push the impure thoughts out of my mind.

"That what you wanted?" I said, putting down my other bag. I'd left most of my purchases in the wagon.

"My gosh. You sure know how to win a fella's heart."

I coughed and stared at him, wondering exactly what he'd meant by that. He must have seen my panic.

"Don't be stupid. I only met you yesterday. I mean, you sure know how to make a fella happy — in lots and lots of ways."

He winked at me and pulled a long, black licorice stick from the bag, waving it in front of his face, going cross-eyed when he focused on it.

"Whoa, Jimmy, you got me a big one. This is so fucking big I can't even believe it."

"Watch your fucking mouth, Oscar," I said, trying not to laugh.

"I'd much rather watch yours," he said.

When I looked again, he had the end of the licorice in his mouth, and he was sucking it and gazing at me out of hungry eyes.

"Stop that."

His eyes widened. "Why? Don't you want me to eat it? You got it for me, after all."

"You showing me how you're gonna act if I decide to bring you on the road with me? Because this is *not* good behavior, Oscar."

He almost choked on the licorice, then slid it from his slack mouth and let his hand fall to his lap. "What did you say?"

I shook my head. "I said, is this what I can expect from you if I decide to bring you with me to Whitehorse?"

"You thinkin' 'bout takin' me with you? Truly?"

"Well, I ain't too fond of the idea of leavin' you here to starve or suck other men for money. So, I'm tryin' to figure out a solution, and that's one of 'em…maybe." I held up a hand. "But I should tell you that the way I am, the more someone tries to convince me to do somethin', the less I want to do it. So's you better keep quiet and show me how good you can be 'bout not temptin' me to go under the sheets with you again."

He took this in and narrowed his eyes. "Why?"

I blinked. "What?"

"Why? How come you don't want to do that, Jimmy? Seems to me you liked it." He nibbled on the end of his licorice stick, and I felt it like t'was my cock he was doing it to.

"I'm tryin' to be an honorable man, Oscar," I said, "now that I ain't hangin' around with thieves and murderers no more."

He nodded, but his face twisted up in confusion. "So...you can't be an honorable man and spank my ass if we both want you to? Among other things?"

I gaped at him, still not used to the frank way he talked about those things.

"No, I don't think so," I said, not at all sure that was the case, but it seemed like t'was — or should be. Or...I don't know. I was so mixed up inside that I didn't know what was up and what was down anymore.

"Oh, I see. Then I guess I'll have to convince you, somehow."

"Convince me of what?"

"Convince you that you can be an honorable man and still satisfy your wantin's with me — and mine, too."

I nodded, knowing what he meant. "Well, you'd better convince me by bein' a good boy, doin' everythin' I say and mindin' your manners. If you're an honorable man in that way, and I'm an honorable man in that way, too, maybe we can be together. But I ain't decided about t'other stuff yet, and I need a clear head to do that. So, I'm askin' you to be good and not deliberately tempt me into doin' somethin' I might regret."

He bit a piece of licorice off. "All right. I promise."

The relief went through me like a cool wave, and I nodded, pleased.

"Thank you."

"I'll respect your boundaries. But we gotta talk about this again sometime soon, when you've had the chance to clear your head, so's I can convince you you're full of some misguided ideas of what's honorable and what's not."

"I suppose you might be right about that, and I promise we will talk about it. But what happened this morning really did turn me upside down and inside out, and I don't barely know what I'm feelin' right now."

"Fair enough," he said, biting another piece off his licorice stick and stuffing the rest back in the bag. "Thank you again for everythin' you done for me. I'm so lucky you're such an honorable man — and that's the goddamn truth."

For supper I had the hostess send up a farmer's plate from the restaurant, with bread, meat and cheese, and some pickles and fresh fruit. We sat on the bed and ate it, talking about all kinds of things, and I felt like I was starting to get to know Oscar a little bit — and him, me.

"Shoot, I forgot to get you to sing the song the maid wanted," I said, remembering right before I fell asleep.

"What?" Oscar said, his voice worn from talking and sleepy sounding.

"The maid heard you and she wanted you to sing a song for her. But I can't remember the name of it, now. And, anyway, it's too late."

"I'll sing a song for you, if you want."

I stared at him in the darkness, wondering why I suddenly felt like crying. I don't know if anyone but my momma had ever offered to sing me a song in my whole entire life.

"You will?"

"Sure. What do you wanna hear?"

I thought about it for a little time. Then I said, "How about *All the Pretty Little Horses*? You know that one?" I was a bit embarrassed, as t'was a baby's lullaby, but that's what I wanted to hear. His voice was so pretty and singing that song, it would probably kill me a little

84

on the inside, but goddammit if I didn't want that sweet pain right now.

He didn't reply as to whether he knew the song or not, but in a moment, he started to sing it and I had to blink back some emotion that came up inside me.

"Hush-a-bye, don't you cry, Go to sleepy little baby. When you wake, you shall have, All the pretty little horses. Blacks and bays, dapples and grays, Go to sleepy you little baby."

He was on his back, and he turned so he faced me in the darkness. I hoped he couldn't see the expression on my face, because it would show how much this was affecting me. He repeated the chorus while he brought his hand out and I felt his finger caress me sweetly on the arm, back and forth, back and forth, in time to the song's rhythm.

When he was done, he was silent for a few minutes, then he said, softly, "Did you like that?"

"Yeah. Yeah, I did. Thank you. Good night, Oscar."

"Good night, Jimmy."

Chapter Eight

The Road to Whitehorse

Oscar had the worst table manners of anyone I'd ever seen. I didn't claim to be the daintiest eater, but he was a goddamn mess. I'd give him some leeway because he was probably still starving a little bit and more concerned about getting food into his maw than how it got there. And I couldn't deny there was something about the way he went for what he wanted that I liked a lot…a real lot.

From what I'd observed so far, he didn't care about anything but what he himself put importance on. He wasn't following the rules of society for the heck of it. He was his own man, and that reminded me of myself in a way. Except it had led to disaster in my case, and I wasn't gonna let that happen to him.

"Golly, these are good eggs. You like yours?" he asked with his mouth full.

I nodded, swallowing mine down before I answered. "I like 'em, sure enough."

"So, you said you're goin' to Whitehorse. That to get more supplies for the man you work for?" He wiped a bit of egg off his lips with the back of his hand.

"That's right," I said, forking a bit of potato.

"How long does it take to get there?"

"'Bout a week or so, if I don't get waylaid and the weather's good."

Oscar nodded. "That don't sound too bad."

"Terrain's a bit wild. There're some rough bits. Hard on the ass," I said, chewing a bite of bacon innocently.

Oscar laughed, little pieces of egg flying out of his mouth. "A sore ass don't bother me none. But I figure you know that already."

I felt my cheeks heat and threw a glance around the room to see if anyone had o'erheard.

"Quiet now. I still ain't decided if I'm gonna take you."

Which was a goddamn lie, because I already knew there was no way I was leaving him in this hellhole of a town. T'was as if I'd discovered a little piece of lefto'er gold in this wasted place, all roughed up and dirty, but it polished up real nice, and I knew t'was a rare thing. I wasn't gonna let go of it—not yet, anyway.

He sure looked nice in the clothes the proprietress had brought. Turned out they fit him real well, even the boots. He was a bit mismatched, but he looked a hell of a lot better than he had when I'd first seen him, that was certain.

The truth was, I'd felt more in the past twenty-four hours than I had in years. Oscar didn't have no place to go, and if I left him there, he'd probably starve or end up on his knees in a brothel—and I didn't want that for him. I didn't want that at all. I had a wagon with space and enough supplies to feed the both of us for the trip to Whitehorse. I was taking him, and that was that. I didn't have to answer to anyone as to how strange it might be to do so.

"That anywhere near to Port Essington?" Oscar asked.

"What?"

He shoveled some fried potatoes into his mouth and chewed noisily. "Port Essington, British Columbia. You heard of it?"

"Nope. But I know where British Columbia is. It ain't in this here territory."

He shook his head. "No, it ain't. From what I know of it, Port Essington's a little cannery town. Not even a town. A village, maybe."

"What of it?"

"My uncle's there. Least he was the last time I heard anythin' about him. I been wantin' to go there for a while."

I nodded, not saying anything.

"He's the only family I got left. Figure he could help me sort things out. Maybe I could stay with him while I suss out what to do with my life."

"That's sensible."

"See?" He smiled and tapped his head with the hand holding his fork. "I got some sensible ideas."

I laughed. "Not many, I bet."

He tilted his head. "Maybe not. But the way I figure it, if you can get me as far as Whitehorse, maybe I can figure out how to get to Port Essington. Whitehorse gotta be closer to BC than this. It's south of here, ain't it?"

"Yeah, that's for certain." I pointed my fork at him. "You tryin' to convince me with logic to take you with me?"

"Sure am. I already tried with" — he licked his lips — "t'other thing. Thought I was pretty convincin' but you're a hard man to sway." He picked up his glass of cider and took a long, slow swallow. I watched his Adam's apple bob and remembered waking up with my dick in his mouth the day before.

I quirked my lip. "When I set my mind on somethin', I can't hardly be convinced to change it."

"I reckon that's true."

"And right now, I've set my mind on takin' you with me."

He almost choked on his cider. He slammed the glass down on the table and wiped his chin where the sweet juice had dripped. I felt a sweet tang of desire as he did it.

"You *serious* right now, Jimmy? You mean it?" he said, voice soft and full of barely concealed excitement that gave me more pleasure than it should.

"I mean it. You need to behave yourself, mind. I expect you to be well-mannered and helpful. And if you ain't, I'll remind you what I expect from you."

He gulped and his cheeks flushed. "How you gonna do that?"

"I'll figure out some way, and believe me, you won't like it. Now eat the rest of your breakfast. We need to buy some food and supplies at the mercantile before we head out."

He blinked and stared at me some more.

"What?" I said, forking more potato into my mouth.

He shook his head. "Nothin'. Feel like I won the jackpot or somethin', though. Don't know how I got so lucky."

I simply nodded and kept eating. Truth was, I felt the exact same way.

* * * *

"So, when are we off?" Oscar asked. "Are we stayin' here for another night, or are we leavin' today?"

"I'd planned to stay in town for a few days, but now I wanna get back on the road."

Truth was, Dawson already felt too noisy and crowded. We were on our way back to the mercantile, as I'd forgotten a few grocery items the day before. The narrow streets were full of people out and about, and we had to step aside a few times to let people pass.

I'd been blindsided by Oscar and what had happened between us, but I wanted more and that was a plain fact. The only thing was that I didn't think t'was right to want what I did. I was trying my best to be an honorable man, and even though I had to admit he made a good point about a lot of things, I was not gonna give in to these unholy desires without a fight. Now I just wanted to be back on the road. At least we'd be on our own and not within viewing or hearing distance of anyone else, in case Oscar got up to mischief with me and I couldn't resist him, even though I was determined to hold out as long as I could.

Nothing about him and me and what we'd done together made a lick of sense but darn it if I could shake him. I had to take him, and I wanted us to clear out of this place tonight. If we were lucky, we'd get to Whitehorse earlier than scheduled and we could have a night or two there before Oscar lit out for Port Essington. Even if all we ever did was cuddle and talk, t'was worth it to keep him close.

That was, if we didn't chase each other off by then, which was more than likely. Neither of us seemed like easy men to live with. I knew I could be a grumpy-ass bastard, and Oscar had already showed me plenty of attitude. We were like firecrackers when we were together, setting each other off...in more ways than one. This was a recipe for disaster.

So why was the thought of being on the road with him so tempting to me? I couldn't fathom it, so I decided to go with it and let the chips fall where they may. I was going to hell anyway, so what were a few more sins?

"So, we're outta here today then," Oscar said. "Just as well."

He seemed pretty happy about it.

"You got anythin' you need to do before we go? Anyone to tell you're leavin'?"

He scoffed and slapped his hat against his thigh. T'was a pretty worn-down felt hat, not leather like mine, but he seemed happy to have it. "Nah. Unless I go tell the guy who put the bruise on me that he ain't gettin' another go. That would be amusin'."

"'Cept he might have another go at you then," I said.

"Not if you were there. You'd fight for me, wouldn't you, Jimmy? You'd protect me, right?"

I laughed and shook my head. "You're crazy."

He turned in the street and walked backward, lowering the brim of his hat and giving me a look. "You would, though. I know you would. You look like you'd be good in a fight. Nobody'd be able to rough you up."

"I been roughed up in my time, and it ain't no fun. So, let's try to stay away from trouble, how about?"

He shrugged and turned back the right way. "Sure enough. I can do that."

"Can you really?" I said, unable to hide the skeptical lilt to my voice.

He swiveled his head and gave me a narrow-eyed glare. "I figure I can, now that I got a full belly and a day's rest, thanks to you."

His words made my cheeks heat and the memories of what we'd done together come rushing back. God, this fella was trouble, whether he knew it or not.

He managed to behave himself at the shop. He helped me pick out some grub for the journey and carry it back to the hotel in paper bags, where we loaded it into the canvas ones in the wagon. I told the stable boy to hitch up the horses, that I was heading out, and paid inside for everything.

"Thought you was stayin' another night," the proprietress said, taking my bills.

"Somethin's come up, and I need to git. I'm sure you can find someone to take the room."

"Sure enough."

"Thanks for the clothes you got for me. They fit my cousin real well, and he's grateful for 'em."

She eyed Oscar, who stood outside the door watching the foot traffic, then nodded with a blank expression. "Seems a lot better today. Cleaner and more talkative. You sure he's your cousin?"

I willed my voice to stay steady as the heat lit my cheeks. "That's what I said, ain't it?"

"You did. Seems like I get a lot of rough men bringin' their young cousins through here. Enough to make me wonder about some things."

I gave her a look. "What things?"

She stared at me silently, as if trying to send a message with her eyes. I knew what t'was, and I was *not* having it.

"Things I don't wanna talk about…or think about," she said, between clenched teeth.

I nodded curtly. "Then you'd best keep your mouth shut and your nose out of other people's business."

"Hmph," she grunted. "I don't care what folks do, as long as it don't hurt nobody. I ain't the minister."

"Glad to hear it," I said. "Good day."

I turned and walked out onto the porch, grabbing Oscar by the elbow. "C'mon. Let's get out of here."

I must have pulled him pretty rough because he stepped back and glared at me. Fella had a flashpoint temper, that was for sure.

"What the hell's wrong with you? I ain't your dog, y'know, what just goes along with you when you whistle."

For some reason, this comment made me want to laugh.

I raised my eyebrows. "You ain't?" I couldn't help smiling all of a sudden because he was too amusing for words, honestly.

"I— Now, you look here, Jimmy. I might—" He gazed around us as we walked to where the horses stood, hitched and ready, at the fence, to make sure no one could hear. "I might be willin' to be your good boy, but I ain't gonna crawl around like a dog for you. Never mind you want it."

My dick ached all of a sudden at the look in his eyes, and the only thing I could think to say was, "We'll see," which about made him choke on his tongue.

At least it shut him up. Then he opened his mouth wide and cackled a laugh the whole town could have heard.

"Goddamn it. For someone so regular, you sure gotta sense for the more unusual side of things."

"If I'm gettin' used to you, then I'd say that's for damn sure. Get up there, now, 'n let's go."

"Hold on. I need to meet your horses."

Horses were so regular and ordinary that I was surprised he wanted to meet them. But I followed him to the fence and told him about them.

"This here's Dixie," I said, scratching the mare on the nose like she enjoyed. She knickered to me, and I was glad to see both horses looking rested and ready to go.

"Hi, Dixie," Oscar said, reaching a tentative hand out. I took it gently and placed in on Dixie's black mane. She was brown everywhere except for her trimmings, which were black, and the white strip down her face. She was sturdy and reliable, most of all.

Oscar flashed me a grin and stroked Dixie's mane then her neck. "She's real nice. So soft."

I nodded. "She's a good horse. This gray gelding here is Sprite. He's good too, e'en though he's younger and a bit more flighty. She keeps him steady, though."

He reached a hand out to Sprite, and the horse sniffed it, then pushed his muzzle against Oscar's fingers, looking for treats.

"He wants a sugar cube or an apple."

"I ain't got those," Oscar said. "I only got some skritches to give you, Sprite." He ran his fingers o'er Sprite's cheeks and down to his chin and scratched him lightly. When he turned to me, I must have been staring at him.

"What?"

"I ain't never seen a person so polite to horses before. Most folks don't even acknowledge they're anythin' more than a means to get from one place to another."

He laughed. "Well, I figure I'm puttin' my life in their hands gettin' up into this wagon. And I want them to know I'm worth keepin' alive."

He climbed up into the wagon seat, his cheeks pink and smile so wide you'd have thought he had a million dollars in his pocket instead of a handful of lint. I swung myself up beside him and picked up the reins. Then I clucked to Dixie and Sprite and glanced to my side.

"You sure you want to come with me? I ain't got time to bring you back if you change your mind."

His smile slowly disappeared, and I felt kind of bad for that. Still, I needed to make sure this was what he wanted.

"Ain't nothin' here for me but starvation and abuse. I ain't felt any hope in a long time, and I feel hope now. If you'll have me, I'll be joinin' you, and I'm mighty grateful for the opportunity. I'll help you out as much as I can, and I'll try not to be a burden. All right?"

My chest tightened at the sincerity in his gaze. The fact he wasn't making a joke or trying to push my buttons proved how honest his answer was.

"I'll have you. And I'm glad to," I said.

He nodded, as if we were making a deal. "Okay. Let's go."

I nodded and *chirruped* to the horses.

* * * *

It took about a half hour to get clear of Dawson City and neither of us looked back. Seemed like we were both ready to get away from other people. The Overland Trail that would take us all the way to Whitehorse was a rudimentary graded highway for wagons and sleds in the winter that wound through the mountains and around gorges and traversed rivers, though we'd be dependent on cable ferries for those crossings. Traffic was not heavy, since the easier way to travel was by boat through the waterways. The only folks taking the Overland Trail this time of year were hard-assed buggers like me who refused to drift down a river crammed into boats with hundreds of others. I enjoyed the journey, hard as t'was, and the landscape, though tricky and treacherous in parts, was more beautiful than any land I'd ever seen or ever would see.

In fact, Oscar was so quiet that I wondered if he was all right. But when I gazed at him, he was staring around us with his eyes wide at the gold and gray landscape that stretched out ahead, cut through with river gorges, rocky slopes and rolling up to huge mountain ranges all around.

"You ever been out of the city?" I asked, already feeling a sense of peace and relief.

"Not very often," he admitted. "Times I have, I enjoyed it. Somethin' awful nice about not havin' so many eyes on you all the time."

"Yeah, I agree 'bout that," I said.

"I been havin' to watch my back a lot. I don't know if men can tell I ain't chasin' skirts, but they seem to know my preferences, and it ain't somethin' that brings a lot of respect with it. Don't really see why it don't. Nothin' wrong with it, in my opinion."

He side-eyed me to see my reaction.

"I s'pose I agree with you about that." I met his gaze and winked. "Though I never expected anythin' like what happened between us back there."

Now we were away from other people hearing, I sort of wanted to talk about what had happened between us. T'was making my head all kinds of confused, and it seemed like he had a lot of experience with that kind of thing. I wondered how *much* experience he had.

"You, uh, you been with a lot of men?" I asked, feeling my cheeks flush, but curious all the same.

His lip quirked. "You mean, for sex?"

"Yeah, that's what I mean."

"Well...sure, I guess. But I ain't fucked 'em all. Lots of petting and sucking an' stuff like that. I don't fuck someone unless I know them real well."

And didn't that make my poor cock plump up right then.

"Shit," I said. "I expect that's sensible."

"That make you hard?" he asked, seeming able to read my dirty mind. "Hearin' about that?"

I cleared my throat. Nodded. Wasn't much point to denying it after what we'd done.

"Sure."

"I wonder if you didn't go along with what everyone else was doing, 'cause you never had the opportunity for nothin' else."

"I reckon I prob'ly did."

"Did you never have wicked thoughts 'bout other men?" he asked.

Well now. He sure knew how to embarrass me.

"Maybe I did. But nothin' led me to try to do anythin' about it. Figured when I was really horny for a woman, my mind did strange things. Soon as I got some relief, the thoughts went away for a while."

Oscar nodded. "I ain't never felt wicked for a girl. Never had any interest in 'em."

My head swiveled sharply, and I pinned him with a look. "You ain't never been with a girl a't'all?"

I couldn't say I wasn't surprised by that. Boy was twenty-one years old. I'd figured he must have been with a girl at some point. He sure was waking me up about a lot of things.

He laughed. "Nah. Can't get hard for a girl. I tried a couple of times, though, but t'wasn't very good. And they weren't too impressed."

I laughed softly. "No, I bet they weren't."

He laughed and nodded. "So, I stopped tryin'. I know my cock ain't impressive, anyway. Though men don't seem to care about that much."

"Nothin' wrong with your pretty cock, Oscar." I licked my lips, remembering last night. "You sure got hard for me."

He chuckled. "I sure did. Maybe I'm hard for you right now."

I about choked, and my dick went full on, then. I coughed. "You jokin' with me?"

"No, I ain't. I'm rock hard in my trousers right now." He was silent for a long time and so was I.

Then he said, "I really liked gettin' spanked o'er your lap t'other day."

Thank heavens we were on the road, or I'd have died of shame and embarrassment that other people might hear him. But no one could hear either of us right now.

"Yeah, I could tell," I whispered.

He cackled a proper laugh then. "*You* liked it, too."

"I did. Don't rightly know why, though. 'Cept you got an ass like an angel's, and all that squirmin' about did me in."

He made a little moaning sound and shifted on the hard wagon seat. "Shit. Stop talkin' about it. Next time this wagon goes o'er a bump, I'll spill in my trousers."

"Shit. You better not," I said, in a warning tone that was pretend but also, I was serious. Last thing Oscar needed was to be wearing damp clothes right now.

He gave a long sigh before saying, "Why, Jimmy? What's gonna happen if I do?"

I hissed, desire swooning inside of me like lava. "I reckon I'm gonna stop this wagon and take you across my knee again."

He made a noise, and I wondered if he *had* spilled. But then, he laughed. "If you think that's gonna stop me, you don't know me very well."

"I *don't* know you very well," I said, amused and horny and, fuck, well and truly spellbound by him.

"I reckon we're gonna change that."

"I reckon we are."

The lurch and sway of the wagon o'er the rough ground had a hypnotizing effect, as did the beauty of nature surrounding us, and we were quiet for a long time as we passed through the stunning landscape. I tried to remember being this happy before, and I couldn't. T'was strange, since I was thirty-six years old, and I'd never felt this good.

Chapter Nine

Right and Wrong

I told him we'd better find a different focus for our conversation if we wanted to get anywhere today, because remembering what had happened between us and what might happen once we made camp that night was too damn distracting.

I asked him about growing up in Dawson City and if he'd always struggled or if he'd had a decent life for a time. Turned out he'd been all right until his ma had died of typhus when he'd been about fifteen. He said his pa had been in a state and didn't know what to do with him, except to say he needed to learn how to make a living, so he wasn't being useless and a hindrance. He'd started doing odd jobs around town for people, which had led him into contact with some older men who'd seemed real nice, until he'd realized what they wanted.

"They take advantage of you?" I asked. "Knowin' you were...the way you are?"

"Guess you could say that. 'Cept I kinda wanted to be taken advantage of, if you know what I mean? I was desperate for anythin' at that point. Wasn't much pleasure in my life, and what I could get, I grabbed at."

I nodded. "Sure."

"And to be honest, I felt sorry for 'em. 'Cause they'd only wanted what I did for so many years without bein' able to get it, an' they were so sick and twisted from the shame and denial. Most of 'em couldn't even look me in the eyes after, couldn't even talk to me. Some of 'em offered me money, but I never took it."

I glanced at him, seeing years of misery and attempts to grasp at bits of pleasure so tainted by society's disapproval that t'was hardly pleasure at all.

"But I wasn't starving or nothin'. My pa fed me and made sure I was safe." He gave a little snort. "Till he up and died from alcohol poisoning a few years later."

"Jesus."

"I told him that moonshine he was drinking was tainted, but he didn't believe me. Said t'was fine. Drank the whole jug one night and didn't never wake up the next mornin'."

Oscar made a noise and looked away, stomping his foot on the floor of the wagon as if trying to keep control of his emotions. "Stubborn old fucker."

"Christ. What'd you do?"

"Whatever I could to pay the landlord, so I could stay in the house, as run-down as t'was." He shrugged. "I worked as an errand boy. Shoveled shit and mucked stalls. Didn't have no proper skills, so t'was rough. Then I got in with a fella who needed a regular assistant for doin' deliveries around town, and that worked out pretty well. I was able to survive all right with that. Didn't have much, but I didn't need it. But then he started gettin' me to stay late in the warehouse, and I had a bad feeling about it. One night, he made moves on me. Said t'was my obligation to 'im for giving me a steady job, to let him do whatever he wanted, that I weren't nobody anyway and he'd toss me out on the street if I didn't."

I swallowed, feeling so sorry for this young man, what he'd been through and how unfair t'was.

"So, what did you do?" I was almost scared to ask.

He shook his head. "Well, you know me. I don't tend to keep my feelings to myself so much."

I chuckled. "Nope. That's true enough."

"I told him he could fuck off, that I wasn't goin' near his sorry dick and he wasn't gonna touch mine, neither." He blushed bright red with anger and shame. "He couldn't understand it. Seemed like he figured if I liked to be with other men, I should like to be with any other man, under any circumstance. That all I existed for was *that* and I was no good for anythin' else."

Oscar cleared his throat, but he wouldn't meet my gaze. The wagon bumped o'er the rough ground and jostled us as he spoke. "He was gonna rape me. Had my trousers off and everythin' and spittin' on his hand when his wife came down and found us. Then he told her t'was me tryin' to get him to sin and that he didn't want to, but I was the devil and he couldn't resist me."

"Jesus, that's turned around," I said.

"Yeah, t'was. Wife chased me out a there with my trousers barely pulled up. Then the story went around town. Much as I tried to tell people t'wasn't my fault, they knew there was somethin' different 'bout me and I got a reputation. Then nobody'd hire me for anythin'."

I narrowed my eyes at him. "You were about to go in that whorehouse and trade yourself for cash when I saw you. You tellin' me that was the first time you thought of it?"

"No, sir, t'wasn't. There were times I was pretty desperate, but I got by without *that*, somehow. Almost did it a few times, then couldn't bear to. But when you found me, I was more hungry, more exhausted and more desperate than I'd ever been. If you hadn't come by, I'd have gone inside and offered my services to the madam. I was that desperate."

"Yeah, I know you were."

"I was a mess, but I thought maybe they'd clean me up and figure out a way to use me."

"Like I done?" I asked. I couldn't help it, because I felt guilty all of a sudden, like I'd taken advantage of him like everyone else had tried to.

He swiveled so fast on that wagon seat that he startled the horses and I had to hold them.

"You ain't done nothin' wrong. You did everythin' right, and I'm so grateful. I wouldn'a done anythin' with you if I didn't want to. You didn't take advantage of me."

He grabbed me by the collar of my jacket and searched my gaze. "You believe me, don't you? 'Cause I'm tellin' the truth. I'm here by my own free will, and I don't regret nothin' we done." He let go of my collar and smoothed it flat. "I hope you don't neither."

"No, I don't. I just don't know what to do about this awful feelin' — like it's wrong, and I should know it's wrong. But it don't feel wrong when we're doin' it."

"Hell, I prob'ly shouldn't have took advantage of you when you were sound asleep and didn't know what was goin' on. I was the one who made the moves on *you*, Jimmy, and I prob'ly should be sorry, but I ain't."

I huffed out a laugh. "No, don't be sorry." I sighed, moving with the motion of the wagon and remembering how nice it had been to be intimate with Oscar. "I needed that. And I liked it a lot, true enough — much as that surprised me."

Oscar licked his lips and blew me a kiss. "Yeah, I guess you did."

"T'was t'other that was more surprising. Most men don't mind getting their dicks sucked by whoever's available, long as they can justify it. But I ain't never had my cock sucked by another man before. And I ain't never spanked another man o'er my lap, neither. Don't rightly know who I'm becomin', Oscar."

He grinned and looked down shyly, even though he was the least shy fella I knew. "Well, whoever he is, I've taken a mighty shine to him."

I cleared my throat and deliberately broke his gaze. T'was nice of him to say, and it made all kinds of emotions swirl around inside me. It had been a long time since I'd had someone like Oscar to talk to. Forever, maybe.

We rode the rest of the day in silence, mostly, except for occasional comments about the weather and the landscape. We stopped a couple of times to take a piss and stretch our legs.

"See those mountains?" I said, after we'd relieved ourselves and got on the way again. I nodded to the west of us, where a long line of peaks could be seen.

"I ain't blind, Jimmy. Course I see 'em." Oscar scoffed, giving me a bit of a smile to show he wasn't mad.

"That's the Ogilvie Mountain range," I said. Then I pointed east. "And those are the Selwyn Mountains o'er there."

He eyed me curiously. "You tryin' to impress me with your geological know-how?"

I raised my eyebrows. "I'm trying to make polite conversation."

He nodded skeptically. "Could be. I think you're showin' off."

I blinked, feeling like I wanted to haul Oscar o'er my knee again. But I put that thought out of my mind. 'Cause he might actually be right. I fought a smile.

"Could be."

I got back in the wagon and picked up the reins.

"That ain't a crime, is it?"

Oscar laughed and climbed up into the seat beside me. He bumped me with his shoulder. "No, it ain't a crime. And I don't mind, long as there won't be a test on all these names later."

I chuckled and got the horses moving. "Well now, I hadn't even thought of that."

He groaned and laughed, and I marveled at how nice t'was to have a pleasant companion with me. I'd thought I enjoyed being by myself. And I surely did, after hanging around with sorry types of men for so long.

But traveling with Oscar was more pleasant and more comfortable than I'd imagined it would be, and I was glad.

When it got a bit later, and he began to complain about being tired and how hard the wooden seat was after a day of sitting, I had to admit I was feeling it, too.

"We'll stop soon. I reckon we can find a hidden spot to camp in that copse of trees o'er there."

"All right. I'm hungry, too."

"I know it. So'm I." I regarded him sternly. "You're gonna have to help me unhitch the horses, feed and water 'em, and all that. E'en though you're tired and sore."

"Yes, sir. I reckon I'm willin' to do that for some grub and a fire."

"Good."

When I found a good spot, I stopped the horses.

"This'll do," I said and swung down from the wagon seat, stretching my body out. I heard some cracks as my bones adjusted, and it felt real good. I might have made a noise of pleasure.

I turned and saw Oscar watching me and licking his lips, which was a strange thing, to be sure, but it made me happy for some reason.

I gave him a wink and said, "Come on, now. You said you'd be helpful."

"Yeah, I will. Sure enough, I owe you that."

"You don't owe me nothin', but I won't object to some help, that's certain."

* * * *

For the next three days, we drove from ten in the morning until around five or six o'clock at night, with only some small breaks in between. I had a pocket watch that I'd got in Whitehorse ages ago, that I only had to remember to wind before I went to bed, and it kept real good time. I was pretty good at judging things based on the position of the sun in the sky, too, although it changed pretty rapidly so far north.

Luckily, those first evenings we were both so tired from traveling that we didn't wanna do much except make camp, have supper and fall asleep under the wagon. But Oscar looked better and stronger every day that he ate three meals and slept through the night, thank goodness. His face had lost its sharpness where the bones had started to show and held color as good as mine. I was glad to see it.

Sleeping underneath the wagon with another person was strange at first, but I soon got used to his soft snoring and occasional muttering. T'wasn't until the fourth day that something sparked between us again. I guess we were getting used to the journeying some and weren't quite so tired when we stopped.

We hadn't talked any more about what had happened in the hotel, and I thought maybe it had been a fluke—a strange thing that wouldn't ever happen again between us. But there'd been enough shy glances and secret looks between us since then, so I doubted that was true.

As we usually did, after some quick grub we laid our blankets out by the fire, but this time I filled his tin cup with whiskey because I felt like celebrating, leaving Dawson City so far behind.

"Bottom's up," I said, passing it to him and drinking mine down.

When I finished and looked at Oscar, he was holding his cup and barely able to keep from grinning.

"What are you smilin' about?"

"You said 'bottom'." He winked.

I blushed, even though I hadn't meant anything by it. "Now stop it. T'wasn't a…sexual reference."

"Oh, I'm pretty sure that must ha' been," he said, taking a sip and closing his eyes with the warmth and comfort of it.

"T'wasn't and you know it," I said.

"I *don't* know it. You seemed to like me being bottoms up across your lap that time." He waggled his eyebrows and stuck out his tongue, and goddammit if my cock didn't stand right up and take notice.

"Oscar, behave yourself, boy."

He sat up straighter as all the mischievousness left him. He regarded me all serious, with a wide-eyed innocence that called to something inside me. The sun was on its way down, since t'was a little after six, and the world glowed with orange.

"Why, Jimmy? What'll you do if I don't?"

We stared at each other as the warm breeze lifted his dark hair, which was still pretty clean and curly from our dip in the river a few days before. I'd let him use my razor when I'd shaved the night before, showed him how to scrape the bits of hair off his skin. He'd preened like a peacock, because he was so proud of doing such a manly thing. I was glad to teach him how, even though he barely had any beard to contend with.

But there was no hiding from this thing between us.

I leaned forward and gave him a mighty stern look, to see how he'd react.

"You want another hidin'?" I asked. "'Cause I ain't scared to take you o'er my knee again."

My mouth went a bit dry after I'd said it, and I wondered what he'd do.

"Hell, I ain't scared of that, neither," he said, in a voice that sounded cautious, even though he'd said he wasn't frightened. Maybe he was nervous, like me, because of how much we'd both liked it and worried of where it would take us if I did it again.

That was scaring me, too, but t'was too late. I'd started something I couldn't rightly take back, and we needed to finish it.

"Well, maybe you should git o'er here then," I said, clearing my throat, pushing forward because I couldn't wait to have him bend himself o'er me. At least this time we didn't have to worry about making noise. There wasn't anyone around for miles.

Oscar stood up slowly, dusting himself off and casually striding toward me. He had a look on his face that said he was searching for something stern and strict, and, by God, I knew I could give it to him.

I *wanted* to give it to him. And where that came from, I had no goddamn idea. But the wanting was there, and I guess that's what he'd meant when he'd said I'd found it. I sure had found it. I'd dug up this thing inside myself that matched the same thing inside of him, and 'a wanting' was a good thing to call it.

Chapter Ten

The Flame Catches

He stood in front of me, so close I could smell him. T'was the smell of sweat and youth and man, and I liked it so much that I closed my eyes and breathed it in. Maybe t'was the memories of my youth, when I was always surrounded by other men. Except, in those days, I only wanted companionship, not whatever was rising between me and Oscar right now.

I knew what was rising, and t'wasn't my memories.

"You want to punish me, Jimmy?"

My breaths came faster as I stared straight ahead at where his rough trousers stretched tight o'er his cock, standing hard like mine was. God, we were a pair. Kind of lucky we found each other, if you thought about it, though I was trying *not* to think. I was trying to go with what we both wanted and not suss it out too much. Some things, there wasn't any sussing out. They just were. And this seemed like one of those.

"Yes, I do." I couldn't rightly deny it, the way my palm was sweating to swat his ass and make him squirm and moan like he had before.

He gave a long sigh, like he'd never heard anything so welcome.

"Good. 'Cause I reckon I'm a very naughty boy and I need to be taught a lesson by someone who knows better'n I do."

A moan left my throat before I could stop it, and I felt a shudder through my whole body as I looked at him, standing there, waiting to have his ass spanked, wanting it as much as I wanted to do it for him.

I cleared my throat. "I reckon that's true."

When our gazes met, Oscar thrust his hips forward as if he couldn't help himself.

"Take your trousers down first," I said, licking my lips. "I reckon I wanna go at your bare ass."

He scrabbled at his belt and undid it, then unbuttoned his fly. He pushed his trousers down, and frantically worked the string on his drawers, cursing at the inconvenience of them. "Goddamn drawers. I ain't never worn such things afore, and I don't like 'em."

When I took a breath to laugh, my chest was so tight with longing that the oxygen burned as it entered.

"Oh, you are so goddamn naughty, cursin' like that. Now get them drawers down and stop your bellyachin'."

"Fuck," he whined, desperate. He got the string untied and pushed the cotton drawers down past his plump dick, what sprang out at me like an eager puppy. But I ignored it and simply nodded at him.

"O'er my lap now, so you can take your punishment."

"Jesus. You gotta grab me and *pull* me o'er your lap or I'm gonna shoot up in flames any second."

My mouth formed a stern line as I did what he asked and circled his wrist with my hand, pulling him down across my lap where I sat. He made a soft grunt as he landed atop me. I shifted my thighs so he was spread between them, with his ass tipped up at an angle very conveniently. We'd been traveling near water and bathed every day before supper, so he was clean, at least. Seemed he never wanted to be anywhere close to the filthy state he was in when I'd found him, and I was glad of it.

Soon as he lay on my lap, I cupped my hand along the curve of his ass, cherishing the soft skin of it and the heat that came from him. I breathed deeply as I tried to contain myself. I didn't want this to be o'er too quick. I wanted to enjoy it.

"You sore from the wagon seat, boy?"

"No, sir. I'm gettin' used to it."

"That's good. I reckon' you'll get used to this, too." I hauled my hand back and brought it down hard, making a loud smack that echoed o'er the grass.

"Je-*sus*," Oscar yelped. He panted quickly a few times. "Don't know as I will, but I sure want to try. I like that so much."

"You want another like that?"

"Yeah. Please, Jimmy."

I swatted him again, and this time he groaned, pushing against my thigh.

"Don't you dare come. You are one naughty boy, Oscar, and if you come before I say you can, you'll get even more of a punishment."

"What would that be?" he grunted.

"I ain't tellin'. But you won't like it."

"Oh, I reckon I will."

I almost laughed, because he was such a damn troublemaker and up for goddamn anything. I didn't even know what I meant, except in the back of my mind, I saw him bent o'er and holding on to the wagon box while I moved in on him from behind. But then my mind stopped working, because t'was so dirty and forbidden, and he called to me like nothing else ever had. I knew we'd probably end up there, but I wasn't ready for that yet, I didn't think. Seemed there were so many ways we could play and learn together, before going that far and blowing my mind outa my head like I was sure it would do. I didn't quite know if I'd recover from it, to be honest—or if I'd want to.

"Quiet now. Take your punishment like a good boy, Oscar."

He nodded and gasped as I spanked him again, and again, not being merciful at all and hoping he'd tell me if it hurt too much. After a little while, I stopped.

"You all right?"

"Yeah." His voice was soft and barely there. It shook like he'd hardly spoken for years.

"Is it too much?"

"No, sir. It's perfect."

I soothed a palm o'er his cheek, admiring the shade of his skin. "God, your ass is bright pink and as warm as a low fire."

"Fuck," he moaned, "stop it."

"You want me to stop?" I asked, surprised and more than a little sorry.

"No! Stop yammerin' and keep punishin' me. I'm a naughty boy, and I deserve it. Give it to me good." He made a noise of desperation and squirmed on my thighs. "Please!"

"Okay, I will," I said. I'd held out pretty good for days, and I couldn't help but give in to what I wanted—what he wanted, too, just as much. Maybe all we wanted was to be like this together and, if that were the case, I didn't see no harm in it. I could pretend I was simply punishing him for being a brat and leave it at that, even though I knew t'was much more complicated.

I gave it to him as hard as I dared, until he was crying and moaning like he might die. Then I got scared I really *was* hurting him, and I stopped, terrified he'd never speak to me again.

"You okay? I'm so sorry, I—" My hand trembled and throbbed from the pain of hitting on him.

"Fuuuuck," he cursed, panting and whimpering. "Don't move or I'll come."

I opened my mouth, surprised. "What? You will?"

"I might. I'm tryin' not to," he said, his voice strangled with the effort.

I felt my heart swell, that he was trying so hard to be good for me, and he didn't sound hurt, not really — only exactly as much as he wanted. But I couldn't do it anymore. His ass was real pink now, and I bet it throbbed.

"You're a good boy, Oscar," I whispered. "You're a real good boy."

He sobbed out a "Yes, sir," and lay there whimpering and shaking until I pushed him off my lap onto the hard ground and dropped to my knees atop him.

The grunt he made when he landed turned into a groan as I bent to take his cock in my mouth. I was working on pure instinct now, only doing what I wanted and not thinking about what it meant about me or him or anything. His sweet little dick jerked in my mouth, and his fingers twined in my hair as he arched and cried out my name, and hot fluid spilled down my throat and o'er my lips as I swallowed like t'was the sweetest wine.

"Jimmy, oh, God. *Jimmy*," he whispered, trembling and o'ercome, pushing his fingers into my hair. I kept him in my mouth, getting used to the feel and the taste of him, until he pushed me away and sat up with a dazed expression on his face. When his spanked ass hit the ground, he yelped and shifted onto his hip.

"Jesus. I never expected you to do that." He cradled my chin in his hand and kissed the mess of spunk off my lips.

"Did I do it right?"

He smiled so wide that it about killed me, and laughed, blinking back the remnant emotion from it all. "What the hell do you think?"

I shook my head, smiling too. "I don't know. I don't know nothin' about any of this."

"You got a dick, right? You got a pretty decent-sized cock, if I recall."

I glanced down to where I was about ready to break through the fabric of my brown twill trousers. "Sure."

"So, I think you know what'd feel good, and what to do to make mine go off like a fuckin' geyser."

I laughed, embarrassed but pleased. I couldn't fault that logic. "True enough."

He sobered, glancing at my trousers, his eyes going wide. "Now, I know you ain't ready to do any fuckin', even though I can't hardly wait for that. But I know a trick that might work to get you off, and it'll be fun to try."

"What's that?"

He opened his mouth and licked along his top lip with his pink tongue, and I couldn't hardly tear my gaze from it. It made my dick throb and shake, simply the sight of that tongue of his.

"We got some grease for the leather, right? To keep it soft and supple?"

"Yeah." What was he getting at? If we weren't gonna fuck, then what did we need grease for?

"You go get it. Then I'm gonna go on all fours, and you're gonna grease up between my thighs, here." He ran his hand along the insides of his thighs under his softening dick, and my eyes went wide, looking at him all soft and vulnerable there. "Then I'm gonna keep my legs tight together while you fuck me between 'em, you understand? It'll feel nice, and you'll spend for sure and make a mess, but I don't mind."

I let out a quivering breath because I could imagine what it would feel like, and suddenly t'was all I wanted.

"Okay. Wait here."

He smiled again, his eyes like two hot coals, keeping me warm. "I ain't goin' nowhere. Anyway, my trousers are around my ankles. You've hobbled me."

"You hobbled yourself, but I'm glad. I'll be right back."

I moved on shaky legs, my cock rubbing against my trousers, and I almost came from that and the thought of what I was gonna do. But I held off because no way was I missing out on pushing between his bare thighs like that.

I got the little pot of grease and hurried back to him.

The sight of him waiting on all fours for me wasn't like anything I'd ever seen.

"Jesus, Oscar. You got a pretty ass. Pretty legs. Pretty everythin'."

"Come on. Use lots of that grease, now, so you'll slide back and forth," he said.

I made a choking sound and nodded as he spread his thighs and waited. When they were all slick and slippery, he closed them together. "Now fuck me that way, like I told you. I wanna feel your big cock between my thighs, Jimmy."

The noise of a twig snapping in the silence of the night caused me to freeze and I waited for something else as I put a hand on Oscar's hip and said, "Shh, I heard somethin'."

"What is it?" Oscar said, turning to gaze all around at the darkness.

"Prob'ly an animal. Hopefully not a bear," I said.

"Jesus!"

"I didn't see any bear scat around when we made camp. I'm sure it's nothin'. Prob'ly a raccoon or a badger. It won't mind us."

"Maybe we should make a lot of noise," Oscar said.

"Yeah, I can do that," I said.

I made panting, desperate noises as I undid my belt and my trousers, and untied the string on my drawers, pushing everything down and sighing with relief as my cock was set free. It bumped him on his ass and he moaned, rocking forward and back.

"Jesus, I'm startin' to get hard again," he panted.

"You are so naughty, Oscar. Such a naughty fuckin' boy. I oughta put you o'er my lap *every* night. Maybe I will."

I used a hand to nestle my cock against the crease of his thighs and pushed forward, groaning loud as it pushed between them. The slide and the heat of his thighs about made me spill right away, but I needed to feel that again. I pressed my lips together and held off, thrusting again and again until I thought I'd died and gone to fucking heaven. The sight of Oscar's freshly spanked ass and the sounds of his excited breaths as I fucked him like that were enough to send me higher than I'd ever been.

"Oh Jesus. I ain't gonna last long." My voice sounded like someone else's—high-pitched and desperate.

"S'okay. I wanna feel you make a mess on me."

Goddamn, he was a dirty, dirty fella, and I loved it so much!

I opened my mouth with a loud cry as I spurted and thrust into that slippery heat, again and again, until I was spent and curling o'er his back like a stud brought to a mare that never made it inside her. I'd seen that plenty of times, and now I understood it. Except Oscar wasn't no mare and I sure wasn't no stallion, and none of this made any damn sense.

Still, I couldn't find it in me to care. Maybe people were more complicated than horses. Or maybe a stallion might be confused and horny and do that to another stallion, if he'd let him—which was highly doubtful.

I made a sound like a laugh at the direction my thoughts were taking, as I stayed there with my still-hard cock between Oscar's wet thighs.

"What's so funny?"

"Nothin'…just us." I pulled my cock out and hitched up my trousers, putting a hand on Oscar's fine ass. "I can't fathom why this feels so good when it ain't what God made us for, is all."

"How do you know what God made us for?" he said, rolling o'er and pulling me down on top of him.

He gazed up at me with wide, innocent eyes, and went on. "How do you know?"

"Well," I said, "ain't it true that God made man and woman to lie together and make children? That's what the preacher says."

Oscar nodded thoughtfully. "I never trusted those preachers to tell me what God did or what he stood for. I seen enough men of the cloth do things that'd make me blush and think twice. I seen them ruin lives with their dishonesty, and actin' like they know exactly what God wants of us. Tellin' *us* how to behave, when they break rules and do things plenty more against nature than anythin' you and I are doin'."

He seemed so sure of this, and I couldn't deny he had a point. I'd seen things, too. And heard terrible things about how the priests treated the tribes around there, and the people they thought of as savages. Seemed they took the word of God and twisted things to suit their own purposes.

"Yeah, well, maybe you're right. Anyway, it ain't anythin' I'm worried about. I couldn't care less about any of that. Not even sure God exists, and that's a fact."

"Oh, I think he exists," Oscar said with a quiet certainty. "I see him in them mountains, and the stars and all the good things in the world. I see God in the things I feel for you, Jimmy."

I snorted, even though I sort of felt the same, but t'was too sentimental.

"What things? Doesn't seem like nothin' we do is very Godly."

He grinned and sat up, swiping some of my spend from his thigh. "Depends on your point of view, I suppose." He put his finger into his mouth and sucked my spunk off it, and I about fainted. I felt like a quivering virgin on her wedding day, all the things he was showing me.

"You are gonna kill me, Oscar."

He pulled his finger out of his mouth with a popping sound and licked his wicked lips. "I sure hope not."

"How are we gonna get all this grease off you now? And my spunk? You can't eat it all off yourself."

"That sounds like a challenge." He grinned and smacked his lips again.

"It ain't. Maybe we can use one of the blankets from the wagon. I'll go get one."

"Hurry back. Don't want the wolves to get me."

I turned back as I walked. "I think one already did. A sorry old wolf with no good intentions."

Oscar put a hand to his chest. "If that's what gettin' eaten by a wolf feels like, I'll offer myself every evenin'."

Chapter Eleven

Outlaws

The next day we traveled along the river, through the tall, autumn grasses, the snow-capped mountains looming around us in the distance. T'was a warm day in late August, but the nights were starting to get cooler, and I'd found an old jacket for Oscar to put on while he slept. I hoped the good weather and mild temperatures would stay with us, at least until we got to Whitehorse.

In the wagon, Oscar was real quiet, and I wondered if his ass was sore.

"You still hurtin' from your spankin'?"

He looked up at me, blushing like a maiden. "A little. But it's fine."

"What's wrong, then?"

He gave me a sidelong glance. "Jimmy, are you only playin' with me?"

I clicked to the horses, hurrying them o'er a small climb in the track. "Huh? What? I thought you liked the playin'?"

He nodded. "Yeah, I do. I do like it. I's just wonderin' if that's all t'was."

I didn't say anything, mulling that o'er.

"What do you mean?"

He rubbed at a spot of dirt on his trousers. "Is that all it is? Is there anythin'…more to it…than fun and games?"

"Oscar, I—" I was about to say, of course, there was, when he interrupted.

"Sorry. It's silly. Never mind."

I reeled in the team. The horses snorted and complained but they stopped. I gave Oscar a stern look that must have surprised him, because he sat up straighter and put a hand on the metal rail of the wagon seat.

"Don't do that."

"Do what?"

"Don't ask me somethin' important then backpedal. You gotta right to ask me things."

He blinked, reddening. "Sure."

"Are you asking me how I feel about you? 'Bout us?" I asked.

He looked sheepish and embarrassed. "Yeah, I guess so. Not sure why I wanna know. You prob'ly think I'm a nuisance, half the time."

"No, I don't."

"Well, you ain't offered to bring me farther than Whitehorse. As far as I know, we'll be partin' ways there. I know you gotta job to do, but maybe—"

"Oscar, I ain't taking you to Port Essington. I ain't got time for that. It ain't anywhere I need to be going.

"Sure. I know." He sounded real disappointed.

I *chirruped* to the horses and got the wagon going again. We drove in silence for a bit. Then I cleared my throat. "Maybe you could stay in Whitehorse with me. Help me out doin' this here job."

He looked at me, surprise on his face. "Stay with you in Whitehorse? You mean, not even go to Port Essington?"

"Yeah. That's what I mean."

His forehead creased. "But I gotta go see my uncle. I gotta find out if I still got some family left."

"Have you ever even met your uncle?"

"Long time ago. Don't remember much about him."

I nodded and stayed silent for a bit. "How do you even know he's gonna help you out?"

"I don't."

"Then why you gotta go all that way?" I asked. I'd hoped he'd take me up on my offer, but maybe t'was for the best if we parted ways after this week. Maybe I could give in to more of my secret longings for one week then go back to being respectable. Well, as respectable as I ever could be.

But t'wasn't only fun and games and, hopefully, my offer would prove that. This week was gonna leave a mark on me, as serious as those welts I'd left on Oscar's ass, but deeper and more permanent. I already felt changed by it.

"I need to, Jimmy. I lost everyone else. I need to find him," he said fiercely, and I knew there wasn't any swaying him.

"All right."

We drove in silence for a bit. Then I said, "Why don't we not think about partin' ways. We still got almost a week till we make it to Whitehorse. Let's enjoy bein' together. All right?"

He nodded, seeming conflicted. I knew how he felt. I didn't want to think about us having to part ways, either, but I didn't have time to go to Port Essington. I had a job to do, bringing supplies back to Dawson City for Mr. Henley, and I couldn't afford to be two weeks late doing that. I was trying to make a solid career and a good reputation for myself.

We made camp farther inland this time, since there was a real nice spot in the middle of a forest glade that offered privacy and protection. I hadn't said anything to Oscar, but I'd seen a man on horseback the other day, riding along the ridge nearby. It didn't make no difference, except if someone stumbled upon us being physical with each other. I didn't even want to think about what might happen. Folks didn't understand stuff like that, and seeing it out in the open could cause a real strong reaction, I figured. So, I thought it made sense to keep our camping spots as secluded as possible.

I set Oscar to getting a fire laid, while I took the buckets to get water for the horses. While I was carrying them back, I sloshed water on myself.

"Goddammit," I said, setting the one bucket down to get a better grasp on it.

As I straightened, the sound of voices came to me through the trees. I heard two men talking before I even got to within sight them, and my skin prickled with gooseflesh. Because I didn't only recognize Oscar's voice. I recognized the other voice, too. And that voice only ever meant trouble.

I walked faster and carried the buckets of water into the camp. Oscar stood near to the wagon, talking to another fella in a worn brown hat, chaps and a fringed jacket, looking like a trapper when I knew he was anything but that.

The fella looked up and gave me a crooked smile that sent a spike of fear through me.

"Well, looka who it is!" he said. "If it ain't little Jimmy Downing, comin' outta the wilderness like a vision."

My whole insides quivered, and I knew Oscar and I were in some trouble now. I only hoped Spook wasn't gonna stay long. Hopefully he and the rest of the gang were on the trail of something and not hanging around there.

"Spook, what're you doing around these parts?"

He laughed and took off his hat, placing it o'er his heart. His face still had that bird of prey look about it, with his angled nose and beady eyes. It was something I'd been trying to forget. "Well, I's simply lookin' for a place to set myself for a spell, maybe get a bite t'eat, Jimmy. You got anythin' for the likes a me?"

Oscar looked back and forth between Spook and me, wondering what was up and seeming uncertain about where he stood in this.

I nodded politely at Spook. I didn't want him hanging around, but there wasn't anything I could do except offer him food and hope he wouldn't stay long. And there was something I needed to know first.

"The rest of the gang nearby?"

Spook smiled long and slow, and I wondered how I could've ever imagined he and the others cared a whit about me, except as to how I could help them do the things they did.

"They's up on the ridge, plannin' a hit. They sent me down to scout around. They ain't gonna rightly believe what I found."

He laughed then, and the familiar sound sent another chill through me.

This wasn't no good. This meant the end to our carefree traveling, unless I could distract Spook and let him believe we didn't have anything of interest to him. Which we really didn't, except he and the gang were probably still peeved that I'd taken off from them, and I didn't know what that might mean—if they wanted to get even, draw me back into the gang or what.

All I knew was, I wasn't going back to the gang. There was no fucking way I would throw my lot in with them again. I'd come too far for that.

I felt some hope for my future now. Except some of that hope was tied in with Oscar here, and I didn't know what they might do with him, especially if they found out what he was to me. I needed to play it cool, and I hoped Oscar would understand that we needed to be careful about the things we said.

"Oscar and me, we's takin' the empty wagon back to Whitehorse. Then I got to load up another shipment."

There wasn't any point lying about it. Our only hope was making what we were doing sound so boring that Spook would lose interest. At least, the gang was on the trail of something, so they wouldn't want to change plans to mess with us or anything. Hopefully.

Oscar met my gaze and raised his eyebrows in a question. I shook my head slightly and stepped toward Spook. "We got some food we can offer you, if you wanna stay for a bit."

"Sure, that'd be friendly, wouldn't it, Jimmy? Nothin' like two friends findin' each other again, is there?"

I gave Oscar a look and it seemed he could tell how unsettled I was. He kept pretty quiet, stoking up the fire and getting things ready for some supper.

"Oscar here seems awful nice," Spook said, looking at my friend with a licentious interest that curdled my stomach.

Spook had absolutely no morals and no conscience. He was a dangerous man. Although I'd never actually seen him take his pleasure in a fella before, I sure wouldn't put it past him. And when Spook took his pleasure, he didn't exactly ask if t'was all right with whoever he was taking it with. He simply took it and left the other person bleeding in the dust.

I grunted. "He's all right. Helps me around the site. Good to have another pair a hands."

"Sure," Spook said, looking Oscar o'er, probably wondering what he was to me. T'wasn't unusual for two men to travel together, but I wondered if he could tell how me and Oscar were more to each other than traveling companions.

Oscar hadn't said a word since I came back. I figured he could probably tell how dangerous this situation was and he didn't want to make it worse. But when Spook walked o'er there and reached out to touch Oscar's hair with his grimy fingers, he pulled back sharply.

"Don't touch me."

Spook backed off, raising his hands in the air. "Sorry. You just got such pretty hair," he said, and he looked at me with eyebrows raised. "Ain't he, Jimmy? Got pretty hair?"

Spook looked at me as if he knew everything. Had he been watching us, somehow, from afar without me noticing? What if that twig cracking in the darkness the other night had been Spook, hiding there, watching all Oscar and I had done that night? T'was possible, as horrifying as that thought was, and if that was the case, we were done for."

Or maybe he was simply fishing for something I wasn't gonna give him.

I shrugged. "If you can call a fella's hair pretty. I don't know."

"He's a bit skittish, ain't he?" Spook looked Oscar o'er with disdain and spat onto the dirt.

"You gonna join us for some grub, Spook? Or you gonna get on your way? I reckon the others'll be wonderin' where you are."

Spook sighed. "That's true enough."

"Who all's there, anyway? The whole gang…or only you and Whitlaw?"

Spook didn't look at me when he replied, his narrow-eyed gaze fixed on Oscar with scornful interest. "Reckon that's none of your business. You made it pretty clear you didn't want anythin' to do with the likes of us no more."

I moved toward the wagon where my rifle was hidden, in case I needed to go for it. But Spook took off his hat and shook his head, turning to look at me. "Don't know why you'd up and leave us, Jimmy. You had it pretty good."

I met his gaze, as much as I never wanted to look into his soulless eyes ever again. "I did have it good. You and Whitlaw treated me all right. We made some good hauls."

"Yeah, we did. We're still makin' 'em."

I sighed and shifted my gaze to the ground. "I decided I wanted more out of life than always bein' on the run, stealin', lootin' and shootin' people."

Spook laughed and shook his head. "You make it sound so bad. We were just gettin' our due. No place else in this world for the likes a me and Whitlaw. And you, neither, I bet."

"I found me a place, and I'm keepin' it."

Spook took another look at the wagon and at Oscar, who stood stock still, holding on to the edge of the wagon box with one hand, looking like he wanted to run. I couldn't rightly blame him.

"Suit yourself. But you know you always got a place in our gang, if you want it." He crooked a thumb at Oscar. "You and your pretty fella."

I didn't say anything for a long moment, wanting to tell him that wasn't ever gonna happen, but also not wanting to make him mad. "Well, thank you kindly. I'll keep that in mind."

"Sure enough."

"You stopping for a bit?" I said again.

"Nah, I best get back. Like you said, Whitlaw gits ornery when I'm late. And he ain't no picnic, normally."

I nodded at that, because that was an understatement. Of the two of them, I'd rather deal with Spook any day. But they were usually pretty close to one another, and if Spook had found us, Whitlaw would know it.

"That's true."

"Maybe we'll run into each other again," he said, tipping his hat to me, then Oscar. "Watch out for them wolves in the hills. They got a nasty bite."

He swung up onto his horse and headed off in a hurry, raising dust from the ground as he did. Oscar and I watched him go and didn't say a thing until he was a long way gone.

I think both of us were afraid to move. Oscar turned and met my gaze with a wary and anxious expression. "Jimmy, I ain't never seen you so pale before."

I raised a hand to my head, wondering on the best course of action with this unexpected turn of events.

"Jimmy?"

I looked up as Oscar walked o'er and stood in front of me, wrapping his skinny arms around himself and looking like he might be sick. "That were one of the men you used to outlaw with."

"Uh-huh."

Oscar shuddered. "I didn't like the way he was talkin' 'bout me."

"I didn't like that, neither."

Oscar swallowed his fear down. "Would he ever — ?"

"I don't know. He done a lot of terrible things. Don't know if it were only to women and girls, or if he done them things to men, too. He's capable of it, that's certain. I don't want him anywhere near us."

Oscar nodded. He looked around us at the quiet forest, then returned his gaze to me. "Who's this other fella? Whitlaw?"

"Whitlaw's even worse than Spook. 'Cept Whitlaw don't play around with people before killin' 'em. He just does it."

Oscar huffed out an anxious breath. "I think I'd prefer that, actually."

I gave him a look. "He ain't gettin' *you*. He ain't gettin' *us*. We're gettin' outta here…right now."

Oscar stared at me, and must have seen how serious I was, because he didn't question it. "I'll help you hitch up the horses, then."

"We ain't hitching 'em up. We're leaving the wagon."

My brain had been going a mile a minute, figuring out the best course of action. The wagon slowed us down, and t'was damn near empty. No goods in it, just a few things of mine that didn't fit in the saddlebags — blankets mostly. And two saddles I'd found cheap, in case we had to abandon it for any reason. I'd been thinking in case we broke a wheel or something, but this was a good reason, too.

"Leavin' the *wagon*?" Oscar said. "Are you serious?"

"Do I look serious?"

He huffed a laugh that was more a release of tension. "Yeah, you look *real* serious."

"You know how to ride a horse, Oscar?" I said, grabbing a saddle out of the wagon box and setting it on the ground.

He looked nervous. "I mean, I can sit on one. Don't know much about makin' one go or nothin'."

Goddammit.

I'd have to lead his horse, then, and he'd have to hold on tight. Or maybe he should ride with me.

"How far you reckon we're goin' tonight?" Oscar asked.

"As far as we can. I wanna put as much distance between us and them as I can."

Chapter Twelve

The Wagon is Abandoned

We let the horses have some food and water, while we took what we could from the wagon box that wouldn't weigh them down too much. While we did that, I tried to get Oscar more comfortable with the idea of riding. Luckily, the horses were seasoned and gentle, although Dixie could be ornery when she got tired and hungry. But I would ride her and put Oscar up on Sprite. He was a steady horse and calm most of the time.

"If you can sit a horse, I'll lead Sprite behind me. You only need to hold on. You can hold the pommel of the saddle and hug with your thighs. We won't be able to go as fast as I'd like, but it'll be faster than using the wagon, and hopefully, you'll find your seat right quick." I winked at him to lighten things up a bit. "You need to put that sweet ass to work, now, you hear? And those slim, muscly legs of yours."

"I will, Jimmy. I'll do my best."

He seemed terrified all of a sudden, and I couldn't blame him—a pure city boy, who'd been face-to-face with a murderous outlaw until a short while ago. At least Oscar was street-smart and not new to life and death struggles.

"I know you will. We'll be all right."

I wasn't half convinced of that, but I didn't want him to worry.

I helped him onto Sprite. He grabbed onto the pommel of the saddle with both hands and nodded. "I got it. I'll be fine."

I squeezed his thigh, then leaned in and pressed a kiss to his knee. "You will. I'll start slow."

"Okay."

Truth was, seeing Spook again and having him so close to what was quickly becoming the most precious thing in my sorry life had damn near given me a heart attack. I would do whatever I had to do to keep Oscar safe. If that meant killing again, then so be it. I was lost, anyway. But if I could keep Oscar safe, maybe he'd have a chance at something. Maybe his uncle in Port Essington could sort him out and help him find an honorable path. Well, mostly honorable...

I swung up on Dixie, and we started forward at a walk. I had to really hold myself back, because I wanted to gallop and get the hell out of there. If I'd been alone, I could have. But there was no way I was leaving Oscar behind. Besides, the horses were tired from a full day of riding and wouldn't be able to go far.

We only had a few hours of daylight left, but I wanted to get away from where they'd found us before we holed up for the night. They'd come upon the empty wagon if they returned, so they'd know we'd left it, but hopefully they wouldn't bother trying to chase us down. I was trying to think positively as much as I could.

There wasn't any point in giving up. I'd worked too hard to get away from those men and make a new life for myself, and now I'd found Oscar. Whatever happened between him and me, I didn't want Oscar to fall prey to men like them. Sure, I had once been an outlaw, just like them, but I wasn't no more. And I'd never been as cruel and heartless as Spook and Whitlaw — and that was a bold fact.

Anyway, that line of thinking was too disheartening to go down right now. I'd changed my life to make it as honorable as I could, and there wasn't no going back. Even if those things I did with Oscar made me not worth saving, I still was a better man than them two.

"Shit," Oscar cursed.

I snapped my head around. He was trying to hang on to Sprite, but t'wasn't looking too good. Guess I'd picked up the pace more than I thought, and we were trotting now.

"Sorry… Sorry," I said, pulling Dixie to a walk and checking to see he was still mounted.

He smiled nervously, but said, "I'm all right. I reckon we can go faster if you want."

"You sure?"

"Naw. But I'm willin' to try it."

I thought about it for a second. If he could handle it, we could get a bit farther with some cantering, and he should be able to sit that.

"Okay, listen. That was trotting, that jerky movement you felt. That ain't much fun and I know it. Hard on the ass." I winked and he rolled his eyes. "But a horse gotta trot before he canters, which is a lot smoother and easier to sit. So, you'll feel the trotting then we'll go a bit faster and things'll smooth out. Still, it's gonna be fast, which might make you nervous."

"I reckon it will. But I can do it, Jimmy."

"I know you can. But if you feel scared or if you feel you're gonna fall, lean forward and grab Sprite 'round his neck. You know, hold your whole body against him and close your eyes. If you can stay on him, he'll keep you safe." I tried to convey my confidence in the horse with the sternness of my gaze.

Oscar nodded again. "Okay."

"Okay. I'll walk a bit, then we'll trot, then we'll canter. Give a holler if you do fall off, in case I don't notice."

His face went pale, and he frowned. "I don't think you need to tell me that, Jimmy. I reckon if I fall off, I'll holler pretty damn good."

I laughed a bit to lighten things up. "Yeah, I reckon you will. You ready?"

"Nope. But let's go."

Oscar ended up doing all right. He didn't fall off, anyways. And I don't think he had to resort to hugging poor Sprite to stay on. I was pretty happy about that, and probably so was Sprite. At this rate, maybe he could handle his own horse soon with a little instruction.

We found a small meadow in the thick of some trees, where we could camp for the night out of the way of things. Hopefully, nobody'd see us. It seemed a pretty good hideout, so for the first time in five hours I was able to relax a bit.

But only a little, because those men were experts at finding people if they really wanted to. But I couldn't be tied up in knots all the time. T'wasn't good for me or anyone, and a man could lose his perspective. So, I did what I could to relax, which included passing around another tot of whiskey.

Maybe t'wasn't smart to get tipsy in this situation, except I couldn't help it. I needed to settle down. I only meant to have one or two small cups of the stuff, but then me and Oscar got to yammering by the low fire, and t'wasn't long before we were both a little gone.

"You think they're lookin' for us?" Oscar asked, pushing a stick in the dirt, making crazy swirls.

I snorted. "Hope not. I'm sure they had plans for some nefarious hit, so maybe that'll occupy them enough they'll forget about us. We ain't nothin' but a couple of insignificant curiosities with no goods and not much money, so I hope they'll move on."

"Gosh, them's big words. You got a lot of book learnin', doncha? Gives me a shivery feelin' when you talk like that."

I side-eyed him. "I got some. Forgot most of it. 'cept some of the words."

"When did you leave the gang? How long ago?" he asked.

I stretched out on my back, my boot kicking o'er a pot that made a small clang — nothing too loud — but I made a face, and Oscar laughed softly at my clumsiness.

"T'was five years ago now," I said. "A lifetime."

"I reckon that's true. Must have been a big change."

"T'was. But t'was a change I needed." I sipped my whiskey, enjoying the burn and the warmth in my belly. "It had got to a point where I either had to break away or step in front of Whitlaw's rifle. I didn't wanna live like that no more."

Oscar stared at me, his face looking fierce as anything.

"I'm glad you broke free of 'em. Would a been a damn shame if I'd never met you," he said, moving closer and sitting by my knee, facing me. "Hell, I'd prob'ly be dead." He took a long sip of whiskey. "Or sellin' my body to the highest bidder at the cathouse or out in the street." He laughed. "Or the *lowest* bidder. I reckon I wouldn't get much."

I stared at him, hurting inside to think he gave his body such a short shrift. "Might be rude to say it, but I'd have paid a lot of money for what we did that first night, if I'd known how nice it'd be. You'd have been worth every penny."

He blushed and laughed again. "Well, my goodness, you are romantic, ain't you?"

I tried to look insulted because I knew he was making fun of me. "You ain't got any idea how romantic I can be, boy," I said softly, his face going all soft and blurry in my vision.

"Hell," he said, opening his mouth as we gazed at each other. "Golly. I'd sure like to."

I licked my lips, my mouth suddenly dry. "That right?"

"Yeah."

I put my cup down and grabbed his wrist, pulling him close and praying to God nobody was anywhere near. I figured we were hid pretty good, and the horses would alert us if anyone came by. And I couldn't resist him anymore.

He fell against me with a grunt, and I took his chin with my other hand, guiding his mouth to mine.

We kissed with an intensity that came from being on the run from *God knows what,* and only having each other to rely on and trust in the whole world, and from the chemistry we'd already skimmed the surface of and could hardly resist no more.

"Jimmy," he moaned, squirming on top of me, shoving his hands between our bodies and working my belt open, then my trousers.

I figured we both needed relief and needed it fast, so there wasn't any point in slowing down. All thoughts of being romantic left my head, and I groaned into his mouth as he wrapped his fingers around my cock.

"Fuck, Oscar. I could come right this second."

"Don't. Don't you fuckin' dare, Jimmy."

I laughed. "Well, look who's makin' all the rules now."

"Yeah, you better believe it. I want you to come in my mouth, not my hand."

My dick pulsed hard, and I almost spilled right then from his words.

"Jesus," I panted, scrabbling my heels in the dirt, trying to back up when I couldn't because of the log I was leaning against.

"I ain't Jesus, but I can maybe get you a little glimpse a God."

"Fuck, Oscar, I bet you can."

He grinned and moved backward down my body, plucking my shirt out of my trousers and working the buttons. He pushed it open and bent to tongue one of my nipples, sending a jolt of electricity right to my cock.

I shuddered a gasp, cupping the back of his head with my hand as he loved all o'er me, ending up down between my legs with his breath on my arching cock. I moaned, throwing my head back and he hadn't even touched my dick.

"Now that's a real hefty cock you got, Jimmy. Not like mine," Oscar breathed, shuddering—and not from the cold, I reckon. "You're a *real* man and I ain't. I only got this small thing that don't measure up none against yours, at all."

It seemed like he was talking trash about himself, so I began to protest, but he smiled up at me.

"Nah, I like that. Makes me go all shivery inside to think I got hardly nothin', and you got that big manly cock on you. Don't know why, but it does—same as likin' to be spanked and told what to do, I suppose."

"Oh. I see."

He swallowed thickly, eyeing my cock like t'was the biggest, manliest thing he'd ever seen. And I can't say it didn't make me feel damn good.

"If *you* could talk about my cock that way, you know, callin' it small and nothin' compared to yours… Hell, Jimmy, I'd really like that."

True enough, he was getting pretty fucking excited talking about it already. Didn't make much sense, I didn't think, but the way he reacted to the thought of it, I didn't much care.

"All right," I said, reaching down and smoothing a hand o'er his soft hair. "That little tiny thing you got ain't fit to be called a cock, I don't think," I said, watching him close to make sure I'd got this right, since it seemed so backward.

He closed his eyes and did a whole entire body shiver that let me know I was on the right track for sure.

"Oh," he breathed.

"I think I got a cock, and you got a little nubby there, don't ya? A small, little thing that I'd love to lick and suck to make it gets as big as it can get, but that still ain't very big, is it?"

Oscar opened his mouth and made a noise, shaking his head back and forth, his face flushing like mad.

"Nope, it sure ain't. Not like yours." He opened his eyes and gazed fiercely at me. "You got enough cock there for the both of us, I reckon."

Next thing I knew, he'd swallowed me down so far that I couldn't breathe. My body shook and my balls emptied into his throat, accompanied by my surprised groan and Oscar's contented humming.

When he finally let me slide out of his warm mouth and moved up to kiss me, I thought I might be dead.

"Oscar…"

"Jimmy…that was so good. The way you teased me about my — *my little nubby*." He shivered again. "That was *perfect*."

"It did seem a strange, but seeing how much you liked me talkin' like that, hell, I'll talk about your little nubby all day long."

He smiled and I laughed. I gazed up at him leaning o'er me.

"Everythin' we do gets better 'n' better. Why is that?" I asked.

He looked thoughtful. "Maybe because we're meant to be together?"

"You think?"

"Yeah. I do."

"Well, how about that," I said, feeling my brain cells start to reassemble. I sat up carefully, pushing him onto his side. "Lie down. I wanna get you off."

He grinned. "You wanna suck my little nubby, Jimmy?"

"I sure do. I never got no dessert yet."

He laughed and smacked his lips. "Well, *I* sure did. You gave me lots, sure enough, outa that big, manly cock a yours."

Dirty boy.

I grinned, opening his shirt and bending to his nipple like he done me. He squirmed so good beneath my kissing and nibbling.

"Oh... Jesus, that feels so good."

"I never knew how much I liked it till you done it. Nobody ever spent that much time with me before. Don't recall anyone touchin' me like you do."

"Well, that's mighty sad. I'm sorry 'bout that. Real sorry."

"I ain't. 'Cause that simply makes this more special than it already is."

Oscar laughed softly. "I'm special?"

"You sure are," I mumbled. "I aim to show you how special," I said, before taking his nubby in my mouth. T'wasn't really that little, only a bit smaller than average, I reckon. But I kind of liked that he wanted to *feel* small and a little less than a real man next to me. Not sure why, and I wasn't gonna examine it too close, but I liked it. Sure made me feel bigger and tougher, even though I knew he was as strong and as much of a man as me. Maybe more of an honorable man, because even though he'd been like this with other men, I didn't think he'd ever killed anyone like I had.

He clutched my hair and made the most delicious sounds as I worked him. T'was only the second time I'd had him between my lips, but it felt so natural, and I relished the taste and feel of him. I wondered if I'd always have preferred this to bedding women, but never knew it because the opportunity'd never come up—or if t'was only *Oscar* I liked. Because I sure *did* like him—the taste of him, the smell of him, the noises he made, the way he went all soft and sweet except for this one rigid part. But I knew how to make him soft there, too.

"Jimmy. Jimmy," he panted.

When I glanced up, he was looking down, watching me, and I felt a renewed jolt of interest in my cock. God, he was like a fire fairy or something, burning me up with a look and his dark magic that I couldn't get enough of.

"Tell me...how small I am. How small my nubby is... Please."

I pulled my mouth off him and teased him with my fingers. "Your nubby is so small I could eat two if you had 'em. I like the way it fits in my mouth, and I can get all around it with my tongue. I'll have to suck you twice as much, I guess, since you're barely a mouthful a t'all."

He gasped, and when I took him between my lips again, he made a strangled noise and spilled in my mouth, sighing sweetly into the night as the pleasure took him. I teased him gently with my tongue and soft kisses as he came down, until he pushed me away with a laugh.

"Stop. That's too much."

But I grinned and shot him a devilish look and held him down, driving him mad with the attention I paid to his sensitive spots. I had him squirming and protesting before too long.

"Stop, stop," he said, but he wasn't pushing me away.

"You really want me to stop?"

"No. Not really. I like it when you torture me like this. 'Cept I might get hard again."

"We need a word you can say when you *do* really want me to stop. 'Cause I like hearin' you say stop when you don't really want me to."

"Yeah, I like sayin' it."

I gave his softening little nubby a final kiss and moved up his body, so we were face-to-face. "What do you reckon your word should be?"

He thought it o'er, pushing the hair out of my eyes with his finger. "How 'bout 'whiskey'?"

I grinned. "That's a good one. All right. You say that and I'll stop, and that'll keep you safe. Keep me safe, too, from doin' somethin' you really don't like."

"All right."

He sighed and I about lost my soul in those brown eyes of his. Figured t'was gone the first time I caught sight of him, anyway.

"Wow, you 'bout startled me with all that romance, Jimmy," he said with a grin.

I wiped my chin, proud as punch. "I know it."

* * * *

Without the wagon for a bit of protection in the night, t'was cold, and I woke up shivering long before morning. I glanced o'er and saw that Oscar was doing the same thing. His eyes were closed but I reckon he was awake.

"Oscar."

"Yeah?"

"You cold?"

"Yeah. Why's it so cold, Jimmy?"

"I reckon 'cause we ain't got the wagon to keep us cozy no more. Even bein' under it were a way to keep a little bit a warmth snug around us."

"Oh."

"C'mere. We can keep each other warm."

"Okay."

I lifted my blankets for him to scooch in next to me, and I wrapped him up tight and spooned him right close. I felt warmer right away, but it took some time for our shivering to slow down. T'was good to have another body so close, and if I hadn't been so tired from the travel and the whiskey, maybe we would've ended up in another clinch. As t'were, I figured we were simply glad to get a bit more sleep before morning.

Chapter Thirteen

Rope and Leather

We slept cuddled together, but I reckon I kept one eye open in case the horses started fussing. Luckily, there wasn't no sign of anyone, and we headed out first thing, again with me leading Sprite and Oscar trying to keep his seat.

It went much better this time, and I figured I'd try to give him some actual riding lessons once we made camp. We didn't see any sign of anyone or anything suspicious, and I figured we must have got away, thank goodness. T'was a close call, but if we kept on and stayed well-hidden at night, I figured we'd be okay.

The cable ferry we used to cross at Stewart went pretty well. I figure t'was easier to manage the simple mechanism without having the weight of the wagon on it—only the two horses and us—so we got across without too much trouble, although we had to pull the empty platform from the opposite shore first off. The horses were used to ferries. Dixie shied a little, but Sprite walked right on without a problem. I let Oscar lead him, and I believe I observed a bond forming between them.

Oscar might have been skinny and rough when we'd first met, but he was regaining his strength from eating regular and from sitting a horse all day. He gave me lots of help with the pulling, and I was glad of it.

We found another hidden spot to camp that night and slept curled up together again. We weren't in no mood for loving this time, because it'd been a long day with high wind and tricky landscape, and we were beat. But t'was nice just to be close to each other in the cold night. I figured the weather was only getting colder from here on out so, we might as well get used to it. Sure, we were heading south, but t'was late August and the temperature was dropping.

I figured we probably had enough food to get us to Whitehorse without going too hungry, but I might try to hunt us a rabbit to add to our protein intake. So far, we hadn't seen sign of either Spook or Whitlaw—or anyone else connected with the gang—so that was promising. I began to feel optimistic that we'd shaken them off our trail or they'd had other important business to attend to that meant they didn't have time to chase us, which was honestly the best-case scenario, and I didn't wanna think about other ones.

The mosquitoes had gotten bothersome, but we rubbed our skin with the marigold juice I'd bought in Whitehorse, and that seemed to help quite a bit. And t'wasn't anything as bad as those bugs got in the spring. That time of the year you had to slather yourself in the stuff, reapply it every couple of hours and you still got bit.

O'er mugs of hot coffee in the morning, I told Oscar I was gonna give him some tips on managing Sprite by himself. I figured he was ready for that, and it would mean we could make more time than we were already.

"You sure? I mean, he's a good horse. But will he listen to me?"

"I reckon he will. You gotta be confident and tell him what to do, that's all."

"How do I tell him?"

"I'm gonna show you before we head out. Here. Put these on." I passed him a pair of old riding gloves I'd kept when I'd bought my new ones. "These'll protect your hands from the leather. They can get pretty sore if you're riding for long periods of time without gloves."

"Okay." He pulled them on and admired the way the worn, brown leather looked.

"There you go. You're startin' to look like a real cowboy now."

He gazed up at me with sparkling eyes. "I reckon I am."

When I boosted Oscar up onto Sprite, I handed him the reins this time.

He frowned and shifted in the saddle nervously. "I don't know about this, Jimmy. I ain't never rode a horse before."

I raised my eyebrows. "You been ridin' this here horse for three days now, and I reckon you found your seat pretty good. This is the next step." I gave him a smile to boost his confidence — show him I was relaxed about this.

He nodded. I showed him how to hold the reins.

"You remember what I said about huggin' him with your legs?" I asked, smoothing a gloved hand along Oscar's slim thigh, wondering if we'd have time today to do anything interesting before sleep took us. Hoping for it, but not certain about anything.

"Yeah."

"Well, if you squeeze him real tight and give him a *chirrup* and a little slap of the reins against his neck, he'll start to move for ya. And if you wanna go faster, squeeze him again or give him a kick like you seen me do with Dixie. They know what that means."

"Okay. But how do I stop?"

"Pull back hard on the reins until he listens and slows down. I know you're strong enough, now that you got some regular meals and exercise."

He looked at me with a bit of a grin. "How d'you know how strong I am? We ain't done nothin' but soft things together."

I wasn't sure what he meant by that, but I grinned. "That may be true. But you did pretty good helpin' me pull the ferry at the crossing. You got a lot of strength in them slim muscles."

He nodded. "Oh, I do. I'd like to show you how strong I am. Maybe we should have a bit of a wrestle tonight before bed."

Seemed like Oscar had some of the same hopes I did.

I laughed. "Sure. I'll go easy on you, though."

He shook his head, blushing like a girl. "Oh no. You go as hard as you want. I can hold my own, I bet. Even if I do have a *little nubby*, I got strong muscles."

Suddenly, I got quite an image of us struggling together by the fire, each of us trying to get the upper hand, and Oscar ending up across my lap at the end. I figured that's what he would want, and the thought of that about made me groan.

"You and your little nubby. I guess that's what we're callin' it from now on?" I asked.

He blushed and nodded. "I sure like it when we call it that."

"I know you do. Now, stop your pretty wiles, Oscar. We got a lot of ground to cover before we can think about playin' like that." I slapped his thigh as I turned toward Dixie. When I glanced back, he was watching me with a right needy gaze that made me feel all kinds of warm things. "But I do like the sound of it."

I swung up on the mare and nodded.

"Tell you what. You do a good job ridin' Sprite all by yourself today, and I'll think about givin' you what you want tonight."

He grinned. "*Whatever* I want?"

"Whatever you want, Oscar. But you fall off that there horse, and I'll make sure your bottom don't only hurt from that."

"Shoot. Now you're makin' me wanna lose my seat."

"What?" I barked a laugh. "You want me to give you a hidin' for *not* fallin' off?"

"Sure. Maybe." He laughed.

"Tell you what. You sit that horse, and I'll give you anythin' you want, e'en if it seems strange to me."

"That's a deal, Jimmy. I figure lots of things seem strange to people before they try 'em out." He waggled his eyebrows at me, making me laugh.

"I reckon that's true."

Hell, I knew t'was true. All the strange things we'd done already seemed like the answer to prayers I didn't even know I was saying.

❇ ❇ ❇ ❇

I needn't have worried.

Oscar did real well, guiding that horse like they were the best of pals and barely looking like he needed assistance. Anyway, Sprite was used to being near Dixie and doing whatever she did, so probably Oscar's instructions were barely needed. But t'was good for him to practice and get used to riding a horse properly, in case something happened to me—which I didn't wanna think about, but anything was possible on a journey like this. He needed to know how to take care of himself.

Now that he was more comfortable and not staring down at the saddle and holding on, Oscar expressed some dismay at the look of the country we were riding through.

"Jimmy, I ain't never seen such country as this. I never knew this was what things looked like outside of Dawson."

I nodded, guiding Dixie along the path that wound around the outer slope of a mountain, so we had a view of miles stretching out in all directions with glimpses of the Mayo River to the east and the Yukon River far to the south of us, that we could barely see. The land was packed with thick, green forests and dotted with rocky gray and brown slopes and outcrops that rolled and settled in places where it looked like there wasn't any possible way to get through. We weren't riding on the main trail anymore, in the interest of avoiding Spook and Whitlaw, but on a less popular, adjacent path that the indigenous people used to get by. I knew the landscape well, from years of outlawing in this area. Unfortunately, so did Spook and Whitlaw, though I hoped to God they didn't have any interest in chasing down the likes of us, since we barely had anything to our name, now that we'd left the wagon behind.

We rode at a slower pace after we'd had some lunch. I was getting pretty tired of beef jerky, t'was true. But I was mighty glad we had what we'd brought. We'd come down from the bottom of the mountain to a flatter area with pockets of trees and open spaces. As we were going along, I caught the flash of a small fox in the distance and brought Dixie to a sudden stop. Oscar wasn't paying attention, but Sprite was, and he stopped, too.

"Whoa. What're we stoppin' for?" Oscar said, looking alarmed.

"Shhh," I said, pointing at the trees ahead as I slowly reached for my rifle. "See that fella there? The brown fox?"

"Right there? That little fella?" he whispered. "You gonna shoot him?"

"I'm gonna try."

"I ain't never ate a fox before," Oscar said.

"You might not yet, if I don't get a good shot in. Now quiet."

"Yes, sir."

I held Dixie steady with my knees and aimed as good as I could. My gun made a loud crack when I pulled the trigger and the fox dropped dead like a leaf from a tree.

"Holy shit," Oscar breathed. "You got him!"

I couldn't help smiling at the awe in his voice. "Yeah, I reckon I did."

"You're an ace shot, Jimmy."

"Nah, just hungry."

I strung it up behind my saddle and kept an eye out for another opportunity. I almost got a shot at a rabbit but I held back, because the crack of a rifle going off made a bit of noise, and I didn't wanna do it for nothing. Anyway, we had a fox and that was good enough for a nice meal tonight for the both of us.

* * * *

"Oh my God. Whoever knew fox tasted so good, Jimmy?" Oscar said, chewing the roasted meat off the bone like he was born to it, grease dribbling down his chin.

"You're makin' a mess of yourself, son. Where'd you learn your manners?" I asked.

"This is so good that I gotta get it into me. Don't care about manners."

"That's plain to see," I said, laughing at his eagerness. I was glad he liked it because he needed to fatten himself up a bit.

"I'm rightly sorry, Jimmy, but when I get this kind of hunger in my belly, there ain't nothin' standin' between me and what I want."

For some reason, that there statement sent a shiver up my spine and made my cock swell. I cleared my throat and paid more attention to the bone in my hand.

"That make you feel somethin', Jimmy? Knowin' I can't help but take what I want sometimes?"

I nodded, keeping my eyes down. "I reckon it does."

"You want me to take what I want of *you* tonight?"

I didn't say anything for several seconds while the desire in me surged, and his words hung between us like sparks ready to ignite.

"I reckon I do."

"Good. 'Cause when I finish this here meal, there'll be other things I'll be thinkin' about."

"I reckon I'll be thinkin' about them things, too. But we oughta let our bellies settle from the meal first."

"I s'pose that's fair."

I risked a peek at him. He gazed at me while he slurped the juicy meat off the bone, like this was only the beginning and I was next. I shuddered and tore my gaze away, because I couldn't rightly wait.

We took the buckets down to the river to get water for the horses and decided to strip down and have a bath. The water was pretty damn cold, that's true, but t'was nice to wash the sweat and grime from four days of travel off us. I stole a couple of glances at Oscar while we washed, except t'was so cold that we finished as quick as we could. I didn't get to see much.

I'd told Oscar not to leave camp without me, and I wouldn't leave camp without him, neither. The shock of finding him with Spook on my return four days ago had scared the daylights out of me, and I knew it could have been so much worse. I wasn't taking any chances, even when it'd been a while since we'd felt any close threat, and I figured they'd let us go because they had more important things to do than chase down a couple of insignificant fellas like us.

Once we'd fed and watered the horses, I caught Oscar eyeing me from under the brim of his hat.

"What?" I said, though I knew what he was thinking.

"I figure you're nervous about wrestlin' with the likes of me," he said, nodding like he had me all figured out. Except, I knew he liked to instigate.

"Oh yeah. I'm terrified," I said, rolling my eyes and pretending to walk past him to get to my bed roll. As I brushed by, I reached out and grabbed his arm, pulling him with me as I used my foot to trip him up and land him gently on the ground. I came down atop him so he was trapped underneath me. T'was easier than catching a greased pig at the fair, that's for sure — which I'd done a few times in my youth.

"Fuck," Oscar cursed, struggling to get away. "Goddammit, Jimmy. How do you move so darn fast?"

I held him firm and nuzzled into the crook of his neck, nipping and licking him. "Don't you forget, I was an outlaw most of my sorry life. I got good reflexes, and I'm used to subterfuge."

He grunted, wriggling and trying to get the upper hand. But he wasn't going to. I wasn't letting him get away until I'd finished what I started. I held him while he struggled, until he winded himself and settled down, finally. I felt his nubby pushing against my hip, and now that he was quiet, I slid a hand between us to grab it where it stood beneath his trousers. "Jesus, you ain't even a handful when you're good and hard, are you?" I teased, knowing he liked that.

He whined and thrust against me. "Goddammit. What're you gonna do now?" His breaths came quick and sharp together, both from his struggle and how turned on he was.

"I don't rightly know yet. I'm turning a few things o'er in my mind. Reckon I should tie you across my saddle with some rope and tan your hide for daring to challenge me."

He made a sound, and I felt his cock move under my hand. "Oh, God. Would you?" The look on his pretty face damn near killed me, he was wanting that so bad.

We breathed hard together for several long moments as I considered. "I reckon I would. You like the sound of that?"

"Fuck, Jimmy. I almost came in my trousers when you said it."

"Yeah, I thought so." I stared down at him. "You gonna do as you're told if I get up?"

He nodded, the look of excited mischief on his face a vision of glory.

I narrowed my eyes. "You better, else I might not do what I said."

"Yes, sir. I'll behave."

I backed off him and stood up, reaching down to grab him by the belt and tug him to standing, which he must have liked a lot because he groaned and clutched my arms.

"You sure are strong. I like that," he said.

I didn't say nothing but marched him to where my saddle was sitting on the grass. "Stand right there."

"Yes, sir." He stared down at it and licked his lips, his chest going out and in like he'd run a race. I figured he was about to.

I went and got my leather gloves and pulled them on, then grabbed a bit of rope from the tack and brought it o'er to him. "Put your hands together behind your back. I'm leaving your shirt and jacket on 'cause it's cold and I don't want you to catch a chill, even though sometime I plan to have you buck naked when I do this. Maybe we can spend a few nights in a hotel when we get to Whitehorse."

He sighed, nodding, and put his hands where I wanted them. "I'd like that."

"Me, too."

I looped the rope around his wrists and tied them tight. I supposed being an outlaw had taught me some useful things. Never new they'd come in so handy when I turned my life around. Though my life was so far turned around now that t'was all topsy-turvy, that was for sure.

"Try to get out of that," I said, stepping back as he did.

"I can't."

"Good. Does it hurt?"

"Nope."

"All right. Don't forget your special word, in case things get too rough for you. You remember what it is?"

"Yeah. *Whiskey.*"

"That's right. Reckon I'm gonna need some after I finish with you. Now stay still while I get you ready," I said, moving in close from behind and finding his belt buckle with my fingers. I undid it and his trousers and his drawers, pushing everything down to just above his knees. I liked the way my gloved hands looked against his skin, and I hoped the feel of the soft leather would be nice for him.

His head lolled back on my shoulder while his bound forearms bumped against my own erection.

"You're so hard," he said.

"Yeah, so are you, *boy*," I breathed, getting more worked up the longer it took to get started. "You spend on my nice saddle, and I'm gonna spank you harder. Got it?"

"Jesus, Jimmy. You keep forgettin' who you're talkin' to. I like a hard spankin', so that ain't much of a punishment."

He was so genuine that I had to laugh. "That's a fact. You do. Never met anyone liked to be spanked as much as you do."

"Well, you been livin' a sheltered life, I guess."

"I guess so. Not anymore," I said, shoving him down to his knees in the grass and bending him forward across my saddle. "I reckon I'm makin' up for that now."

He made a little squeal and scrabbled his feet in the grass, trying to find some purchase. I pressed on the back of his neck firmly with a gloved hand and swatted his behind a couple of times.

"Jesus Christ. *God*!" he groaned.

"You like that?" I figured he did, but I wanted to make sure.

"Yes! Fuck, yes!" he gasped. "More."

"You want more, naughty boy? You deserve more of my hand on your sorry ass?"

"I do deserve it, Jimmy! I'm so naughty. You wouldn't believe the things that go through my mind when I look at you sometimes."

"I reckon they're pretty bad. Pretty fuckin' dirty," I said, swatting his ass so hard he shifted on the leather of the saddle.

He grunted, shaking his head. "They are. So dirty. Such impure thoughts I have 'bout you."

"That little nubby of yours better not spurt before I say it's okay. If you shoot onto my saddle, you'll be cleanin' it off with your tongue."

He shuddered and almost choked, and I thought he might have come.

"Jesus, did you spend, Oscar?"

"No! *Almost*. Jesus, I almost did. Not sure how you ever learned to talk like that, but I like it. I like it *so* much."

"Quiet now. I'm giving you ten strokes of my palm for all your naughtiness, then you can pull up your trousers and tidy up from supper, you hear?"

"I hear you. I'll try not to spend."

"Good boy. I want you to count, now. Make sure you know your numbers."

"Je-*sus*."

I slapped his already pink ass. "*Count*."

"One," he said, squirming and rutting against my saddle. "Two."

"Good boy. Now I'll let you spend on number ten if you want, but you gotta hold out till then."

He whined and wriggled under my hand. "Don't know if I'll make it."

"I wanna see you try."

"Okay. Three. Four. *Five!*"

He was panting now, and my arm was starting to get sore from holding him, but I couldn't tear my eyes away from the sight of him held down like this, o'er my saddle, ass in the air for me.

"You got five more n' then you can spend if you want," I grunted, starting to feel it in my hand now.

"Six! Seven! Oh God, I ain't gonna make it!"

"Yeah, you will."

"Eight! *Fuck*! Nine! Goddammit, *ten*, Jimmy. Oh. *Oh!*"

I made a ragged noise in my throat and let go of him, fumbling with my trousers and underthings. I pushed them down, whipped out my cock and jerked it hard, so my jizz splattered onto Oscar's pretty pink ass before he'd even finished spending himself. Our noises of pleasure melded together as I kneeled with my cock in my hand, staring at the beautiful sight of my spunk all o'er his bare bottom.

"Fuckin' *Christ*, Oscar."

"I spent on your saddle." His voice was quiet and soft and ashamed—maybe even a little sorry.

"I figured you did. You remember what I said 'bout that?" My voice was none too steady neither.

He gave a soft little gasp that was almost pitiful in its desperation. "That I gotta lick it all off?"

"Yeah." I chuckled, reaching out to swipe a bit of my jizz off him. "I spent all o'er your ass. Reckon I oughta lick that off?"

"Oh, God. Would you? Would you do that?"

"Try'n' stop me," I said, bending down and lapping at my spend on his smooth flesh.

"Oh, fuck, that feels so good and so goddamn dirty. I can't believe you're doin' that."

"I wanted to claim you. Figure I have done it, good and proper."

"One day, you gonna fuck me? Leave a bit a yourself deep inside me?" he hissed through clenched teeth, in order to keep his moans in.

I groaned, spreading his cheeks and tonguing at his hole like I was starved for it. There wasn't any spunk there, but I licked it anyway, thrilled by the noises he made. He smelled like sweat and leather and man. Don't know why it made me so wild, but it did.

"I can't wait for that. I think I'll about up and die if you do that," he continued.

"I will do it, Oscar. I promise, I'm gonna—maybe sooner'n we both thought I would."

My cock was plumping up again with all this talk of fucking him and the taste of my own spunk on my tongue. "Now I wanna watch you clean up my saddle, then we'll see what'll happen."

"Yes, Jimmy. Okay."

Good thing we were camping deep in the middle of nowhere, hidden by trees and darkness. I wasn't responsible for any trauma to the wildlife that witnessed what we were getting up to. I couldn't fucking help myself.

Chapter Fourteen

Gone

I kneeled in the dirt, stroking myself, while Oscar licked up his spend from the leather of my saddle, eyeing me while he did it, looking dirtier than the Whore of Babylon. By the time he was done, I was ready to show him he was mine and only mine.

"Lean o'er my saddle again. I'm gonna untie you so's you can brace yourself."

His eyes widened. "You gonna fuck me now?"

"I sure want to. You gotta problem with it?"

He shook his head. "Nope. I've wanted you to since I first laid eyes on you."

"Back when you was sassin' me and talkin' back?"

He grinned. "That's my version of sweet-talkin' a man, didn't you know?"

I winked.

"I didn't know it, but it sure worked. O'er the saddle now," I said, untying his wrists. "Brace your hands on the ground. I ain't never done this with a man before, but I liked to ride women pretty hard when I fucked 'em. Figure it'll be the same with you."

"Goddammit. I sure hope so," Oscar replied, voice high-pitched with excitement.

"Shut your mouth, now, or I'll put a gag in't."

"Holy shit. Thought you left your outlaw past behind, Jimmy?"

"Most of it. There are some skills still come in handy." I slapped his ass again, making him moan. "I need to get some of that grease. Stay still."

I brought the grease back to where he bent o'er my saddle, looking at me like I was bringing him salvation. Maybe that's what this was—salvation from a life living like everyone else, settling for things that were supposed to make you happy but didn't, because you thought nobody would wanna give you what you really needed. Sure felt like salvation to me.

Greasing him up between his soft cheeks almost made me ready to come again. I figured I wouldn't last long once I got inside him. T'was different from a woman, that's certain, but the same in a lot of ways, too. I wanted to be gentle enough that I didn't hurt him but hard enough that he got what he needed. That we both did. Figured I could manage that.

But sliding my dick along his warm crack, gazing down at his pink cheeks, warm from my own hand, made me desperate. I lined up the head of my dick at his hole and pressed forward, surprised when there was barely any resistance and it went in a short ways, accompanied by a shaky gasp from Oscar.

"Y'all right?" I said, between jaws clenched with trying to hold myself back, because all I wanted to do was slide right in there, go deep and sure and fuck my boy hard and good. When I thought about leaving a bit of myself inside him when I was done, I could barely hold on. It set off something in me that never got lit when I'd done that to a woman. There was something more depraved about this, that's for sure, even though it felt right and good, too. I was so confused about my feelings for this bratty boy-man, I couldn't think straight — but I didn't want to.

"Oh, that's so good. *God*. You can go in farther. Please. Can you? I been so empty..."

I cried out as I sank in pretty near all the way at that sweet urging and felt the heat of him swallow me up right good. "Goddammit. Goddammit. Jesus Christ. Oh fuck. *Jesus fuckin' Christ.*"

He laughed, and I felt it in my dick.

"You like it?" He pushed his backside out, forcing the remaining inch of me into him.

I whimpered and closed my eyes, gripping his hips tight and instinctively pulling back and thrusting forward again, making Oscar groan and having to bite my tongue to keep control. It felt so fucking good that I could hardly believe it, better than any woman I'd ever bedded in my whole sorry life. And wasn't that a revelation.

"I like it so much, Oscar," I panted. "I like it so much."

"I knew it. I knew you would. I like it, too. You don't need to baby me, either. You can fuck me good and hard. It's been a while, but I like it like that."

"I ain't gonna last long," I said, quickening my pace and going harder. "I'll try, but I ain't makin' no promises."

"Oh, God. Oh, God. Your dick is so big, Jimmy. When it slams inside me, it feels like it's comin' out my throat."

"Jesus, you got a nasty mouth on you." I was frantic now because I knew I was close, and I wanted him to enjoy this too. "You able to jerk yourself off while I do this? I ain't gonna last much longer."

He groaned but moved his hand underneath him and grabbed his nubby. "Harder, Jimmy. Harder. Fuck me hard. Fuck me hard and spill inside a' me. *Please!*"

I made a garbled noise of assent as I picked up my pace, hitting somewhere inside him that made him shudder and gasp as he must have come in his hand. His body clamped around me and that was it. I stiffened and I fell onto him, staying deep and buried as I spent myself deep inside him, like I'd said I would.

We lay there for bit, trying to come back to earth after hurtling past so may stars and planets that I couldn't rightly keep track of how far we'd got. When I made it down, my cheek plastered against Oscar's warm back, my cock still in his warm ass, listening to both of our heartbeats slow down, I felt dizzy.

"I gotta pull out of you, but I don't want to," I said.

He reached back and grabbed my hand off his hip, holding it in his. "I don't want you to, neither. But you'll fall out soon anyway, I reckon."

"True. That's true. I can feel it shrinkin' already. It's tired."

"I bet it is. You wanna watch your spunk leak out of me?"

"Oh fuck. Oscar, you shut that dirty mouth. I'm too tired to come again, but you're gonna make me want to, talkin' like that."

"You wanna see, though. Dontcha?"

Jesus Christ. He was so fucking dirty, and I loved it. "Yeah, I reckon I do. Stay still. Keep your legs spread when I pull out."

"I will."

I slid what was left of my dick out and leaned forward so I could see the bit of white spunk that followed it, the sight of that unbelievably erotic as Oscar's shiny's hole opened and closed.

"Goddammit," I whispered. "That looks…"

"I wish I could see it," Oscar said, craning his head to look at me watching.

"Shhh," I said. "I'm tryin' to focus here."

I slid my thumbs between his cheeks and pulled them apart, watching more of my spend leak out of Oscar's pretty hole. And I couldn't fucking help myself. I leaned forward and licked it up, swirling my tongue around his soft hole, pushing the spunk back into him and teasing him like the bastard I was.

"Ooooooh," he moaned. "Oooooh, that's so *dirty*. That feels so good, Jimmy. That feels *so* good."

I spent a bit of time playing with him until he was hard yet again, and so was I, but I didn't barely have the stamina to chase another spend. So, I turned him o'er on my saddle and sucked him off, pretending I was disappointed with the size of his penis, calling it sweet names and playing up to the fact that he liked to be small and dainty next to me. When he came apart under my attentions, I swallowed what he spilled while he stroked the hair back from my forehead and watched with those dark and beautiful eyes.

Afterward, I got a cloth, wet it with the water we'd brought from the river and cleaned us both off as best I could.

When we headed to our bed rolls and cozied up for the night, loose and boneless and exhausted, I hoped we wouldn't have to deal with any unexpected events, because we would have been pretty fucking vulnerable, after all that.

* * * *

We made it through the night undisturbed and woke to birds singing, animals foraging and what seemed like the entire forest cheering us on our journey. For the first time in a long time, I felt hopeful about getting to Whitehorse, having a couple of days together at a hotel then setting Oscar on his way. I figured we could find someone for him to travel with, so he wasn't entirely on his own. It would hurt my heart to see him go, that was a certain fact. But I'd be damned if I'd hold him back because I wanted to keep him near me. I wasn't selfish that way, and he was probably better off without me, as much as we'd gotten close on this journey.

Two men weren't meant to be sweethearts, and if we stayed together, it'd end in arguments and hurt feelings eventually. T'was better to part friends after having shared such intimacies.

Mayhap it had scared me how much I'd enjoyed fucking Oscar. Because I *had* enjoyed it, and sure enough, we'd shared something special. I couldn't rightly deny that. But our futures lay in two different directions, and I knew it wouldn't be like this forever. That thought made me sad, but t'was the way of things, mostly.

You learned to deal with it.

That day, while we traveled, I thought about a lot of things. How, if my life had gone better or more according to the way of things, I'd have had a wife and maybe a couple of wee ones, be living on a ranch with some cattle or sheep, living a regular life. But would I have been happy doing that?

I used to think I would, back when I was all tied up with Spook and Whitlaw and couldn't see a way out of it. I'd daydreamed about being a regular, law-abiding man with a wife and children and a home, and I'd thought that was the thing I should be reaching for. But I wasn't sure about that no more — not after the things I'd done with Oscar and how they'd made me feel. I wasn't sure I could ever bed a woman again, to be honest. Or maybe I could, but it would never feel as good as what Oscar and I had done.

Oscar was getting better at riding, and he and Sprite had developed quite the close relationship. I heard Oscar mumble to the horse on multiple occasions while we traveled, and he gave him little pats and strokes to encourage him o'er especially difficult terrain. We had to ford a few low streams, and Oscar clucked to that horse like he was his baby the whole time, not that Sprite was new to picking his way across rocks and gravel. After so many days riding, he had become a seasoned horseman in a short time. I was proud of him and figured t'was a skill he would always have. I shot a couple of rabbits that we cooked o'er a spit at our hidden camp before turning in with some cuddling and sweet-talking that I liked as much as the fucking we'd done the night before.

But when I woke up in the darkness and noticed right away that the warmth of him was gone from beside me, I didn't feel good about it at all.

"Oscar?" I said, my voice rough from sleep. I patted the bed roll beside me to check for warmth, but it felt cold, which sent a scare through me right quick. I scrambled up and gazed around me in the early morning dimness. Both the horses were there, and all our gear, too — what little of it there was.

But no sign of him.

"Oscar?" I said loudly, moving around the camp and peering into the trees. Mayhap his belly'd been upset, and he'd had to take a shit and gone somewhere private, even though I'd told him to stay nearby. I made a quick circle of the camp, becoming more and more nervous when I couldn't find him.

This was bad. This was pretty fucking bad, and I hated that I'd kept sleeping when he'd left me. Why hadn't I noticed when the heat of him was gone? What the fuck was wrong with me? I was a sorry-ass protector if I couldn't keep one skinny, bratty, man-child safe.

T'was hard to believe he'd wandered off and got lost, though that could have happened, especially at night in the middle of the bush. But my mind thought back to our encounter with Spook, and an arrow of fear sliced through me.

What if he'd gone to have a shit or a piss and they'd snatched him? They could have been watching us for days, seeing *everything* we'd done together, and now they were holding Oscar and God knew what they were gonna do to him.

I knew I had to stay calm and do the rational thing, which was to go looking for him. T'was hard not to let myself spiral into panic, but I worked for it and saddled up the horses, both of them, so when I found him — and I would — we could continue on as if nothing strange had happened. That was the hope I held close to my heart as I got ready to ride.

Sprite nudged my back as if asking where his friend was, so I turned and rested my forehead against his broad one.

"We'll find him. Don't you worry. We'll get him back, wherever he is."

I hoped to God that was true. I couldn't bear to think about the odds and how they were stacked against us.

* * * *

I made the rounds of where we'd camped, to make sure he wasn't anywhere on the site before we headed out. I didn't see any proof of his existence at all, but for his hat, which was where he'd put it before bed, and a branch he'd been whittling while we sat around the campfire. I had both of those things with me so's I could give them back to him when I found him.

I was going on pure instinct now, because he could be anywhere, in any fucking direction. But I reckoned I'd start out going alongside the river, back the way we'd come and hope I'd see some sign of him, anything, to give me an idea what had happened. If I didn't, I reckon I'd be riding around in circles for days.

The forest thinned near the river, and the landscape became sparse and rocky. When I came out of the trees, the wind cut through me from the north. I hoped he had his jacket on still, and I wished he had his hat.

T'was going on two hours since I'd left camp when I heard a gunshot nearby. My heart about leaped out of the top of my head as I urged the horses faster. But I wanted to sneak up to it, because there was no point galloping right into the midst of whatever was happening.

Sure, t'was possible Oscar was already dead, but t'was possible he was alive and, if so, I needed to form a plan to get him away from them what had him. And it might be Spook and Whitlaw — or it could be anyone else. I didn't rightly know, yet. So, I had to be careful and assess what was going on before I figured out what to do.

I swear to God, those next ten minutes were the longest damn minutes of my life. Felt like hours, before I heard yelling and pulled up behind a copse of trees and got off Dixie, tying them horses up and grabbing my rifle, then slinking around to get a look at what was causing the racket.

I saw Whitlaw first, the sight of him making me sweat before I figured out what was going on. He was yelling at someone, and waving his pistol, and sure enough, there was Spook with a pissed off look on his sorry face, yelling back at Whitlaw. Something about leaving him alone to deal with whatever t'was.

Then I saw Oscar, and I damn near almost blew my cover. He was on the ground and all I wanted to do was run o'er there, see if he was still alive or whether he'd been shot dead by the two men who'd already ruined *my* life, and now were out to ruin *his*.

Then Spook kicked him in the shin, making him groan, and I almost fainted with relief. He was alive, then, but for how much longer?

Spook glared at Oscar like he was a piece of shit come off his boot. I kept myself quiet and listened, but I cocked my rifle slowly and silently, and got ready to shoot if I needed to. I didn't wanna kill nobody, but I would. If it meant protecting Oscar, I'd be glad to have an excuse to kill either one of these men.

Whitlaw spat onto the ground and sneered.

"We ain't got time for this shit. Shoot the kid and let's go. Not sure why we didn't shoot Jimmy when we took the little 'un. He was layin' there so sweetly.

Prob'ly dreamin' of a homestead, or somethin' stupid like that."

Spook laughed, and t'was a dangerous sound. Meant he'd found something amusing that might keep him entertained for a while. Whitlaw oughta know there wasn't no rushing him, which worked in my favor, but I didn't wanna think about what he was planning. Reckoned I was gonna find out pretty soon.

"'Cause this'll hurt 'im more, seein' what I done to his precious slut afore I kill 'im. Prob'ly break his heart."

"You're disgustin'," Whitlaw said, spitting into the dirt again. He sighted his gun on something in the distance and pulled the trigger, the sound ripping the air. Oscar jerked against the ground but didn't dare move. "Don't know why you wanna sully yourself with a goddamn boy. Seems wrong in all kinds a ways."

"Well, for one thing," Spook murmured, poking at Oscar with the tip of his black boot. "He ain't a boy. He's a full-growed man, with hair on his privates and everywhere else. But I reckon I can make him cry, sure enough."

My pulse was going a mile a minute, but I knew I couldn't get a decent shot in, so I waited. T'was the hardest thing I'd ever done to watch Spook playing with Oscar, but I needed to wait until I got a good chance with a bullet. I inched closer, staying in the cover of some bushes, hoping my hands weren't so sweaty that my rifle would slip when I took aim.

Spook grabbed Oscar and pulled him up, standing him against a tree and tying his wrists together quickly. He shoved a rag between his lips and tilted his head back with dirty fingers. T'was hard for me to watch, especially since I knew how scared Oscar must be.

"You sure are pretty," Spook said, grinning like a lunatic. "Never understood why men'd take their pleasure in other men afore I saw you. Can't say as I blame Jimmy for tryin' it. Sure looked like a lot a fun."

He drew his hand down Oscar's neck and o'er his chest, then drifted it o'er his shirt and bound hands until it landed on Oscar's belt buckle. He worked the belt open and unbuttoned the trousers.

Chapter Fifteen

Blood in the Dirt

Oscar's eyes were wide and staring, but not at Spook. They were glazed and distant, like he'd gone inward to protect himself from what was happening, and I didn't blame him. I had to take a shot soon, whether I had a good chance or not, simply to make Spook stop what he was planning on doing.

"You ain't even hard for me, kid? Well, that's a shame. I was gonna play with you for fun afore I raped you, but it seems like that'd be a waste a time, don't it? If you can't even get hard for the likes a me, I reckon I ain't that ugly. Do you think I'm ugly?"

I'd watched Spook play this game with enough women to know how t'was gonna end, and I wasn't gonna let him do that to Oscar. Didn't care if it meant the death of us both, honestly.

"Anyway, doesn't matter what I look like if your face is in the dirt, does it? You don't need to be hard for me to fuck your pretty ass till you cry or I finish — or both — do you?" Spook's chest rose and fell rapidly, and he looked crazed, like he'd been waiting all his life for a chance like this.

Maybe he had.

I glanced at Whitlaw. He sat on a rock, resigned to watch Spook like he was most entertaining, and the show was only getting started. The hand holding his pistol lay relaxed in his lap.

I didn't waste time watching Whitlaw but turned to watch Spook shove his hand into Oscar's trousers. I reckon he twisted his balls because Oscar made an awful sound and doubled up. And that was my chance.

I already had my rifle aimed at Spook's head, so when Oscar bent down, I pulled the trigger, praying to God my aim was true and I'd get him.

As if t'was in slow motion, I watched Spook's head explode into bloody bits and splatter all o'er the tree and Oscar. I turned toward where Whitlaw was sitting.

Whitlaw stared in dumb shock as Spook's body crumpled to the ground. In slow motion, his head swiveled to where the shot had come from, and his hand with the pistol followed. I had less than a second to get him in my sights, but at least I didn't need to worry about hiding no more.

I stood up, aimed at his chest and pulled the trigger. My bullet found its target a moment after Whitlaw's gun went off, the bullet whizzing by my ear in the luckiest moment of my goddamn life, since he was generally an ace shot. Whitlaw clutched his chest and fell back onto the rock he'd been sitting on, rolling off and landing in the dust.

I was frozen, mostly because I couldn't believe I'd killed them both in such little time. But they were quiet and still. I knew Spook was done for, and I figured Whitlaw was dead—or soon would be. I didn't even care that I'd almost been killed. Seemed to be a price I'd pay any day to keep Oscar safe.

I heard a small groan above the sound of my own pounding heartbeats. I looked to where Oscar had been to see him stretched out on the ground, covered in bits of brain and blood, reaching out for me, looking like he'd seen the fires of hell and lived to tell but wasn't ever gonna be right in the head again.

I was torn, because I needed to make sure Whitlaw was gone before I let my guard down.

"It's okay now," I said to Oscar, moving quickly toward the rock where Whitlaw had fallen and peering at where he lay. His eyes were open and he locked onto me, but he wasn't going nowhere. There was blood bubbling out of his mouth and his skin was pale and clammy. He tried to say something but only made a sorry rattle in his chest.

Suddenly my anger o'ertook me, for everything I'd ever witnessed at their hands, and for the fact they'd made me a part of it. I lifted my rifle in the air and stepped closer, bringing down the butt of it on Whitlaw's head again and again, until he lay still.

"That's for what you done to me, leading me into this sorry life, making me help you do your robbing and killing and making me watch Spook doin' all those terrible things, so I'd be too scared to leave. 'Cept I did leave, and I found a new life—then you *still* come after me, stealin' everythin' that was good about it and almost killin' *that*, too." Tears coursed down my cheeks as I collapsed to my knees, sobbing in great, ragged jerks for all those wasted years and all that fear and suffering I'd witnessed and endured.

By the time I'd collected myself enough to turn back, Oscar had wriggled his way through the dirt and grass to me, his hands still tied and trousers open. He was so close that I only had to lunge for him so's I could gather him into my shaking arms.

"I'm sorry. I'm so sorry. I shoulda woken up when you left me. I'm so sorry," I gasped, holding him against me and stroking his hair, even though he was covered in Spook's blood and brains. "I'm so sorry. I got you now and ain't ever lettin' go."

He was crying, too, and we huddled together on the cold ground for a long time, relieved to be free of the threat of them two outlaws.

"Oscar, I need to check somethin', all right? But I'll be back with you in a minute, and I ain't going out of your sight."

T'was a moment before he nodded against my chest and loosened his hold on me. I kissed him on his bloody forehead, then stood and walked back to where I'd left Whitlaw bleeding in the dirt.

I didn't look too close at what I'd done to his head with the butt of my rifle, but I used my shaking fingers to open the big pockets of his coat and see what was in there. The first one had a half-eaten roll of bread and some crumbly cheese, but the pocket on the other side proved my instincts were correct. I hauled out a wad of bills so thick that they barely fit in there. It looked to be nearly five hundred dollars at first glance, and I reckoned he had more of that in his leather pouch, so I stuffed that money in my own pocket, slinging an apology up to God and the authorities for taking dirty money. But t'was a sure thing Spook and Whitlaw didn't need it no more, and Oscar and I did. And even though I knew they'd got it through thievery, I didn't reckon anyone would be able to connect us to it.

Sure enough, I found another three bundles of bills in Whitlaw's leather satchel. I quickly counted it, and although my brain spun from everything that had happened, I felt a load lift off me, knowing we had some means to survive once we got to Whitehorse and money to replace some of the supplies I'd had in the wagon.

And the wagon, too, if I was gonna keep hauling supplies to Dawson City. But that would mean leaving Oscar to travel on his own to Port Essington, and I didn't really know if I could do that, after what had happened. Because the truth of t'was, almost losing him to Spook and Whitlaw had shown me clear how much he meant to me. And I didn't ever want to leave him, truth be told.

I stuffed all the money into my own satchel and closed it up, making sure the buckle was fastened so's it wouldn't fall off me on the road, now that t'was carrying our future inside it. Then I returned to Oscar and helped him stand, before making our way down to the river with the horses.

I stripped him and myself and took us into the cold water, glad to see him pink up and come to himself after his terrible ordeal, gasping from the shock of the frigid river.

"You gonna be okay?" I asked, trying to get all the blood and gore off him, watching him shiver and shake from the bracing cold.

"Yeah. Th-thanks to y-you." His teeth chattered and I reckoned he was still in shock from the fright and having Spook's brains blowed out on top of him.

"It's my fault you were in that mess, and I'm so sorry. I should have left you in Dawson City. You'd have been safer, prob'ly."

Oscar shook his head violently back and forth. "I'd a prob'ly been dead by now—or wished I was. You saved my goddamn life for the *second* time, Jimmy."

I wrapped my arms around him, holding him close, so grateful I'd found him and that I'd been able to save him. If they'd caught me and made me watch Spook do what he was planning to do, like I'd seen him do to people in the past, I'd have lost my mind. Or I'd have tried to stop him with my bare hands and got a bullet in me.

T'was a miracle it had turned out the way it had, and I didn't wanna let Oscar go.

I wrapped him in one of the blankets and sat him on a rock by the river, got myself dressed and started a fire so he'd be warm. Then I spent half an hour beating the blood and guts out of his shirt and trousers and laying them out to dry near the flames. I didn't want to camp here—so close to where the horrible memories were gathered and where two men lay dead from my bullets. So, when Oscar's clothes had dried, he put them on, and we got ready to ride out.

"I don't know if I can sit a horse right now," Oscar said, looking smaller and younger than I'd ever seen him, thanks to Spook and his goddamn sadistic side. "I feel all dull and dizzy—like I ain't real or somethin'. I don't know."

"S'okay. You can sit up on Dixie with me. I wanna keep you close, anyway."

"Okay." He started breathing quick again and his forehead screwed up as he fought back tears. "I'm all right. I'm all right."

"No, you ain't. Nobody'd be all right after what you been through, not yet anyway. But you will be. I aim to make sure of it."

He nodded, not quite believing me.

"Here... Get up onto Dixie, and I'll sit behind you. That way I can hold you and keep you steady."

"Okay."

I helped him onto my horse and swung up behind him, cradling him with my body and making sure Sprite's lead was still tied to the saddle. It felt good to have him so near, and I'd kill anyone else who tried to take him from me.

He shivered and shook in my arms. I knew t'was partly from the cold of the river but mostly from his body going into shock after everything, and all I could do was hold him steady and share my warmth and find us a place to camp—a place that was hidden, secure and away from anyone who might want to cause us harm.

I wanted to get us far away from the scene of violence, so we could put it behind us and get back to our journey. I was relieved that both Spook and Whitlaw were gone and not a threat to us anymore. But I didn't know if there was anyone else from the old gang with them, who might find them and hunt us down—and that thought worried me. Then again, the way gangs worked sometimes, maybe they'd take it as an opportunity to gain control. I can't imagine that Whitlaw or Spook would be much missed by the other men. I hadn't been the only one with regrets or who'd been ready to get out. Then again, maybe that had already happened, and the two of them had been on their own.

We rode about ten miles before we stopped and set up camp. I settled Oscar on another rock and told him to put his head between his knees and take deep breaths to calm himself. Then I got some kindling and bigger branches to start a fire, without leaving him out of my sight. While I was getting things going and making things comfortable, I talked to him, using my tone of voice as a settling influence. I spoke about ordinary, regular stuff, like how it'd be nice to look for some more rabbits tomorrow, so we could have a good supper. All we had for tonight were canned beans, but I figured neither of us was very hungry.

Once I'd stoked the fire and cooked up some beans, I offered him a cup full. He shook his head.

"I ain't hungry."

"All right."

I spooned some into my mouth and chewed, even though the events of the day hadn't done much for my appetite, either, but it wouldn't do for either of us to get sick because we weren't eating. I sat close beside him on the log in front of the fire, staring into the flames, same as him, and grateful things had turned out the way they had, but wishing Oscar hadn't had to go through any of that.

"Here… I want you to eat this," I said, holding the spoon in front of his lips.

"I said I ain't hungry, Jimmy."

"I heard you say it. You need to eat, son."

He turned to glare at me. I hadn't seen him look so fierce since that first day, when he was so lost and wild that he was biting at everything near him.

"You gonna force me to?"

I tried smiling. "I reckon I won't. But I'm askin' you to please eat a spoonful of beans to make me happy. Will you?" I figured I'd catch more flies with honey than I would trying to make him.

His eyes lost some of their fierceness and softened. He kept his gaze locked on mine and opened his mouth.

Very gently, I put the spoon between his lips and watched as he slowly licked the beans off. I can't say my dick didn't decide to get interested in what he was doing, though I mentally scolded it to settle down.

"Will you eat a bit more?" I asked softly, glad to see him swallow and keep it down.

"I reckon I will, if you keep feedin' me."

I grinned, spooning up more beans and feeling better about everything, all of a sudden.

"You like that?" I asked.

"Yeah," he said, with his mouth full. "I reckon I do."

"So do I," I said.

He raised his eyebrows.

"Not because I enjoy the sight of your pretty pink tongue, though I can't deny that's a part of it."

He flashed a small smile that I was so glad to see. He ate two more helpings before he said he'd had enough.

I finished the rest of them and put my elbows on my knees, enjoying the warmth of the fire, holding the cup in my hands to be doing something.

"I could use a bit of whiskey," Oscar said, "to wash them beans down."

"Yeah, I reckon I could, too. We best be careful, though. We only got about half a canteen left."

He nodded. "I reckon a little would go a long way right now."

"Yeah, that's true."

I swished some water in the cup to get the last of the beans out, and grabbed the canteen of whiskey, pouring about half a cup's worth.

"You want me to feed you the drink, too?" I asked, half joking but half serious because I'd love to do that for him. T'was like caring for a hurt baby bird, and it pulled at something delicate and breakable inside me.

He nodded.

As I lifted the cup to his lips, I suddenly had an awful thought and pulled it back.

"Spook didn't do anythin' to you before I got there, did he?"

Oscar's face lost a bit of its color for a second, but he shook his head.

"Nah. Only rough words and hints of what he was gonna do is all," Oscar murmured. "But that was enough. Jimmy, I was so scared." His voice was a whisper of itself. "I tried to find a place in my head I could go and not feel anythin', not be scared of nothin', but t'was hard. I used to be able to find that dull, quiet place pretty good, before I met you. But you keep me wantin' to be in the world most of the time, and it's hard to find that place now."

"But he didn't touch you? Didn't hurt you, except with the horrible fear that he was gonna?"

"No, sir."

"Thank hell for that," I said, the relief a palpable thing. "I reckon it's gonna take some time for you to forget about what happened and the way it made you feel. But at least you ain't been...physically violated...more'n I saw him do before I shot him."

Oscar nodded.

"Why'd you leave me in the night?" I asked.

Oscar swallowed. "I... I couldn't sleep, and I figured walking around might help. I didn't want to wake you. I know now that I should have, and I'm sorry."

"S'okay."

"No, it ain't. You told me, and I didn't listen. I was walking by them rocks near the water when Spook grabbed me and held his hand across my mouth so I couldn't yell. I thought I was dead, right then. But then he took me to his camp where t'other man was and spent the rest of the night explaining exactly what he planned to do to me in the morning."

My stomach sank. "I'm so sorry, Oscar."

"I figure he must have seen you fuckin' me, because he said he was gonna do better."

"Jesus. I'm sorry."

"Can I have that whiskey now, Jimmy? 'Cause t'wasn't very nice to have a man's brains blowed out all o'er me, even though t'was a lot better than the other thing. You know?"

"I know," I said, holding the cup to his lips and letting him have a couple of good long sips. "You're an awfully brave man, Oscar—" I realized I had no idea what his family name was, and that made me embarrassed, after all we'd done together. "Jesus H. Christ. I don't even know your last name."

He smiled, and I was glad to see it. "I reckon we know most everythin' about each other now, and my last name ain't so important. But it's Yates, if you're interested."

"I am, for certain. You're an awfully brave man, Oscar Yates, and I'm glad to know you."

"Well, I'm really glad to know you, Jimmy Downing. And I'm happy you're an ace shot with that rifle."

"Goddammit, so'm I."

The relief of what had happened and how I'd stopped it, hit me all of a sudden, and I took a shaky breath. "Don't know what I'd have done if Spook had…if he'd…done *anythin'* to you."

Oscar nodded soberly. "I'd a prob'ly wanted you to shoot us both."

I stared at him, the reality of how close I'd come to losing him so fresh in my memory that I couldn't hardly bear it. Then I nodded and took a sip of the whiskey myself.

When we finally bedded down for the night, I pulled Oscar close and held him tight with my arms wrapped around him.

"This is how we're sleepin' tonight. You ain't goin' nowhere. You gotta take a piss or a shit, you wake me up an' I'll come with ya."

"Gosh, Jimmy, you say the most romantic stuff."

I scoffed at his teasing. "G'on now. Get to sleep."

We lay there for a while before Oscar whispered my name.

"Yeah?"

"I can't seem to settle. E'en with your arms around me and the heat of you keeping me warm. Seems like my nerves are never gonna stop fussin'."

"I know. I remember feeling like that sometimes. When I was small, my momma would sing me a song to get me to sleep."

After a long silence, Oscar said, "Would you sing me somethin', Jimmy?"

I thought about it. Seemed like there was nothing I wouldn't do for him right this second.

"I reckon I will. I ain't no balladeer, though. But I'll do my best."

"All right."

I lay my mouth close to his ear, enjoying his scent and closing my eyes so's I could savor it. Then, I started singing. I sang him *All the Pretty Little Horses* like he sung to me that one time, then I remembered some more of the sweet, soft songs my momma used to sing me, so I sung him those, until I felt him loosen and jerk subtly as he sank into sleep.

Thank goodness.

I couldn't even imagine how scared he must have been when Spook and Whitlaw took him. He must have figured he was dead and gone right then—that I'd never, ever find him, they'd do what they wanted and shoot him—and that would be it.

Chapter Sixteen

A Soft Bed in Town

"How're you feeling this morning?" I asked Oscar while we drank our coffee by the fire.

The weather was growing cooler, and I'd woke a couple times in the night to make sure Oscar was still there and to pull him closer to keep him warm. As the sun broke o'er the horizon, I cupped my coffee mug and enjoyed the steam rising from it and the heat that seeped into my cold hands. We'd been real lucky with the weather so far, and it looked like it would be another sunny day that would warm up as it went on.

"I reckon I'll live," he said, giving me a sweet smile. "I slept pretty good, once I started."

"Glad to hear it. T'was good holding you in my arms all night, making sure nothin' got you." I didn't say anything for a little bit. The memories and heightened emotions of what we'd been through the previous day still lingered. "Don't know if I'll ever be able to let you sleep alone, after what happened yesterday."

He gazed at me with a strange expression. "But you ain't gonna come with me to Port Essington."

"I know what I said." I looked at my boots and shrugged. "That was before I almost lost you to them two." I took another sip of my coffee and cleared my throat. "That was before I realized how much you mean to me."

He didn't say nothing for a minute. I glanced up to see him blink fast, like he was holding back a waterfall, and I smiled, blushing, and shrugged again. "I ain't gonna fight it no more. I figure I'm yours and you're mine and there ain't nothin' we can do about that no more except go along with it."

"Jimmy, I—"

"That's as long as you feel the same as I do."

"Of course I do. I don't wanna be parted from you. But I can't stay in Whitehorse and help you. I gotta find my uncle. He's the only one I have left who cares about me, 'cept for you."

"I know it."

He blinked hard as he tried to hold my gaze. "You mean...you're gonna come with me *all* the way to Port Essington?"

"Yeah. I reckon I am."

He swiped a trembling hand o'er his eyes and sipped his coffee, nodding quickly and grinning.

"I'm thinkin' that maybe we can stay at a hotel for a bit before we head out. We can prob'ly be in Whitehorse in a couple of days. We can get a bath, find some other clothes or at least get these properly laundered, have a few good meals and sleep in a proper bed...along with some other things."

"We ain't got the money for that, do we?" Oscar said, his face twisted up in confusion at my words.

I smiled slow and patted my leather satchel. "I reckon we do now."

His eyes went wide. "You get some money off them outlaws?"

"I did. A lot of it. More'n I've ever had at one time, and that's a fact."

He stared at me, searching my face for the truth of it. "I guess they owe us that, right, Jimmy? For what they done?"

"It ain't nearly enough for what they done, but I'll take it to smooth out our lives and give us the chance to get you to Port Essington, safe and sound," I said. "But first, we're gonna have us a rest in town."

"I'd like that a lot." He thought for a while, sipping his hot coffee and watching the sunrise through the trees with me. "They gonna wonder we be sharin' a room?"

"Nah. A couple of 'poor' cowboys like us? Why'd we wanna pay for two rooms? We'll ask them for a pallet for the floor, so we can pretend we ain't sharin' one bed. And we'll have to be careful. No loud spankings or nothin'. Don't want all of Whitehorse hearing me tan your pretty ass or your loud wails and sobs, now, do we?"

"I reckon I can go along with that," he said. "We'll save those for the road."

"I reckon."

We gazed at each other, both of us feeling more like ourselves now that we'd put a night between everything that had happened the day before and the more optimistic outlook of today.

"Now, go give that horse of yours a kiss. He missed you yesterday. Didn't know what was going on, since you weren't ridin' on him."

"*My* horse?"

"I reckon he's yours now."

"I ain't never owned nothin' like a horse before. I ain't hardly owned anythin' in my whole life."

"Well, you do now."

He nodded and stood. I watched him go to Sprite and *cluck* to him. Sprite nudged at Oscar with his muzzle, poking at his pockets for a piece of carrot or something good. But when he couldn't find that, he simply rested his forehead against Oscar's chest like he was happy to be there. I reckon that horse had belonged to Oscar the first time they'd met.

Just like I had.

Fella had a way with horses *and* men. He didn't rightly know it, but he was something hard to resist…and I'd quit trying.

And I wasn't gonna let anyone else have him, and that was a fact. If his uncle truly did care for him and wanted to help him, I'd find a way to stay in Port Essington and get some honest work so's I could stay near, and Oscar and I could continue with our loving, somehow, some way, that wouldn't call the law down on us or disrupt the orderly flow of society.

If keeping him meant living a part of my life in secret, I'd take it any day o'er losing him. Surely wasn't the worst thing I'd ever done, and mayhap it might be the best.

Seems that scare with Spook and Whitlaw showed me real good that nothing about what Oscar and I did together was wrong or sinful. Sure, the world had taught me that it must be, but I believed my own heart and eyes o'er those teachings.

What I felt for him *wasn't* wrong. T'was *every* bit of *right*, even if it involved playing at power and punishment like we did. That was nothing like the real evil games people played that hurt and killed folks.

AE Lister

T'was nothing like that. It came from loving another person and wanting to please them, no matter how strangely some things did that. T'was going off instinct and the way two people meshed together and not questioning things that felt good, and right. I figured the world could do with more of that.

* * * *

We rode hard for two days, seeing more and more travelers as we hooked up with the main road into town and finally made it to Whitehorse.

T'was good to be near civilization again, particularly after the incident with them outlaws. I knew nobody'd be looking for their killers. If the law found them, they'd be silently thanking whoever'd done it, and that was a fact. I didn't feel one slip of guilt for putting an end to their sorry lives, but that was gonna be the last bit of killing I ever did, if I could swing it. I didn't want no more blood on my hands after that.

We found us a hotel and got the horses looked after. Then had a proper meal and arranged for a room with a bath and a pallet for another bed, to keep up the ruse that we were two tired and dirty nomads who needed housing for a couple of nights.

After we got inside the room and locked the door behind us, Oscar turned and pressed himself against me, nuzzling into my neck and wrapping his slim arms around me. Instinctively, my arms encircled him, and I slid my hands up to cup his face as I kissed him all o'er his cheeks and forehead, finally landing on his mouth. The passion of our connection reared up, as did other parts, as Oscar welcomed my tongue and kissed me back greedily. This was the first time we'd embraced in

189

such a way, and I was startled at how regular and right it seemed. He felt like a woman, except for some obvious differences that I didn't rightly care about. Or, that I did care about, but that only enhanced his appeal. I figured lovin' on someone was lovin' on someone, and what body parts were involved didn't rightly matter.

But I forced myself to pull away after a time, because we were filthy, and I wanted to be clean before we came together.

I let Oscar bathe first, though I helped him to wash his hair and other parts and he returned the favor for me. By the time we'd finished and dried ourselves, we were so hot for more that we couldn't hardly stand it.

"Jimmy, I want you so bad. I never wanted anyone so bad as I want you," Oscar said, tumbling onto the bed and speaking in low, soft tones, so nobody'd hear him. His little cock was standing up against his belly, so I wrapped my fingers around it as I gazed into his eyes and kissed him sweetly.

He sighed and thrust into my hand for a minute, then rolled onto his back so's I could climb o'er him, which I did and was very happy to.

"You make me feel so safe," he said.

"I wish I could have kept you safe. I will from now on."

"I know it."

I sighed, running my lips along his neck and inhaling his clean scent. "You're like this precious thing the universe gave me, and I aim to take care of it. Take care of you," I said, giving him small kisses o'er his cheeks and chin, while he stretched and squirmed underneath me.

"I know I don't even deserve you."

"You *do* deserve me and everythin' I'm givin' to you—this soft lovin', as much as the harder, dirtier stuff."

"But I *love* that stuff," Oscar muttered breathlessly.

"Yeah, I know. So do I. But right now, I wanna take my time and be gentle, so you'll lie still and take it, y'hear? I can be strict, even when I'm bein' kind, right?"

"God, how did I ever find somebody who would know what I liked, what I needed?"

"Quiet now, n'let me love on you," I scolded.

"Yes, sir. I won't talk no more, but I ain't promisin' I can be very quiet," he said, moaning a little at the end of that statement.

"Well, you better figure it out, or I'll be puttin' a soft bit of cloth between your teeth to keep you that way."

I froze then, remembering about Spook and the gag.

"I'm sorry," I said quick, sitting up and gazing down at him, horrified I'd said that. "I didn't mean—"

He looked at me fierce and shook his head.

"No, stop it. Ain't the same thing. I know what you mean, and I reckon if you were t'do that, if I gave you *permission* to do that, I'd like it a whole lot. It's not the same thing."

"I know it's not. I'm sorry. I don't want to—" I rubbed a shaky hand o'er my face, collecting myself, pushing those memories away.

"I know. Now kiss me. I want you inside me soon, y'hear? And I'll be as quiet as I need to so's you can do that, all right?"

"All right. All right."

T'was good to sleep naked in a soft, warm bed instead of on the ground, wearing all our clothes. Even though we were safe now, I kept Oscar wrapped in my arms all night. T'was so much better with his naked flesh pressed against me, the sweaty and sticky results of our joining wiped off with soft cloths, so the baths we'd had wouldn't be wasted.

I needed a haircut. Reckoned I would look out for a barber in the morning. Oscar's hair was getting long at the back, but his curled in the most charming way, and I liked it. I couldn't bear to see it cut. I'd told him that, playing with them soft, brown waves before we'd fallen asleep, and he'd said he didn't mind keeping it a bit long, that he'd get it trimmed when we got to Port Essington. He could always tie it back with a piece of string or leather if t'was getting in the way.

"It don't make me look like a girl?" he'd asked.

"Nope. It makes you seem like somethin' in between—a beautiful, mysterious creature, with the properties of both. I like that a lot."

He'd smiled and kissed me on the cheek, then sighed and closed his pretty eyes, falling asleep against my chest. He was so precious to me now that I almost couldn't bear it. There wasn't no one could take him from me. I'd like to see them try.

* * * *

In the morning, we got a basin of warm water and some towels and shaving gear sent up and took turns shaving each other. On the road, we'd used the rough razor I kept with me, and it had done a decent job, but I needed to get me a new blade. At least the ones here at the hotel were nice and sharp.

"Whoa," I said, smoothing my hand along Oscar's cheek when I was done with him. "Softer than a baby's bottom, I reckon."

"You prob'ly ain't never had your hand on one of them," he said, grinning.

"Nope, I'm happy to say. But I hear they're pretty soft, being brand new to the world n'all."

"I reckon they are."

I stared at him for a long moment, humming with contentment. Then I rubbed my fingers along my chin and smiled. "Well, ain't we a couple of fine city slickers? Now we only need to get some new clothes, and we're all set."

He frowned. "You got enough money for that, this room *and* supplies for the trip?"

"I reckon I do, if we can find some clothes cheap. There's usually shops where you can buy clothes what other people got rid of that're still in good shape. They'll do for us fine, and won't cost as dear as new," I said. "The only good thing to come out of our meeting up with Spook and Whitlaw was the money I found in Whitlaw's purse."

"How much money *did* you find?"

"Never mind. But it's enough to get whatever we need, between here and Port Essington."

T'was a shame to put on our old, soiled clothes after getting so clean, but hopefully we wouldn't have to wear them too long.

We left the hotel after getting some breakfast. Eggs and bacon and bread and cheese tasted pretty good after canned beans and cured meat for so long, and we lingered before heading out into the crowded streets of Whitehorse.

There were lots of people about, and I kept Oscar close, though I tried not to hold on to him like he was a child...or my woman. He was a grown man, and it would look strange. But I kept my eyes on him, that's certain, and he seemed happy to stay near me. Once or twice, he took the edge of my sleeve when the crowd was jostling him, but I don't reckon anyone saw that. And t'was something a friend or a cousin might do, to keep from being split from someone on a crowded sidewalk.

We were lucky enough to find some suitable clothes in a used clothier's shop, not too far from the hotel — trousers of fine cloth that fit us decent and soft cotton shirts in a couple of colors so we'd have a change — even vests to give us some warmth under our jackets and new braces, socks and underthings, too. I told the shopkeeper to burn them other clothes, and we wore out what we bought. I also picked up a couple of pairs of soft leather riding gloves that the proprietor offered us at a great discount because of our other purchases, and a fishing pole with some gear for a penny. Figured we could try our hand at catching supper when we camped, if I wasn't able to shoot anything. It came apart to fold up nice and small into a little carry bag, so t'wouldn't be hard to bring with us.

Oscar cut a pretty fine figure in his new clothes, I have to say, since the ones he'd been wearing had been worn and old-fashioned. He looked so handsome, and I couldn't stop staring at him, to be honest.

"Why're you lookin' at me like that?" he said, as we walked back to the hotel in our finery.

I blushed and shrugged. "I can't say out loud. Not on the street, anyways."

"Oh."

He walked taller now, too, knowing he looked good in his clothes and feeling proud to be so presentable.

"Well, I feel very good to be walkin' beside you, Jimmy, in your new vest and shirt, and those delectable trousers that hug you in all the right places."

I stopped dead, glancing around us to see if anyone had heard him, but people were going about their business and paying us no mind.

"See? I know some big words, too," he said.

"Oscar, behave yourself now," I said, embarrassed and on guard, but pleased by his words, no less.

"I'll try, Jimmy, but you look like a schoolteacher or somethin' e'en more respectable in them clothes. I reckon it'll be that much more fun to misbehave, now."

My eyes widened as my cock plumped up in my new trousers, and I realized Oscar was right. They hugged me pretty close, and I felt a little obvious.

"Stop it. I'm gonna make a spectacle of myself."

"Gosh, I sure hope so."

He was trying not to laugh, and following me close as I quickened my step, wanting to get back to our room, right quick. Mayhap I couldn't lay into him like I wanted to, but I could figure out *something*. He was looking for some discipline, I could tell, and I aimed to give it him in whatever way I could. Perhaps I could make his being quiet a part of the game without using a gag.

Even though he said he'd probably like it, it reminded me too much of what we'd been through with them outlaws, and I were trying to forget. Figured it'd be a little while before I'd be comfortable tying him down across my saddle again, too. But we'd get there, knowing us. He was right. T'was completely different, since he was allowing me to do that, and had a word to use if t'was too much. And I was doing it out of love and desire, and not real, evil violence.

T'was the difference between night and day, even though it might not look that way from an objective viewpoint.

When we got back, I followed him upstairs, loving the look of his sweet ass in his new trousers. When we went into our room, I locked the door behind me and turned to face him. He was watching me, waiting for something only I could give him.

So, I did.

"Take off them nice clothes, Oscar, so they don't get mussed now, y'hear?" I swallowed, my mouth going dry at the thought of having him to myself, in the privacy of our room right this minute.

"Yes, sir, I will," he said, my good boy, sounding breathless and excited as his fingers went to the buttons of his new vest. T'was a dark blue silk material that looked real nice with the light brown shirt he was wearing. I reckon I'd have paid any price to get him all dolled up like he was. He looked sharp and distinguished, but so young, too.

"You sure you're as old as you said?" I asked, giving him a stern, skeptical look.

He lifted his chin. "How old did I say I was? I can't rightly remember. I was slingin' a lot of bullshit your way, back then."

I felt a chill go down my spine and my eyes widened. Then he grinned and laughed at my reaction.

"Wow. The look on your face. I'm only pullin' your leg. I'm twenty-one, like I said. I just look like a bratty-ass boy."

I narrowed my eyes. "You *are* a bratty-ass boy, I swear, Oscar. Your age don't matter."

"Oh? So if I said I was eighteen, t'wouldn't make any difference?"

"It'd make a bit of difference. I'd feel worse about wantin' you the way I do," I said, taking a step toward him. "But since you're twenty-one, I figure you're old enough to know if you want me or not."

"Oh, I *want* you, Jimmy," he said, pushing the braces off his shoulders and pulling his shirt out of his trousers. He unbuttoned it and took it off. I reckon he'd put on a bit of weight, and it looked good on him. Real good.

"You fold that nice, y'hear? I just bought that for you."

He looked right at me and tossed it to the bed, giving me a wicked smile that about burned me up from inside.

"Why? What're you gonna do if I don't listen?"

Chapter Seventeen

Subdued

I didn't say a thing, only nodded and walked silently o'er to pick up the new shirt to fold. I set it on top of the vest Oscar had placed on the nearby chair, but had to push past him to do it, and I saw him track me with his gaze, as his bare chest rose and fell quickly.

This already felt like a practiced dance between us, the way he provoked and I followed-up with some much-needed discipline, to make him feel controlled and safe. I didn't question it no more. T'was simply the way we worked together, and the way we liked to be.

I turned back to him, splaying my hand against his smooth throat and tilting his head back, so he was looking me in the eyes.

"I'm gonna teach you to show some respect, that's what," I said, then kissed him on the mouth, hard and possessive, while I slid my fingers down his chest and belly and slowly unbuttoned his trousers.

"Shit," he whispered, his breaths coming even quicker. "Okay."

I chuckled at the way he just gave in. But he was gonna find this challenging, I had no doubt.

When I reached into his clean drawers and wrapped my hand around his erection, scrunching the fabric down so's he wouldn't soil it, he made a gasping noise.

"Shhh-h. You are gonna have to be quiet so I can have my way with you. I ain't gonna gag you, boy, 'cause that would be too damn easy."

He whimpered and thrust into my grasp, raising his hand to hold my arm as he swayed. "Fuck, Jimmy. That's gonna be so hard."

I grinned against his neck as I kissed and licked him there. "Yeah, I know. You're so hard, ain't you? So hard, but still so small in my hand that I nearly can't stand it."

Like I said before, he wasn't actually that small and he knew it. But he liked to pretend I was the real man with the real big cock, and he was something else, so I indulged him.

"Fuck," he cursed, as I let go of his cock and moved my hand around to cup his ass cheek and slide my fingers between, pushing at his sweet hole. "Goddammit, Jimmy."

"Don't you swear at me, Oscar Yates. You keep that pretty mouth shut, unless I tell you to open it so's I can stick my cock in it. Mayhap *that'll* keep you quiet." I whispered those wicked things in his ear and licked at the lobe as he damn near fainted with obvious desire. "Now I don't wanna hear another word outta you. I want you to take them trousers and underthings off and fold 'em neatly on the chair. Then I want you to lie down on this here bed and spread your legs for me. And I want to watch you play with your little nubby for a bit. Nod if you understand me."

His breath caught in his throat as he nodded frantically, his mouth open, eyes wild and full of need. I stepped back to give him space.

T'was hard to keep a hold of myself, but I was determined to, because dragging this out and making him behave was gonna make for a fun distraction. And when I finally got inside him, he was damn near gonna go crazy trying to keep quiet. And I sure as hell wanted to see that.

Now that we were in a safe place, with a bit of privacy behind locked doors, I was planning to take my damn time enjoying him and driving him mad in the process.

He kicked off his boots and took off his socks, putting them neatly under the chair. Then he stripped off his trousers and underthings while I watched and tried to be silent, even though I felt like cursing because he was so damn beautiful. Instead, I crossed my arms and waited silently, as if I had nothing better to do and that seeing him strip wasn't affecting me at all.

He kept glancing at me as if he wasn't sure of himself like he usually was—like I'd given him something t'think about, now that I'd told him he couldn't talk or make a noise. He was probably wondering how he was gonna do that and realizing about now how challenging it would be. I had found a way to control him and feed into his wanting, while keeping the noise to a minimum. At least, that was my plan.

When he was naked, he crawled backward onto the bed, his long legs splayed out for me like I'd asked, wrapping his fingers around his nubby as he pulled on it slowly, his gaze meeting mine as his mouth opened wider.

God, he was a vision. It took all I had to stay where I was and not attack him, put my hands and mouth everywhere at once, push those thighs apart and suck his cock and eat his ass like I wanted to.

What the hell had happened to me o'er the last little while? T'was like I'd found something inside me that I'd never imagined was there, but now that I'd found it, I could barely satisfy it. T'was exhilarating and terrifying, all at the same time.

I kept myself planted where I was and began to slowly take my own clothes off, starting with the vest. The silk felt soft and smooth under the rough pads of my fingers, and when I took it off, I made sure to place it neatly on top of the pile of Oscar's clothes.

"You're bein' a very good boy, Oscar," I told him, watching him fist himself while he kept his gaze on me. "Nice and quiet. I'm sure you want to say all kinds of things, but you ain't, and I know you're tryin' to be good."

His forehead crinkled in concentration as his hand sped up on his nubby. I thumbed the braces off my shoulders and pulled the tails of my shirt out of my trousers.

"Don't you come now. You jerk yourself for me, but don't you come, you hear me? I got lots of plans for you tonight," I said. "That little thing of yours is gonna get a workout."

He closed his eyes and swallowed, then nodded twice and opened them again, slowing his hand down a bit.

"You need more slide?" I asked, brows raised.

He made a small noise and nodded frantically.

"Okay. Stay still now," I said, moving closer and placing my hands either side of him on the mattress while I leaned o'er and hawked up some good spit, letting it slide out of my mouth right onto the head of his nubby, while he watched with crazed eyes.

"Oh, fu —" he said, almost disobeying my command, but caught himself and shut it down quick, gathering my spit with his fingers and using it to slick his nubby, so he could slide his hand more smoothly. He threw his head back and sighed, jerking that thing like he could go all afternoon. I doubted that were true, but mayhap we were gonna try.

"Shit, that looks so good, boy. You gotta sinful way 'bout you, that's for sure. And I like it a whole lot."

I finished unbuttoning my shirt and took it off, folding and adding it to the pile, though I could barely take my eyes off him. He looked like a fallen angel, lying there teasing himself, his legs splayed so I could see the dark cleft between his cheeks where I wanted to end up before the evening was done, tossing his head back in ecstasy and torture, both.

I kicked off my boots and peeled down my socks, putting them nearby. Then I moved to the bed and stood at the foot of it, right in front of where he was lying with his eyes closed and mouth open, quiet little gasps the only thing coming from him.

"Oscar Yates," I said, with a stern tone I figured he would like, "look at me, *now*."

His eyelids flew open, and he gazed up at me as I put my hands on my hips and raised my eyebrows again. His hand stilled on his nubby as the tip of his tongue appeared briefly on his lower lip. He stayed silent.

"Good boy."

Every time I said them two words, his cheeks flushed a little darker.

"Now I want you to let go of yourself. That's enough of that for the moment, though it sure looks nice."

He did as he was told, letting his fist drop to the mattress, as the fingers of his other hand curled in the sheet.

"Now, turn o'er onto your hands and knees."

He looked like he was about to jump out of his skin, but he did it, moving gracefully and quickly, so's my own dick jerked in my trousers as he got into the position I'd asked for.

"Now spread them legs and put your chin down to the bed, on top of your two hands. And don't fucking move or make a sound, y'hear me? You say 'Yes, sir,' if you understand, then be quiet."

"Yes, sir," he squeaked as he did what I'd asked of him.

I got on the bed behind him on my knees, palming my cock under my trousers that I was keeping on for the moment. T'was the only way of postponing fucking him right this minute, I figured.

"Now I'm gonna do somethin' that'll make you wanna scream and beg, I reckon. But you're gonna have to figure out a way of not doing that, else we're gonna have the law bangin' down this door—and neither of us wants that."

He swept his head around to gaze at me with wide eyes and a crazed, excited look that made me thrill to the power I had o'er him, simply with my words. He made me feel like a king or something, I don't know. I only knew I liked feeling that way.

"Nope. Turn around and stare at the wall like the good boy I know you are, or I ain't doing nothin'."

He quick turned around and pushed his ass out, making me smile before I laid my hands flat against his plump cheeks that looked fuller now he'd had a couple weeks of regular meals.

His skin felt smooth and warm, though t'would have been nicer if I'd been able to heat them cheeks up with a good spanking. But I figured there'd be lots of time for that when we were on the road to Port Essington and camped out in hidden spots like we'd done before. Port Essington wasn't like Whitehorse, and not a lot of people knew about it, so there shouldn't be many people heading in the same direction. We might run into some folks from the local tribes, but they usually avoided white men, and I didn't half blame them. They been treated terribly by my brothers, and I were full ashamed of what my people had done to them.

I heard him make the smallest gasp when I spread his cheeks to expose his sweet pink hole, what looked so small and vulnerable. Except I knew how damn powerful t'was, how much he could take inside him and how good it felt to be in there. He had hair there, but t'was soft and feathery-looking and only made me hungrier.

The sounds of our breathing filled the space as I waited, prolonging his torture and the anticipation of what I was gonna do. I figured he knew by now what I was planning, except he probably couldn't hardly believe I'd do such a thing in a fancy hotel room.

But the truth is, I *wanted* to do it. I very much desired to feast on him like he was the tastiest buffet, like I'd already done that one time when I was crazed from spilling inside him. There was no part of him that was distasteful to me, and I wanted to give him the pleasure of my tongue where it would feel real good. I wondered if mayhap he'd want to do it for me, someday, but I didn't rightly care about that right this minute.

I rubbed the pad of my thumb across the wrinkled skin, and it fluttered under my touch. He was still clean from the bath and from my tending the past night, and I wanted to taste him so bad. But first, I blew a soft breath onto him while I held his cheeks apart.

He choked on a moan and tried to surge forward, but I held him still. Before he could recover from that, I swept the flat of my tongue o'er him and his whole body stiffened as he tried to hold back his pleasure sounds, little gasps the only thing coming from his open mouth.

"Good boy. You are doin' so good. This is gonna be tough, but you'll like it, I reckon."

He nodded his head frantically and stretched out like a cat, pushing his ass toward me again.

"Okay, I got you," I said, before I bent to attack him with my mouth and tongue.

His ragged breaths were the only thing to be heard besides the slurping and sucking sounds I made as I slavered on him, like a starving beast on a bone. I tried to be quiet, but he was so delectable, especially with all the squirming and gasping.

When he brought his hand down to wrap around his nubby, I pushed it away and scolded him. He let out a quiet whine but went back to the gasping and heavy breathing while I tortured him some more.

I finally had to let up because I figured he was gonna come apart from that, and I wanted to get into him before that happened. I backed off the bed and grabbed the saddle grease from the table, putting the little tub of it on the bed while I pushed down my trousers and underthings.

My cock was raging, and I was so ready to bury it inside him. I had to stifle my own sounds as I slicked it up, then added the grease to the spit on his hole and lined myself up.

"This is gonna feel good, I reckon, but you'll need to stay quiet," I said, to remind him to keep it down. We only had a short way to go, but this would be the most difficult time to keep quiet, and we had to be circumspect.

He nodded frantically and gazed back at me with half-lidded, glazed eyes, as I grabbed his hip with one hand and pressed forward.

Both of us let small sounds escape when I breached him, and I didn't stop to make sure he was okay before going in all the way, because it felt so good. The focused attention I'd paid with my tongue must have loosened him up, because he didn't complain or cry out, just pushed back to welcome me. He pressed his forehead to the mattress and arched his back, as I grabbed his other hip and thrust into that beautiful tight heat again and again. I was in heaven and never wanted to come back to earth.

His body flushed with heat, and he bit the goddamn pillow to keep from screaming, his eyes closed tight and hand fisting his little cock. I couldn't stop him and didn't want to, since it would only be moments before I spent and this would be finished.

He stiffened and I heard the longest muffled groan as he exploded onto the sheets o'er his fist. I followed soon after, and I couldn't stop the sound that came out of me. I could only hope anyone listening figured I'd hurt myself or something because it sounded right like agony as I stilled deep and shot my load into him, clutching like he was the only thing keeping me alive.

And he was. I swear to God, he was. I lived for him — and for *this*.

Oscar collapsed flat onto the bed with me atop him, my twitching cock buried in his ass, both of us breathing like we'd finished a race. I kissed his cheeks and nuzzled his warm neck, the scent of his sweat a comfort and a sweet reminder of our coupling. My cock slowly shrank, and when I slipped out of him, he made the sweetest sound — a whimper of regret or surrender. I don't rightly know what t'was, but t'was lovelier than anything I'd ever heard from anybody, ever.

I pushed myself onto my elbows as I hovered o'er him, so's I wouldn't crush him. He snaked his hand toward me with his palm up and I slid mine into it, clutching tight as he threaded his fingers with mine. His eyes were closed but his lips formed a smile as he lay there in his own mess, recovering from the fucking I'd given him. There wasn't no sweeter sight in the whole damn world.

"Jesus, Jimmy," he said softly after a while. "I don't know if I'll be able to sit my horse tomorrow. You're so damn big and perfect, and I can still feel you there."

I kissed the back of his head then his shoulder. "I reckon we can stay another day in town before we head out."

He sighed happily. "Truly? I could take another day a this."

"Yeah, me, too, now that you've learned to be quiet, like a good boy. I reckon I can spend all of tomorrow making sure you get lots of practice."

* * * *

We spent all the next day holed up in our room, kissing and touching and giving each other soft, quiet pleasure. At times, t'was a challenge for me to be good, like when he climbed atop me and rode me while I lay on my back and clutched the bedsheets, closing my eyes so's I couldn't see what a profane figure he made there, pleasuring himself on my cock like he was a king's consort. T'was the dirtiest and most amazing thing I'd ever seen, his nubby thick and rising from the pleasure he was getting from my cock inside him.

If I hadn't closed my eyes, I would have spent as soon as he sat on me, and that's a fact. Because every time I peeked a little bit and saw him there, abandoned to ecstasy, his mouth open and glazed eyes watching me, t'was a close call again.

Finally, he told me to shoot and t'wasn't nothing to obey him, since I couldn't hold on no more anyhow. I figured I'd spank his ass for taking control like that, once we were on the road, and he'd like it—which worked out, because I didn't think I could live the rest of my life without him doing that again.

We kept the straight-out fucking to the morning, and I only used my fingers and my mouth to get him off the rest of the day, so's he wouldn't be too sore to ride out. We only took breaks to go downstairs to eat or visit the privy.

If anyone in the hotel suspected we were up to such lascivious mischief, nobody seemed to care. We were treated as regular travelers who mayhap needed to catch up on some sleep. And even though some of what we did together was technically illegal, it sure seemed benign compared to some of the stuff I'd done when I'd been hanging around with Spook and Whitlaw.

Figured I'd start drawing my own ethical boundaries, now that I was a self-made man. Long as I didn't hurt nobody no more, I was free to do as I pleased. If I had to keep circumspect because of the random rules of a prudish society, then I would.

Chapter Eighteen

Punishment

"After breakfast, I'll look at those maps and plan out a route. Then we need to get ourselves a mule and pack up. Hopefully we can head out after lunch," I said, chewing on a piece of crispy bacon while Oscar spooned egg into his pretty mouth—the mouth that had been on every damn part of my body the day before, and I could barely forget it.

"Sure. I miss ridin' that horse." He glanced around but we were in a corner and away from listening ears. "E'en though I've enjoyed ridin' *you* these past two days."

I felt the heat rise in my cheeks and gave him a stern look, pointing at him with my fork. "Behave. Stop tryin' to provoke me."

"But, Jimmy, I reckon that's become my life's goal."

"Fuck if I don't know it. Don't forget, once we get on the road and away from pryin' eyes and ears, you owe me at least a couple turns o'er my knee. At *least*."

He shuddered and squirmed in his seat. "Jesus. I know it."

He grinned as he shoveled more egg in his mouth and chewed eagerly, as if he couldn't wait to be off.

Didn't take us long to find a mule for sale and swing a good deal. Just because I had a satchel full of cash didn't mean I wanted to spend a small fortune on an ornery animal that may, or may not make our journey easier.

"Aw, he'll be good. I know it," Oscar said, stroking the nose of the sturdy animal. Its name was Poke, we'd been told, only because it liked to butt at your chest for a chin scratch. I only hoped it didn't have the oppositional nature of most mules.

"Well, he has his moments," the seller said with a grin. "But mostly he'll be good for a carrot or an apple. I seen worse."

"Why're you selling him?" I asked.

The man shrugged. "I don't need him no more. I'm staying put for a while. Keep the wife happy, you know?" He winked at me as if I *did* know, even though I'd never had a wife and didn't plan to get one.

"Sure," I said. "We'll take him, then."

After leading the mule back to the hotel—he *did* seem to come willingly once we'd given him some apple—we spent the morning loading up everything we'd purchased, in order to make our journey as comfortable as possible.

That included a canvas tent, so we'd have some protection from the elements and wild animals that roamed about. 'Twas small, but big enough for the two of us to move around enough to enjoy the privacy the tent afforded, even though there weren't likely to be many other people about. I'd perused the map for an hour or so and decided on a circuitous route that avoided the most extreme landscape and passed by a handful of small towns along the way, in case we found ourselves in need of assistance. Still, it would be a rough journey, and the weather was getting colder. I only hoped the snow would hold off until October. T'was the last week of August and, where we were, the winters started early. T'wasn't unheard of to get snow in mid-September. At least we'd be moving south.

We had purchased enough basic supplies to get us to Port Essington as long as there were no delays. Water would be accessible along the route, and we had the fishing pole and my rifle to take down small game.

Oscar, in his new clothes and jacket, with the gray knit scarf and leather riding gloves, sitting atop that handsome horse, was a sight for sore eyes. He must have seen how I was looking at him.

"I got somethin' on my face from breakfast?" he asked, his forehead creasing.

I shook my head. "Nope."

I wanted to tell him how good he looked, how much like a young gentleman, but I didn't dare say something like that out in the open in case it came out like I really meant it, and people understood how much I wanted to grab him and bend him o'er the feeding trough, take down them soft trousers and have my way, right this damn minute.

"You're moonin' at me like I was a girl. Quit it, now."

My eyes widened and I glanced around, only to see the stable hand laugh like he thought it a funny joke between friends and not the goddamn truth. My gaze shifted back to Oscar, who grinned and waggled his eyebrows, as if he were happy he'd got away with it. And now I wanted to spank his sorry ass into Sunday, which wasn't helping my trousers feel any looser.

I shook my head like I was annoyed, which I *was* so t'wasn't a stretch, and swung up on Dixie, clucking at her to move it.

"Let's go," I said. The sooner we got out of the public eye, the better.

* * * *

I figured we could be in Port Essington in ten days if we made good time. T'was colder now, the days getting shorter fast, so there wasn't a lot of time to waste. We'd be forced to winter in Port Essington, regardless of whether we located Oscar's uncle or not. Hopefully there was some honest work I could get to cover our needs. I was pretty handy with all sorts of things, and there wasn't much I wouldn't do for a buck except whore myself out — and who'd pay for the likes of me, anyway? — or steal, or anything outside the law.

I figured between the two of us, me and Oscar could manage, and I could get a hold of a wagon somehow in the spring and start my cargo business again. Not that I wanted to be traveling all the time, but if Oscar would come with me, it wouldn't be so bad. I enjoyed having him all to myself in the wilderness and not worrying so much o'er what most folks would think about what we did together. I figured it would be harder to keep that a secret living in town together, but we could sure manage for one winter. And mayhap he'd be staying with his uncle anyway, and we'd have to find secret moments to get away and find some privacy.

At any rate, t'was no use thinking that far ahead. First task was to make it there safely. I stressed to Oscar the importance of not wandering off on his own, anywhere. Even though we'd taken care of Spook and

Whitlaw and it didn't seem like anyone else was looking for us, there were a million dangers out there that could get him, especially since he wasn't as versed in the ways of the wilderness as I was.

That first day we rode pretty far and both of us were exhausted by the time we camped, so there wasn't any funny business. And anyway, we'd enjoyed two days in each other's arms at the hotel, so we were well and truly satisfied. Though I reckon, from the look on Oscar's face when we woke up the next morning, that the sun wouldn't set on another day before we were fucking again. But that was fine by me.

That night by the fire, I bent him o'er my lap, took his trousers down and spanked that beautiful ass until he begged me to stop and offered all kinds of favors if I'd let up. I wasn't even spanking him so hard but, boy, did I love it when he squirmed and begged as if I were killing him. Eventually, I stopped, lay back and let him suck me off in thanks, while his nubby didn't get no attention.

"You gonna make me go to bed like this?" he asked, pointing down at his erection while I lazed on my back, happy and spent.

"Why don't you take care of yourself, if you're so upset about it? I like watching you do that. Watching you take that little nubby in hand and play with it like the dirty boy you are. Sometimes, I feel like that thing is only good for a hand job. Barely enough to fill my mouth when I bend to it," I said with a sly grin, so he'd know I was joking.

"Oh yeah?" he said, wrapping a hand around himself and moving it slowly, pointing his dick at me. "That a fact?"

I chuckled.

"Here," I said, grabbing the tub of leather grease and passing it his way. "Slick your little nubby up."

He closed his eyes and groaned. "When you talk like that…" he sighed. "Fuck. Makes me so damn hot."

"I know it. That's why I do it. I think your dick is plenty big enough, but I'll tease you 'bout it if you want me to."

"I do. I like to feel like I ain't even half a man when I'm with you, 'cause it makes me feel little and cared for. I don't know…"

"I know you do. And I'll care of you, Oscar, as well as I know how."

He laughed. "Good thing we got a new tub of that stuff in town. This one is almost used up." He scooped most of what was left in the tin and tossed it back to me, rubbing the soft grease o'er his hard nubby with a fair eager hand.

"I know it. Can't barely stop gettin' hard now whene'er I use it on my saddle."

He chuckled. "Yeah, me too. Mind you, can't barely keep from gettin' hard from bein' around you, Jimmy. Funny how we met outa the blue by pure chance but we're so good together, huh?" he glanced up at me from under those long black lashes as he smoothed the grease onto himself.

I nodded. "I think of that pretty often. I'm glad you were there at that cathouse, even if t'was because you were starvin' and desperate. I'm so glad I found you."

He came closer and fell to his knees in the dirt beside where I was sitting. "I'm glad, too. I was about ready to do somethin' I'd probably end up regretting, and by then there wouldn't be no turning back from it, I'm sure."

I nodded, staring at his fingers moving o'er his nubby and licking my lips, feeling my cock stir again then settle, because t'was so satisfied from his tending. "Maybe. Anyway, I love feeding you and making sure you're okay. I don't know why. Ain't never wanted a kid of my own — figured that was too much responsibility. But I like lookin' after you."

He winked and sped up the movement of his hand. "I like lookin' after you, too, Jimmy, in all the ways I can."

The little devil. I knew what he meant, and t'was true. He took care of me in so many ways, and I took care of him in them ways — and others — too.

He was getting breathless now, close to his climax I reckon, from the look of him and the way the head of his nubby was turning red and leaking.

"Open your vest and shirt, Jimmy. I wanna spend on you but I don't wanna ruin your new clothes."

I grinned at the way he made those sinful words sound so normal. "That's mighty thoughtful of you, Oscar," I said, my gaze on his pretty cock as I quickly unbuttoned my clothes and pulled the cloth back, revealing my chest and belly to him. "Those new clothes of yours must be makin' you act like a proper gentleman, and that's a fact."

He looked far from a gentleman right now, and we both grinned.

"They surely are," he panted, moaning and shifting closer, pointing his rosy, ready dick right at me. "I'm gonna make a mess of you, Jimmy."

"Can't hardly wait to see that," I said, reaching my hand out to cup under his testicles, which were tight and full.

His mouth dropped open as I stroked him there and behind with two fingers, teasing o'er his hole.

"Oh, fuck it, Jimmy, I'm comin'. I'm comin' *now*," he groaned, jerking his cock so that ropey jizz landed all across my belly and chest like sugar icing. T'was the hottest thing ever, and I smiled my pleasure at him as he came down from the high of it.

"That was lovely to watch," I said, swiping some off my chest and putting my finger in my mouth, sucking as I locked eyes with him.

He shuddered and closed his eyes. "*Jee-sus.*"

* * * *

I woke up in the dark and reached for him, but he wasn't there.

"Oscar," I said. "Oscar? Where are you?"

The panic surged through me instantly. I'd told him to wake me up if he needed to leave my side in the night, because I knew there were more dangers out there than he could even imagine.

I pushed up and stood, peering into the darkness to see if he was nearby, but I couldn't see nothing but the two horses, munching on grass and making soft, friendly noises to each other.

Shit.

What if he'd gotten lost out there somewhere, or worse, got taken again, by someone else this time? There were evil people roaming this country and that was a fact.

And I'd told him to stay near. I'd *told* him.

My steps got quicker as I wandered around, calling his name, becoming more and more worried as I got farther from our camp.

Finally, I heard him.

"I'm here, Jimmy. I'm right here."

I looked where his voice was coming from and sure enough, there he was, walking calmly toward me with a smile on his sweet face. The relief hit me like a wave, followed by another wave soon after of pure, unfiltered anger.

"I told you to *stay* near me." My voice was all choked up with rage.

"I'm sorry," he said, shrugging. "I woke and couldn't get back to sleep. And the moonlight was so pretty that I wanted to see the river with it shinin' down like that."

I blinked, not expecting that. I'd figured maybe he'd needed to take a crap or something, not that he was going sightseeing.

I closed my eyes to try to calm myself. "You wanted to *see* the *river*?"

"Yeah."

"With the *moonlight* on't?"

"Yeah. Why you sound so mad, Jimmy? I ain't done nothin' wrong."

I opened my eyes and glared at him. "You ain't done nothin' *wrong*?" I repeated, like he was speaking another language I didn't understand.

I took a couple of deep breaths, then looked around us. The night was quiet and empty and peaceful, and Oscar was there and safe. But I couldn't settle my nerves, and I needed to make him understand how dangerous t'was for him to go wandering around in the dark all alone.

I took my warm jacket off and threw it to the dirt. I was so hot under the collar right now I was burning up.

There were a couple of big rocks nearby, and I walked o'er and sat down on one.

"Come here," I said between clenched teeth, pointing at the ground in front of me. "*Now.*"

Oscar seemed confused, like he wondered why I wanted to play a sex game in the middle of the night. But that wasn't what this was at all.

"Why?" he said.

"Because you disobeyed me, and you need to be punished."

I saw when he realized what I meant — that I wasn't gonna haul him across my lap for a fun, sexy spanking but that I was genuinely *furious* that he'd disobeyed me for a pretty river in the moonlight.

"I didn't mean to make you worry, Jimmy. I figured you wouldn't even wake up."

"Well, I did. And I found you out." I pointed at the ground again. "Now get o'er here and let's get this done."

"I'd rather you fucked me, Jimmy. You can fuck me if you want." He gave me a little grin and rubbed a hand o'er his trousers where his nubby was.

I chuckled but t'was a dry, annoyed sound. "I have no interest in fuckin' you right now, *boy.*"

He stared at me, and I wondered if he would run back to camp and hide behind his horse or something.

"Now if you ain't o'er here in one minute, I'm comin' to get you. And it won't be my hand on your sorry ass but a birch switch I'll get you to find yourself and bring to me. You hear?"

I saw him swallow and lift his chin, and for a second, I wondered if that idea might appeal to him. But he must have thought better of it because he walked o'er to stand where I'd pointed.

"I'm sorry, Jimmy."

"I know you are."

"I didn't mean to make you worry."

"That may be true. But you did, and I need you to understand that when I tell you somethin', it ain't for my own enjoyment. You need to listen to what I say. I'm older than you, I'm used to being on the road and I know what kind of dangers are out there. Now, I know the river looks pretty in the moonlight, and I'm glad you're one to appreciate those things, I truly am. But the next time you wake up and want to go look at the sparkling water, you *wake* me up! And I'll go look at the pretty river with you."

"Truly, Jimmy? You'd do that?" he said, not quite believing it.

I gaped at him. "I *told* you I'd come with you if you needed to take a shit or somethin'. Don't you think I'd rather come along if you wanted to take a walk in the moonlight?"

He shrugged. "I figured you'd think t'was silly."

"Well, I don't. Now stop talkin' back to me and get yourself o'er my lap so's I can take care of this right now. If you won't listen to what I say, then maybe you'll listen when your ass is red from the beating I'm about to give you. Take off your jacket and pull down them braces first."

He stared at me for a second. "But it's cold."

"The spankin' I'm about to give you will keep you real warm."

He thought about that for a second and swallowed. Then he slowly took off his jacket and layed it on the ground, then thumbed the braces off his shoulders like I'd told him.

I reached out and took hold of his wrist and pulled him across my lap, fed up with his nonsense.

He made a squeaking sound and fell on top of me, scrabbling his boots in the dirt.

"Stay still. I'm gonna start o'er your trousers, to warm you up and get some a my anger out, then I'm gonna pull them down and spank your bare ass till you're cryin' real tears," I said. "And you can use your word if you want and I'll listen, but if you don't get through this now, I'm gonna do it again in the morning."

Before he could say anything, I wrapped an arm around him to keep him steady and brought my hand down hard a few times, to give him an idea where this was gonna go.

"Aw, fuck, that hurts!"

"Supposed to."

I spanked him some more, until he stopped his squirming and settled in for it. Then I reached under him and undid his trousers, pulling them down to his thighs, and started spanking his bare bottom. T'was a little pink still from the night before, but I didn't rightly care.

"Don't you ever wander off like that again, you hear me? You scared the crap outta me, like you did that first time when Spook an' Whitlaw had you. I thought someone else came and took you from me, and I wasn't gonna be able to find you and—" The words choked in my throat.

My breaths came hard and close together and I squeezed my eyes shut, because suddenly I was seeing someone else and I didn't want to remember him.

"I'm sorry," Oscar panted, squirming on my lap but not trying to get away. "I'm sorry, Jimmy."

I kept spanking him, harder and harder, until he was crying and moaning and sobbing. "Don't be sorry. You listen to me when I tell you what to do. You listenin' to me now, Robert? You listenin' to me tell you to stay close and not wander off?" My hand slowed as tears streaked down my cheeks, and I shoved Oscar off my lap and scrambled away from him, memories I'd buried for years coming back in a rush.

He lay there in the dirt for a long moment, sniffling, while I tried to get a hold of myself. I felt awful for treating him that way, and the other feelings inside me got all tangled up with that. I hugged my arms around myself and let the horrible sobs take me, as my body shook with grief and guilt and all them awful memories I'd spent years burying.

At some point, I ain't even sure how long after that, I felt his hand on my shoulder and heard his soft, familiar voice.

"Who's Robert, Jimmy? Why did you call me *Robert*?"

Not, "Why did you dump my ass in the dirt?" or "Why did you spank me so damn hard?" but asking about the name I'd called him by mistake.

I forced myself to look at my boy — my lovely, beautiful, brave boy who had showed me so much love and mischief and took care of me in so many wonderful ways — and I told him who Robert was.

"My brother."

My voice was too soft, and I had to clear my throat to make it louder.

"Robert...was my baby brother."

Oscar squeezed my shoulder and I focused on his face. His cheeks were flushed and wet from his crying, from that spanking that had ended up a lot harsher than I'd intended.

"Are you okay?" I said, my voice breaking. "Did I hurt you too much? I'm so sorry. I— I don't rightly know what happened."

I wiped my face with the back of my hand while Oscar fell to his knees and wrapped his arms around me, ducking his head in my lap and holding me tight.

"I'm fine, Jimmy. Reckon' I won't disobey you again, though. I learned that lesson." He rubbed his forehead against me. "But maybe your baby brother never did?"

The grief rose up inside me again and I nodded, though I knew he couldn't see. A fresh sob took me again, but I stomped it down.

"What happened to Robert?" Oscar asked in a small, scared voice.

Chapter Nineteen

Declarations and a Treacherous Crossing

God, this fella was sharper than a whittled stick, but I suppose it didn't take a genius to figure out there was a painful story there. It took me a long time to find the words to explain to him what had happened. But finally, I did.

I told him how Robert had found me after I'd joined in with Whitlaw and Spook and insisted on being a part of the gang, even though I'd tried my hardest to keep him out of it. Spook and Whitlaw had liked having him with us, because they could control me easier with the threat of making his life miserable if I did something they didn't like, made too many demands or tried to impose my ethical arguments on them. And they had got him to do all the grunt work they thought was beneath them. And Robert had liked being near me and being a part of an outlaw gang in the way a lot of young men did. Made them feel big and brave and like they were playing a big joke on the world. I had been planning on getting us *both* away from them, because I couldn't bear to see him caught up in that life with me.

"He was a lot like you, now that I think of it," I said, holding tight to Oscar and dipping my head down so's I could speak to him softly, now that my crying had eased. "He liked to look at pretty things. He was good with animals and couldn't stop jokin' and grinnin' all the time. He loved that horse Spook gave him, and he taught it to do all kinds of crazy things. The others made fun of him, but he didn't rightly care. He loved his life, as little as t'was."

We were silent for a bit. I didn't want to go on, because this story didn't have a happy ending.

"What happened to him, Jimmy?"

It took a minute for me to start up again. But Oscar needed to know.

"He wandered off one night and a rival gang got him. Shot him in the chest and left him. I woke up and he wasn't there, and Spook and Whitlaw didn't even wanna go lookin' for him.

"That was when I knew I couldn't stay a part of that gang. Even before I found him lyin' there with his chest blown apart and his" —I gasped and forced the words out—"face in the dirt. He wasn't smilin' no more and never would again."

Oscar nodded against me then pulled back gently and stood in front of me. He brought his hand under my chin and tilted my face up to look at him.

"I ain't Robert. And we ain't in a gang. But I will do everythin' you tell me from now on, Jimmy, 'cause I know you're only trying to keep me safe like you couldn't do for him. And I love you for it."

My face collapsed on itself again and I let out a sob — just one—then I got hold of myself again and looked into his soft eyes and nodded.

Oscar wetted his lips and continued. "T'wasn't your fault, Robert's death. He was the one wanted to be in the gang with you."

"But if I wasn't in the gang in the first place, Robert would never have joined it."

"You don't know that, for sure. Maybe he'd have found his own gang. Sounds like he really enjoyed that kinda life — maybe even more than you did."

I nodded, because that was true. And it gave me a little bit of relief to hear it. Even though I'd always blame myself for Robert's death, maybe t'wasn't truly my fault, in the end.

I reached out a hand and circled his wrist with my fingers, stroking the soft spot on the inside. "It's a little strange you remind me so much of him," I said softly. "Considerin' what the two of us get up to together."

He laughed. "Well, I reckon I'm not your brother, so it don't matter. I'm glad I remind you of him. Seems like it's a good thing to remember a fella who was so close to you at one time."

I nodded again, my eyes burning with more unshed tears than I could handle right then.

"Did I hurt you, Oscar? Are you all right?" I said softly.

He shrugged, giving me a shy look. "I reckon I got what I deserved. It'll make me think twice about goin' for a walk in the moonlight all alone again."

"Good."

"Reckon I'll wake you up and bring you with me next time."

"Good. I'd like that."

"And, Jimmy?"

"Yeah?"

"I don't mind you lookin' after me like a brother in some ways, as long as you look after me in other ways, too."

He started to pull away, but I held on to his wrist and didn't let him. I looked up into his eyes again and smiled. "I reckon you got my heart all wrapped up with yours now, Oscar, and I can't stop feelin' the way I do about you. I reckon I love you, too, strange as that seems."

He moved forward, clutching my arms and kissing me on the lips with such gentleness it almost brought the tears back.

"It don't seem strange at all, Jimmy. It just seems right."

* * * *

In the morning we were quiet, getting things ready to head out.

"Your bottom sore?" I asked when we mounted up. I already knew t'was, from the wince he made when he landed on his saddle.

"I reckon I deserved it," he said, giving me a sorry smile. "Every time I bounce, I'll remember what not to do no more."

"That's a fact. That's why I done it."

"I know, and I'm thankful."

I blushed and nodded, clucking to Dixie and moving out.

About an hour or so later, we arrived at a river that wasn't exactly on the map. Well, the river itself was on the map, but this must have been a tributary to the main river, and t'was directly in our path. We rode up alongside it a ways to find the easiest place to cross, but t'was gonna be a job, no matter where we picked.

"Can we get across?" Oscar asked, gazing at the fast-moving water with some doubt and a good degree of wariness.

"I reckon we're gonna have to," I said, "somehow."

Fear coiled in my belly at the look of the water, but there was no other choice than to cross it or we'd be stuck. We needed to go forward. As far as I could tell, there wasn't a cable ferry or anything like that to make it easier.

"The trick is gonna be to get this damn mule across," I said, eyeing Poke with some distrust. "The horses'll be all right, and if we stay with them, they'll help us. But that mule..." I cocked my head at the animal that was loaded with all our supplies. "He ain't gonna like it."

We'd had to cross some milder spots of water with Poke, and he'd been hesitant every time. Oscar and I could swim, so at least we had that in our favor. But it'd be tough if either, or both of us, lost our seats on the crossing. We were better off on the backs of Sprite and Dixie if they could keep their footing — or even if they had to swim a bit.

But leading that damn mule was a problem.

If he balked when we were halfway across and held up the horses, I didn't know what I'd do. I'd have to let go, and hope to God he didn't drown or go back to shore. T'was risky, and that was a fact. I talked it o'er with Oscar, because he was fairly new to riding and this was gonna be tricky.

"First rule when we go is you gotta listen to me and do what I say, no questions asked. Even if you think it's not right, you do what I tell you. I've crossed a few rivers in my time and I know better'n you what to do. All right?"

"Yes, sir. I reckon I'm used to doing what you say, most of the time," Oscar said, giving me a wink, though he was pale and looked pretty darn scared of the water.

There wasn't any knowing how deep t'was exactly, and that was the other problem. There was a chance the horses wouldn't need to swim at all, which would be the best-case scenario. But there was a bigger chance they would, and I hoped to God they'd be okay and wouldn't get tipped o'er or fall into a panic. If a horse panicked during a river crossing, you were in trouble and so was the horse.

"Dixie and I'll go first, and I'll hold Sprite's lead rope to help you. But I'm gonna have to let it go if Dixie and I get into trouble, so you'll have to be ready to guide Sprite best you can on your own. All right?"

He nodded, his forehead creased with worry. "Okay, Jimmy. I'll do the best I can."

"I know you will." I put a comforting hand on his shoulder. "These are good horses and they're good swimmers. But anythin' can happen attempting somethin' like this, and you need to know that."

He stared at me as if processing what I was saying. "Okay."

I didn't want to say it, but we'd been extremely lucky so far, except for the encounter with them outlaws. The rest of our travel had gone fairly smoothly, which was well-nigh a miracle in these parts with the dangerous terrain and so many uncertainties. I couldn't help the feeling that our luck might be about to run out.

But if we wanted to keep making our way to our final destination of Port Essington, we had to cross this here river.

I'd spent some time figuring out the best spot to make our attempt, with a flat solid grade of packed sand going down to the water and what looked like a decent spot to land at the other side.

If we made it.

I shook my head and cleared my throat. We'd make it—or we might die trying. I was under no illusions about the life or death situation we might be facing. But we'd give it our best shot. I hoped maybe t'wasn't as deep as it looked.

"Come on," I said, to Oscar, after we'd made sure the supplies were fastened securely to the mule's broad back. I wrapped Poke's rope around my gloved hand three times, and Spike's lead once on my other hand, then clucked to Dixie. "Go on, girl. You've done this before. You know the drill."

Dixie whinnied, as if in reply to me, and I fancied she was saying, *Don't you worry, Jimmy. I got this.* Except, for all I knew, she was saying, *Not again, you old fool. You'll kill us all, yet.* Hopefully, t'was the former.

Anyway, she started into the water and didn't seem to be spooked or nothing, so I took that as a good sign. Sprite followed, stepping carefully, and I thanked the Lord for these two sensible horses. They were strong and sturdy, and I had a lot of faith in them.

Poke balked at first, like I'd known he would, but after one complaining bray of indignity, he followed Dixie into the cold water.

We started off all right, and it didn't seem too bad. The horses moved easily in the water as it got deeper, but the current didn't seem all that strong and Poke was doing okay. I thought everything was gonna be fine until we got about midway, and the water climbed up to my knee. I glanced back at Oscar. He was gripping his saddle horn like I'd told him to do and holding tight with his legs, but his face was white as a sheet, and he looked fucking terrified.

"It's all right," I said, trying to sound confident, and not worried about how deep this water was getting. "Steady on."

He nodded and gripped the saddle tighter. "The water's *cold*, Jimmy."

"I know it. But we'll be across soon and I'll—" Dixie's feet lost purchase and we went down sharply, then she was swimming, neighing and snorting in disgust, as she was forced to keep us afloat in the cold water.

"Oscar!" I shouted. "They're gonna have to swim, but you'll be okay! Just hold on tight and let Sprite do his thing."

I felt the powerful muscles of my horse working hard to get us through the strong current, when there was a pull on the rope as Poke felt the bottom give way and realized he had to swim with all our supplies on his back, and I reckon he was scared. He brayed and his head went under. I had to let the rope go, in case he pulled us down. I quick unwrapped the rope from around my hand and released it.

At the same time, Sprite's rope pulled out of my other hand as he started to swim in the wrong direction from where me and Dixie were going.

"Oscar! Hold on!" I shouted.

There wasn't much else I could say. I saw Poke's head come up out of the water and his wild gaze as he swam for us, knowing by now he needed to follow

Dixie, no matter what. Thank God. That mule was smarter than I'd thought. Smarter than Sprite right this minute, honestly.

I whistled to Poke and told him he was a good mule, and there'd be carrots and apples waiting if he kept going, trying to give him encouragement with the sound of my voice. Meanwhile, I saw Sprite branch off toward the other side of the river where the landing wasn't as good, and I hoped to God he'd be able to get out and Oscar wouldn't fall off.

Things were dicey now, that was for sure. So much for the best-case scenario. But t'wasn't the worst-case scenario — not yet, anyway.

Right as I had that thought, Dixie's hooves hit ground again as she gathered her legs under her and stumbled forward, lifting me out of the water and surging forward.

"Come on, Poke. You can do it!" I shouted to the mule, who saw that Dixie was getting a purchase and swam harder to gain it as well. He gave out a loud bray as he found the ground and scrabbled to follow us. I felt a surge of relief, then Oscar's frantic call took it away in an instant.

"Jimmy!" he cried out as Sprite found his footing and surged to the side. In slow motion, I watched Oscar slide off the side of that horse and into the current like my worst nightmare.

"Oscar! Oscar! Hold on to somethin'! Oscar!" I yelled, trying to turn Dixie, but she wasn't having it. She'd gotten her footing, and all she wanted was to get to the bank and up out of the water. All I could do was try to stay on, keep looking back at Sprite and hope like hell to see Oscar's head above water.

"Oscar!" I screamed again. His head bobbed about a meter away from Sprite and he stayed close as his horse pulled toward the bank where t'was steep and rocky, and neighed with the same fear and panic threatening to o'ertake me.

"Sprite, you're all right!" I hollered with confidence I didn't feel quite yet. "You're a good boy, Sprite. You come here! Come here!"

I whistled, trying to get Sprite to come to where Dixie had climbed onto the sandy slope.

It seemed useless for a second, and I feared Oscar would get cut up on the rocks or end up under Sprite's hooves, with him so desperate to get out of the water. But then Sprite's head turned and he started coming back to us.

"Hold on, Oscar. Don't you let go of that horse!" I yelled as I slid off of Dixie and gave her a slap to the rump to keep her going onto dry land. I saw Poke haul himself and all our supplies out of the river and follow Dixie onto the grass, shuddering and breathing hard and looking like he never wanted to see another river in his life.

I couldn't say I blamed him.

Then I went into the water, calling to Sprite, who was trying to get to me. Finally, I was able to get a hold of his bridle and help lead him to where he could get out easy. Oscar had a hold of one stirrup, and Sprite's saddle was starting to come off, but I grabbed him by the neck of his shirt and hauled him toward me.

"Oh fuck, Oscar," I said, pulling him into my arms and letting go of Sprite, who was climbing the bank now and shaking the water off, as if he'd only thought to go for a leisurely swim, and that was all.

"Jimmy!" Oscar gasped, coughing and gagging. Seemed like he'd swallowed water, so I hauled him to shore and laid him out on his side in the wet sand, thumping his back as he retched and coughed.

"Breathe, son. Breathe," I said, o'er and o'er again, until he took a shuddering breath and let out a moan of sheer terror. I grabbed him up in my arms and held him close, saying encouraging things into his ear as he calmed down and settled into the warmth of my embrace. We were soaked and cold, and I needed to round up the horses and start a fire, but I couldn't let go.

We'd made it and so had the horses — and the goddamn mule, too. We had a good deal to be thankful for.

Chapter Twenty

A Desperate Rescue

While we dried our clothes by the fire that afternoon, we discussed staying put or making our way farther until nightfall. According to the map, we were getting close to a little town or outpost called Telegraph Creek, and both of us felt it would be nice to see other people and a bit of civilization again.

"Looks like it'll take most of a day to get there, I reckon. But if we ride out in a bit, we can maybe get there by lunch time tomorrow."

"Sure," Oscar said, frowning. The river crossing had spooked him — and rightly so. It could have ended pretty badly, and Oscar was too sharp not to realize that.

"You okay?" I asked, checking the clothes we'd hung on a string near the fire. We'd mostly kept on what we'd been wearing, 'cept I'd given my almost-dry shirt to Oscar since his was drenched. The bulk of our supplies were laying out to dry, and the horses and mule were grazing in the sunshine, letting it do the work of drying them. The heat of the fire soothed our spirits as much as it warmed and dried the two of us.

"Yeah. Just, I was scared when I fell off," he said, gesturing at Sprite. "I barely managed to grab that stirrup before the current took me." His voice was soft and timid, like he didn't dare admit he'd almost drowned less than two hours before.

I walked o'er and sat beside him on the log.

"I know. But you did real well. You grabbed it and you held on tight, like I'd told you," I said, trying to make my voice solid and comforting, giving him the praise he needed right now. "You're a good boy, Oscar. You listened to what I said, and you did it."

He gazed at me through his long, dark lashes. "I fell off, though. I know I scared the crap out of you…and myself."

"That wasn't your fault. That was Sprite's fault."

Oscar was about to protest, in defense of his horse, so I waved my hand dismissively.

"T'wasn't anyone's fault. Accidents happen, that's all. And we're lucky t'wasn't worse."

He nodded. "That's a fact. Makes me sick to my stomach to think of it, and how it could've gone bad."

"Then don't. Let's load up Poke again, and everythin' else and keep going. There's no more crossings until Telegraph Creek, and the sooner we get there, the sooner we can relax and plan the next part of our journey."

By the time we headed out, the animals seemed no worse for wear, since they'd got a little break after the crossing and a bit of feed to bolster their spirits and energy. I wanted to make good time, so we kept up a good pace while we circuited a network of pathways that led along the mountain ridge toward the town of

Telegraph Creek. I reckoned t'was one of them mining outposts with a handful of stores, a church and a school—maybe a cathouse or two for the men who'd travel through—and hopefully an inn or hotel, though I had my doubts about that. Either way, it'd be nice to see some signs of human life after being so long in the wilderness.

T'was near suppertime, and we were starting to get hungry and look out for a place to set up camp. We'd covered a good amount of distance, and I reckoned we had about three hours to go until we got to the town, but we'd have to do it in the morning. It had been a long day and we needed food and sleep.

"We should prob'ly look for a place to set up for the night," I said to Oscar, as Sprite made a startled shriek and reared up in front of me, causing Dixie to stop sudden and twist around.

I had to fight to turn her back, and by the time I'd done that I saw Oscar falling and watched as his head hit a big rock and bounced as he slid limply to the ground.

"Aw, fuck! Oscar! No!" I shouted, sliding off Dixie as Sprite almost trampled me in his haste to get back from whatever had spooked him. I figured t'was probably a snake, but I didn't see any sign of it now, thank goodness. My main worry was Oscar and the blow to his head.

He lay in a strange position on the ground, and he was out cold, which didn't surprise me but worried me immensely. His head wasn't bleeding or anything, but I'd seen it hit that rock and knew t'was a serious blow that might cause trouble. And here we were, out in the middle of the wilderness, and what the fuck was I gonna do if he didn't come to in a little bit?

I felt the panic start to rise in me, but I pushed it down and told myself he'd come to in a few minutes, for sure, and we could ride gently to find a stopping place for the night. We could always stay in camp for a day or two, so's he could rest if he needed to. We had enough food, and I could get water from the stream that flowed nearby.

I sat down and pulled his head into my lap, soothing my fingers along his cheek and forehead. "Oscar... Oscar, you had a fall. You need to wake up now."

But t'was no use. He was out cold and with no sign of waking. I felt the spot on his head where he'd hit, and sure enough, there was a lump forming, and I knew it'd be a doozy.

I didn't know what to do. Every minute that passed without him coming to made me more worried. There was three hours to Telegraph Creek, but it would be tough with the dark coming, and how was I gonna get a passed-out man there, anyway? I could manage easier to get him to a place we could camp for the night and hope for the best.

But that didn't seem like a good idea. He needed to be looked after and looked at by a doctor. But that wouldn't happen until we got to town, assuming they had a doctor there. At least they'd have other people, and maybe one of them could take a look and tell me what to do.

I'd have to get him there, somehow. And if we were lucky, Oscar would come to along the way.

I went through all my options, looking at the three animals who probably wanted to rest, at this point. Sprite had settled a few meters back on the trail, and Dixie was grabbing weeds out of the ground and chewing them, wondering what me and Oscar were doing and when she'd get her supper. Poke was standing still, and I imagined he'd be rolling his eyes if he could manage it.

After looking at my options, I decided the best bet was to take a few things off Poke and put them onto Sprite, then tie Oscar spread out on Poke's back, so that some of Poke's supplies would cradle his head, and he could ride as cushioned and secure as possible, on his belly. T'wouldn't be very comfortable, but t'was the best I could do, and since he was unconscious, he'd be spared the worst of it.

While I re-distributed the load, leaving enough on the mule to help put Oscar in a good position, I gave the animals a bit of feed and some water. We had at least a three-hour journey.

I tossed back and forth the idea of walking and leading the animals, so I could make sure Oscar didn't fall off. But that would turn a three-hour journey into twice that, and we didn't have that kind of time. I decided to tie him down real good and lead the mule and Sprite as I rode Dixie. T'wasn't gonna be easy, but I couldn't think of any other way it could be done at all.

After I'd organized the packs on Poke's back, I hefted Oscar up on top and arranged him as best I could, hoping every minute that he'd come to and be able to sit his own horse, or at least ride in front of me. But that didn't happen.

I ended up splaying him out backward on top of Poke on his belly, with his head resting on a soft pack of blankets and clothes o'er the mule's wide rump, while his legs wrapped around Poke's neck. I roped his ankles together so his legs wouldn't dangle too much and fastened the rest of him down, best I could, to hold his body still as we rode. I'd have to keep Poke near me and hold on tight to that lead rope, because if he spooked and got loose, running off with Oscar tied onto him... Well, I didn't even want to think about that.

Once Oscar was secure as he'd get, I checked his breathing again, gave him a kiss on his pale forehead, sent up a silent prayer to God or Jesus — or whoever might have a mind to help — then swung up into my saddle on Dixie. I'd tied Sprite's lead to my saddle, but I held on to Poke's with my hand so's I could control him better. I knew Sprite would stay with Dixie anyway, but the lead tied on made it easier to keep him close.

The stress of this endeavor was already killing me, because I knew anything could go wrong at any moment and Oscar's life was on the line. But I also knew that I had to get him some medical attention before he up and died on me out here in the middle of fucking nowhere. I cursed myself for not riding out in front like I usually did, in which case it would've been Dixie that would've seen the snake and reared up, and I'd have been able to sit her, probably. Anyway, there wasn't much point to that line of thought. What had happened had happened, and I could only move forward now.

The longer he stayed out of it, the more worried I got. I knew a hit on the head like that could kill a man. Oscar wasn't dead. I knew that much, at least. But the longer he stayed unconscious, the worse of a sign t'was. He could be brain-damaged if there was bleeding or swelling going on in there. It made me so frustrated and scared to know there was nothing I could do except get him to some care, somehow. Whether t'was a doctor or a kindly citizen who could take him in and nurse him back to health, I didn't rightly care. But he needed a bed and some warmth at the very least, right now.

My head filled with fears and terrors of what I'd do if this were it, and Oscar never came to or didn't ever recover. As long as he wasn't dead, I'd look after him, no matter what. I figured I could give him that much, when I wasn't able to do nothing for Robert.

I didn't rightly know how much time passed before I started to feel like we were close to something besides trees and water and nature. By now, darkness had fallen, and I could see a glow up ahead, where surely there was some kind of a small town.

I felt a renewed burst of energy and I urged Dixie on a bit, as I held fast to Poke's lead rope. I didn't want to go too fast. We'd been lucky, and my rigging of Oscar onto Poke's back seemed to be working well. I'd stopped to check his breathing too many times to count and it had stayed the same, and his pulse, too. T'was weak, but t'was there. Still, I could hardly wait to find us a place where he could rest properly.

Soon, I was able to make out buildings and hear the sounds of other people, even though t'was late.

There was a town. It looked a pretty rough spot, too. Probably one of them mining outposts where travelers stopped for a night or two then went on their way. But I knew what to look for, even in a small place like this. And anyway, it found me.

As I turned down a well-lit, dirt road, a shawl-wrapped young woman on the porch of a very large house stepped down and waved at me.

"Hey, handsome. You fancy a soft spot to rest your head?" she asked, gazing behind me as Oscar made a pitiful noise. "Shit, what you got there, mister?"

I jumped down off Dixie's back and rushed to check on him, half hoping he was coming to. But he was still out cold.

The good-time-girl in too much face paint looked at Oscar and frowned.

"He don't look too good."

"No, he don't," I said, turning to her with a worried expression. "You gotta place he can lie down for a bit? I need to find a doctor."

She snorted. "Ain't no doctor in Telegraph Creek. But I reckon Miss June can have a look at him."

"Miss June. That your boss?"

"Yes, sir. She knows a lot about what bodies need to stay well and vital, and that's a fact. Not unusual, in her line a business."

"Do you think she'd take a look at my friend here? Maybe give him a bed for the night?"

The woman smiled kindly. "My name's Claire."

I nodded. "My name's Jimmy, and this here is Oscar."

She peered down at Oscar's sleeping face. "He's a cutie, that one. You're not bad yourself, there, Jimmy."

"I'll give you some money if you help me. I won't be needin' no physical attention, but I'll pay you all the same. He needs help."

"Come with me, then." Claire smiled, wrapping her ratty shawl closer about her shoulders and leading us inside.

T'was true, I'd been in my share of cathouses, and this one looked about the same as the rest on the outside, although t'was a bit more fancy on the inside. I'd seen hotels that looked worse. I was pleasantly surprised by the cleanliness and orderliness of it, and it gave me a good feeling about finding help there.

Sure enough, the young women and men who worked in these places may not have the manners of ladies and gentlemen, but that didn't mean they were stupid and classless. In fact, some of the women I'd come in contact with had been sweet and smart, and surprisingly optimistic for people of their station. If the pattern held, the mistress of this establishment would be enterprising and whip smart, with a maternal care for her charges and a pride in her work that belied its less than savory reputation.

As soon as we got inside, Claire went to find the mistress, and a young man in eye makeup and a corset came close to look at Oscar.

"My lord, he don't look too good," the fella said.

"Nope," I replied, trying not to stare at the way the boy's chest and nipples were pushed up by the tight boning in the silk fabric. When I met his gaze, he blushed and smiled.

"I beg your pardon," he said, "but we don't see too many handsome cowboys come through these parts. Mostly rough miners with a bit of gold in their pockets that makes them think they own the world."

I didn't know what to say, but I felt flattered with the way he was looking at me. If I hadn't already found my way with Oscar, I might have asked the madam how much for a few hours with this handsome fella. Then again, I probably wouldn't have dared. I would maybe have been tempted, but I would have thought it a passing fancy and not indulged in it.

I was glad Oscar hadn't ended up working in a bawdy house in Dawson City, because them things were like factories, chewing up whores and spitting them out so quick they'd be dizzy and broken. But this place seemed to run at a slower pace, and the employees seemed calm and content. A few gathered around, clucking o'er Oscar and showing a genuine interest in his welfare.

"Here... Lay him down on this settee," a plump, blonde woman told me, standing and giving the seat up for Oscar's benefit.

"Thank you," I said, laying him down and making sure his head was pillowed comfortably.

"What happened?" the delicate boy asked.

"His horse shied at a snake and he fell off, banged his head on a rock," I said. "I'd hoped he'd come to before we got to town, but he's still out. Don't know what I'm gonna do now."

"Miss June'll know what to do. Here she comes now," said the plump girl who'd given us her seat. "Miss June, this here fella got knocked out pretty bad."

Miss June was a tall, older woman, whose beauty had begun to decline but who still possessed a certain charisma and stature. Her hair was wrapped up in a purple scarf, and she wore clothes that didn't show off her figure as much as the others.

She looked all business as she met my gaze. "Did you bring him?"

"Yes, ma'am."

"Do you mind if I have a look at him?"

"No, ma'am. His name's Oscar...and I'm Jimmy."

"Well, Jimmy, let's see how he is now that he's lying down and comfortable." She sat beside Oscar in the small space left on the settee and examined his face. She glanced back at me. "How old is Oscar?"

"Twenty-one."

She regarded him with some skepticism. "He doesn't look older than eighteen or nineteen. Are you sure?"

She spoke well, as if she'd had some education before she'd fallen into this line of work. And it gave me hope.

"Yes, ma'am. He told me twenty-one, and I believe him. He's had a rough life."

She nodded and touched my hip briefly. "Haven't we all. You say he banged his head?"

"Yes, ma'am. On the back, there." I was holding my hat and wringing the brim, I was so nervous and scared for Oscar.

She turned his head a bit on the pillow and felt gently with her fingers. "Oh yes, he's got quite the goose egg here. Any bleeding after he fell?"

"No, ma'am, not much."

"Good. That's good." She lifted Oscar's wrist and held her index and middle finger against it for a bit. "His pulse is a bit weak, but it's steady. That's a good sign."

"I reckon I can pay you to keep him here for a couple of days, if you have the space."

Miss June turned and looked me o'er carefully with her sharp eyes. "Who is this man to you, Jimmy? Is he your brother or your friend — or is he something else?"

The way she looked at me, as if she could see through my skin and right into my heart, was alarming in one way and comforting in another. Figured I might as well tell her the truth. We were all on the other side of the law and society here. I might as well lay it out.

I glanced around at the others who stood clustered around, waiting for me to answer Miss June.

"I reckon we're sweethearts, if you want the honest truth, ma'am."

She nodded and gave me a smile. "Thank you for being honest with me, Jimmy. I do appreciate it. And I can see how much you care for Oscar. So, yes, we can look after him here, for as long as he needs it."

I felt the relief hit me like a bull knocking me o'er, and I had to fight the tears that threatened to come.

"Thank you kindly...all of you." I looked around at the group of people peering o'er my shoulder, caring for Oscar the way folks a lot higher in society surely wouldn't.

The fancy boy put a hand onto my shoulder. "He'll be all right, I'm sure a'it, Jimmy. Miss June has a lot a learnin' 'bout these things. 'Bout all things, really. She coulda been a doctor if she weren't a girl."

Miss June looked at him and laughed outright. "I could have been a lot of things, Cal, if I wasn't a girl."

The others chuckled and nodded.

"That's sure enough," Cal said, smiling.

He was pretty in a strange way, like Oscar, but since he was made up, he looked even more feminine. He seemed something in between a man and a woman, and I liked the look of him. I didn't doubt the services he provided to the men that wanted them were appreciated in a big way, since most men couldn't find them things out in the open. I only hoped he was treated well.

But it looked like Miss June ran a good business there, and I reckon she had rules to keep her boys and girls safe — and enough learning to give them proper care, as well.

Chapter Twenty-One

Sanctuary and Kindness

Miss June had me take Oscar to one of the upstairs bedrooms that wasn't being used. Despite what I'd seen of other cathouses, this particular establishment was expansive, well-maintained and clean as anything I'd ever seen. There were folks scrubbing floors and bringing up laundry, as well as women leading men into private rooms. I heard the sounds of pleasure coming from several.

"You say there ain't no doctor in this town?" I asked again. T'wasn't that surprising. "There can't be many people living here, then."

"That's true. There aren't many—and not many families or married folk. Telegraph Creek is made up of mostly bachelors trying to survive on their own, working for nearby trade. We get a lot of single men traveling through here." She grinned, creating a dimple in her cheek. "That's where most of our business comes from."

"I see. You seem to be doin' all right. I ain't never been in a nicer cathouse, an' that's a fact. An' I been in several."

Miss June laughed. "Well, thank you kindly. I do pride myself on running a fine establishment, Jimmy."

She opened a door and gestured for me to go in. "This room's just been cleaned, and you and Oscar are welcome to use it for as long as you need it. Cal will help you get settled in, all right?"

"Yes, ma'am. And thank you."

Cal came into the room with us and pulled back the bedsheets, so's I could lay Oscar down.

"I can help you get his clothes off, if you like. I ain't offerin' that to be rude. It's true that I do like the look of other men, and you two are both cute as punch, but I ain't gonna drool o'er him or nothin'. I reckon I can help."

"Thank you kindly, Cal." I said, not caring at this moment what his inclinations were. "Would you get us a pitcher of water and a bowl, please? I'd like to clean him up a bit."

"Yes, sir, I surely can do that. In fact, I can prob'ly get one a the girls to come in and help, if you'd rather?"

"No, Cal, I like you, an' that's a fact," I said, because t'was true. There was something familiar about Cal, even though I'd never seen a young man dressed in women's clothes that wasn't in a show or something. "I don't mind you helpin' me make him comfortable."

He beamed under his makeup, and it made him glow with pleasure. "Good. I like you too, Jimmy."

Between the two of us, we got Oscar undressed and washed up so's he could rest peacefully in the soft bed. He made small noises and even tried to push us away as we messed with him, which I took as a positive sign.

He'd been stone quiet and completely out of it while he'd been strapped onto Poke's back, so I was relieved to see him coming back, at least a bit.

I noticed some bruises coming through Oscar's pale skin as I cleaned him carefully, and I figured what hadn't come from his fall had come from the rough ride on Poke, and I was sorry for it. But there hadn't been another way to get him here, to this strange haven in the town of Telegraph Creek. Things could have gone a lot worse.

Once Oscar was cleaner and resting, with the blankets pulled up to his chin and a soft look on his sleeping face, I turned to Cal.

"Thank you," I said, taking my time to look him o'er now.

He was a pretty fella, that was certain. Along with the purple basque, he wore a pair of satin black ladies' bloomers with ruffles around the edges, black stockings and a pair of scuffed men's boots. His hair was short but waved delicately around his ears and atop his neck, giving him a feminine air. His eyes were blue, and he had long lashes that didn't hardly need the fancy paint on them.

He blushed and looked down at the floor, giggling. "I reckon you ain't seen anyone like me before," Cal said shyly. "But you gotta stop lookin' at me like you wanna eat me up, Mister Jimmy."

I cleared my throat, embarrassed and a little guilty, because Oscar was lying here unconscious while I was letting my lustful thoughts wander.

"I'm sorry, Cal. I didn't mean to. My thoughts are all messed up right now and I can't control the way I react to you."

"S'okay. I don't really mind, 'cept you're makin' me wish things I shouldn't rightly be wishin' right now, with your sweetheart lyin' there."

We both laughed a bit and Cal cleared his throat.

"I reckon I'll go down and tell Miss June that Oscar was makin' sounds and motions while we cleaned him. That's a good sign, for sure."

I sighed. "I sure hope so. Thank you."

He nodded and left with a shy little smile. I wondered what Oscar would think of Cal, and hoped I wouldn't have to wait long to find out. I sat on the bed beside him and rested my hand on the quilt above where his heart was, looking at his familiar features resting, as if only in sleep and not the terrible void that was unconsciousness.

I gently took his hand that was laying motionless on the counterpane, so's I could feel that he was warm and alive, and he hadn't left me yet.

"Oscar, you need to wake up soon, you hear? You can't leave me all alone in this world, not after wakin' me up to you and everythin' we do together."

I looked at the floor, trying to put into words everything he meant to me.

"I love you, an' that's a fact. I don't wanna live without you. You gotta wake up, and besides, you gotta meet Cal and Miss June and t'other people what live and work here. This ain't *like* the bawdy houses in Dawson City. This is a good place with good people, who happen to offer their intimate services to other, like-minded people."

There was a knock on the door.

"Come in," I said, letting go and moving back from Oscar's bedside. Not that it mattered, except to be polite. They knew what Oscar was to me.

Miss June came in with Cal at her heels.

"Cal said Mr. Yates was moving and making noises." She came in and moved close, to bend o'er Oscar and examine his face.

"Yes, ma'am."

She checked his pulse again and listened to his breathing. "It's stronger now. I have a feeling he'll be awake soon, Jimmy."

"Truly?"

"I think so. You stay with him. When he wakes, you send Cal for me, all right?"

"Yes, ma'am. Thank you."

She stood and patted me on the back. "You're taking such good care of him. He's sure to be all right, if he gets enough rest over the next few days."

I was so relieved I couldn't gather the words together and simply nodded.

Sure enough, after another half an hour, Oscar's eyelids fluttered and opened. He saw me, then his gaze drifted around the room in confusion. "Jimmy? Where am I?"

The relief hit me like a cool wave, and I grabbed his hand where I'd left it, squeezing and fondling it—and fighting back tears. "Oscar…you're awake? God, thank God. I was worried you weren't gonna wake up…"

"My head hurts."

The fact that he'd recognized me and said my name gave me an untold amount of happiness.

"You're all right, Oscar. We're in Telegraph Creek now. It ain't much of a town and there ain't no doctor, but we're in a safe place with good people to look after you."

Oscar squinted, as if the lights were too bright, when there was only one small lamp lit on the table.

"What happened? All I remember's ridin' Sprite, and you were sayin' how you thought there was a small town comin' up soon."

"That's a fact, and we're in that town now. Sprite spooked at a snake in the grass and threw you. You smashed your head on a big rock and got knocked out. This is the first you woke up since."

"Golly. That must be why my head hurts."

"I reckon. I have to tell Cal to get Miss June." I started to get up, but Oscar held on to my hand tight.

"No. Stay with me for a bit. I need to catch up to you."

I nodded and stayed where I was, my eyes filling up again.

"No, Jimmy. Don't cry. I'm all right."

I nodded but didn't dare say anything. If I opened my mouth, I'd start bawling. As t'was, the tears streaked my cheeks silently, while my eyes feasted on the sight of Oscar awake and talking.

"I'm all right. I'm gonna be fine. My head hurts a bit, but I know what my name is and, well, I recognize you all right." He gazed around him at the room. "Only, I'm so thirsty."

Cal had brought me a glass of water, and I picked it up now and helped Oscar to take some sips of it.

"What's your name, then, since you're so smart?"

Oscar scrunched up his face as if he could barely recall it, but I knew he was teasing.

"Hmm. Must be somethin' tough like…Jake?"

I shook my head. "Nope."

"Buck?"

My smile got wider. "Wrong."

"You tell me, then. What do you think my name is?"

I raised my eyebrows. "You tell me your name, silly boy, and I'll kiss ya. Deal?"

"Fine." He gazed at me with an impish smile and gave me what I needed. "It's Oscar. Oscar Yates."

I nodded and cupped his chin, leaning in to press my lips to his as a sob rose inside my chest that made me shake with relief and make a strangled noise.

"Oscar Yates, you about scared the life outta me," I murmured, then kissed him hard and pulled back.

The door creaked open, and I glanced o'er to see Cal.

"He awake?" Cal asked.

"Yeah. Can you get Miss June, please?"

"I surely will."

"Who was that?" Oscar asked, gazing at the door that Cal had closed behind him.

I smiled. "That's Cal. He's a very nice boy who's been helpin' me."

Oscar's eyes narrowed. "Helpin' you how? Are we in a cathouse?"

My mouth dropped open. "How do you know that?"

"That boy had on more makeup than most a' the whores I ever seen," Oscar said, sounding more shocked than I'd ever heard him. His voice sounded raw and tired, but he had his wits about him, it seemed.

I laughed. "True enough. I reckon he likes to look pretty for his clients, that's all."

"Jimmy," Oscar said weakly, blinking at me. "Are you tellin' me I'm bein' looked after by whores and molly boys?"

"I know it seems strange, especially considering how we met outside of one in Dawson City, and I dragged you away like t'was the devil's playground. But this one's different. This one's a nice place with nice people. And Miss June? She's book-smart *and* street-smart, and caring, and Cal's gone to get her so's she can have a look at you." I smiled, showing him how relaxed I was. "Anyway, I've only seen one molly boy and that's Cal — and you'll like him. There may be others, I don't know."

He looked at me like I'd gone plumb crazy, and I couldn't blame him.

"What?" I said.

"I feel like I done gone and woke up on a whole different planet."

I laughed and took off my hat, bending to kiss his forehead. "Yeah, I can see that. But this here's a friendly one."

Miss June came in, followed by Cal, who stayed by the door, giving us some space. Oscar's eyes flitted to him before they landed full on Miss June as she grinned at him and put her hands on her wide hips.

"Well, good morning. The sun isn't up yet but I'm glad you are, Mr. Yates."

He glanced at me, surprised. Then he looked back at Miss June and gave her a little smile. "Thanks. You can call me Oscar. I'm glad to be awake, too. I reckon Jimmy here saved my life...again." He looked at me. "That's three times now," he said softly.

Miss June looked at me and I nodded. "Sure enough. And I'll save it again if I have to. But hopefully I won't."

She looked back at Oscar. "You're a lucky young man to have such a devoted paramour."

Oscar's eyes widened and flew to mine. "You told 'em?" he whispered. "You told what we are t'each other?"

I nodded, and Miss June made a disdainful noise.

"Oscar, Jimmy knew he was in the one place he could be truthful, and I appreciate him for being honest with me. Nobody here is going to send the law on you." She gestured at me and Oscar and Cal. "We're all operating outside the law here."

"I reckon," Oscar said, sounding unsure. I couldn't blame him, seeing as he'd only woke up a few minutes ago and had a headache and perhaps other issues. He was squirming around in the bed a little.

"Do you need to relieve yourself, Oscar?" Miss June asked bluntly.

Oscar's cheeks flooded with embarrassment. "I reckon I do."

She nodded. "That makes sense. You've been unconscious for a while." She turned to me. "There's a bowl under the bed he can use. Cal and I'll leave you two, but I'm going to have the cook heat up a batch of broth and some toast for Oscar, and fix something more substantial for you, Jimmy."

I blinked at her, again fighting strong emotions. "Thank you kindly, Miss June."

"Thank you," Oscar said, "I'm sure Jimmy was scared outta his mind I wasn't gonna wake up."

"He was mighty worried, and that's a fact," Cal said from beside the door. "You got yourself a fine man, Oscar."

Oscar looked at Cal, assessing, before he said, "I know it. Thank you."

Cal nodded and ducked out of the room ahead of Miss June.

Once they'd gone, I hauled out the chamber pot and helped Oscar out of bed. He was a little embarrassed to have me so near while he pissed, but I didn't trust him not to fall, and I guess he didn't neither, so he put up with me holding on to him.

"I'm sorry," he muttered.

"What're you sorry for? Bein' alive? I'd rather watch you piss in a pot than land in a grave."

He made a little sigh of relief as his piss hit the bottom of the pot with a clang. "Oh, fuck, that feels good. Wasn't sure I could hold it."

"I imagine if you'd have pissed the bed, Miss June and Cal would have taken care of things. I imagine she's seen a lot worse."

"That's true enough."

When he was done, I nudged the pot back under the bed with my foot and helped him get back in.

"Does your head hurt bad?" I asked.

He smiled up at me as I arranged the bedclothes around him. "Nah, I'm all right. Figure in a day or two I'll be good as gold."

I narrowed my eyes at him. "Oscar Yates, you do as Miss June tells you. She says to stay in bed for a week, that's what you do. All right?"

"All right. Gosh, you'd have made a good nanny, Jimmy. Or a daddy."

"I'm your daddy, sure enough, and you listen to me good."

His eyes widened. "Well, that fall didn't do nothin' to my nubby, Jimmy. You just woke it right up."

"I'm glad about that, although I would keep lovin' you, nubby or no nubby."

"Jesus, don't even say that."

I laughed. "Fine. But I'm sure glad you still got it and that it works okay. But that ain't the only thing about you I love, you know."

He smiled. "I know it. You like my ass."

I sighed, rolling my eyes. "I surely do. But I reckon you ain't recovered from the last spankin' I gave you, and you gotta get your head better, too."

"Jimmy?" Cal's voice from the doorway startled me and I whipped my head around, wondering what he'd heard.

My face flushed. "Yes, Cal?"

"I got some food here for you and Oscar. Shall I bring it on in?"

I stood up and hoped to hell Cal hadn't heard us talking about spanking and such. Although, living in a bawdy house, it probably wouldn't shock him. Still...

"Yes. Thank you kindly."

Cal smiled and came into the room, bringing a tray with the broth and tea on it. He approached Oscar and placed the tray on the table at the bedside.

"You're lookin' better and better every time I see you," Cal commented. He was wearing a pretty blue shawl o'er his shoulders now, so his state of nakedness wasn't so startling. Except, he was still dressed in women's clothes, so there was that.

Oscar looked him o'er with a curious appraisal. "Why're you wearin' clothes like that, if you don't mind my askin'?" He lowered his voice. "Does Miss June make you dress that way?"

Cal blushed slightly but shook his head.

"Oh no." He giggled. "I like wearing corsets and things—and a little rouge and eye makeup, even a bit of lip color, sometimes."

He turned to me. "You might have to hold the bowl and spoon it to him, Jimmy. I reckon he might like that anyhow."

While he was talking, Oscar reached out and touched the edge of Cal's delicate shawl with his fingers. When Cal noticed, he grinned from ear-to-ear.

"I know it's a bit strange, but it makes me feel more myself somehow, to wear fancy and delicate things. And Miss June, she don't mind. And t'other girls? They help me find things that'll look fetchin' on me. And the men? Well, they don't mind a t'all." He grinned with a devilish air. "I reckon they like somethin' a little out of the ordinary, y'know? And that's me."

Oscar smiled at Cal, and I was glad they were getting along. The more I got to know this young fella, the more I liked him. He was so unabashedly who he was, and he didn't rightly care how strange it might look at first.

Truth is, a person got used to it. I reckon if I saw him in men's clothes, I'd think t'was strange at this point.

As If reading my mind, he said, "If I have to leave this place, I wear regular men's clothes, but I don't like to. Makes me feel strange and reminds me a things I'd rather forget."

"Is Cal your real name?" Oscar asked.

"Well, no, it ain't. But it's my name now, I reckon. Don't nobody e'er call me by my old name, so this one's more real to me than anythin'. Cal is short for Caliope, which I think is real pretty, and I chose it. Everyone here calls me that."

Oscar blinked up at Cal as if he was the most beautiful creature in the world all of a sudden. "I think Caliope's a real pretty name, too."

"Thank you, Oscar."

Cal turned to me. "Miss June says to give him that broth and tea, and make sure he stays in bed at least two whole days. He needs to rest his brain, and let it heal after it been jostled about in his head so much."

I nodded, thanking my lucky stars we'd landed in this place.

"An' e'en after that, he should stay here an extra day or two, and take it easy. Maybe longer, if you don't got no particular place to be. Miss June says you can stay a whole week, if you like."

"That's mighty kind of Miss June. Mighty kind of all of you. Truth is, we're heading to Port Essington, British Columbia, but there's not a set day we need to be there. I'd rather Oscar rests up and gets healthy for the rest of our journey. I reckon we can stay a week with you folks."

Cal smiled. "I'm glad. I like you, Jimmy, and I'm gettin' to know Oscar a bit, and I reckon I'm gonna like him, too."

"We don't wanna be a burden. I can let Miss June know there's lots of things I can do around here to help out."

Cal nodded. "I'm sure she'd appreciate that."

I blushed, nodding, wanting to say something else.

"And for the record? I think you look real nice in them things. And I think the name you picked is real pretty, too."

I glanced at Oscar, and he was smiling at me, so I knew he understood I was trying to be kind and not showing a sexual interest in Cal. Though the more I saw Cal, the more I thought I might like to see Oscar dolled up like that, just to see how he'd look. But he probably wouldn't be comfortable with it, and I wasn't gonna bring it up, anyways.

"Why, thank you. You fellas are makin' me blush like a twelve-year-old virgin. And God only knows, I ain't *that*."

He laughed, and we did too.

He shut the door behind him and went downstairs. I found a seat on the bed near Oscar and picked up the bowl of broth.

"You really gonna feed me, Jimmy?"

"I reckon I will. I like caring for you like this," I said, spooning up the broth and holding it to his lips. "Open up now."

He opened his mouth and I placed the metal spoon on his tongue, tilting the warm broth into it. He swallowed and gave me a saucy glance.

"You like lookin' at my tongue," he said softly.

I grinned. "There's that, too. Quiet now and eat."

Chapter Twenty-Two

The Angel of Telegraph Creek

Once Oscar had eaten all his broth and drunk most of his tea, he settled back on his pillow and looked up at me with tired eyes.

"You best get in and cuddle with me, Jimmy. I reckon you could use some sleep, too."

All of a sudden, the last twelve hours caught up with me, and exhaustion hit me hard.

"I reckon I could."

I got undressed and climbed into bed beside him, happy to snug him into my arms and hold him, knowing he was safe, that we were both safe, and we could let our guard down for the first time in almost a week.

* * * *

I woke up with a start. Yellow rays from the sun streaked through small gaps in the blue curtains to sprawl on the polished wood floors of the room we were in. I marveled again at how clean the place was.

With men of a certain outlook being the usual customers, cathouses normally had less than pristine standards, since the men didn't care as much as they wanted a quick fuck with a reasonably attractive woman. They generally didn't stay long and wouldn't have noticed dust on the furniture or streaks on the floors.

But Miss June's place was immaculate. Her whores were not only attractive but were also clean and content. If anyone could run a decent, respectable bawdy house, it seemed Miss June could—and was doing that exact thing. I was grateful we'd ended up here—more than mere words could express.

After roaming o'er the sparse but well-made teak furniture with nary a spot of dirt or dust, my gaze landed on Oscar in the comfortable bed beside me. He slept soundly on his belly, with his head resting sideways on the soft pillow, his sweet mouth slightly open with a bit of drool shining in one corner. I resisted the urge to swipe it dry with my finger, as that might wake him, and he needed the rest. He looked like an angel lying there, his back rising and falling softly, and I pushed down the emotion that threatened to crest again at the thought that I could have lost him. He could have died from the journey on Poke's back, and I could be accepting Miss June's assistance in burying him, instead of her care to help him recover.

I tamped those thoughts down. There wasn't no use in entertaining them. We still had miles to travel to get to Port Essington, and I had to focus on the fact that he was alive and would recover and hope to God that we didn't have any more close calls on the next part of our journey, when I knew full well we might.

I eased myself out of bed and dressed quickly, all of a sudden remembering Dixie and Sprite and the mule. In the chaos of getting Oscar looked after and the confusion of meeting all these nice people, I'd plumb forgot about the animals. I hoped to God they were still outside, but I wouldn't be surprised if they'd been stolen or if they were suffering from the cold and having nothing to eat or drink. I felt awful, and this was not usual for me. I normally made sure my horses were well looked after.

I ran down the stairs in my shirtsleeves and skidded to a halt at the bottom of the fancy stairway, gaping at the sight of Cal lying in the arms of a man on the settee. He was asleep and it looked like the man was, too. I didn't know if they'd had relations or if the stranger had simply paid for a sweet cuddle, but Cal looked peaceful, and the man was snoring contentedly.

They were dressed, so they must've gone upstairs if they'd done anything more than be sweet together. I knew some men paid whores to cuddle and didn't even care about anything else. T'was a harsh world out there, and if you didn't have nobody, t'was worth some coin to feel comforted and safe in another person's arms from time to time. And for the whores, t'was easy money. Sad that some folks had to pay for it, but better to get it that way than not at all, I s'posed.

I opened the door and stepped out, crestfallen to see no sign of Sprite or Dixie — or the mule that had carried Oscar.

One of the girls I'd seen last night stood on the narrow porch with a thick wool robe around her, smoking a pipe.

"Good mornin', Jimmy," she said warmly. "Miss June won't let me smoke inside, so I got to come out here."

I looked around frantically for a sign of them horses, but I couldn't see anything. Figured they got stole in the night, and that meant Oscar and me were pretty fucked.

"Do you... Do you know what might have happened to my horses?" I asked, hoping against hope they were somewhere safe, but pretty sure I'd been robbed.

"Yeah, sure do. Miss June sent someone to put them in the barn, to feed 'em and water 'em and put 'em up for you."

My heart stopped beating frantically as I realized we were, all of us, in good hands.

"Truly?"

"Yes, sir. Miss June said you were our guest, and we needed to look after your sweetheart and your horses."

I didn't know what to say. I stood there gaping at her for several moments.

She smiled and lowered her pipe, giving me the once-o'er.

"I, uh, I can take care a you, free a charge, if you want. If your sweetheart's too tired and recoverin', why, I can give you somethin' quick and fun, if you like." She quirked her lip in a coy invitation.

She was pretty enough, with thick brown hair coiled loosely on her head and fresh, pink cheeks around a bow mouth, and if I'd not so long ago been terrified about the horses and whether Oscar was gonna live or die, I reckon I might have took her up on it.

She winked. "Take the edge off?"

"Well, I thank you kindly, miss. That's a very sweet offer. But I reckon I should go check on them horses and make sure they remember me."

"Suit yourself," she said, shrugging, but not in an unkind way. "If you change your mind, let me know. My name's Trick."

I stared at her, my gaze going to her plump breasts that were busting out of her chemise and wondering what kind of tricks she might know. "That ain't your real name, though."

She laughed. "No, it ain't my real name."

I was mighty curious now. I cleared my throat. "Uh, why'd you pick that one, then?"

She looked me up and down, slowly this time, and it felt almost like a caress. "Well, wouldn't you like to find out?"

She wasn't gonna tell me, I supposed, and I wasn't gonna get her to show me.

"Go on," I laughed. "I reckon you'd be mighty entertainin', but I got work to do. I'll see you around."

"See ya." She grinned and took another pull off her pipe.

I was shaking my head as I walked to the stables to visit my horses and see if they were all right, although it sounded like they'd been well looked after. Everyone at this place seemed well cared for. I'd never ever been in a whorehouse that seemed like such an honorable and happy place. Seemed like a place people wanted to be and weren't forced to exist in a state of lechery and pain. Seemed even though they took care of others' most basic needs, they had respect and care for themselves.

T'was a revelation. I'm sure t'wasn't perfect and maybe some of them regretted this life, but t'was better than a lot of other things, like starving in the streets or being with someone that looked after you but beat you, too. I'd seen enough of that in my lifetime to appreciate people trying to make an honest living, even though t'was doing things others saw as morally questionable. Hell, what Oscar and I did together was seen by most as morally questionable, but t'was the sweetest thing that ever came into my life, so I would've argued that point with them until I was blue in the face, if t'would ever do any good. I reckoned t'wouldn't. But t'was nice to find a place with people who believed what we did.

T'was so early that there wasn't much activity in the small town. The street where I'd stumbled upon Miss June's establishment was sparsely dotted with other buildings. Now, in the daylight, I could make out the names etched into the signs on their fake fronts.

Hansen's Distillery, Masterson's Dry Goods and Hair and Teeth Care by Jakob Callender. Convenient to have a barber-slash-dentist on hand, I supposed. Although I would rather go to someone who specialized in dentistry, rather than sit in a barber's chair and have him attend me with a pair of pliers.

It occurred to me that I didn't even know the name of Miss June's place. When I stepped down off the porch, I turned around to look up at the brightly painted sign.

The words 'The Angel' in all capital letters, painted bright white against the brown boards, with the words 'Rest House' following in smaller letters, faced the narrow street. My heart beat louder with the fact that I'd brought Oscar to this place when we were in dire need of both heavenly intervention and rest and recovery, and that's what t'was named.

I shook my head and walked around the porch to head down an alley beside the large house, where Trick had indicated the stables could be found.

The barn was a dark brown building behind the large house, with its doors wide open to the fresh clean air of early morning. It smelled of fresh hay and horse dung, and a young lad glanced up from where he was cleaning out a stall with a wide shovel.

"Can I help you, mister?" he asked, brushing his dirty blond bangs out of the way of his green eyes with the back of his hand.

I smiled at the boy, who looked about twelve, with a bit of peach fuzz on his top lip and pimples on his hairless chin.

"Yeah, you got two horses and a mule in here? Name's Jimmy."

He nodded. "Yup. They's in the first three stalls at th'end, there. Nice horses. And the mule's all right, too. I made sure they was dry and warm."

"Thank you kindly. I was worried about my friend and plumb forgot about 'em."

He looked grave. "I know it. Miss June told me and said to take good care of 'em for you."

There were other horses in stalls and the stables were quite large. The boy must have noticed me looking around.

"We put up horses for the men what visit The Angel. They give us coin for that, on top a what they pay for their leisure." He blushed. "I ain't got nothin' to do with *that*. But Miss June pays me good coin to look after these here horses, and I like doin' it. I got a warm and dry place to sleep here, too, and enough money to buy food for myself—or I can get somethin' inside, if I want."

I nodded, walking o'er to check on Sprite and Dixie and Poke. "Miss June seems like a very respectable woman, in spite of running a place like The Angel."

"She is, mister. She's smart and kind and I like her a lot. I'd be on the streets if it weren't for her."

I nodded, sure that were true. "How old are you, son?"

"Fifteen, mister."

A late bloomer, then.

"Old enough to know 'bout what goes on in there and want no part a'it. And anyway, Miss June won't have nobody younger'n eighteen workin' them rooms."

"Glad to hear it."

I *was* glad, though it didn't surprise me. Miss June seemed to have some pretty high standards.

"But I don't care if they wanna do it. There ain't nothin' wrong w'it, I figure."

"No, that's fair. Everyone I've met at The Angel has been sweet as punch. That ain't always the case with cathouses."

"I'm glad I found Miss June," the kid said, folding his hands on the handle of his shovel and resting against it.

"I'm glad I found her, too. I was pretty worried 'bout Oscar."

Dixie peeked her nose out of her stall when she heard my voice. She whinnied as I approached her.

"Hey, girl, how are ya? Glad you got in outta the cold. I'm sorry I left you," I said, scratching her under the chin and wishing I had a carrot for her.

"My name's William."

The young lad had followed me o'er to Dixie's stall and stopped beside me.

"Good to meet you, William," I said, turning to shake his hand.

He cocked his head at me. "You met Cal, yet?"

I smiled. "Yeah, I met Cal."

William nodded. "I reckon I like Cal the most of all a them," he said, gesturing toward the house.

"Oh yeah?" I raised my eyebrows.

"Yeah. Some a them girls like to tease me, tell me what they get up to with the men. But Cal ne'er does that."

"He seems like a very nice person, Cal does," I said, and I meant it.

"Yeah, Cal is. Y'know, Cal likes if you say 'she', though, when you're talkin' bout her." He glanced at me to see my reaction.

I nodded. "I reckon that makes sense. I'll try to do that from now on."

William smiled. "You think it's strange that he — I mean, *she* — wears women's underthings?"

I shook my head. "I seen things a lot stranger. I reckon it don't do nobody any harm." I smiled at William. "I think Cal looks nice."

"Yeah, I do, too." He frowned. "Not in a queer way. I mean, it don't make me wanna — y'know..." He cleared his throat.

I knew what he was trying to say, so I helped him out.

"I don't reckon it'd matter if it did. But I understand what you're sayin'. Those clothes suit Cal. They feel right on her, so she feels right wearin' them — and that comes through somehow, I guess."

"Yeah, that's right." William grinned.

"I reckon there's all kinds of people in this world, and if they ain't hurtin' nobody, I reckon they can wear what they like."

William grinned. He straightened up and grabbed his shovel, as if to get back to work. But before he did, he said, "I like you, Jimmy. You think the way I do 'bout those things."

"Well, I like that you took such good care of my horses. I reckon Oscar will be glad too, when I tell him."

He cocked his head again. "Is Oscar your sweetheart?"

I blushed. "I reckon he is."

"Is he gonna be okay?"

"Miss June says he will be. He's doin' much better — thank you for asking. He's gotta stay in bed a couple of days and rest for a few more. I reckon we'll be hangin' round here a week or so."

I moved to Sprite's stall and petted him on his neck, cooing at him. He seemed as glad to see me as Dixie was.

"Good. I'm glad. I'd like to meet Oscar when he's up and movin' around," William said.

"I'll be sure to bring him out here. He'll wanna see his horse, I reckon."

"Which one is his?"

"This one. His name's Sprite, and that's Dixie. She's my horse. And the mule is named Poke."

I glanced at the gray-brown mule in the next stall who seemed content to eat his hay and ignore me.

William laughed. "He's a bit of a case, that one. But he only needs a bit a care, that's all."

I gazed at the animal with a real fondness. "That mule carried Oscar strapped to his back like a sack of potatoes for miles to get him here safely. He never shied or spooked or gave me any trouble on that journey. I was scared to death that either the blow to Oscar's head would kill him or that animal would take off with Oscar on his back, and it'd be all o'er. But he never even pulled on his rope. He came along with me and Dixie and Sprite, carrying the extra load of a man, and never complained. I owe him a lot, and that's certain. Thank you for lookin' after him and the others so well."

I unsnapped my pouch and took out the wad of bills. William's eyes went wide as I counted out twenty dollars and handed them to him. "That's for the week. If we stay longer, there'll be more."

He stared at the money like I was handing him a gold bar. "I ain't never seen that much cash all at once. You sure, Jimmy?"

"Yeah, take it. I value my animals and the care they're given," I said. "Figure you got a little packet of cash you're savin', or you can start with that."

"I will, surely. Thank you."

I left William in the barn and went back into the house. The settee was empty, and I walked around looking for someone. Seemed like most of the workers were asleep, which made sense, since they'd be up most of the night with clients.

I eventually found a scullery maid in the kitchen, who was scrubbing the counters.

She looked up and blew a hair out of her face. "Hey there, mister. What can I do for you?" She said it like she was trying to be polite, but she had a lot of work to do and didn't much care for the interruption.

"Hello, ma'am. I'm a... I just come here with my friend, Oscar. He's upstairs recoverin' from a fall. Is there any way I can have a tub of hot water brought up later, maybe after lunch? I reckon I'll be waking him to eat, then we can both scrub the travel dust off, maybe?"

She eyed me cautiously. "You Jimmy?"

"Yes, ma'am. That's me."

She nodded and seemed to decide she didn't hate me.

"I'm Cassie. Miss June told me to get you whatever you needed. And to get some broth and bread ready for your friend, and some a the lefto'er stew for you at lunch time."

"Thank you. That would be very kind."

"And I s'pose I can get a bath brought up, too, and some towels."

She didn't smile but she didn't say to get out of her sight, neither. She went back to her cleaning.

"Is everyone asleep?" I asked.

"I reckon. Most of 'em what do th'entertainin' stay up pretty late, so nobody's usually up around here until around noon, except for me and t'other maids who can do some work in the main areas without disruption."

"Miss June sure seems to run a tight ship."

"That she does." Cassie finally smiled and I expect she was just busy with all the cleaning Miss June expected, and it was hard to relax enough to be friendly. "She's an angel, I reckon, so the name of this place makes sense. Though she'd laugh if she heard me say it."

"She's gotta lotta staff. More'n I've ever seen in a cathouse."

"Miss June charges high coin for her girls. And the men pay it, 'cause they know the place is clean and the girls are too." Cassie smiled wryly. "And there ain't no other cathouse around here, anyway, so, they're stuck. And they have to behave themselves. You met Gus yet?"

I shook my head. "Don't think so."

"Gus is six foot seven and prob'ly two hundred, eighty pounds. He's a big fella. Miss June pays him to toss out anyone who gets too big for their britches."

"I see. She's a smart lady."

"She is smart. She's had some schooling. More'n the rest of us. But she never treats us like we're any less deserving of respect than she is."

"I can see this place is a haven for people what might not fit in anywhere else — like Oscar and me."

"You're lucky you found us."

"I know that, truly. Thank you in advance for the hot water, Cassie. It'll be nice to freshen up after such a harrowing journey."

I took my leave and went back to the room, sneaking in and taking off my clothes and crawling under the covers with Oscar, so's I could get a few more hours of sleep.

* * * *

T'was a knock on the door that woke me later.

"Jimmy?"

T'was Cal's voice.

"Yes, Cal?"

"I got some food for you and Oscar, if I can come in?" she asked.

"You can," I said. I reckon Cal had seen more interesting things than two men in the same bed, so I stayed under the covers but sat up halfway, leaning o'er Oscar and whispering to him that he needed to wake.

Cal smiled when she saw us. "I'm glad you got some rest. Did you meet William, Jimmy, when you checked on the horses? Trick said you was fit to be tied when you stepped out the front door and didn't see 'em there."

I kissed Oscar on the forehead as he slowly woke. He blinked in the bright, late morning light, and moved to sit up with my help, then looked at Cal. She'd changed her clothes and now wore a dark blue silky robe o'er whatever underthings she had on. She had a matching blue ribbon in her short hair, and she'd taken off most of the makeup.

"I figured they'd been stole, honest to God," I said, referring to our animals. "But Trick sent me to the stables, and I did meet William. Very nice boy. He took good care of 'em."

"Took good care of who?" Oscar asked, gazing at Cal then me, before he yawned.

"Good mornin', Oscar," Cal said, laying her tray on the bedside table. "Well, it's almost noon now. Anyhow, did you sleep well?"

"I did. Thank you."

"How's your head?" I asked Oscar.

"Feels a whole lot better," he said. "I feel real good, honestly."

"Good," Cal said. "You hungry? There's some beef broth here and some bread and butter. A bowl of stew for Jimmy."

"Thank you, Cal. Did *you* get any sleep?" Oscar asked with a grin.

Cal's eyes flashed to Oscar, then to me. "Well, I...I had a bit of sleep this mornin'. Somethin' kept me up most a the night."

"Somethin'? Or someone?" Oscar said.

Cal winked. "I ain't tellin'."

"Well, that ain't no fun." Oscar made a face.

"I'll only say t'was a good night, that's all." Cal lifted a hand to her cheek and blushed.

"I'm glad to hear it," I said and gave Oscar a stern look. "Now you stop askin' rude questions and pass me the broth, so's I can feed you."

"Shucks, Jimmy, I reckon I can feed myself now," Oscar scoffed.

I glared at him, and he recognized the look I gave him.

"Shoot, what're you gonna do, Jimmy? Haul me o'er your lap with Cal watchin'?"

"I reckon you're not well enough for that, much as I'd like to do it." I glanced at Cal. "I'm bettin' Cal wouldn't have a problem with it."

Cal seemed to be trying not to laugh. "Well, I... No, I wouldn't. Not a t'all. But Jimmy's right. You ain't up for such games yet, I reckon."

"It ain't a game. Jimmy paddles me for real," Oscar said, his lips twitching.

"Now stop tryin' to raise eyes," I told him. "It's a game and you know't. Well, except for that one time."

"When you said you was doin' it so's I'd learn," he whined, watching Cal's reaction. He was acting like a child trying to aggravate a parent. Honestly, when he *was* well enough, I was gonna spank him pretty good for this.

Cal's eyes were about as big as saucers as she backed her way out of the room. "My goodness. Please don't make me picture that, 'cause it's makin' me a little bit flustered. Good day. I'll be back to get the dishes, and Cassie's sendin' up a bath for you boys. Goodness, I can't rightly get away from these thoughts I'm havin' now. Good day."

Poor fella. Oscar laughed softly and I gave him a look.

"What?" he said.

"I'm of two minds. Part of me is glad you got your gumption back, 'cause it means you're feelin' better, but part of me is regretting that lip of yours, 'cause I can't spank you for it at the moment."

Oscar flicked his tongue out and licked along his bottom lip, looking me o'er. "I reckon you could give me a *little* spankin', Jimmy."

"Oh no. I ain't doin' that. If you listen to Miss June and rest in bed, the way your s'posed to, and take it easy after that for a bit, then maybe I'll give you what you want. But *I'll* be decidin' when. You have to be a *good* boy."

Oscar shuddered and looked down at his lap.

"Well, look what you gone and done now."

"*You* did that. You're the one can't shut up about spankin'. In front of poor Caliope, too. I reckon she's pretty darn flustered now."

He looked at me strangely. "She? Ain't Cal a 'he', Jimmy?"

I shrugged. "I thought so at first, but William — he's the stable hand — says Cal likes to be called 'she' and 'her', rather than 'he' and 'him', so's I reckon I'll try to do that, from now on. Out of respect for Cal."

"Well, that's…interestin'. I suppose it makes some sense."

"Do it have to make sense even, if that's what Cal wants and it don't hurt nobody?"

"No, I suppose not."

"Now, I'm gettin' up and dressed, and gonna feed you your lunch. Then I'm gonna eat mine. Then we're gonna get a bath."

* * * *

The maids that brought up the big tub and filled it with hot water from jugs told me to strip the bed when

Oscar was in the bath and throw the sheets outside the door. They would take them and wash them, and when we were done bathing, one of them would come in and make up the bed with fresh sheets.

"Seems like you're always bathin' me, Jimmy," Oscar said when I insisted on helping to wash him.

"Miss June said you were supposed to rest. But I know it'll help you to feel better if you're clean, and we both got pretty dirty on the journey. I'm sure everyone will appreciate us polishin' up. But you need to be still and let me do the work."

"Yes, sir. I guess I can let you do that."

He watched me with soft eyes as I used the linen cloth and flower-scented soap to wash him everywhere. I treated him like a newborn lamb, I was so gentle. I was so damn thankful to be able to do this for him and to know he was gonna be all right after the scare I'd had. My hand started to tremble, remembering what I went through when I thought he might never wake up, or that he might be dead when I was leading Poke behind me.

"You all right, Jimmy?" Oscar asked. He lifted his hand and put it on my cheek, dripping water down my face that mixed with the tears. I shook my head.

"No. No, I ain't. I thought—" I said, my words catching in my throat. I cleared it and tried again. "I thought I'd *lost* you. I thought you were almost dead, or you'd hurt your brain so bad it would never work properly again."

I drew in a harsh gasp at those dreadful thoughts I'd had and just now spoke out loud.

"Hey, shhh, it's all right. I'm all right. I'm *fine,* and that's thanks to you, and to Miss June, and to Cal. You brought me here to them, and they're lookin' after me and so are you. I'm so lucky I got you. I am, and I'm sorry you had to go through that. I *love* you."

I blinked the tears away and nodded, leaning down to kiss him on the lips, losing myself in that familiar warmth and the feel of his mouth under mine.

After a while, when I felt better, we pulled apart and I smiled at him, so relieved he was really all right and we were in a safe, warm, friendly place together.

"Feel what you done to me."

T'was a bit of a dare, but I couldn't resist putting my hand into the water and wrapping my fingers around his hard nubby that was standing up in the warm water, raring to go, even if Oscar wasn't quite ready yet.

"You sure feel like you're all right," I said, cupping his erection in my hand and stroking along it.

"Oh, I am. And when Miss June lets me outta bed, I reckon I'm gonna go grab you and pull you right back in with me."

I kissed his forehead and let go of his cock. "I reckon I'd like that."

Chapter Twenty-Three

Miss June's Wisdom

I spent that day and the next nursing Oscar and helping out Miss June and the girls while he rested. Turned out, there were a lot of things to get done when you were trying to run a clean and orderly business.

I helped to move some furniture and fix some things around the place that needed fixing. They sure appreciated some free labor, and I knew how to do a lot of simple things. I was glad to be able to contribute, but I also offered Miss June a handful of bills for the food we were eating and the room we were occupying.

I was lucky to be able to do that, and t'was thanks to Spook and Whitlaw's tainted cash, but I reckon Miss June wouldn't mind that. And it seemed proper that some of their take should pay for Oscar's welfare.

"It's not necessary. I wasn't going to ask you for anything," she said.

She was speaking to me while she brushed and braided Trick's long hair in the parlor. From what I'd seen, all the girls helped each other out with things and didn't stand on ceremony. It was a pleasant atmosphere to be in. I expect Miss June didn't put up with petty squabbling among her employees and cultivated that level of behavior.

"Miss June, you're putting us up for a week, now, giving us space and helping to nurse Oscar back to health. I reckon you deserve some money for that."

"I get plenty of money running the Angel, Jimmy."

"I don't doubt that one bit, Miss June. I've never been in a place like this, what tended to men's needs with such grace and respect. It's truly a fact that being a whore ain't ideal work for anyone, but the way you run this place, it turns out it's a lot better than a lot of things, I reckon. There's money in it, that's for sure."

"It's been a nice change for the girls to have you and Oscar here," she said, urging Trick up and off, since she'd finished. Once Trick had gone with a sly wink at me, Miss June gave me her full attention. "Things can get a little boring day in and day out, seeing travelers come through and nothing else in this little town. Even though this is a respectable place in my eyes, my girls still face stares and judgment in town, and they don't like that. And Cal? She has to wear men's things if she even wants to leave this place, except to go to the barn to talk to William." Miss June sighed. "I've done what I can to make this an accepting place for all of them and let them do their jobs in peace and with care. I won't tolerate anybody being mean or vicious in my establishment—and the men know that and they behave."

I'd met Gus—Mr. Hanover—and he was massive and completely devoted to Miss June and The Angel—and dedicated to keeping everyone safe.

I nodded. "Seems pretty damn civilized if you ask me. We were lucky to find this place, 'specially with…"

I cleared my throat and gestured at the stairs. "'Specially with the way me and Oscar are with each other."

Miss June smiled and put a hand on my arm. "You and Oscar are a lovely couple. Don't let anybody tell you different, Jimmy."

"No, ma'am, I won't. But I reckon we won't tell many people the way it really is between us. I wish we could, but—"

"I know, and that's wise. Too many people don't understand. It scares them or something, I don't know." She shrugged. "And the law thinks they're protecting people from their baser instincts." She cocked her head. "Buggery." She shook her head and scoffed. "As if that's only something shameful done between men. You know how many men bugger their wives and nobody gives a damn? Some of my girls can charge a lot for that if they don't mind it. And Cal? Well…Cal gets a pretty high fee for her services, let me tell you."

I shook my head, blushing to hear her talk about something so private and shamed by society.

Miss June folded her arms across her chest and said, "Most of them do it. And most of the wives, if they're being honest? They like it. So, what the hell is the goddamn problem if two men want to do it? That's my question. Goddamn government, peeking their noses into everybody's business, except where it should be when the men are beating their wives, controlling them and nobody gives a good goddamn."

"Yes, ma'am."

"Seems to me there's too much evil and cruelty in this world to care about how two people want to express their love for each other."

I smiled at how ornery she was getting. Miss June was a fiery cat, and I liked her a hell of a lot...for so many reasons.

"I reckon you're right about that. I've seen that cruelty and evil up close, and I'd rather see love in any form than that."

Miss June regarded me thoughtfully, then broke into a laugh. "Maybe you and I should run for office. Pretty this whole world up with molly boys like Cal and couples like you and Oscar. It would be a better place, I think."

I laughed at the thought of it. "I reckon it would. Maybe that'll happen someday."

"Maybe. I'm not going to hold my breath, though. I'm going to simply keep making my corner of it the way I want it to be," she said. She took both of my hands in hers. "I want you to *hold on* to that money, Jimmy, and use it to start a life for you and Oscar in Port Essington."

I stared at her for a bit. "I don't rightly know what life the two of us can have, Miss June, seein' as most people would think we were sinners or worse for being how we are together."

"It's true that the world isn't ready for men like you and Oscar to kiss each other in the street. But you have to figure out what you want and what price you're willing to pay to have it. Now you can either pay the price of giving each other up, or you can pay the price of living in a way that requires you to keep that part of your life a secret."

She gazed at me with intelligence, perception and in an all-knowing kind of way.

"I imagine there are probably many more people like you and Oscar than most folks suppose. But they're living as brothers, or sisters, or cousins, or very good friends, on their own homesteads and going into town every day like everyone else, doing their work and contributing to the society that hates them. But inside the walls of their own homes, they're loving each other and giving each other as much pleasure as they can, in order to make up for that."

We looked at each other for a long time, and I reckoned she was probably right.

"But Oscar...well, he's lookin' for his uncle, and maybe he'll wanna stay with him instead a me," I said quietly, voicing my main worry to the woman who'd done so much for us both.

She smiled in a kindly way. "Oh, Jimmy. Do you honestly think that young man would give you up for someone he hasn't ever met? Even if they are family, you two are more than that by now. But you make sure he knows how you feel about him, and you tell him my advice about living your own private life together, beyond the interests of 'society'. All right?"

I nodded, hope blossoming for the future she described, if Oscar wanted that. "I will."

* * * *

Oscar rested like he was supposed to and got better and better. On our fifth day at Miss June's, I took him out to the barn to meet William and visit the horses.

"Oh, Sprite, I missed you!" Oscar said, wrapping his arms around his horse. "I'm sorry you saw that snake and it scared you so much you had to rear up. And, I reckon, you're sorry I fell off," he said, leaning his head against Sprite's broad gray neck while Sprite looked to see if he had an apple or a carrot. "Yeah, I got somethin' for you."

He brought out the carrot he'd brought, with permission, from Miss June's kitchen and gave it to Sprite, while I fed Dixie an apple.

"You're a good rider, Oscar," I said, because he was. I was amazed at how quickly he'd taken to it. "T'was simple chance Sprite got so startled, and you weren't expectin' it. You'll be more prepared now, if t'was to happen again, I reckon."

"Yeah, I reckon. Guess you gotta be prepared for all kinds of things out on the road."

I sighed, not looking forward to leaving for Port Essington in a few days. But there wasn't much in this here town we could do, and besides, Oscar was still fixated on finding his uncle.

"Are you two really sweethearts?" William asked Oscar.

Oscar glanced at me and winked at William. "Oh, yes, sir. That man is taken."

I laughed. "Yes, sir, I am, an' that's a fact."

William smiled and blushed. "Well, I think you look good together. It seems right to me."

"Thank you for sayin' so," Oscar said. "Jimmy says you're lookin' after our horses and the mule real good."

"I surely am doin' my best. I like workin' for Miss June. And I like bein' with the horses."

A thought occurred to me. I was almost afraid to ask but I needed to know, now that I thought of it. I scratched Dixie on the chin and looked at William.

"You ever have any trouble with the men that bring their horses to you, son?"

He turned red and looked away, giving me my answer.

284

"Sometimes. But Miss June'll ban 'em for life if they do anythin' to me. She tells 'em that right off, and they listen. She says she got employees to satisfy all their desires, and they got no excuse goin' after other things."

I was glad to hear that, but it still seemed William was in a vulnerable position out here all by himself. He must have seen my concern.

"Gus checks on me pretty often. And I got me a knife in my boot, Jimmy. One a them tries anythin' and they's gonna get a cut-up face—either that or lose their balls. Miss June gave it to me, and she told me to do that."

Oscar laughed loud and shook his head. "I reckon you can look after yourself pretty good, William."

"Yes, sir, I can. I learned to on the street, that's certain."

"I'll bet you did," I said, ruffling William's hair.

"G'on," he said, pushing my hand away and grinning. "Maybe you should take Oscar back to th'house and give him some lovin'. The way he's lookin' at you, with those moony eyes, looks like he might need it, now that he's well."

I laughed, my gaze going to Oscar, who was indeed looking at me like he wanted to climb into my lap—or bend o'er it. "I reckon you might be right."

Oscar grinned and there was a twinkle of mischief in his eye. "Let's go."

But when we got inside of Miss June's, he set me in one of the chairs in the parlor and told me to stay there.

"Why?" I narrowed my eyes, suspicious.

"'Cause I told you to. I got a little surprise for you, but you gotta sit there and wait for a bit." He looked real excited about something, and I couldn't guess what t'was.

"All right. I reckon I can do that."

I was alone in the parlor when a knock on the door sounded, so I got up t'answer it, thinking t'was probably a customer. But standing there were two men, who looked like they were ready for church rather than wanting a bit of slap and tickle.

"Good afternoon, sir. May I please speak with Miss June?" the taller man said. I noticed he was clutching a bible, and my hackles immediately went up.

"What for?"

The man smiled, but it held no warmth in it at all. "I'm sorry, but are you a client a Miss June's?"

"That ain't none a your business, I reckon."

He cleared his throat and glanced at the other man, who seemed to want to be anywhere else. "Well, if you would tell Miss June we stopped by, I'd much appreciate it. I'm Reverend Mallory and this is my assistant preacher, Mr. Desmond."

"I'll let her know," I said, aware that, generally, a reverend approaching a cathouse was intent on saving folks and increasing attendance at church — or wanting a donation. I didn't think Miss June or any of her girls were interested in that, but I'd tell her they came by, certainly.

"Thank you. Good day."

I closed the door and went back to my seat, feeling a little down now. Miss June's establishment had seemed like a different world to the real one, for a while. Now, it appeared the real world was knocking on the door like it tended to, with evil disguised as good, God-fearing men who only wanted more money in their pockets, and more power to influence folks when they had no business to do that. Most of them weren't speaking for God at all, but only for themselves, from my experience.

My brooding only lasted for a second, though, because down the stairs came Trick and Cal with mischievous smiles on their faces, leading another woman in a very fancy peignoir by the hand, toward me.

What in tarnation?

All kinds of scenarios flashed through my mind as I raised my hand and shook my head.

"Now hold on a minute, I got no interest in a woman, no matter how pretty you got her dressed—"

At that moment, they swung the girl toward me. She almost tripped o'er herself as she posed in front of me, her made-up face hidden coyly behind a large fan. Before I could process any of this, the girl spoke in a strangely familiar but not-familiar voice.

"Awe, shucks, a big man like you prob'ly got somethin' extra nice for a pretty girl like me."

She batted her darkened eyelashes at me and I almost fainted.

That voice…

The fan lowered and I almost had a heart attack, because staring at me out of that made-up face was a very familiar expression.

I squinted my eyes and backed up a step. "*Oscar*? What in *tarnation* are you *wearin'*?"

Cal giggled as Trick cursed and said, "Jesus, that were so good, Cal! You did Oscar up so good. Jimmy ain't never knew who t'was till just now!"

I stared at Cal then at Trick, both of them pleased as punch at their joke.

Oscar dropped his fan and stepped back, putting his hands on his hips and sashaying like he was born to it, while I gaped and examined him.

The black peignoir with gold embroidery was open in the front and spread wide by his stance. He had on a black, boned corset, that pushed his chest up like Cal had worn that first night. And he had a pair of frilly, white, women's bloomers on, and stockings, and a pair of men's boots. He was dressed exactly as Cal liked to be, as I'd secretly imagined, and I had to say, he looked pretty darn good in them clothes.

I'd always thought Oscar seemed like something in between a man and a woman, and these clothes brought that out in spades. He didn't exactly look like a woman. But the flesh above the corset bulged almost like small breasts, and his pink nipples looked scandalous, out in the open like they were, even though he was a man. He looked different, that was for sure, and it brought something out of him, the way he moved and preened and came up to kiss me on my cheek.

"You're a mighty handsome man, Jimmy Downing," he said softly.

"I—uh, I…don't know what"—I shook my head, unable to stop my gaze from going o'er him again and again—"I don't know what to say."

"Well? You wanna go upstairs with me?" Oscar said in a smoky, sexy voice. "I reckon I could use a good man like you up there."

Cal and Trick were trying not to laugh. I shot an accusing look at Caliope.

"*You* did this."

She blushed and looked down, then back up, and t'was fetching in a most singular way.

"Yes, Jimmy, I surely did. But Oscar asked for it. He came to me, I swear. Wanted to show you how sexy and sweet he could be, for the fun of it. Don't he look nice?"

I turned back to Oscar, who shucked off his peignoir, turned and slowly bent himself to pick up the fan he'd dropped, showing me and everyone else how nice he looked from behind in them things.

"Aw, shucks, I seem to have dropped my fan."

"Good lawdy, boy, stop this teasin'," I groaned, moving forward to shield his backside from prying eyes. I grabbed his hips and brought him standing up against me, sliding my arms around him and holding him close. My breaths came rapid at the feel of that corset around his middle, and his fine ass in women's bloomers against my hardening cock was a trip.

He snorted a laugh and wiggled that ass against me.

"Oh, my goodness, you seem to have a very big problem there, Mr. Downing. Maybe you can take me upstairs and we can see what we can do about that, hmm?"

I spoke in his ear, running my hands all o'er the silk of his corset and rutting against him. "I reckon that's a good idea. You're a very naughty boy, Oscar, gettin' dolled up in them pretty things to tease me. I reckon I should pull down those bloomers and tan your hide."

I heard a gasp behind me, from Cal probably, and a loud laugh from Trick. I didn't think I'd spoken loudly, but perhaps they'd heard what I'd said.

"You'd best go upstairs, the both of you," Miss June said as she came into the room, and took in what was happening pretty quick with her sharp observational skills. "Last thing I need is for this house to go up in flames."

I smiled at her o'er Oscar's shoulder and let him pull away and lead me toward the stairs.

"My, my," Miss June said, taking in Oscar in all his feminine glory. "You fit in very well here, my dearie. Now go give your man some attention, now that you're feeling better."

"Oh, I surely will, Miss June." He turned to address the others. "Now if y'all hear any strange noises from upstairs — like, say, spankin' and yellin' and whinin' noises, maybe some beggin' and pleadin' — y'all just ignore it, all right?"

"Ha!" Trick said, her cheeks rosy with amusement. "We're sure enough used to doin' that! G'on with you, now. Ride your cowboy into the ground, you hear me?"

"I surely will. Come on, Jimmy. We got some catchin' up to do."

I went with him, my brain still tripping at the way he was dressed and what it did to me. At the bottom of the stairs, I remembered the Reverend.

"Oh, Miss June? There was a Reverend Mallory and a Mr. Desmond here to see you a little while ago. I told them you were busy because they looked like bible pushers to me." I hoped I'd done the right thing.

Miss June rolled her eyes and made a face. "Thank you. They visit me every so often, lay out some bull about God and Jesus, and how I should close my doors and stop causing my girls to sin." She laughed and put a hand to her forehead. "It's not me forcing them to make money the only way they can. That's the men who are in charge of this world. I'm only making it safe for them."

"I reckon that's true," I said. "In fact, I know it is."

Trick laced Miss June's arm with hers. "You've done more for us, Miss June, than God or them preachers e'er would, an' that's a solid fact."

Miss June gave Trick a kiss on her cheek and gestured to me and Oscar. "Go on then and have some fun upstairs. We won't pay attention to any noises we might hear." She winked and Oscar pulled me after him.

When we got in the room, Oscar led me to the chair and pushed me down into it. When I started to protest, he held up a slim finger in front of his lips and shook his head.

"Shh, only sit there. I wanna put on a show for you, Jimmy."

My breaths were coming hard already at the sight of him and the thought of all the things we could finally get up to. My dick stood aching for him already. It'd been that way since he'd bent o'er in them bloomers.

"No. C'mere... I wanna pull them bloomers down and spank your naughty ass."

Oscar put a hand to his face, as if he was a lady and I'd shocked her. "My goodness. The mouth on you, Mr. Downing. Do you speak to all the girls that way?"

I laughed at him. He was so damn good at this. Who'd have thought it?

"No, I do not—only the ones that deserve it. Only the ones that wave their asses at me in fine company, tryin' to provoke me."

"Did I, Mr. Downing?"

"Pardon?"

"Did I...provoke you?" Oscar asked, his voice going deeper, as if breaking out of character.

"You surely did." I rubbed a hand o'er the bulge in my trousers. "This look provoked to you?"

He nodded then he frowned, and he looked so darn cute standing there in his bloomers and corset, with such a focused look on his face that I had to smile.

"Gosh darnit, Jimmy. I was gonna do a dance for you and everythin'. Now, I only wanna lay o'er your lap."

I shook my head and crooked a finger at him. "I don't wanna watch you dance," I said, sitting up straighter. "What I want, is to watch you wiggle and squirm o'er my lap. And I wanna slowly peel them bloomers down, so your bare ass shines in this lamplight while I'm pinkin' it up."

"Shit," he said, dropping his mouth open and letting his tongue coming out to lick his lip.

I raised my eyebrows and said his name in a firm voice. "Oscar."

His eyes went wide, and he made a sound that went straight to my dick.

"Get your smart ass o'er here and bend o'er my lap if you wanna spankin'. If you don't wanna spankin', I reckon you should pull down them bloomers and get onto the bed, because I'm gonna need to fuck you, whether we do t'other stuff or not."

"God, I love it when you talk like that."

"Get the fuck o'er here, Oscar."

"Yes, sir," he giggled, moving quick so he was near me in the blink of an eye. "Put me o'er your lap for a spankin', 'cause I been a very naughty girl."

I took a deep, shaky breath because I felt like I might pass out from the desire that surged inside of me. Then I wrapped my fingers around Oscar's slim wrist and pulled him across my knees.

He made a startled sound as he landed and put his arms out to brace himself against the floor. His long limbs stretched out beside me, and the legs of his bloomers rode up to expose the straps of the garters, that were fixed to the tops of his stockings.

I grasped the top of his bloomers in my fist, pressing him down on top of me, and groaned. "Fuckin' Christ, Oscar. I swear you're gonna kill me."

"I don't mean to. I'm just lyin' across your lap, like I'm supposed to be."

I made a desperate sound, letting go of the bloomers and reaching below to run my fingers under the black garters. "This is messin' with my mind. The fact you're wearin' these things... Oscar, it's so damn arousin'. I don't know why, and I don't fuckin' care."

He wiggled his ass and peered up at me, his hair falling in an adorable way. "I don't care either. Only tan my hide like you promised."

"I will. I will," I panted, feeling his hard nubby poking at me through his bloomers. I stopped playing with the garters and slid my fingers under the band of his sweet, white bloomers, pulling them slowly down o'er his ass and leaving them around his thighs. I could see the garters coming down from the corset now, and it looked even better than before.

"You are such a naughty, naughty boy, Oscar, dressin' up in these women's things because you knew it would drive me plumb mad." I rubbed my palm o'er his bottom, so pleased to be able to treat him like this again and give us both what we needed. "And Cal helped you get dolled up, didn't she?"

"You know she did."

"Yeah? Well, maybe I should give Cal a spankin' after I give you one."

"Oh, Jimmy. I'd pay good coin to see that," Oscar moaned.

"Really?"

"Well, maybe not, 'cause I declare I want you to myself. But, hell, the thought of it is sure settin' me on fire."

"I can feel that it is. I'm gonna spank you now," I said, my voice strangled.

"Do it o'er the bloomers first. I wanna see how that feels."

"I reckon you ain't makin' the demands right now. I need to spank your bare ass. Maybe I'll pull the bloomers up after and spank you again."

I stopped talking then and started spanking him—not too hard at first but building up to how we both liked it. Not as severe as the punishment I'd dealt him that one time, but hard enough that I had him wiggling pretty good and begging me to lay off and fuck him.

Which I did. I pulled him off my lap and dragged him to the bed, laying him down and pulling off them bloomers so fast that I almost ripped them. I shifted his knees up, so I could move in behind and push inside him, with the help of some of the saddle grease I'd kept near the bed, knowing it would soon be needed.

Oscar moaned. "Ah, fuck, Jimmy, yes. God, get in me. Come in me, *please*. I need you so bad."

I choked on my own breaths. "Goddammit, you feel so tight, so warm! Your ass cradles my cock so good. I wanna claim you. I wanna come inside you and be leakin' out after. God. God. *Jesus*."

I came hard, jerking into him like I was possessed, grabbing his hips with white knuckles. He didn't complain.

Through the haze of my pleasure, I heard him cry out and come beneath me, onto the sheets and probably on Cal's nice corset as well. We tumbled and finished together in a tangle of sweaty limbs and silk, and I reckon we'd not have an experience like that ever again.

Chapter Twenty-Four

Riding Out

T'was sad leaving Miss June's a few days later.

Cal let me keep the frilly white bloomers to dress Oscar in whenever he wanted. I folded them up nice and small, and stowed them away in my saddle bag, safe inside a big handkerchief.

Miss June pulled me aside while Oscar said his goodbyes to everyone.

"Jimmy Downing, I reckon there's a place in my house for you and Oscar, if you ever need it. I could use another strong man like Gus to help dissuade certain bible pushers and other undesirables to stay away. We don't usually have too much trouble with the locals — they accept us for what we are and ignore it — but those preachers have a way of thinking they have to do God's work as a part of their own faith. Even though, in my honest opinion, a good half of the world's troubles come from that."

I nodded. "I reckon you're right." I offered her my hand. "Miss June, thank you for everythin' you done for us. I am more than grateful. If we hadn't found this place, Oscar might be dead by now, or we'd have been robbed and set upon, at the very least, with him so vulnerable and me tryin' to look after him on the road."

Miss June ignored my hand and grabbed me into a big bear-hug. She was warm and soft, and t'was nice to feel how strong she was, too. She was a woman to be reckoned with, that's for sure, in mind *and* body, and I was proud to know her.

"Bye, Jimmy. You take good care of Oscar, now. But don't forget to spank him from time to time." She glanced at Oscar with a grin. "I suppose he needs it. And so do you, no doubt." She gave me a wink that made me blush.

"Yes, ma'am."

When I said goodbye to Caliope, I leaned in and gave her a sweet kiss on the cheek. She hadn't shaved for a couple of days and her whiskers were starting to grow in.

"Miss Caliope, I reckon you'll need to shave soon," I said, smoothing my fingers o'er her rough cheek and chin, staring into her wide blue eyes.

She smiled and placed her hand o'er mine. "Well, y'see, sometimes I want to be smooth-shaven, and other times I like to have a bit a rough there, to make my disguise even more allurin'. I reckon you understand that, from when we dressed up Oscar for you?" She batted her eyelashes at me. I felt my cock plump up and my cheeks flush.

I smiled. "Yes, miss, I reckon I do. You're a fascinatin' person, Miss Caliope, and I'm very glad to know you." I backed up and gestured to Oscar. "We'd best be goin' now. Figure we can make it to Port Essington in less than a week, if we get good weather."

"Did you pack those warm blankets I gave you, Jimmy?" Miss June asked. "The nights are getting colder and longer, as they do in October."

"Yes, ma'am. Thank you. We'll be all right. We can surely keep each other warm inside the tent at night," I said, looking at Oscar, who grinned.

* * * *

T'was nice to be on horseback again, though I was uneasy about the rest of our journey. Oscar was a fairly new rider, and something like what had happened before could happen again. At least at Miss June's, I knew he was safe and on solid ground.

But I couldn't think like that. We couldn't live our lives staying in one comfortable place and hiding out from the real world, could we? We had to get to Port Essington to find Oscar's uncle. I hoped to hell the man was there and hadn't gone someplace else, because I didn't feel like chasing Oscar's uncle around the whole country. If that were the case, maybe I could convince Oscar all we needed was each other.

The landscape in northern British Columbia was an extension of what we were used to, traveling through the Yukon — mountains and valleys, cut with rivers and streams. Water was always near unless one traveled high into the mountain ranges, which we avoided. T'was better to take a longer, circuitous route, than risk the treacherous heights where panthers roamed, and one misstep could mean the end of everything.

Our first night of camping, we were tired and sore from riding and the change from our sedentary habits, so we went straight to bed in the tent after supper. T'was warm enough, and those blankets Miss June had given us came in handy. I woke up a few times to the sounds of wolves howling.

The next evening, while we warmed ourselves by the campfire, I brought out the topped-up canteen of whiskey and poured us out a couple of mugs.

"To Miss June, pretty Caliope and saucy Trick. What a crew they were." I raised my glass and Oscar clinked his with mine.

"I'm almost glad I fell off my horse."

I narrowed my eyes at him.

"What?"

"Don't say that. You almost fuckin' died," I groused.

"Well, I didn't," he said, waving his mug. "I'm right here, alive and kickin'."

"Mm-hmm. Thanks to *them*."

"Thanks to *you*."

I shook my head. "If they hadn't been there…"

Oscar put down his mug and rose, stepping o'er to me. He gazed down with a fierce expression on his face.

"If they hadn't been there, you'd have figured out somethin' else. You got me all the way from where we were to that town, strapped like a sack of potatoes on Poke's back. I was blacked right out, Jimmy. I don't even know how you done it."

I shrugged.

"It's thanks to you I'm standin' here right now."

I gazed up at him. The fierceness on his face changed to something different.

"What?"

He looked me up and down, then slowly grinned.

"You know, we're really alone out here."

"Yeah. So what?"

He kicked at a rock in the dirt. "So…nobody could hear us if we wanted to get up to somethin'. Right?"

I squinted up at him. "You want a spankin'?"

Oscar shrugged, a blush coloring his cheeks. "I don't know. You got me rememberin' how good you are with a bit of rope and a saddle."

Oh Christ. I remembered that, too. The way the crotch of my trousers felt tighter, my dick remembered it pretty good.

"You want me to do that again?" I asked in a husky voice, my muscles tensing as if I'd have to chase him down to get him, when he'd probably willingly go o'er. Then again, a bit of a chase might be amusing.

Oscar thought for a moment. "Maybe. Maybe somethin' else. 'Cept I don't know what."

I scrabbled my feet in the dirt and stood up, so close I could smell his clean sweat. We'd had baths before leaving Miss June's, so we were still pretty clean compared to how filthy we'd be in a week.

"I got an idea, but you tell me if you don't like it. It's a bit strange," I admitted.

"Tell me."

"We spoke about wrestling one time. I'd kinda like to do that."

He grinned. "Oh, yeah?"

I nodded, my cock getting harder at the thought of holding him down, subduing him. Then I wondered if t'was right to react like that. I put a hand to my head, feeling a bit less eager now.

"What's the matter?"

"I prob'ly shouldn't like the feeling of capturing you and keeping you close, keeping you subdued, but I think I will. But then I— Am I like *them*?"

He came close and put his hands on the sides of my face, making me look at him.

"You ain't anythin' like them two."

"But I like to spank you and hurt you a little. And I reckon I'd like to chase you and bring you down and…and settle you, and" —I whispered the next part—"force myself into you. But that's…that's rape, and that's violating someone, and why do I want to do that?" I felt horrified and afraid of my desires, suddenly.

"That ain't rape." Oscar shook his head and licked his lips. "What we do together, it ain't the same. 'Cause I want it. And there's a stop word I can use, if I decide I don't want it no more. Right?"

I nodded slowly, trying to believe he was right.

He continued. "What you said there, a minute ago, about chasin' me and catchin' me? I really like the sound of that."

When I met his gaze, he was smiling and eager and had that twinkle in his eye I knew so well.

"You *ain't* like them outlaws. And *you* ain't an outlaw a t'*all* no more. You're a good man, Jimmy, and you're mine, and I'll make sure you don't do nothin' I don't agree to, even if it's a bit rough or it seems like force. You'd never force yourself on me, not really—not if I told you to stop and used my special word. *I know you.*"

I nodded, feeling better and knowing he was right. T'was only games we played that made us feel good, and there was nothing wrong with that.

He stood there rubbing my cheek with his thumb. My whiskers were growing, even though we'd both shaved back at Miss June's before heading out on the road. He winked at me.

"You wanna chase me?"

The way he said it in that breathy voice made my balls ache. I nodded, not saying anything. Then I met his gaze.

"I reckon I do."

He nodded, smiling like a mischievous prince. "Okay. I ain't gonna run too far or too fast. We'll keep this simple the first time, all right?"

"All right."

He let go of me and backed up.

"Bet you can't catch me," he said, then turned and ran in a circle beyond where the tent was set, and back around, while I stood there. As he got close, he lifted his arms in a questioning gesture and ran by, taunting me.

I watched him run. He was wearing the new clothes I'd bought him, minus the jacket since t'was warm near the fire. He looked good, and I liked to watch him move. Oscar had a grace to him — a fluidity of movement that I liked to watch — and I was watching it now.

"Come on! You gonna catch me or what?" he said.

I scratched my chin with a finger and took off my hat, slapping it against my thigh as if I was thinking about what I was gonna do, while Oscar ran around the campsite like a lunatic. Then I ambled o'er to my saddle laying on the ground, and picked up the coiled rope near it, stringing it out in my hands as slow as molasses.

When Oscar saw what I was doing, he slowed and righted the hat on his head. "Oh shit. You ain't gonna rope me, Jimmy?"

I smiled a devious smile, because that was sure what I was gonna do. I figured I needed to keep my skills sharp, and I might as well practice on him.

"Don't slow down, 'less you wanna make it easy on me," I said.

"Shit," he said again, and picked up his pace. But t'was too easy to land the lasso around him when he came near again. I pulled it tight and kept him in one spot, walking to where he struggled with his arms pinned, then fell o'er, onto the ground.

"Jesus. You got me good."

I looked down at him lying there, not struggling at all, only staring up at me like he wanted to be caught. I reckon he felt relieved, since he panted with the exertion after the lazy time we'd had in Telegraph Creek.

"I thought you were gonna chase me," he said.

"Changed my mind. Decided to rope you instead. Less work."

He laughed. "You gotta get this rope off me now."

"Oh, do I?"

I crouched down and loosened the rope a bit, so's he could move his arms and get out of it. He lifted it off him and tossed it to the ground.

"What are you gonna do with me? You decided yet?"

I nodded slowly and gestured to the tent. "I want you to get your ass in that tent, strip off your clothes and wait for me."

He stared at me for a long moment, deciding if he wanted to fight me or do as I'd asked.

I guess he was too tired from his running to fight and maybe too eager to find out what I was gonna do next.

"All right."

He turned and walked away from me, ducking into the shelter as I gathered the things I needed. I got the saddle grease and a softer length of rope from my bag.

I didn't want to use the rough lasso on his bare skin. The last thing he needed were rope burns to deal with on the road.

I ducked inside the tent and saw him kneeling there on the blanket, buck naked and quivering with excitement and anticipation. He didn't look up when I came in. He kept his eyes on the ground, and I reckon he was trying to show me he was gonna be a good boy and obey me.

I started looping the rope through my hands, while I stood there assessing him and deciding how I wanted to proceed.

"Oscar, you ever been hog-tied?"

He let out a breath and looked up, then, his eyes wide and mouth open. He seemed to process what I asked him then said, "Nope." He moved his gaze along my body and locked on the rope in my hands. "I reckon I'd let you do it, though."

I nodded thoughtfully, in no rush. The horses were taken care of, and I'd banked the fire. T'was a milder night than we'd been having, and we had the entire evening to ourselves, with only the owls watching.

"I reckon I want to hog-tie you right now. Then take my time havin' my way with you." I cocked my head and raised my eyebrows. "You on board with that?"

He nodded his head rapidly and made a little gasp before he said, "I reckon I'm on board with anythin' you wanna do to me."

"You remember your stop word?"

"Yes, sir."

"Tell it to me."

"Wh — whiskey. It's whiskey." His voice came out in breathy pants as his eyes widened and a darker flush crept up his neck.

"Yes, that's it. You tell me that word if you wanna stop this at any point, you hear? I don't care if it's because you're hurtin' too much, you've changed your mind or it's too much, in any damn way."

"God, look at me Jimmy," he said, leaning back and pointing to his nubby, standing against his belly and leaking. "Do I look like I have a problem with any of this?"

I smiled. "Well, not yet. I reckon you won't. I'm gonna try to keep everythin' nice and gentle, except you're gonna be tied up pretty tight. All right?"

He closed his eyes and nodded, swallowing thickly. "Yes, Jimmy."

"All right."

First, I got every single blanket and bit of padding we had to make a comfy little nest for Oscar, so's he wouldn't be strained too much beyond the confined position he'd be in. Then I spent the next twenty minutes rigging him up well and tight with the rope.

I had to figure it out, because t'wasn't as simple as hog-tying a calf, although it did remind me of that. Oscar was a similarly young animal, with gangly limbs, but he didn't bellow like a calf would — least not yet. He might when he got closer to his finish. That thought made me laugh to myself.

That was my goal, really. To get him to make that kind of primal noise when I got him off finally, after lots of teasing and tasting, while he couldn't do nothing about it.

Since I wanted access to his sex, both in front and behind, I made the necessary adjustments to the regular hog-tie method. Instead of binding his ankles to his wrists so that he was bent in a backwards bow, I kept him flat and bound his wrists together at the small of his back. Then I used a piece of rope to bind one calf to one thigh and repeated that on the other side. After that, I took a separate piece of rope and tied it between the wrist rope and each calf rope, so that Oscar was rendered immobile, but could open his legs as wide as he wanted or needed to, and I could play with him in those very tempting areas.

I thanked God them outlaws hadn't tied him up this way, so he had no terrible memories of it. If he'd had bad memories of this, I wouldn't have done it.

But Oscar was right. This was completely different from being strung up by two fellas who didn't give a damn about whether you lived or died, or suffered, or what not. Oscar was giving me permission to do this every second he didn't say that stop word of his, and I was grateful every moment that he trusted me enough to let me. Because when I was finished, and he lay there in the knotted ropes that squeezed his pale flesh in the most alluring places? T'was prettier than anything I'd ever seen in my whole life—and I'd seen a lot of things.

"Oscar. You look…" I didn't even know a word for how beautiful he was.

"How do I look, Jimmy?" he said, voice quivering, dark eyes gazing up from where he lay on his side on the soft blanket, his nubby pointing out at me with a drop of fluid at its sweet tip.

"I can't even—" I inhaled shakily and put a hand to my forehead. "I wanna eat you the fuck up, then fuck you so gentle it makes you cry with the pleasure of it."

He moaned and his eyes closed. He licked his lips and nodded. "Okay. I say hell yes t'all that. *Please.*"

I nodded, unbuttoning my vest then my shirt, taking both off and putting them aside. I left my trousers on for the moment, so's I could maybe keep my hands off myself for a bit. Before I started, I turned him carefully to arrange him on his side, so that I could access every little bit of him that I wanted to get to.

This was gonna be all about Oscar—about worshipping him from head to foot while he couldn't do nothing but lie still and feel it, and experience how much I loved him and wanted him on a physical and a spiritual level. I wasn't no good explaining these things in words, but I hoped I could do it with the way I treated him for the next hour or so.

Chapter Twenty-Five

Roped and Hog-tied

I started with soft, simple kisses all along his body. Like I'd said I would, I took my damn time, enjoying the taste of his smooth skin, the tickle of hair and the little sounds he made as I went along. I felt the tension rise in him and saw the way my attention affected him, whenever I glanced at his nubby. His eyes would open, then the lashes would flutter closed again. I knew I wasn't putting him to sleep, but into some kind of erotic trance, maybe. All I knew was that I loved every minute of it.

He did good at being quiet for a long while, but as I got closer to those spots where he was probably aching for attention, he started squirming and trembling – and begging me to hurry.

"Please. Please. I can't take this gentle teasin' no more."

"Oh yeah, you can. 'Cause I ain't nearly done yet."

He groaned and jerked against the ropes. "Jimmy…"

I chuckled and ran my hands up the insides of his thighs, beneath the taut ropes, my fingers spread and my palms sliding along until I had his pretty ass cupped in my hands. I used my thumbs to spread him, so I could see his sweet little hole.

"Jimmy!" he yelped.

I ain't even touched him there, yet, but he sounded so desperate.

"What?"

"Oh please. *Please.*"

I shook my head, clucking at him to be quiet while I made soft, slow movements with my thumbs around the edge.

"What do you want?"

"Only…touch me there…or lick me… Oh, hell," he panted. "I need you to do somethin' more. *Please!*"

"Hmm. But I'm likin' just doing this a whole lot," I said. "'Cause I can see you tense and quiver, and it looks so goddamn good."

"Fuck," he whined. "I swear, you're gonna kill me with this. Honest to God."

I laughed harder this time, then leaned close and swiped my tongue across his hole with a quick, firm motion.

He choked and struggled, the breath swooping out of his lungs so fast, followed by a long groan that was almost a yell. When I repeated the motion, he made the same noise. I glanced at his little nubby, as a stream of clear fluid strung out of him like spider webbing, glistening in the lamplight.

T'was my turn to have trouble swallowing. I made a desperate sound.

"Lookit that sexy little nubby of yours. Tryin' to stand tall and be a real cock. It's so fuckin' cute."

"Jimmy!" he yelped, as more fluid pushed out. I knew my words affected him deeply, and I kept at it.

"When is it gonna learn it ain't ever gonna be that? It's gonna be my little nubby to play with forever, while I get ready to fuck you with the *real* thing I got."

"Oh, fuck. You're gonna make me spill just with words, I *swear*."

I grinned and bent to attack Oscar's secret place with enthusiasm.

Now Oscar jerked under me, straining to stay still beneath the unrelenting eagerness of my onslaught.

"Oh fuck! Oh fuck!" he moaned, whimpering and gasping as I teased him hard with my tongue and mouth, even gave him a hint of teeth on occasion, enough to make him shout out in surprise. T'was a good thing he were bound tight, because if not, he'd have plumb wriggled right out of the tent, I figure. He both wanted it and didn't want it, because t'was teasing and tasting and nothing enough to give him what he really needed.

But what he really needed was pushing at my trousers, like t'was gonna break free of them if I didn't open them up. I kept eating at his ass as I scrabbled my fingers at my flies, opening them and pushing my trousers down enough to get some of the saddle grease and slick it on up. I couldn't hardly wait no more neither.

"Oh, fuck...Jimmy..." He was almost crying now, he was so desperate.

I backed off and used one of my grease-covered fingers to push inside his hole, so slowly that it about near killed him. He made a loud, long "Oooooh," sound and stiffened so quick that I looked at his nubby to see if he'd spilled by accident. But t'was only more of that clear fluid leaking out, like he was ripe for the fucking—and I knew he was. He was so ripe that he was about to burst.

But I'd said I'd be gentle, and I would be. While I got him ready with one finger, I curled around him and teased his balls with my tongue, running it up the side of the little, not-so-little thing, but avoiding the tip for now. I used a light pressure to tease him, while I added another finger in his ass and made things nice and loose for me to get in there.

"Oh my God. I think I'm gonna die now. Bury me under that pretty tree out there, all right? And tell Sprite I'll miss 'im." His voice was shuddery and shaky and interrupted with gasps and stutters. I heard a wolf howl in the distance.

"You're gonna be fine. You can take it."

"Jimmy…" He groaned, his entire body tensing and shaking. "If you don't come into me soon, this'll be all o'er."

I laughed, but it sounded more like a string of gasps. "O'er for you."

"Please! Please, I need you. Please…"

"All right. All right."

I crouched on one knee and a forearm, right up close behind him, using the fingers of one hand to spread his cheeks as I rested the head of my cock against his hole. I had to remind myself to go slow and gentle as I eased into him, barely enough to spear him with it. Then I stopped.

We trembled with the need for more, but I stayed still, and Oscar cursed me.

"You behave, Oscar Yates, or I ain't giving you more than this, and you'll have to find a way to complete yourself."

T'was an idle threat, but he stopped cursing.

I continued. "You lay still, and I'll continue. When you start strugglin', I'll stop. Suit yourself. And say your word if you don't like it."

Oscar nodded, his bound hands grasping and releasing at nothing, as I eased myself into him, going all the way while he lay quiet and still. One of my arms wrapped around his chest and held him tight, as I breathed hot in his ear.

"I love you so much, and this is my favorite fuckin' place to be. Inside you, feelin' you all around me, knowin' you can feel me so deep."

He whimpered and nodded. I slid my hand up his neck and o'er his chin until my fingers pushed at his lips. He parted his mouth and welcomed them inside, tonguing them and sucking them like they were candy.

"Oh fuck," I murmured, pulling all the way out then breaching him again and going deep. I liked that a lot, and so did he, I reckon, if the sounds he made were an indication. I did that so many times — so slow and leisurely — as if we had a thousand years to fuck and play together. I'd settle for thirty more with him.

Finally, after a good long time, I couldn't help moving faster. I fell into a quicker rhythm that felt so nice and good. Oscar moaned and sighed, his nubby leaking. I wrapped my fingers around it, and he about exploded right then, screaming and finishing like he never had before, and it seemed to go on forever. I thrust a few times, hard, and let go inside him, trembling and moaning, and clutching onto him like he might float away from me if I let him.

And I wasn't ever gonna do that.

* * * *

The next morning, when we were getting the horses ready, Oscar turned to me and said, "I ain't never been loved the way you loved me last night. I never thought anythin' could be like that. I feel like — " He paused to think o'er what he was going to say. "I feel like we were the same person for a little while, y'know? Sounds strange, but I felt so close to you."

I nodded. "I know. I felt that, too." I glanced at him as I tightened the belt on Dixie's saddle. "Did you like bein' roped up like that?"

Oscar nodded, gave me a wicked smile. "I reckon I loved that. I'll be your roped calf anytime you want, Jimmy. If you're gonna treat me like that, you can rope me up anytime, anyhow, anyway."

I couldn't hide the grin that broke out on my face as I swung up on Dixie's back. "Good. 'Cause I got lots of rope and lots of ideas."

Oscar mounted up and tipped his hat to me. "I know you do, Jimmy."

* * * *

The next few days were a mix of hard riding and hard relaxing wherever we decided to set up camp. We kept hearing wolf howls, especially at night, but we hadn't caught sight of a one.

"It's almost as if they're following us," Oscar said, staring into the darkness. "Sometimes I fancy I can see a pair of glowing yellow eyes, but then I blink, and they're gone."

His words made me nervous, because I'd felt the same way for a while now. The gray wolves that roamed these lands were large, viscous beasts — strategic pack hunters that planned their kills and worked together to vanquish their prey. Sure, we had guns and horses, so we were probably safe. Still, if a large pack decided you were dinner, it could be a nasty fight.

"It'll be nice to get to town, that's for sure," I said. "I don't really know what to expect, but for sure there'll be people, shops and saloons, hopefully. God, I could use a visit to one of them. It's been a while."

We were too tired to get up to much, but t'was nice sleeping under the warm blankets Miss June had given us, with Oscar close in my arms. In the morning, we found time to get each other off quickly before heading out, and we hoped we'd have time for more leisurely lovemaking once we got to Port Essington.

The plan was to find a hotel and get a room, then start looking for Oscar's uncle. If I looked deep into my heart, I kind of hoped we wouldn't find him right away, so's we could spend a few nights holed up, the two of us, in our room, getting cleaned up in one sense, but keeping things filthy in another.

Then again, we realized we wouldn't be able to do some of the noisier things we liked to do together, so a couple of nights before I expected we'd ride into Port Essington, I put Oscar across my saddle again and spanked his pretty ass until he finished on the smooth leather. Then I made him lick it up like before and suck me off. Maybe t'wasn't very romantic, but it worked for us.

The next morning, we packed up early and headed out. We were about a day out of Port Essington, though I imagined we'd have to camp for another night before we made it.

While we rode beside the river, in a deep valley between two mountains, I saw the first one. T'was only a gray blur to the left of us, but it sent a chill through me.

"Oscar," I said.

"I seen it. There's more," he said, voice sharp with fear.

"Where?"

"Behind us. Look."

I turned my head, keeping Dixie to a calm trot because I didn't want to show them any fear. I didn't want Oscar to know how scared I was, either. Especially when I caught sight of the three large wolves loping along a good distance behind us.

"Shit," I said, turning forward as my heart started to pound. If they had us surrounded, which is what packs of wolves generally did to their prey, we could be in serious trouble.

"Oscar," I said again.

"Yes, Jimmy?"

"I'm gonna need you to stay as calm as possible, so Sprite don't get any more spooked than he already is. I reckon these horses knew the wolves were there before we did."

"Yes, sir."

"I wondered why Dixie's gait was jerky. Now I know."

"How many are there?" Oscar asked, his back ramrod straight and his eyes wide. "I saw four so far."

I'd seen another two o'er to the right of us by then, but I didn't tell Oscar. I forced my voice to be steady and low, though I felt like yelling out a warning.

"This is what I need you to do. You keep Sprite with me, y'hear? Stay as close to me and Dixie and Poke as you can. If we get split up, those wolves may see their chance. Together, we're more of a threat to them than they are to us."

"Okay." He didn't sound too sure of himself.

"You can do it. And Sprite'll wanna stay close to us, anyway, so just let him."

"Yes, sir."

"And I'll tell you when we're gonna go faster, yeah? For now, we're gonna keep at this pace. When we get closer to the trees, I'll tell you to go. Then you kick that horse and make sure he keeps up with us, you hear?"

"Yes, sir, I will. I'll do my best."

I thought I'd seen a couple more wolves to the left, and the three behind us were gaining ground. We were out in the open still, and I didn't want to make it a chase yet. I figured, once we got closer to the trees, we could lose 'em.

"What about your gun?" Oscar said.

"I ain't got enough bullets to kill them all. We're better off getting to them trees. Then maybe, I can try to shoot some of them."

We were about a hundred meters out when a howl from ahead of us pierced my spine like a splinter of ice, and I shivered. The other wolves joined in. It sounded like more than I'd expected. Seemed like a cacophony of creatures, and the dread in my belly felt like a lead ball.

I glanced behind us and saw the wolves were almost abreast of us, now. It took all I had to hold Dixie to a trot, and Sprite's eyes had gone wide and frantic. We couldn't wait any longer.

"Go!" I yelled to Oscar, as I kicked Dixie into a canter, then a gallop, and held tight to Poke's lead rope, so if he bolted, I'd still have him.

But Sprite shot out ahead of us, Oscar unable to hold him.

"Shit! Oscar, hold on! Don't you fall off!" I yelled, urging Dixie to catch up. She tried her best, but Sprite was out of control, racing toward the cover of the trees. For a second, I thought he'd make it. We could catch up, and we'd all be okay.

Then a gray form blurred out of the trees up ahead, and Sprite swerved to the left and turned, racing back in the other direction, which was the worst thing he could have done. Oscar clutched the saddle and bent close, holding for dear life to Sprite's sweaty back, as the pack of wolves converged on them.

Dixie had seen the trees and was trying to get to them, ignoring Sprite and Oscar when they went past us. My frantic breaths hurt my chest as I pulled on the reins and yelled at her to slow down and turn. We had to go back for them. I had the rifle, and I planned to use it. But first, I had to turn her.

Poke had seen the shelter ahead and pulled hard on his lead rope. I let him go and watched him streak ahead as I pulled hard on Dixie's mouth with the reins.

By the time I'd brought Dixie around in a wide arc, away from the cover of the trees she so desperately wanted, t'was to see a wolf grab Sprite's hind leg in its powerful jaws. The horse screamed, its eyes crazed with fear and pain, and stumbled, as Oscar tumbled off his back and landed in the dirt.

At that moment, I feared he was done for. I scrabbled for the gun on my saddle. But the wolves ignored Oscar in favor of the larger meal, and Sprite went down with the whole pack on him, the sounds of his shrieks echoing in my ears as Dixie and I thundered toward Oscar.

I had to give up on the gun in order to get to Oscar as quick as I could.

He pushed himself off the ground, and I swear, he was about to run back to that horse when I blocked him with mine.

"Get up here! Now!" I said, reaching down and extending my arm. He hesitated for one short second as the snarls of the wolves, the snapping of their jaws, the tearing of horseflesh and the howls of his dying horse blended together. Then, with a sob, he grabbed my hand so I could haul him up on Dixie behind me.

"Come on, girl. Go!" I said, and turned her toward the trees. To Oscar, I said, "Hold on to me, tight! I won't lose you — not now, not after everythin'," I said as I pulled his arms around me and felt his trembling body cleave to me.

There was no point in getting my rifle out and shooting those wolves. Sprite was dead, his screams silenced and only the horrible sound of bones cracking under fierce canine jaws remaining.

We raced to the trees, and by the time we were well-hidden from the pack of wolves, they'd be gorging themselves on Sprite anyway and would hopefully leave us be.

We were able to round up Poke, who had made it into the trees before we did and didn't get far before the load on his back slowed him down. We got as far from the scene of Sprite's untimely demise as we could, before we camped for the night. I tied Dixie and the mule to a tree, right by our tent, so's they'd be safe, and we'd hear if any wolves came close. I figured after the events of the day, they'd let us know pretty quick if they felt threatened at all.

Oscar sobbed in my arms about the loss of his horse and about being sure when Sprite went down that t'was the end for him as well, and he'd never be with me again. I felt the truth of that fear, and thanked God, or whoever was looking down on us, that he'd been spared, even though we'd had to pay a dear price.

* * * *

The terrain became more uneven as we neared the coast — and the weather more variable. The day we rode into the town of Port Essington was windy, wet and cold, and we were glad to be back in civilization.

Not to mention, t'was an appealing spot. Even in the middle of a downpour, we could appreciate its beauty, settled between the water and the mountains. The smell of fish and the sea pervaded the air, and the docks were busy with workers scaling and filleting the fresh catch.

We were tired and soaked to the bone, shivering with the cold. We needed to find somewhere to put up.

The first hotel that looked amenable, we turned in and had Dixie and Poke stabled and looked after, as we got ourselves a room for the night.

"I think you'll be comfortable here, gentlemen. Did you want to dry off upstairs before you come down to dinner? It's served between six and eight in the dining room."

The dapper gentleman gestured to the left of us.

"Thank you. That'll be fine."

Oscar stepped forward. "We're actually on the lookout for someone who's supposed to live in this town. Could you tell us the best place to start if we're hopin' to find a man? He's my uncle."

Oscar's excitement and hope was palpable, and I prayed we'd be able to locate him. But I had my doubts. Times were hard, and people didn't always stay in the same place for long.

The man nodded. "I think Jensen's Saloon would be the place to start. They see most of the men in town and know where they live. Unless this fella you're looking for is a teetotaler?"

Oscar shrugged. "I don't really know much about him, but we can start there. I reckon the church would be the place to try if the saloon ain't heard of him."

"Yes, that makes sense. Here's your key, gentlemen. I hope to see you down for supper."

"Thank you," I said.

The proprietor — at least I assumed that was who he was — was a very nice, older man who seemed glad to assist us. I had a good feeling about the hotel and the town itself.

"Thank you kindly."

A young maid went up with us and started a fire in our room. I gave her a coin for her assistance.

"Thank you kindly, mister. If you need anythin' else, please ask downstairs."

Pretty much everything we owned was soaked, so we stripped down and set our things to dry by the fire before we headed down to supper.

Oscar was so excited to start looking for his uncle that he could barely sit still. At least it seemed to distract him from the horrible events of the previous day.

"I know you're eager to find this man," I said, "but what're we gonna do if we *do* find him?"

"Whataya mean?"

"I mean, are you gonna go live with this uncle of yours? I doubt he's gonna want me taggin' along, and we can't explain how it is between the two of us, can we?"

He frowned. "I didn't think about that. I was so focused on making it here that I didn't truly consider what was gonna happen next, beyond findin' my uncle and tellin' him who I am."

"Yeah? Well, I've thought about it," I said softly. "I reckon if you wanna go live with your uncle, you have every right to. And it would be a comfortable life for you, that's certain, at least, if he's doing well and he's a nice person, which I reckon he will be." I looked down at the wrinkled, waterlogged skin of my bare feet, that I'd moved close to the fire. "If he's related to you, he'll be a good man, I reckon."

Oscar shrugged. "I don't really know nothin' about him, Jimmy. But I'm hopin' he'll be a good man. I'm hopin' he'll want to meet me."

"I'm sure he will," I said, even though I had some doubts about it.

Surely, most men would be glad to find out they had a nephew like Oscar, but anything was possible. This man could be a derelict, for all we knew — or a drunken disaster.

Chapter Twenty-Six

Port Essington

While we ate our supper in the dining room, I managed to convince Oscar to wait until morning to search for his uncle. We were exhausted and emotionally wrecked from the loss of our horse and still trying to get warm. I didn't relish leaving the comfort of the hotel on what could be a wild goose chase.

But as tired as he was, Oscar had trouble getting to sleep. He tossed and turned, even after I'd settled him with some leisurely attention that he offered to reciprocate.

"All right. I ain't gonna say no to that," I said, pleased to be in a comfortable, safe bed after camping in the wilderness and being chased by a pack of wolves.

When he began, I closed my eyes, grateful to be in this warm room with the red glow of the fire in the grate, and Oscar treating me so kindly.

After a time, he pulled off me and asked, "Jimmy?"

"Yeah? You wanna stop?"

He laughed. "Hell, no. I wanted to ask you somethin'."

"What's that?" I reached down and ran my fingers through his soft hair, determined to enjoy having him with me now and trying not to worry about what might happen the next day.

"Do you think you'll ever be ready for me to be the one to…" He looked down shyly, grinning with some mischief. "I mean, you don't have to do that. I'll understand if you always want to do it to me. I don't mind that one bit. I'm only wonderin' if you thought, you might want to—"

"Yes. Yes, I do," I said, smiling down at him. "I'd trust you to do that to me, Oscar."

"You would? Truly?"

I nodded. "I ain't sayin' it don't scare me a little. But after seeing how much you enjoy it when I do it, I reckon I'd give it a try. Luckily, your little nubby isn't all that intimidatin'," I said, with a twinkle in my eye. T'was smaller than average, true, but t'was still bigger than anything I'd had in my ass before. "I ain't quite ready tonight, though."

He laughed and rubbed his barely stubbled cheek against my dick, making me groan. "Yeah, I know." He started to say something else, then thought better of it and went back to teasing my cock.

I circled my fingers under his chin to make him stop and look at me. "You were gonna say somethin' else."

"I was gonna ask if you might be okay with me touchin' you there tonight? But if you really ain't, say so. It's just that…if you ain't never had a cock there, a finger can feel almost as good, and I can show you why I like it so much."

I stared at him, looking so shy and bashful, asking me that—his soft brown eyes glowing. "Are you askin' if you can put your finger in my ass, Oscar Yates?"

He grinned, pleased as punch that I was taking his request so lightly. "Yes, sir, I reckon I am. T'would be an honor."

I raised my eyebrows. "An *honor*?"

"Yes, sir. For a lowly fella like me to give you an introduction to that kind of pleasure? Well, I can hardly wait."

He certainly did seem to be excited about it. I supposed I was slightly less so, but I figured I could let him and see how it felt. I knew that if I decided I didn't like it at all, Oscar would stop.

"All right."

"All right?"

"Yes, Oscar. You can do that, if you promise to use the saddle grease — *lots* — be very gentle and stop if I ask you to."

"Of course, Jimmy. Of course, I will. Wait there, an' I'll get the grease." The excitement in his voice made me smile.

I lay there, watching him move around the room naked, his pale skin glistening in the lamplight. He found the tub of grease pretty quick in my saddle bag that I'd brought in with us.

I noticed his nubby hardening again, and I hoped to God we could get some sleep after he tended to me, because I'd almost been drifting off before he mentioned about his finger, though that would've been the height of rudeness. Now I was awake and kind of looking forward to it, though I'd never had anything stuck up my rear and never imagined I'd want to.

But the way Oscar acted when I fucked him made me want to see what all the fuss was about. Miss June said lots of married men did it to their wives, so there must be some reason. I reckon they wouldn't let their husbands do that if there wasn't some pleasure in it for them. Then again, what did I know about married people? All I knew was that when I did that to Oscar, whether t'was my fingers or my cock, he got such enjoyment from it. So, I guess I could suspend my doubts and fears, and let him open me up down there, and see what t'was like.

He started to suck and lick my cock again, probably to distract me from what he was about to do.

"Now, I'm gonna start touchin' you" —*lick*—"down there, Jimmy" —*suck*—"but slow and gentle and only on the outside for now." He hefted my balls and slid his tongue up my taint, making me choke on a groan. "And I'll keep suckin' and lickin' you while I do it, and we'll see how it goes."

I nodded, unable to speak.

I felt his slippery finger start playing around at the bottom of my balls, circling and stroking—gradually getting closer to the spot that was his goal. When he finally touched me there, the pleasure spiked in me, and I had to stifle a cry.

Holy hell. If it felt so good when he only used a light touch, what the hell would it feel like when he did *more*? My breathing ramped up as I began to be less afraid and more eager for it.

He stroked my hole again and again, at the same time as he slobbered o'er my cock the way he knew I liked. T'was almost poetic, the way the tip of his finger finally slipped inside me like t'was nothing, but it set off an explosion of nerve endings inside me.

I cried out and half sat up, surprised at how good it felt.

"You okay?" Oscar asked, keeping his finger in me, but not moving it, so's I could get used to the strange sensation.

"Yeah," I said, staring at where his hand was and meeting his pleased gaze with my surprised one.

"Does it hurt?" he asked.

"Nope," I said, shaking my head slowly.

"Does it feel good?"

"Yeah," I admitted, then gasped as he wiggled it a bit. I let myself fall back to the bed. I parted my thighs as I gave myself up to him and whatever he wanted to do.

I felt...subdued and so vulnerable...but in such a good way, since t'was Oscar, and I'd agreed to it. T'wasn't a feeling I was used to.

Then Oscar licked my cock from root to tip, sliding that finger deep at the same time.

I arched off the mattress, then settled back as fireworks exploded in my body and brain.

"*Jesus*, Oscar. *Fuck*!" I swore, widening my thighs even more, and pushing my ass against his hand.

"Hold on. I wanna try somethin'," Oscar said, breathless.

"You *are* tryin' somethin'. What else you wanna do?" I panted, still nervous but more amazed than anything.

"This," he said, turning his finger and pressing against some secret spot that lit up like an electric storm and sent lightning to all my limbs.

I made a strange sound, and I felt my cock pulse fluid out of the tip. "God. Oh my *God*."

"I thought you weren't a religious man?"

"I ain't. But *Jesus Christ*, Oscar. That was..."

326

He did the same thing again and I moaned, then whimpered. "Oscar... Oscar..."

"I'm gonna make you shoot, and it's gonna feel so good everywhere—not only in your dick. Your body's capable of things you haven't even imagined."

I couldn't speak, just stared with wide eyes at the low, stained ceiling, while Oscar swallowed my cock and moved his finger inside me. In a moment I was o'ercome with waves of bliss that moved through my whole body, as my dick spurted inside his mouth and he stroked me with his finger on the inside. My body convulsed with it, while Oscar held me down and swallowed my spend. I made a low keening sound as it took me, and when the sensations subsided, I felt like I'd seen God, sure as anything.

I couldn't talk for a little while after. I could only stare at Oscar as if he'd revealed a wonderful secret.

"I promise you, Jimmy, that when you're ready for it, my little nubby will feel even better in your sweet backside than my finger."

I trailed my gaze from his face down to where his nubby was standing again. I reached out with my hand and circled it lazily, too tired and o'ercome to do much else.

He pushed my hand away. "Don't worry 'bout me. Lie still like you are, and I'll take care of myself, while I think about how good it's gonna feel to fuck you some day."

I gave him a soft smile as he got some more grease and stroked himself to his finish, aiming his nubby so his spend landed on my hip while we gazed into each other's eyes.

When he was done, he gave me a saucy wink, then bent to lick me clean. I watched him for a moment before closing my eyes and drifting into darkness.

* * * *

"Where did he say this saloon was?" Oscar asked, as we walked along the street, trying to avoid the rush of people moving about. T'was a little like Dawson City the way t'was so busy, but the people here seemed more gracious and less desperate.

"Is it me or are there a lot of Easterners in this town?" Oscar asked, gazing about us at the people. "Seems strange, but only 'cause I'm not used to it, I s'pose. There weren't a lot of them up north in Dawson, but we did see one or two."

I nodded. "Does seem to be a lot. I guess they come on boats to this part of the world, and find a way to make a living with the fish factories here." I'd noticed a lot of Easterners working on the docks.

The town wasn't as dirty as Dawson City neither, though it smelled like fish from all the canneries. I reckoned I'd get used to it if I stayed more than a few days.

I checked the street sign at the corner. "This one. He said t'was on Second Street. Here." I pointed at the sign. "I think he said to go right?"

"Yeah, that's what he said. It should be along here somewhere."

"There it is. Jensen's Saloon."

"You reckon it's open this early?" Oscar asked.

"Guess there's only one way to find out. Anyway, if it ain't, we'll come back later," I said.

"Sure enough."

But t'was open, so we went in. There weren't many customers yet, but a young man stood behind the counter.

"Howdy," he said with a smile. "What can I get you gentlemen?"

I glanced at Oscar, since he was the one on a mission. I figured he could do the talking.

"I'm looking for my uncle," Oscar said, stepping up to the bar and respectfully removing his hat. "The man at the hotel said you might know of him."

The young man frowned. "Well, my daddy might. I've only been working the bar for a couple of months. I'll get him."

"Thank you kindly," Oscar said, tipping his hat.

The young man returned with a middle-aged fella, who looked like he was angry to be interrupted but was covering it up in the interests of not offending new customers.

"Hello. I'm Timothy Jensen, the proprietor of this here establishment. What can I do for you?"

"Hello," Oscar said. "My name is Oscar Yates, and this here's Jimmy Downing. We traveled all the way from Dawson City."

"Well now. That's a mighty long way. What brings you to Port Essington?"

"I'm looking for my uncle," Oscar said. "You know of someone named Henry Purcell Yates?"

The proprietor's eyes narrowed and he glanced at the young fella, who quickly moved off and grabbed a rag to clean the bar top. Then the older man turned back to us and shrugged.

"I *did* know a Henry Purcell Yates," the man said slowly, "but he ain't alive no more."

Oscar's face, what had been filled with anticipation and excitement since we'd arrived, lost its color, and his eyes glazed o'er as Mr. Jensen explained how Henry Yates had killed himself with the drink o'er the death of his wife from consumption. He'd been gone a year.

"Thank you, Mr. Jensen. That was what we were tryin' to find out," I said.

"I'm sorry t'wasn't the information you wanted." He glanced kindly at Oscar, who seemed to have got lost in his own head.

I nodded, taking Oscar's elbow and leading him toward the door.

"C'mon," I said. "Let's go for a walk."

T'was a beautiful, sunny day, though t'was cold, and Oscar remained silent and only came with me because he was so used to it, I reckon. He stared straight ahead of him like he was in some kind of trance. I knew he'd pinned all his hopes on finding his uncle, but he must've known he wasn't completely alone in this world. He had me, and we had Miss June and Cal and William and all the girls what thought so highly of him in Telegraph Creek. I only needed to remind him of that. But maybe I oughta let him have some time to despair for a bit, too, so's he could process his disappointment then get o'er it.

I led him to a quiet place by the water, a little out of town, where we could sit on some rocks and look out at the pretty view. He didn't say anything for a long time. When he did speak, t'was in a soft voice that was barely there.

"I don't know what to do now, Jimmy. I set all my hopes on finding him and he's dead. All my family's gone now—every single one of 'em."

"Yeah, I know." I looked at him like I'd never seen him before. He was so goddamn handsome, and I think he'd growed up a lot since we'd left Dawson City. He looked like a man now, instead of a boy, even though he was the same age. It'd only been a month since I'd found him.

He kicked at the ground. "I feel so alone."

I stood up from my seat on the rock beside him. "But you ain't alone, Oscar. *I'm* with you."

He looked up at me. "You have to get back to Whitehorse, don't you? To get another wagon, and supplies to deliver back to your client in Dawson City?"

I took off my hat and slapped it against my thigh. "I reckon my client in Dawson City has figured out by now that I ain't comin'. I was supposed to have them supplies to him a couple of weeks ago."

Oscar stared at me. "You never told me that."

"It don't matter," I said firmly.

"But...that was your livelihood, wasn't it? You gave it up to bring me to this place?"

I shrugged. "You needed to find out if your uncle was still here."

He stared at me, some life returning to his eyes. "Jimmy, I didn't know you weren't planning to head straight back to Whitehorse. What're you gonna do now?"

I shrugged again, and glanced at him from under the edge of my hat. "Miss June told me somethin' before we left Telegraph Creek. She said you had to make choices about how you were gonna live if you were men like us, who enjoy being together the way we do, in the *way* we do." I stared at him head-on, to make sure he knew what I was talking about.

"I reckon she's right about that."

"She said you could choose to live the way society expected and lose what you had together or you could choose to live the way you wanted to live and keep that part of your life hidden and disguised. She said t'would be better to live with no apologies the way you wanted, but society weren't ready for that yet. Maybe it will be someday," I said. "Anyway, she gave me a lot to think on."

He glanced around to see if anyone was near, but t'was only the two of us.

"You wanna do that, Jimmy? You tellin' me you wanna make a life with me here? One that'll mean we can keep being together like we" — he choked back a sob — "like we *are*. Like we *love*?"

I nodded quickly. "Yeah, I reckon I do. I reckon I don't give a damn about society, 'cept to see if we can circumvent it somehow." I touched my pocket. "I still got most of Spook and Whitlaw's cash left. Now, I know it's dirty money, but I reckon they won't be lookin' for it once they find the two of 'em been murdered."

Oscar nodded, his face full of life again, and I was glad to see it. I figured both of us wanted to come together right then, but we couldn't, not out in the open like this. But we had a nice room in a hotel waiting for us.

"I tried to give Miss June money for lookin' after us so well, but she wouldn't take it. She said I should use it to set us up in Port Essington, if things didn't work out with your uncle."

He blinked quickly and even swept at his eye with his hand. "You reckon we should do that, Jimmy?"

I nodded, a strange sound coming out of my throat, like something between a sob and a laugh. "I reckon we should...if you want to."

"I want to," he said, without giving it any thought. "I *want* to."

* * * *

We spent the afternoon back at the hotel with each other, bathing and cleaning up, then getting *dirty* all o'er again like we tended to do. I was thrilled to pieces Oscar was on the same page as me, wanting to set up house like we were a married couple, except having to hide that when we were in town or in public.

"I reckon we can be cousins," I said. "That don't seem too farfetched."

Oscar frowned. "Except we already told Mr. Jensen we were lookin' for my uncle. Wouldn't he be your uncle, too, if we were cousins?"

"True, true."

"I mean, we could be good friends. I reckon there's lots of friends livin' together, what aren't gettin' up to what we are. I don't suppose anyone would question it, lest we give 'em a reason to."

"You don't think folks'll figure it out eventually?" I said.

"I don't think so. Long as you keep them moony eyes under control," he said, laughing.

"*You're* the one with moony eyes."

"Anyway, if they did figure it out, who the hell would have the courage to ask us if we were more'n friends? I suppose someone might, but then we'd deny it. If we're likeable enough, which we *are*, and if we don't come into town that often, which we *won't*, and if we don't cause no trouble, which we *won't*, I reckon folks'll leave us alone. Folks usually believe what's most convenient for them, anyway."

"I reckon that's true," I said.

I rolled o'er and pinned Oscar against the mattress. "You wanna do some celebratin' tonight?"

"I thought that's what we been doin' all afternoon?"

I grinned and kissed him gently. "I mean going to the saloon and gettin' shit-faced. Been a long time since I did that."

"I don't think I ever did that. Never had the money." Oscar shrugged.

"I reckon you don't hold your liquor good as I do, anyhow."

"Is that a dare, Jimmy Downing?"

"Maybe, it is."

Oscar grinned and picked up my hand from where it lay on the sheets. He kissed the back of it and gazed at me with glowing eyes. "Then let's go get drunk, Mr. Downing."

Chapter Twenty-Seven

An Unexpected Gift

We got dressed in our fine clothes that we'd had the hotel wash for us. I felt a bit o'erwhelmed with the idea of trying to make a life for the both of us there, when all we had was a wad of cash that was gonna dwindle pretty quick if we didn't find some kind of work. There was always the cannery, I supposed. Even though t'would be hard, manual labor with the smell of fish constantly about, t'was respectable work, at least. I figured I could do that, and Oscar could perhaps be a server in one of the hotels or restaurants. He was cute enough, and I figured he could learn to be polite so's he'd get lots of tips.

I reckon he'd be polite if he were being paid to be, and if I threatened him with a good hiding if he wasn't. Might be fun teaching him.

There was half the town in Jensen's Saloon when we got there. I felt a little strange with all the attention on Oscar and me, since we were so new to this small town. But we found ourselves a small table in the corner by the fire and started drinking. Soon enough, we were feeling pretty good and relaxed.

We'd had a conversation about how we had to watch what we said to each other in public, especially if we were gonna drink. We needed to remember to keep the special feelings we had for each other hidden. So, except for a couple of meaningful glances now and then, and one time when Oscar licked his lower lip purely for my enjoyment, we acted like two good friends having a much-needed jaunt after a long journey. Nobody had to know he probably still had some of my spend inside him or that I'd finished hard in his mouth while he'd stuck a finger in my ass. That was between the two of us, and I'd keep it a secret until my dying day if it meant we could continue with it.

"Do you mind if I have a seat?" The voice at my elbow startled me.

I gazed up to see the young fella we'd met yesterday, who'd been cleaning the bar. He took off his hat and extended his hand.

"I'm Carson Moore. Mr. Jensen is my boss. He told me to welcome you both to town and that he's real sorry about your Uncle Henry."

"I thank you kindly," Oscar said.

I told Carson to go ahead and take a seat at our table. He was a plain-looking fella, but I liked the way he showed a genuine interest in us and how his apology about Oscar's uncle seemed sincere. He was older than Oscar, but not by much.

"Ain't you gotta work the bar?" I asked.

He smiled. "I'm done my shift. Grayson, he took o'er." He gestured to the bar where an older man was pouring drinks and taking orders.

"You wanna drink?" I asked.

"Sure."

"Beer?"

"Yes, sir."

"Oscar? You want a whiskey?" I said, deliberately using his stop word, so's he'd get a kick out of it. I liked having all these secrets that only we knew the meaning of. Made life a little more interesting and fun.

He did blush a little. "Naw, I'll have another one of these," he said, raising his empty tankard. I took it and my own up to the bar.

"Three ales, please, and thank you," I said, starting to feel good after a day of resting and fucking, and now having a couple of beers in my belly. The future that stretched out before me and Oscar was uncertain, but I felt as long as we were gonna be together the way we wanted, we could do anything.

When I got back to the table, Carson and Oscar were speaking about Oscar's uncle, and how he was before his wife got sick.

"He was a good man, I'll have you know. I knew him for a long time, since we worked together in the cannery for a number of years."

It seemed like Oscar was glad to hear anything about his Uncle Henry, but finding out he was a good man was something extra special.

"Tell me about him—like what he enjoyed doing and what his thoughts were about stuff. I don't know." Oscar laughed. "I lost everybody I ever cared about, 'cept Jimmy here, so I wanna know."

Carson smiled. "Well, he loved Annie, that's for sure. He married her when she was outta school. He was a good bit older than she was, but he courted her for a long time, with her family's blessing. Guess he figured that since she was so much younger, he'd be the one to go first, y'know? When she took sick, he looked after her as well as he could, but he had to keep workin' to put food on the table. Her sister helped when she could, but t'was a long time when Annie was sick and Henry had to leave her to go to work. He hated that so much. In the end, his boss give him two weeks off to watch her die, and that was that. Once she was gone, he didn't have no interest in anythin' anymore — not working or eating or nothin'. He'd go to work, but he was dead inside, and nobody could break through his grief. Then he'd come spend his evenings here, gettin' drunk till he stumbled home."

"Where did he live?" I asked.

"Well, that's the thing I wanted to talk to you fellas about. T'was a house outta town, about an hour's walkin', maybe half on horseback or in a wagon."

"He'd walk an hour, drunk, to get home from here every night?" I asked.

Carson nodded. "He did that for a while, till the weather got too cold. Then he'd come into town and buy enough whiskey to drink at home. They found him in the spring, an' he looked like he'd spent most of the winter surviving on nothin' but that, 'cause he was so skinny. He must have froze to death and nobody checked. They found his horse in the stable, too, starved to death." Carson cleared his throat and looked at the table. "Both me and Mr. Jensen feel pretty terrible about that. We never thought t'was so bad, and we thought Annie's sister was still in touch with him."

Carson looked ashamed and a bit guilty, but also genuinely sad. "I reckon we had our own problems, but I am sorry neither of us thought to go and see how he was. In the spring, we realized it'd been some time since he'd come into town, and we went out there. Not a very nice thing to find a man and his horse that plumb died in the middle of winter, 'cause nobody thought to go check." He rubbed a trembling hand o'er his face and looked at Oscar. "Anyway, I wanted to tell you that and say I'm sorry."

Oscar nodded sadly. "I reckon t'wasn't your fault. Sounds like he didn't have nothin' left to live for."

"I reckon." Carson cleared his throat again and looked back and forth between the two of us. "You fellas gonna stay in Port Essington? Or you headin' back out on the road soon?"

I glanced at Oscar. "I reckon we're gonna stay. We went through a lot to get here, and I think we'll try to make a go of it. We're used to the harsh cold and darkness up north. Might be nice to spend some time in a warmer spot.

Carson nodded. "Well, I reckon I should tell you that Henry's homestead's still there. I suppose it belongs to you now, Oscar, if you even want it. The place is pretty run-down and the land o'ergrown. But it's there, if you want it. Nobody else in town does, 'cause it's got such a bad history. But I reckon, with a bit of love and forgiveness, it could be a real nice place."

I felt a strange feeling in my chest, like a sudden breaking of the sun through the clouds, when I realized what Carson was saying. I saw Oscar sit up straighter and lean in to speak.

"You mean there's a house near town that's mine if I want it?"

Carson laughed. "Well, 'house' may be stretchin' it. It used to be a house, but it needs so much fixing up it sure ain't what it used to be. Between working and looking after Annie, Henry'd been neglectin' the place for a while.

I cleared my throat, excitement bubbling up inside me. "Can we see it?"

"Sure. I can show you tomorrow."

We didn't end up getting shit-faced. We walked back to the hotel in a daze and not speaking of the hope we suddenly had for a future there.

As we ambled along a road that angled up toward the hotel, with a view of the harbor and the fish plants, we noticed a young lad standing against the wall of a barber shop.

"Hey, mister, you want a kitten?" he said, holding up a tiny ball of fluff that made a pitiful mewl as Oscar's eyes widened. He glanced at me quick with a hopeful expression.

I was about to say, 'no thanks', but the way Oscar was, silently pleading with me, made me pause.

"How much?" I said gruffly, hardly believing I was considering this.

"Free to a good home, mister. Though, I won't refuse a penny or a nickel." The boy held the little gray-and-white kitten up in one hand, and Oscar took it and pressed it to his chest.

The deal was done. That kitten snugged right under Oscar's chin, and I fished a nickel out of my pocket.

"Here. Thanks," I said. I supposed t'was fitting, since Oscar had just found out his uncle had died and recently lost his beloved horse.

"Is it a boy or a girl?" Oscar asked.

"She's a girl...and feisty. My pa wanted me to put her in a bag and throw her in the river, but I reckon she's better off with you."

Oscar's hand tightened o'er the kitten, and I knew there was no getting her away from him now.

"She weaned?"

"Yep. I been givin' her fish and milk, and she likes that. But I reckon she'd eat any kind of meat, long as t'was soft. She's about eight weeks old now."

I nodded. "Well, thank you."

"No problem, mister. She'll be a good mouser, like her ma. Bye now. I gotta get back before my pa figures out that I didn't do what he said." The boy took off down the street the way we'd come.

I met Oscar's gaze. "She's your kitten. You gotta look after her, now."

"Oh, I will, Jimmy. I promise."

The kitten mewed again, resting its tiny paw against Oscar's cheek, and I couldn't help smiling.

"See? You like her," he said. "Don't say you don't."

I held my hands up in the air. "I ain't said anythin' about it. She's cute, that's for sure. Hope we can sneak her into our room."

"I'll hide her in my jacket," Oscar said, grinning.

It worked, and we were able to smuggle the kitten upstairs. When we got to the room and shut the door behind us, Oscar lifted her out of his jacket and plopped her onto the bed.

The gray kitten sat there, bewildered for a second, before standing on wobbly legs and making her way back to Oscar.

I grinned, taking off my jacket and hanging it on the back of a chair. "She wants her pa."

Oscar gazed at me, then back at the kitten. "I'm her pa?"

"Soon as you picked that kitten up, she claimed you, I reckon. You belong to her, now."

Oscar scooped the wee thing up and brought her to me. "Maybe I'm her ma, and you're her pa."

I smiled. "Maybe that's so."

"We're a family now, ain't we?"

"Sure," I said, wrapping my arms around Oscar and the kitten.

"I'm gonna name her Sprite, Jimmy," he said quietly. "It's only right."

I nodded, nuzzling Oscar's neck as softly as if I was a kitten looking for warmth and comfort. "I think that's a real good idea."

She slept with us in the bed, curled up under Oscar's chin. We'd put a bit of dirt into a little box in the corner and she did her business in there. And I'd gone down and paid for a supper of chicken and potatoes for me and Oscar that I'd brought up to the room, and she'd eaten slivers of the chicken from Oscar's fingers, a low rattling in her throat the whole time.

In the morning, with little Sprite tucked under his arm inside the jacket, Oscar walked with me to meet Carson.

"Good mornin'," he said, smiling and shaking our hands. "I told Mr. Jensen I was taking you out there, and he was pleased. Neither of us are sure you're gonna want to take it on, but it makes sense for you to see the place. Maybe if you're brave enough to put in a lot of work, somethin' good can come out of Henry's death."

"Thank you kindly. We're lookin' to set up near town, so this might be the perfect thing. Neither of us are afraid of a bit of work."

Carson nodded. I let Oscar climb onto the wagon seat and I sat in the wagon box with my legs hanging down, feeling like a boy hitching a ride. I watched the town peel away as we headed out on the main road into the countryside.

* * * *

"See what I mean? It's a disaster right now, but I reckon it could be fixed up."

It sure was a disaster, there was no mistaking that. Then again, Oscar'd been a disaster when I'd first seen him, and look at him now. I figured, with a bit of love and care, you could bring back just about anything.

Carson led us around the yard and o'er to the barn before taking us through the house.

"This place is big," Oscar said, gazing around us at the size of the parlor and the kitchen. "I ain't ever seen such a big house." He held little Sprite in his elbow now, keeping her close and stroking her soft fur.

Carson nodded. "You a city boy?"

Oscar laughed. "Yeah."

"I mean, this is a regular country house for these parts."

"I reckon my family and I were pretty cramped back in Dawson City in our one-room shack."

There was some bitterness in Oscar's voice, and I imagined it had been pretty hellish. Being dirt poor in the country was a little better, usually, than being dirt poor in the city. At least in the country you had beautiful scenery and the opportunity to plant or hunt your food.

Carson regarded him with sympathy. "Anyhow, you can have this place if you want it. The land ain't exactly ideal for farming or anything intensive. But I figure you could have some vegetable gardens and keep some animals, if you wanted — on a small scale. And you've got the little creek o'er yonder for water."

I was getting more and more ideas as we walked the place, and from the look on Oscar's face, he was feeling excited about it too. We'd never get a better deal than this in our lifetime, and I was eager to get started clearing the land and shoring up the house to get through the winter.

"Could we have a moment to talk about this?" I asked Carson. "This is a big decision, so's we need to discuss it, but I reckon we can give you our verdict in a bit."

Carson nodded. "Of course. I'll walk back to where we left the horses while y'all talk about it. I only want to say that it would take a load off my mind if y'all would have this place. It would make me feel a bit better about what happened to your Uncle Henry, that's certain."

"Thank you," I said, taking Oscar's elbow and pulling him aside.

We stood inside the ramshackle house and watched Carson walk out of the space where the front door used to be. I led Oscar out of sight of Carson and took him by the arms with hands that trembled with excitement.

"If we take this here land and fix it up and repair the house, we could make a *home* here — a home for the two of us where we could do whatever we liked. I reckon this is the best offer we're ever gonna get."

Oscar's forehead wrinkled and he frowned, like he was scared to think of something so promising. Sprite lifted her paw and gave it a lick with her pink tongue. I could hear her purring.

"It's a wreck, Jimmy. Gonna take years to fix this place." For once, Oscar was trying to be sensible while I was the one filled with irrational excitement.

I gazed around us, trying to look through sensible eyes and not foolish ones. But I still saw our future here.

"Oscar, look around. The walls are still standin'. Sure, there ain't no door, the windows need fixin' and God knows it's gonna need a ton of work. But I figure we can get this here room good enough to live in come winter, and maybe the kitchen, too. I mean, it'll be kind of like camping, sure. But inside walls and with a fire in the fireplace, it'll be cozy enough."

He looked like he was thinking about it, maybe seeing what I saw. He chewed his bottom lip. "You reckon we could do that?"

I nodded, squeezing his arms because I was so hyped up with the visions in my head. "I know we can. I'm handy and strong, and you're strong and can learn what I know. And I figure we can learn new things, and ain't that the reason for livin'? To learn new things and grow together? T'would be an ambitious project but *I know* we could do it." I swallowed and smiled, letting go of his arm to bring my hand up under his chin. "You and me, we can do anythin'."

He stared at me, hope starting to blossom, as if he hadn't let himself see anything in this here place until I told him I did.

"I reckon you're right. We ain't got nothin' to lose, I suppose."

"No we ain't, long as we're together."

He looked slowly around him again, and nodded. "All right. I reckon I'll set up house with you here, Mr. Downing, s'long as you promise to love me and spank me and tie me up now an' then, even if we're plumb tired from all the work we gotta do."

The smile broke o'er my face like a new dawn.

"That's a promise I'm happy to make, Oscar Yates."

He snugged the kitten against his chest and laughed, that sweet dimple showing. "I reckon we got ourselves a mouser, anyhow. Might as well put her to work."

"That's so. She'll need to work as hard as us, now." I reached out and pet the wee thing on the head. "Let's go tell Carson we're taking this place. Right now. I don't want to waste another minute."

"Look at you, Jimmy. You're about to bust outta your skin, you're so excited."

"That I am. This here's what I left the gang for — a life of promise and hope, with a person I care for more'n anythin' in the world."

Northern Horizons:
Repentance and Absolution
AE Lister

Coming November 2022

Excerpt

Jimmy

Oscar was gone, and I couldn't find him.

The brush surrounding the new homestead — if that's what you could even call it — grew dense and completely impenetrable in some spots. A fella could easily get lost, especially a city fella who couldn't tell an Oak from a Birch and fell over his own outsized feet on occasion. There were wolves in these parts that could kill a man Oscar's size in an instant — not to mention the bears, the coyotes and the panthers.

I'd told him time and again not to go wandering around without me, to stay near the ramshackle rooms we were fixing up and not to go looking for whatever he thought he wanted to see.

The kid was trouble. Had been since I'd first laid eyes on him, back in Dawson City, and there wasn't any way of taming him, much as I'd tried. I suppose, when it came down to it, I didn't want to tame him any more than I'd want to smother the fire that kept us both warm at night and reared up inside me when he looked at me the way he did. He'd nigh burned me with a primal passion that I was still trying to control — or at least understand. It still didn't make no sense how the two of us came together like we did. But there was no turning back now.

"Oscar!" I shouted into the trees, trying to see my way and take heed of any movement ahead of me. I'd searched all around the sorry excuse for a house that he'd inherited from his dead uncle, and he was nowhere to be found. So now, I headed into the brush toward the creek. I'd already checked the well and he wasn't there, neither fallen into it nor trying to get water up for a drink. I didn't know where he was, and I was beginning to panic.

"Oscar! D'you hear me? Get back here right now or I'm gonna tan your pretty hide so bad you won't be going anywhere for a week!"

As I stepped past a big boulder, something caught my eye. T'was the peacock-blue frayed edge of a shawl, and I stopped in my tracks when I saw a familiar person standing there, looking off into the distance.

"Cal? Is that you?" I said.

But it couldn't be Cal. Cal was back in Telegraph Creek, whispering scandalous things into the ears of men who paid her for her time and attention. The person wearing the shawl turned with a languorous ease and smiled at me. T'was Cal sure enough, even though it couldn't possibly be.

"Jimmy! My, I'd almost forgotten how handsome you were."

I blushed, taking off my hat and giving her a puzzled look. "What are you doing here? How did you get here?"

Cal simply smiled, the dimple in her cheek on the opposite side to Oscar's. "Has that naughty boy wandered off again?"

She'd rouged and painted her face 'till there was no sign of the handsome boy underneath, the boy who was a girl for all intents and purposes, except for the tackle between her legs. I reckon that didn't really matter.

"Yes, he has," I said. "And I'm gonna haul him over my knee when I find him."

Cal laughed and pursed her lips. "Oh, I don't think he minds that, do you?"

"He'll mind it this time," I promised. "And he'll mind me."

No matter what games we liked to play involving my hand on his behind, giving him a pretend walloping for being a brat, I'd give it to him this time — like I had once before when he'd wandered off and scared me half to death.

"You know which way he went?" I asked Cal, since I had nothing else to go by.

"There," Cal said, pointing through the brush. "I heard a gunshot by the river."

My blood went cold. *Fuck.* God only knew what he'd wandered into, and for a goddamn second, I almost fell to my knees.

In a moment I'd moved past Cal and I was running, tearing through the brush toward the river, terrified of what I'd find. The crack of a rifle pierced the silence, and it echoed for long minutes as my breaths ripped through my chest.

When I found him, if he hadn't been shot or eaten by wolves, I was gonna kill him, truth be told.

Just as I reached the edge of the brush, where it opened up onto the river, another shot echoed through the trees and I opened my eyes, gasping huge gulps of air and blinking at the darkness.

"Hey, hey, shhhh, it's okay. It's a nightmare. You're dreamin'."

Oscar's shadow loomed above me in the darkness of the room that was barely a room — just a space with four walls and a fireplace, the fire banked now but the coals glowing red.

I grabbed him and pulled him down to me, hugging him so fierce that he squirmed and protested.

"Stop. You're hurtin' me. I can't breathe."

I loosened my hold a little so he wouldn't try to get away, but t'was hard not to hold him in a death grip after that god-awful dream.

"What the hell's wrong with you?" he said, clutching my shoulders.

"I couldn't find you," I whispered, my heart beating a drum in my chest. "I couldn't find you." I was breathless, even though I'd not left my bed.

"I was right here — right here in this bed beside you, all night long."

I nodded against him, keeping him close to prove to myself he was here and he was all right, and so was I. His hair smelled of wood smoke and sweat, and I reckoned we could both use a wash by now.

"You need a bath," I murmured, kissing him under his ear where it smelled of his own special musk that I loved.

He snorted. "So do you. I reckon we oughta change into fresh underwear, too, and wash these ones."

I slid a hand under the blankets, popping the buttons of the flap of his union suit so's I could skate my palm o'er the swell of his ass, making him squirm in a delicious way, his small, stiff cock pressing against me.

"Well, dammit, it sure is you, Oscar. No one else has a nubby so small and cute what wants to pretend to be big enough to cause any mischief," I said, teasing him the way he liked to be teased, so that he felt small and delicate and half the man I was. It had seemed strange at first and like he should be offended by that kind of talk. But he loved it, and that was a fact. And I didn't question it at all no more.

Sure enough, he groaned and pressed his fingertips into my shoulders, rutting against me like a dog.

"Goddammit. What were you dreamin' about? You were sayin' my name then you said *Cal*. Was it a *dirty* dream?"

"No. It was terrifyin'. You were lost, and I couldn't find you."

He pressed against me, his nubby rubbing against my thigh through the fabric of his union suit. We'd bought the sets of red flannel underwear when the weather turned real cold at the start of November. Guess we'd had enough of freezing our asses off on our journey and we wanted to be warm, e'en if it meant looking ridiculous. "Well, you did, didn't you? You found me good, since I was right here all along."

"That's a fact. Thank the Lord," I murmured, turning his face to mine and finding his lips in the darkness. He opened to me in that sweet way he had of assuring me there weren't nothing I couldn't do that he wouldn't want, as far as any intimacy with his body went. We'd nigh explored every damned inch of each other by now, and I never could get enough of him. I wasn't sure I ever would.

I pulled away from his mouth and nuzzled into his neck, just to sniff that scent of him I was so fond of. "I'm just so relieved you're here and it was all a dream."

He relaxed into me and offered his long neck for my kisses and for me to run my nose along. The bit of stubble there did something to ignite me, and I lapped my tongue o'er his Adam's apple, then bit it gently.

"Oh. Jimmy. Hell," Oscar breathed. "It ain't even dawn yet, and you wanna keep me awake?" He yawned.

"I'm sorry. Never mind. Just cuddle under these here covers with me. I need to know I got you."

Oscar stifled another broad yawn. "You got me, all right, in every sense of that word. You prob'ly won't want me after a few more months. I'm already a nuisance most of the time, ain't I?"

I didn't know if he was playing up being a brat or if he truly thought he was a nuisance.

"No, you're just— My ma used to call it restlessness, when I couldn't sit still. Said I'd grow out of it, and I guess I did."

"Yeah? What if I never grow out of it, huh? What if I'll always be like this?" Oscar said, snuggling into me, wiggling his ass, e'en though he'd just told me he wanted to sleep.

"Keep still. I'm tryin' to go back to sleep and you ain't helpin'."

"What if I'm always this restless?" he asked again in a whisper. "Will you still love me?"

I laughed. He was all that and more, this twenty-one-year-old boy-man.

"I reckon I will. Can't seem to help it," I grumbled, as if me loving Oscar was an inconvenience rather than the miracle of a lifetime that had been wasted with broken men.

"Good," he said, laying his head down on the feather pillow. "I reckon I'll still love you, too."

* * * *

In the morning, we woke to bright sunshine streaming in the new glass windows. We needed curtains. Next trip into town we had a list of things to buy. The big wad of cash I'd looted from Spook and Whitlaw—the outlaws who had stolen and almost raped and killed Oscar—still had some bulk to it. I reckoned that the money was rightfully ours, what with all the heartbreak and fear they'd put us through. Although, in the end, it had shown me plain as day how I felt about him—that I'd go through hell and back just to keep this man safe and by my side. I'd shot both of them outlaws dead without a thought, e'en though I'd sworn off killing when I'd left the gang. Figured I was doing the world a favor in that case.

Oscar and I—with help from Carson Moore, Timothy Jensen and Timothy's son, Frank—had managed to shore up one small room of the broken-down homestead that Oscar had inherited from his late uncle. It was a decent-sized space with a fireplace and a cookstove to keep us warm and fed, but with the big bed on the other wall and a chair and a table in it, the room felt small and close.

That suited the two of us, though, for now, and made it cozy and easy to heat, although we were eager for spring to come so's we could finish the job and get at least a couple of more rooms added on to this one. T'was a huge job, for sure, but we had a will and the means, and I reckoned we could get some kind of decent home built for the two of us in time.

For now, I was content to wake up under the wool blankets and quilts we'd bought, snuggled beside Oscar, who sighed softly and blinked like an angel, e'en though the thoughts in his pretty head were more devilish, surely.

"Mornin', Jimmy."

"Oscar. How'd you sleep?"

He rolled onto his side and watched me. "Well, 'cept for you makin' so much noise and hollerin' my name, pretty well I guess."

I'd forgotten about my nightmare. Now it came back to me with all its ball-shriveling fear and sense of loss. I frowned.

"Don't remind me. I never want to have it again."

"I'm sorry. Maybe you won't."

I shrugged. The truth was, I'd been having a lot of bad dreams. Most of them were flashbacks to long-gone days, when I'd watched Whitlaw and Spook do some horrible, bloodthirsty things. And I'd done some myself. Seemed all that was coming back to me in my dreams, and I couldn't hardly get rid of it. I woke from those nightmares feeling hopeless and riddled with guilt, full of disgust at the way I'd lived my life. But this last one, when I was out of my wits trying to find Oscar, brought back all the terror of losing him to Spook and Whitlaw near the beginning of our journey, and how lost I'd felt when I didn't know where he was or how I would find him before they killed him—or did something worse.

I gazed at Oscar, wondering how I'd ever deserved this handsome, heartbreaking lamb of a man and feeling like any moment God was gonna take him away from me. I didn't deserve Oscar. I felt that deep down in my bones, and I guess it was coming out in my dreams. But for whatever reason, he loved me, he wanted me and he'd stayed with me all this time, and now we were setting up a home together, the way we'd do if Oscar was a girl and I wanted to marry her, make her happy and protect her.

I honestly didn't see a difference. The fact that he had a cock instead of a cunt seemed entirely inconsequential. I'd bedded whores more masculine than Oscar. He had the sensitivities, delicacy of feeling and ability to nurture that a woman might. He'd taken care of his horse, Sprite, and he'd nursed the kitten we'd got when we'd first arrived in Port Essington. He'd coddled her like she was his baby, and now she was a big mouser with a fierce disposition that still the tendency to curl up in his lap for loving when she needed it.

Of course, we couldn't let on in town what we were to each other, and that was a shame. But it was a price I'd pay to keep Oscar close. I reckoned I didn't have to tell anyone what they didn't need to know. What me and Oscar did in our home was a private thing, and it was gonna stay that way.

Oscar yawned and gazed back at me out of his sweet brown eyes.

"You look like you're havin' your deep thoughts again, Jimmy."

He kneeled up and took my face in his hands.

"You know it don't do to brood about stuff. You just wind up workin' yourself into a mess of feelings you ain't got no control over."

I nodded and sighed, because he was right.

"I guess t'was different when we were on the road. I was too busy getting us safely from one place t'another, I didn't have time to dwell on things from my past — or worry beyond our immediate survival."

"The past is the past," Oscar said. "I told you that once, and I'll tell you that again. You ain't the same man. You told me a bit of what happened back then, and it truly is horrible. But you was misled and mistreated, and you ain't responsible for the things those men made you do. You gotta believe me."

I nodded in order to placate him, but I still felt responsible. The truth was, I could have left the gang earlier than I had. I could have distanced myself from those men when I'd realized what they were capable of—and I hadn't. I'd run with them for years, helping them with their thieving and killing and all-around terrorizing, because I was too lily-livered to leave. True enough that I'd hung in the background, but that wasn't an excuse.

But Oscar was right. There were things to be done and we'd better get at them, rather than brood under the blankets on this chilly, late-November morning.

"Let's get them horses fed and watered," I said, as a lump under the blankets at my feet started moving and making little mewls.

Oscar reached a hand underneath and pulled Sprite out into the day. The gray and white cat with enormous ears, named for the horse we'd lost to wolves just outside of town, blinked and stretched on the top of the blankets. She let Oscar pet her for two seconds, then jumped onto the floor to search for mice.

"I swear, those ears get bigger every day," I said. "She part rabbit?"

Oscar laughed. "Maybe. Anyhow, I think they're cute."

He hopped out of the bed and grabbed the poker from where it leaned against the iron stove, opening the hatch and stirring the embers that had mostly faded.

"We'd best get this stove goin'," he said, "before it gets too cold in here."

"Sure," I said, grabbing my pants and pulling them on. "Don't forget to do up your access hatch," I said, reaching out to cup his bare bottom in my hand.

"Fuck. That's your fault," he said, reaching behind him to button up the fabric flap.

I grinned. "It mostly always is. Pretty convenient to have that bit of cloth be moveable, I'd say."

Oscar laughed and gave me the wide, impish grin that I loved.

"That's a fact."

He winked as I pulled on my pants and shirt, then sat to do up my boots, while Oscar threw a couple of logs in the stove and stoked it so that they caught and crackled.

We'd spent close to a week chopping wood that now stood in a huge pile against the outside wall of our makeshift house, helping to keep the cold out and in a convenient spot to grab when we needed it. Oscar had learned real quick how to use an axe, and his muscles had bulked up somewhat, although he'd always be on the lean side.

He was strong and he was healthy, and that was all that mattered.

Back when I'd found him—an aimless, wisp of a stray in Dawson City—he'd been skin and bones, and filled with a desperation so raw that it hurt to look at. I'd fed him and taken him back to my room to get him cleaned up so's he'd have half a chance. But what had happened the next morning I don't think either of us had expected.

Oscar had been full of gratitude for the kindness I'd shown him, and I'd been horny for something I couldn't hardly imagine until he'd put his lips around me and got me off that first morning, to my shock and his satisfaction. Those were the only skills he thought he had at the time, and I guess he'd wanted to show them off and thank me for what I'd done.

I'd been blindsided by his bold actions and the confusing feelings he'd aroused in me, but I should have known there wasn't any going back from that moment — that he'd claimed me then and there, and it wasn't no use to fight it. As if something had possessed me in that room, I'd hauled his naked ass over my lap and spanked him like he was a misbehaving child, when he was the farthest thing from that. But it had happened we'd both got off and my world had tipped upside down and backward.

And now we were here, in Port Essington, building a home and making a life together. Back when I'd left the gang and taken up a good, honest career hauling supplies, I never would have expected anything near to this, and now I couldn't rightly imagine anything else.

About the Author

AE Lister/Elizabeth Lister is a Canadian non-binary author with a vivid imagination and a head full of unique and interesting characters. They have published 10 books, one of which received an Honorable Mention from the National Leather Association – International for excellence in SM/Leather/Fetish writing.

AE Lister loves to hear from readers. You can find their contact information, website details and author profile page at https://www.pride-publishing.com

PUBLISHING

Sign up for our newsletter and find out about all our romance book releases, eBook sales and promotions, sneak peeks and FREE romance books!

www.ingramcontent.com/pod-product-compliance
Lightning Source LLC
Chambersburg PA
CBHW030811260626
47169CB00001B/282